SYNDICATE OF SINS

MARIE MARAVILLA

AUTHOR NOTE

This book was my life raft these last few months. Scar's story has been with me from finding out my first book hit a million page reads, to my father's cancer diagnosis and his eventual passing.

I used it as an escape, and it will probably read like that. This book is built on vibes. Maybe it's the sequel self-doubt, but I worried about this book being as good as Ryan's, and maybe it's not. But it is special.

—xoxo Marie

A LOVE LETTER TO THOSE GRIEVING

"'I'm sorry' is a bullshit condolence. Unworthy of being laid at the feet of someone who's being consumed by the greedy maw of grief. So instead, I'll offer up my hope that enough of your tarnished soul survives, so that you may live again."

—Marie Maravilla

TRIGGER/CONTENT WARNINGS

Syndicate of Sins is book two in the Toxic Paradise series, a mafia romance trilogy. Each book features different couples, all in the same fictional world. The relationship dynamic in this book is a Why Choose, meaning the FMC is involved with more than one man. This book is also rivals-to-lovers, and they are NOT kind to one another initially.

This book revolves around the mafia and other criminal organizations, and due to the nature of that, this story is on the darker side of romance. **It is for those 18+ as it contains explicit sex/language, violence, and death. This book is NOT meant to be a guide to sexual positions or kinks.**

Trigger warnings: MMCs are mean to the FMC, graphic torture/death, mentions of human trafficking (off-page: this does not occur to the main characters, but it is a subject addressed in this book more than once), mentions of childhood abuse (not sexual and not on the page), assault, manipulation, misogyny, and abuse

ONE
SCAR

NOTHING ITCHED QUITE like dried blood.

Well, dried cum was a bitch too.

Try as I might to keep my jobs relatively clean, some assholes didn't give me an option. Like, damn, just because a dress showed off my thighs didn't mean I wanted them touched. It had worked out fine tonight since my mark's prints were needed to open the safe. Easier to carry a severed hand than drag a body. Problem was, now I had to walk home looking like an extra from a horror film.

The night air carried the sounds of laughter and conversation from citizens none the wiser to the fact that a killer walked among them. Saliva pooled in my mouth from the aromas wafting off the local food vendors' stalls. I hoped Matsumura's death was painful, because the fucker was keeping me from some of my favorite late-night snacks.

It wouldn't be long before his men were out searching, offering money to anyone with information. The thought had me digging into my pocket for my phone. Tapping into their security network was child's play, and they still hadn't discovered the breach. A pixelated video popped up on the screen. The static made it look like the men were in a snowstorm, losing their minds over their deceased leader lying there with a missing limb. There wasn't any sound, but it was easy enough to tell I'd be in deep shit if I stayed out in the open too long.

I tugged at my hood, drawing it farther over my face. Thank God for the poor lighting in this section of the city because my blood-spattered clothing and limp were pretty large red flags. Most of Tokyo was bright and alive, but if you found the right parts, you'd be greeted with my favorite things: darkness and death. Those two held me tight, like a mother's warm embrace.

Not that I'd know what that was like.

Keeping my head ducked, I shuffled through the familiar streets, favoring my left side. Every step sent blood seeping into the field dressing. A prickle of irritation ran through me as another round of buzzing went off, marking the fifth call in a row. There was only one person who'd attempt shit like that with me. I rounded the corner of an abandoned alley and ducked into a darkened doorway, holding my breath against the stench of whatever coated the walls and floor while I lifted my phone to my ear.

"What? Make it fuckin' quick," I snapped.

My nerves ratcheted higher as the distant sound of shouts hit my ears. It wasn't ideal to be here, partly exposed, not fifteen minutes after robbing and murdering a Japanese drug lord. But it was evident he wouldn't stop calling until I answered.

"*Bella*," Enzo replied, drawing out the term of affection. His Italian accent was smooth and comforting in my ear. The palm of my hand stung as my nails dug into the calloused flesh, attempting to keep my mind clear and my senses sharp. I hated how he tried to disarm me, acting as if his phone calls weren't prison sentences.

"Enzo, what the fuck could you possibly need from me?" I bit out, hating that I still had a handler at twenty-seven. The gray strands that insisted on popping up amid my brunette locks were thanks to the stress he—no, *they*—brought into my world.

"I came by your apartment yesterday. And then again tonight. You weren't there. Where are you, Bella?"

My eyes rolled at his prying.

"Enzo, I might be at Dominick's beck and call, but I don't have to give you a fucking play-by-play of my life. I don't sit around on my ass, waiting for the Mafia don to summon me for a job," I shot back.

Years ago, I *diversified* my career and skill set because the New York Italian Mafia didn't pay me jack shit. Dominick said the work I did for him was paying off my father's debt. So, while Scarletta Romano might be under the Mafia's thumb, my alias, Cain, was available for hire to anyone with a sizable enough bank account. Or something worth trading for.

Tonight's client was one such person.

Two million. That was my price to take out Matsumura. The former Yakuza member had made the mistake of becoming too powerful in Japan's criminal underground, all without their permission. Had he still been active Yakuza, my client would've had to seek someone else to take the kingpin's life. The Yakuza's position as one of the Four Families in New York ensured their safety. Although, truthfully, they wouldn't know who attacked them if I'd decided to. But I kept the peace just the same, not willing to risk my uncle finding out about my side gig.

My eventual key to freedom.

"Did you hear me, Scarletta?" he asked tightly, his words pulling me back to reality.

"No, I wasn't listening, Enzo. I'm busy. Now get to the point of your call," I snapped, poking my head out to glance down the alley. I needed to move.

"*Bella,* what the fuck is that supposed to mean? *Busy* with what? Or who? Are you with someone?"

Concern was rich coming from him. Enzo still told me sweet nothings, trying to string me along. While we'd dated, I'd believed those pretty little lies. Faux promises of loyalty to me—of caring for *me.* Fuck, at one point, I was stupid enough to assume he loved me. But it was all bullshit. The affection was a lie, and I'd believed it hook, line, and sinker. All to stave off the emotional drowning of feeling alone.

Uncared for. Unwanted.

He'd painted this picture that we were in this life together. But under the facade of the fantasy was the truth.

No one was fucking saving me but me.

Looking back, it was ironic that I'd thought Enzo cared for me. He was only loyal to my asshole of an uncle. I was nothing more than a tool to both of them.

My lids closed under the emotional heaviness settling in. I avoided talking to Enzo for this very reason. Speaking with him threw salt onto a still-fresh wound. I swore he sensed when the damage he'd caused was finally scabbing over, and he'd pop back in to peel off the protective flesh.

"Just tell me why the fuck you're blowing up my phone, *stronzo,*" I threw back, deciding to keep moving. Each step sent a burning sensation shooting through my leg.

I'd had worse, but walking with a stab wound was still a bitch. Luckily, I didn't have to figure out how to get past a lobby of tourists while covered in blood like in the old days. I did enough work in Japan that I'd acquired a safe house here.

The graffiti marking the entrance came into view as I waited for my uncle's second-in-command to tell me what the fuck was so urgent. *That* had me more concerned than the potential gangrene.

"You have a job…and a family event your uncle is asking you to attend," he finally answered when it was clear I wouldn't elaborate on my whereabouts.

I couldn't contain my condescending laugh. Dominick only had his lackey contact me when he needed to exploit me. The fact that Enzo thought I'd accept that lie was insulting. I'd bet money, though, that he was scowling on the other end of the line at my reaction, ever the good lapdog.

"Bullshit. He's not asking. He's demanding my presence, Enzo." His silence spurred me on. "Quit the lies. It's unbecoming. Have the balls to tell me how it is," I said, sagging against the smooth metal panel. It pissed me off that it took more than one attempt to press my thumb on the biometric scanner. Lights flickered on, and my eyes tried to adjust to the change as I made my way to the first aid equipment in the bathroom.

"Maybe one day you'll be smart enough not to bite the hand that feeds you, Scarletta," Enzo spat out. The vitriol of his words caused me to stumble as anger thrummed in my veins at his accusation. He'd even added a fucking sigh of disappointment. Like I was a petulant child who chose to act like a brat.

I bit the fucking hand because it never bothered to feed me, and I'd cannibalize that fucker before ever going hungry again.

But golden boy wouldn't understand. If Dominick asked him to jump in front of a train, he'd ask which one.

"And maybe one day you'll stop kissing his ass, Enzo. But honestly, hell will probably freeze over before either of those things happen," I threw back, putting the phone on speaker to strip out of the blood-soaked clothes before playing doctor for the thousandth time.

"Bella, you aren't still upset, are you? I told you she—"

"This has nothing to do with that. And use my fucking name when you talk to me." I squeezed my lids shut, attempting to slow my quickening heart. He did this every time he sensed me pulling away. Laced his tone with tenderness, knowing it stirred up memories of our bodies tangled in ecstasy and the emotions I'd believed we had for each other.

"What's the job?" My voice sounded small, tired.

The sharp scent of rubbing alcohol flooded my nose, giving me flashbacks of a frail child huddled in a dirty corner with her wrist hanging at an odd angle and a young boy with dark hair cleaning the cuts. I needed this conversation to end before I spiraled into an emotional pit of memories that would take me all night to climb out of.

"What. Is. The. Job?" I demanded again when he didn't answer. My adrenaline and patience were waning.

"Where are you, Bel—Scarletta? I'll tell you over dinner."

At one time I would've swooned at the bare minimum he was willing to do for me, but now I heard the undercurrent of irritation in his words. He was pissed I wasn't bending to his will.

"Answer my fucking question, Enzo."

The need to think about anything other than him and me together had me pouring a *generous* amount of alcohol on the wound, welcoming the cleansing burn. A groan slipped from my lips as the liquid hit the gouge on my thigh. My lungs hurt with each deep inhale through my nose as I fought the pain.

"What the hell is going on, Scarletta? What are you doing? Are you…with someone?" he asked, his tone making a full one-eighty from what it had been seconds ago. Now it was laced with jealousy.

Fucking ironic.

"You have two seconds, Enzo. Are you answering me or not? Because my time is valuable, and I'm tired of this little game you play. If you know you're not telling me shit, say that." Silence stretched between us. He hated being tested.

"Two Mississippi, motherfucker," I yelled as I slammed my middle finger on the End button. Instantly, the phone began vibrating, but I ignored all ten calls, focusing on keeping my sutures as neat as possible.

A sigh left my lips as I took in my handiwork twenty minutes later. Another scar to add to the list. A single short vibration rattled against the countertop, accompanied by a text notification banner flashing across the screen.

ENZO:

Job's on Friday. File retrieval.

ENZO:

You'll get details later for the event. Don't run
this time.

Bloody towels hit the floor as I glared at the texts, ice flooding my veins. I'd only tried running once. I was twenty-five, and I'd figured Dominick wouldn't be able to find me—that I was finally free. Three broken fingers and a shattered orbital later, I'd learned my lesson. A lot of lessons were learned that day. The most important one was that I didn't need a hero.

I'd rather be the villain. A walking nightmare for those who got in my way.

So Cain was born, spilling the blood of others onto the earth.

The fucking problem was, I still had to keep up the charade with my uncle and Enzo. Bowing like a bitch when they beckoned me.

I winced at the slight pulling of newly stitched skin as I made my way into the small kitchen. The cold from the stainless-steel counter chilled my flushed skin. I stared at the phone screen like more context would appear the longer I looked.

"What the fuck does Dominick need now?" I mumbled, reaching into my little fridge to grab an Orion beer and mulling over the warning not to run.

Maybe I'd get caught during the job and wouldn't have to go to the *famiglia* dinner. I chuckled at the idea.

I never got caught.

TWO
CALEB

ARE THEY HOT OR ARE THEY JUST ASSHOLES?

SHOUTS OF AGONY RANG OUT, disrupting the peaceful night and feeding my hungry soul. The salty air was usually a reprieve from the stifling city mugginess, but not tonight. Tonight, the invigorating scent carried the promise of death.

Pain and suffering—the building blocks of my being.

Turned out, fucked-up-childhood trauma manifested in interesting ways. Mine created a coldhearted bastard who only cared for my found brothers. There was probably a direct link between the number of backhands to the face I'd taken and why I was such a jackass.

Relentless, obsessive, manic.

The words whispered behind my back so often that I tattooed them on there to let everyone recognize what my fucking strengths were. The memory made me hyperaware of the dress shirt clinging to my body thanks to the humidity on the pier.

"The weak think those traits are negative."

My fists curled at the words. I hated how the old bastard still whispered in my mind, but I bet *Da* regretted creating the monster he had now that I was coming for his empire. Of course, he wasn't cognizant of that little fact yet. He'd been furious about my leaving the family criminal organization. Not because he gave a shit about me—he just didn't want the Irish Mob to look bad.

Still, like Kenji and Niko's families, he was convinced this was another one of my *rebellious* phases and that I'd soon crawl back home, ready and willing to take my beating and beg for forgiveness.

My anger flared at the idea.

That was the problem with turning your back on a predator you'd attempted to tame: you missed the signs of their attack. Gael Callahan might be the head of the Irish Mob, but he was an idiot who'd become far too comfortable on his throne. They all had.

A low groan drew my attention. The dim glow from the lamppost barely cast enough light for me to witness Kenji's handiwork. With each blow, the rippling of his back made his *oni* look alive. He'd once told me that in some Japanese lore, as the denizens of Hell, *oni* doled out punishments and torture.

Making his tattoo very fitting.

"I wasn't fuckin' talking to no one. I swear," the man heaped on the floor pleaded. His voice was raw from all the screaming he'd done over the last hour.

Kenji's manic laugh made me move closer in case I needed to remind him that dead men don't speak.

"See, I don't believe that. A little birdie told me you've been auctioning off a file of information on us. I thought we were friends, Boris." Kenji's hand flew to his heart in mock distress. "How do you think this makes me feel?"

He rammed his black Doc Marten right into our rat's rib cage, pulling a scream from the asshole's lips and a smile from mine.

Kenji moved closer, the light revealing the blood spatter coating his bare chest. He'd ditched his shirt to help speed up the cleanup. "Where's the fucking file, Boris? And I suggest you tell me the truth, or it will be a *very* long night for you."

Boris lay in the fetal position on the deck, arms tied behind his back, ankles cinched together. His face was a play-by-play of his beatings. His pale skin was barely visible, replaced by shades of black and blue. Sweat and spit joined the blood pooled under his face as he violently shook his head, blubbering on about not betraying us, which was bull-shit. He'd been posting about a file everywhere online. He didn't have any important details in that file, but we still didn't want that shit floating around.

"I didn't want to do it, I swear. But I was in the hole three grand. There wasn't much in there, I swear. They haven't picked it up yet. Let me go, and we can get it together."

The desperation in his voice was pathetic.

Kenji let out a cruel laugh as he pushed his sweat-drenched hair out of his face. "You're not fucking going anywhere. Tell me where the drop is, or I'll cut off your fingers one by one and use them to gouge out your eyes."

That was a new threat, but apparently effective, because Boris started talking immediately.

"It's back at the club. Shoved above the middle drawer of the desk," he sobbed, his heavy accent making him hard to understand.

The sudden ringing of a cell phone ramped up the tension. Even in the poor lighting, I saw how Boris paled when Kenji reached for the burner we'd pulled off him.

"Embalming Bitches Services. Fuck us over, and we fuck you up. How can I help you?" Kenji's overly chipper tone had me pinching the bridge of my nose. His crazy manifested differently than mine. In all honesty, it made him the dead-liest of our merry band of psychos because people often mistook his laid-back demeanor as being friendly…safe. But in moments like this, when his lips turned up in a sinister grin and violence shone in his eyes, the truth was clear. He was dangerous.

"My boy Boris isn't available at the moment. Can I pass him a message?" His dark eyes narrowed, his smile slipping. Apparently, he was no longer amused with the caller. Bad news for whoever was on the other end of the line.

Kenji's voice was deadly when he spoke again. "Listen, fucker. You really should be careful of who you talk to in that tone. They might be the kind of person who takes tongues for disrespecting them." He pulled the phone from his ear, glancing at the screen. "Lock your doors, E. I'm coming to collect."

Without waiting for a response, he ended the call and stalked forward, crouching before Boris. The man was back to shaking like a leaf and murmuring pleas of mercy or bribery.

"You're a dumbass, Boris. You aren't supposed to save numbers on your burner. If we weren't gonna kill you, whoever this E is sure would've."

Boris's eyes widened with surprise when I spoke from the dark corner I'd been hiding out in. "What did he want, Kenji?"

"Didn't say. He wasn't a fan of the way I answered the phone." Tattooed fingers lifted Boris's chin, giving me a better view of his battered face. "Where were we, Boris ol' boy? Oh yeah, you were about to tell me when this drop is happening."

Our rat's dirty face morphed into a look of relief. "Tonight. In an hour. We can fix this. I'll go get the file, and this won't happen again." He smiled up at Kenji, who continued to look at the man in disgust.

"Naw, Boris. It would. Once a rat, always a fucking rat." He stood, delivering another punishing blow to the ribs.

The man pulled against his restraints in a last-ditch attempt to escape as I prowled closer. His reaction brought a smirk to my face. He was about to be added to my growing list of lives I'd taken.

"Kenji, call Niko and get him down there," I said, keeping my gaze trained on the pathetic mess of a man at my feet. "Tell him to wait for us. I don't want him killing someone before we get what we need."

The tip of my shoe met Boris' shoulder, rolling him to his back. "Boris, I thought you'd be smarter than this. We've been so good to you, and this is how you repay our kindness? It's a shame."

My slacks pulled taut over my muscular thighs as I crouched. Even with the swelling, I saw how he flinched.

"Now not only do I have to kill you, but I have to make an example of you. Can't have assholes thinking we allow this type of behavior." I leaned in closer, hissing in his face. "We've spent years setting up all the pieces so we can fuck over our fathers. Get our pound of flesh for the shit they put us through. You're not fucking that up, Boris," I said, sending my fist into his gut.

A sob fell from his mouth, his rancid breath invading my air as tears streaked down his dirty face. The rattle in his chest told me he had a damaged lung, making what would happen next even shittier for him. The knowledge made me smile as I stood.

Kenji pushed a blunt to his spittle crusted lips. "Take a hit. It's the last happy moment you're going to have," he said, chuckling as Boris eyed us warily but followed the suggestion.

"You're about to be a movie star," I said, pulling out my phone to record before nodding to Kenji.

Screams filled the night air when Boris realized that the heavy chain he was wrapped in was attached to a concrete block—a concrete block being shoved off the pier. He could yell as loud as he'd like. No one was out here to save him.

Splinters lodged into his skin as he was dragged across the weathered dock.

In a few minutes, his lungs would fill with the icy waters of the Atlantic, and his only company would be the fish that fed on his waterlogged flesh. Well, and the others who'd suffered the same fate.

The silence that came when he slipped below the water's surface was deafening. Kenji sauntered toward me, staring down at the camera. He looked like a demon personified, chest covered in tattoos and blood, with a blunt hanging from his lips as he mussed his black hair with one hand, the other tucked into his black Dickies.

"There a reason you're staring down the camera and walking like a dick?" I asked, ending the video.

"Of course. I plan on editing that bitch and sending it to chicks. Women think that shit's hot." His smile fell when all I gave him was a blank look.

"You haven't watched any of the videos I sent you, huh? Fuck, Caleb. How are you going to impress the ladies?" he asked.

I shoved the silky material of his shirt into his hands before walking toward our SUV as he grumbled behind me.

"Get in the fucking car. If the call was from the buyer, then they might move their timeline up. And try to wipe that fucking blood off. We don't want to draw too much attention," I said hotly, ignoring his earlier question.

"This the same attitude you're going to have with your new wife? Ignoring her while being all moody and terrifying?" he asked teasingly as he jogged to catch up.

My feet faltered at his words. Tonight's activities had been an excellent distraction from the latest way Dominick Romano was being a fucking thorn in my side. I couldn't wait to put the mafioso in a ditch, but until that opportunity arose, we had to stick to the plan. Un-fuckin-fortunately, that plan included taking some sniveling bitch's hand in holy matrimony.

Fucking archaic.

I yanked the vehicle door open, the need for violence once again flowing through my veins. "Who gives a shit about my attitude with her? I won't be touching the bitch. You know how Mafia *principessas* are." I paused as everything I knew about the don's daughter flooded back. "Fuck, she's going to cry at first sight of a gun…or Niko," I said, sliding into the driver's seat.

You'd think she'd be used to terrifying armed men. But the Mafia tended to keep their women sheltered.

"Ugh. I hate women's tears. They always want me to say some comforting shit. How would I know what to say? I cut off people's tongues when they say shit I don't like. Why can't they just be happy with orgasms?" His head whipped to face me. "Did I tell you about the chick who was pissed I had an Uber waiting for her downstairs?" Kenji asked, his voice taking on an incredulous tone.

Tension released, and I unclenched my hands from the steering wheel. "You mean the Uber that was dropping off another woman to come fuck you?" I asked, smiling as I reminded him of the other detail of that night.

I appreciated what he was doing by bringing up one of his escapades. Kenji was the master of deflection. It was an issue for romantic relationships, but it was a welcomed skill for helping calm me down.

He shrugged a shoulder. "Why waste an Uber already headed my way? I didn't think it was unreasonable." He sat up in his seat, turning his body to face me while digging out his phone. "Honestly, she was the unreasonable one. How rude of her not to accept my generosity. We live in fuckin' New York. I could've made her take the subway or walk."

"Right." I dragged out the word, eyeing him while he typed away on his phone like a madman as I drove. "Is there something happening that I should be aware of?" I asked, worried about the scowl on his face—usually, it meant shit was going down.

He waved off my concern. "Oh, no. Everything's fine with Niko. He's already there waiting for us."

"Then are you writing a fuckin' novel or what?" I asked, nodding toward where he was still typing away.

"I'm sending that chick a request for the cost of the Uber." His eyebrows pulled together in confusion. "Hopefully, I picked the right girl…"

I barked out a laugh. Kenji was an asshole, and he didn't give a shit about it. From the corner of my eye, I caught him shaking his head as I pulled onto the road.

"Your poor fiancée. She's about to be in for a nightmare, and women rarely like those."

He was right. Most people weren't the same special type of fucked-up as us, especially women. We thrived on the nightmares—there was truth to them, unlike bullshit fantasies. People wasted away waiting for those pretty lies to turn into truths.

My fingers dug into the steering wheel as I ground my teeth. "It's how it has to be. Hopefully, for her sake, we can confirm she doesn't know shit. Then I can lock her up in an apartment and let her be until we finish this. Otherwise…"

I felt Kenji's eyes studying me.

"Otherwise, she's about to pay for the sins of another man," he replied.

I gave a single nod. If she was of any value, we would exploit that. We weren't good men, and anyone who was part of the Four Families received no love from us.

THREE
NIKO

THICK THIGHS SHOULD SUFFOCATE FACES.

THE STENCH of piss and garbage stung my nose.

Why were the best vantage points always next to fucking dumpsters? I pulled at the fabric of my shirt. If I had sweat marks, I was kicking their asses for taking so long. For ten minutes, I'd battled the beads of perspirations rolling between my pecs while I waited for the two people in the world I considered family to show up so we could go into my father's club.

Of course Boris hid the fucking files here.

There was no fucking way I could go in alone without slaughtering every man who looked at me the wrong way. The Bratva had made my life a living hell.

"Kolay, you represent me. Your body is mine. Your life is mine. There is no weakness in the Bratva."

Those words had been true until a few months ago. Now I was dead to him—to all the Volkov Bratva. A vibration in my pocket distracted me from my walk down memory lane.

"What?" I asked, my words coming out harsher than intended.

"Why is it you never answer Caleb's calls like that?"

In the background, Caleb mumbled about how he wasn't

an annoying ass, which was pretty much the truth. That, and Kenji didn't do well when I treated him too seriously outside of when he was working. A reaction from his childhood. We all had them—quirks and traits we didn't ask for but bore, nonetheless.

"Are you two close? It's hotter than Satan's balls out here tonight, and I already don't want to be here," I responded, glancing toward the ugly black building littered with women teetering on heels while slimy men chased them around, attempting to get their dicks sucked. The Bratva had put zero effort into the club's aesthetics because this crowd didn't come for the high-end atmosphere. They came for the drugs and a taste of danger.

"Yeah, be there in a few minutes, fucker. Don't murder anyone before we get there. Or do. I don't give a shit. I'm already coated in blood," Kenji responded before ending the call. Knowing him, he probably hoped I would start some shit.

Our exits had caused quite the panic. Everyone was scrambling for information on our moves. The Four Families didn't normally worry themselves with the emergence of new players on the scene, but the others weren't the second sons of the most notorious and powerful crime families. Caleb and Kenji and I knew shit. We'd been bred for this life. Even if we'd never been destined to take over, our knowledge made us a genuine threat.

A pained yell cut through the white noise of the city. On instinct, my hand went for my gun at the small of my back as I scanned the area, fully expecting the sound to have come from a woman. This wasn't the club any female should attend, alone or in a group. There was a reason the drugs were freely flowing at Neon Nights, and it had nothing to do with the Bratva being generous with their supply. Compliance was easy when people were high out of their fucking minds.

It was dark as shit in the parking lot, the only lights a dim glow from the club's sign and a shitty streetlamp across the way. Pain shot through my jaw from how hard I was clenching it, my brain already painting a picture of what I'd find when I located the noise. Movement by the private entrance caught my attention.

"What the hell?" I whispered, moving closer.

Ivan was on his knees, his arm twisted at an angle that meant it was probably broken, and there was a hand slapped over his mouth, silencing him.

The garbled screams had come from him?

From my position, I couldn't make out the details. But the figure standing at his back was not a man. She appeared to be about five-nine in her heels, with legs that went on for miles, and she was obviously strong. She'd have to be to take down the six-foot bouncer.

The smile I hadn't realized I wore fell when Ivan reached for his waistband with his functioning arm.

He's going for his gun.

Without thinking about the consequences, I moved out of the shadows, ready to run to her aid. But a black SUV whipped into the parking lot, blocking my path and view.

"Fuck," I exhaled, darting around the vehicle, only to find the door standing ajar and abandoned—no woman, no Ivan.

I tried to piece together what was going on as my brothers' voices sounded behind me, paired with the slamming of car doors.

"I don't give a shit what she thinks about any of us. She's getting locked in an apartment so we won't have to deal with her. What's wrong, Niko?" Caleb asked.

Mossy eyes met mine, his face mostly unreadable, as always. The only indication of his concern was the faint lines between his brows and how his hand had moved toward where he concealed his Glock.

I considered what to tell him.

He didn't need to know about what I'd witnessed. It was

probably nothing. Neon Nights had a reputation for people vanishing—no one knew this better than me. The mystery woman wasn't our concern.

Besides, for all I knew, that could've been some kinky role-playing shit Ivan had going on. My gut protested at the thought of leaving her, but we had bigger things to do here tonight.

"Nothing. Just tired of the heat. How'd tonight go?" I asked, changing the subject.

Caleb stared at me for a few brief moments before giving a slight nod. Fucker was perceptive. It was why he ran point for our crew, but that skill of his was a bitch when *I* was the one trying to keep something from him.

"Boris was very helpful in providing us with information. Tonight's the pickup, so we gotta move fast," he answered, running a tattooed hand through his hair before glancing at the expensive watch adorning his wrist. "We've got maybe thirty minutes before whoever's making the pickup is supposed to be here."

Kenji rounded the front, and I quirked a brow at his appearance. "Nice blood. I'd say that's a new look for you, but that'd be a lie," I teased.

He winked as we fell into step with Caleb. "I told you I was coated in the shit. I'm a little sad you didn't kill these fuckers," Kenji threw back as we approached Alexei.

"Kolay. What are you doing here?"

I tensed at the use of the nickname, irritation spiking in my blood. "It's Niko, and what's everyone doing here, Alexei? We're having a night out," I replied, my tone flat, pushing past him as he snickered and mumbled about my "American-tainted" preferences.

Kolay was the correct Russian version of a nickname for Nikolay. One I'd never gone by because it reminded me of when my father spat it at me in disgust. He hated that I wasn't from Saint Petersburg like my older brother. Most of the men in Bratva were born in the mother country and then sent to the United States from the main Bratva branch in Russia. I was the disappointment because I'd been born an American citizen and lacked the accent. As if I had any fucking control over where my mother was when I popped out of her vagina.

The scents of sweat, sex, and weed assaulted us the moment we exited the hall into the heart of the club. People parted, giving us a wide berth, minus the blond chick who'd attached herself to Caleb's side.

"Damn, Caleb, your wife's already old pussy, and she hasn't even spread her legs yet," Kenji joked, slapping my shoulder with his hand. "He told me I could have her since he doesn't want a wifey."

There was no way to stop my eye roll at his statement.

"Why would you want her? Dominick's daughters are complete bitches," I asked.

"Exactly what I said," Caleb added, grabbing a handful of the blonde's ass. "I'd never willingly touch a Romano." He gave Kenji a pointed look over his shoulder.

"Psh, I'll fuck the entitled attitude right out of that pussy." Our brother waved his tattooed hand dismissively. "You may not *want* a Romano, but if she's hot enough, you'll fuck her…" His statement sounded more like a question, making me chuckle at how Caleb's silence had shaken his confidence.

Dominick had two daughters, Milania and Adriana Romano, and they were real pieces of work. I might cut men down with weapons, but those women cut people down with their words. Fuck, the shit they said to people was cruel.

Spent their early twenties trying to fuck anyone with a dick and money. All behind Daddy's back, of course, since they would be wed off in business deals. Some unlucky bastards ended up with bullets in the brain for touching the *principessas*. And now Caleb would have to take one for the team and marry the youngest cunt. The oldest one had been wed off to Dominick's second two years before. The don didn't have a son by blood, so he'd finessed the system and made Enzo his heir through marriage.

Supposedly Enzo had been in a relationship at the time, and he'd broken the news of his engagement to his girlfriend by sending the chick a wedding invitation. Fucking asshole move.

No one really knew what had happened to the girls' mother, only that when Adriana was little, the mafioso had announced the passing of his wife. He'd never remarried, leaving the position of matriarch of the Romano clan to his sister, Giana.

A viper was cuddly and sweet compared to her.

There was a rumor that Giana had once been married, and that she'd had her husband killed. But it was so long before my time that I didn't know if there was any truth to the story. All I knew for sure was that the Romano family was fucked up, ruthless, and better off in the ground.

A prickle of awareness slid over my skin as I *felt* someone's eyes on me. I never could explain the sixth sense to my father, and he'd called me foolish for believing in it.

But I'd yet to be wrong.

"Someone's watching," I announced, my hand sliding to my gun. Neither of my brothers questioned my announcement. They never did. My gaze bounced around the club, attempting to suss out the culprit. The harsh strobing lights and sea of writhing bodies made it impossible to determine who was watching and why.

"Anything?" Caleb asked as we approached the VIP stairs.

I did a final sweep, but no one caught my attention. "No one sticks out so far." I noted the bouncer sending death glares my way. "Let's get this over with," I said, taking the stairs two at a time.

Thank fuck, the music wasn't as loud up here. I led the way to the cluster of armchairs rather than one of the c-shaped velvet booths that lined the walls. Those were basically death wishes. How the fuck was someone supposed to get out of one of those quickly?

Kenji plopped down into one of the leather seats. "Did you ladies know we're criminals?" he asked, winking.

Blondie and her friend, who'd shown up at some point, giggled, thinking he was messing with them. Or maybe they didn't give a fuck. How could they be so careless with their lives? Kenji had a fuckin' katana strapped to his back and was coated in blood spatter. I looked like I could pop people's heads off with my hand, and Caleb wore his dress shirt unbuttoned to show off the stab wound above his heart.

But that's what women were like around here. They were interested in what a man could get them instead of what we might do to them. They were lucky we didn't sell skin—a rarity in this club.

Caleb followed Kenji's lead. Plopping down and pulling the blonde onto his lap, his eyes scanned the room for any Bratva members watching us too closely. We weren't banned from the club, but they didn't welcome us either, and too much attention wasn't ideal since Caleb needed to sneak into the club's office tonight.

"All right, I think that's enough of this shit," Caleb said, practically dumping the blonde on the ground as he stood. She wasn't his type, and her annoying vocal fry apparently moved his timeline up. Or maybe it was the very unsexy way she'd essentially made out with his ear.

I smirked over the rim of my glass. "Eager to get it on, brother? We've barely been here five minutes. Make sure you fuck her *real good*," I taunted, knowing full well he was planning on putting her in a cab. The glower he gave me would've had most men shitting their pants, but I just let out a laugh.

"I'll see you in a minute," he bit out, pulling the two women along.

Kenji yelled out after them, "He's a grower, not a shower. Don't give him a hard time about it. Oh, and keep licking his ear like that. He loves it."

We fell into a fit of laughter at the look of horror on her face and the middle finger from Caleb.

Thank fuck, this should be easy for him.

FOUR
SCAR

"DO YOU HAVE FUCKING HOLLOW
POINTS POINTED AT MY BALLS?"

THE NIGHT WASN'T SUPPOSED to start with me hiding an unconscious body in a random coat closet. Yet there we were. Asshole should've let me into the club. I'd asked nicely. Now he'd wake up with a dislocated shoulder and a killer headache. And what a bitch move, yelling out like he had.

Thankfully, the thumping sound of bass coming from the speakers had drowned out any noise besides the track. The air in Neon Nights was thick with sexual need. Inhibitions were thrown out the window. Writhing bodies scattered all around, moving like they were in a music-induced hypnosis. More than likely, they were all high out of their minds. There was no way you'd stick around this club if you weren't heavily under the influence—the stench of blood and death seeped from the dark, recessed corners.

Nasty shit happened in here, and I hoped the feeling of foreboding prickling across my skin wasn't for me.

"Can I get you another one, miss?"

I glanced over at the handsome bartender, whose eyes held a little too much interest. "I'm good, thanks. Just waiting for my man," I responded with a little more attitude than intended as I wrapped my fingers around the stem of my martini glass, which was still practically full. His flirtatious smile fell, and with nothing more than a curt nod, he left.

"Men. If you're not sucking their dick, they'll be a dick," I spoke into the rim of my drink, chugging down a generous gulp. The drugs might be free, but the drinks were expensive and watery as shit.

Movement from the corner of my eye caught my attention. I honed in on the commotion, weak drink forgotten. The crowd parted like the red sea, making room for the pack of intimidating men making their way to the VIP stairs.

What the fuck was he doing here?

Caleb Callahan. Criminal, asshole extraordinaire and someone who should not be in a Russian Bratva club. Broad shoulders filled out every inch of his black button-up. It was impressive that I could even see his shoulders above the crowd. Men normally lied about their height, but it seemed Caleb was every bit of the six foot three inches his bio claimed. The lights shone off his hair, revealing its auburn hue. A chiseled jaw was accented by his trimmed facial hair. Caleb managed to toe the line of put-together and rugged.

Honestly, it pissed me off that he was so hot. Fucker probably just woke up looking good.

Also, it was a major tool move to put his height in the magazine article about being one of New York's hottest bachelors. Funny how it left out that he was the son of Gael Callahan, head of the Irish Mob. Maybe because they'd have to address Caleb's place as the less desirable second son, who wouldn't inherit any of his daddy's kingdom. The rumors about him being a major man whore were accurate based on the leggy blonde plastered to his side. My eyes lingered longer than necessary on how his large, tattooed hand grabbed her ass.

I'd give the grab a four out of ten. Where was the kneading? The second slap? Hell, with hands the size of his, I'd want him to grab my ass and let those long fingers get close to brushing my pussy.

Did the tattoo on his knuckles say fuck?

Something drew my attention away from his bold choice in body ink.

Well, that's interesting.

I turned my body to fully face the dance floor, making sure I wasn't seeing things. Not only should Caleb not be here, but neither should the two men flanking him. Especially not together.

One was a real-life, goddamn giant with buzzed hair and tattoos running up the side of his neck. A neck so thick I'd have to use my legs to choke him out if we ever got into a fight. He had a reputation for being able to find anyone trying to escape punishment and had a knack for getting them back.

A shiver ran down my spine at the thought of him throwing me around—and it wasn't entirely from fear. I'd never seen Nikolay Volkov's face. The Russian boogeyman usually lurked around in the dark, but his backside was delicious.

Then there was Kenji Jirocho. He was narrower than the other two, with long, lean muscles, but he was as tall as Caleb. He may not have the mass of the others, but he was very much deadly. And damn good with a knife. Kenji was the interrogator for the Jirocho Yakuza Clan. His ability to break men was whispered about in every circle. Hell, he was flown out to Japan on several occasions when they needed his *special touch*.

From my spot at the bar, it looked like his silk shirt was unbuttoned, and the rolled sleeves showed off the ink covering his arms. I'd seen Kenji's face when we were both working a job in Tokyo. Honestly, he'd deserved a cut from that gig since he'd done all the work of getting the asshole to sing like a canary while I'd watched from the shadows. And as much as it pained me to admit, the man was gorgeous. Sell your soul to the devil gorgeous. Caleb was too, but I was trying to gaslight myself into thinking he was ugly as fuck.

"Why are you three together?" I whispered, tracking their movements.

As if he could sense my gaze, Nikolay turned and scanned the room, sending me scrambling to turn in my seat to face the wall of cheap liquor. I threw back the rest of my drink, the burning sensation of vodka sliding down my throat helping me to refocus. Why had it felt like he knew he was being watched?

I rolled my eyes at the vibrations interrupting my thoughts. Enzo always fucking called me during jobs, and it pissed me off. It was such an unnecessary distraction, and I'd told him so more times than I could count.

ME:

You know how I work, Enzo. I'll text you when the job is done. Until then, don't bother me.

I shut off my phone the moment the message said delivered, not needing this job to be jeopardized by my jailer sending me texts the whole time. Pushing off the stool, I allowed the crowd to swallow me up, becoming another body among the masses. Hands trailed over my flushed skin, attempting to entice me to join their drug-hazed trip. Molly was a favorite in the Bratva clubs. Low risk of ODs in the bathroom and high profit margins.

This place was definitely not my style. Grimy as shit, with an off-brand Hot Topic vibe going for it. I swore the walls were spray-painted black, like they couldn't be bothered to use a damn brush and roller. The flashing lights and house music were helpful, though. It made slinking into the private hallways so much easier.

Amazing how many places you could get into with confidence and a little black dress that practically showed your ass cheeks. No one batted an eye as I strode through a door clearly labeled staff. Still, I was careful to keep any identifying features out of sight of the cameras as I moved up the back stairwell to the third floor. The precaution was probably unnecessary since I had a mini jammer stuffed in my bra, but one couldn't be too careful when stealing from the Russians. Ironically, they were supposed to be our allies. Well, the Mafia's ally.

But as the saying goes, there's no honor amongst thieves.

The quiet click of the door behind me centered my focus. My fingers wrapped around the thick fabric of the ski mask, trying to shove under the brunette locks that poked out at the bottom.

I took a moment to orient myself, recalling from memory the footprint for this part of the club. Most people didn't realize that their building blueprints were readily available. *If* one knew where to look—or hack. Came in handy for a thief. This storage closet had a discreet door inside that led to an office. I pressed my ear against the wood, trying to filter out the sounds of the club and what might lie behind the door.

Silence.

A simple deadbolt was all that was on the door. They probably assumed no one would be ballsy enough to walk right into their club and steal from them. Not unless someone had a death wish—or an over-lording uncle who held your fate in his hands.

The corners of my mouth tilted up at the clicking of the disengaged deadbolt I'd picked.

That was well under thirty seconds.

I slipped inside when no one started yelling or shooting. The only light in the room came from the windows behind the giant desk. New York had enough light pollution that I didn't need to take out my small flashlight. I toed off my shoes and shoved them in my bag. It was easier to get away on bare feet than in heels.

I crept forward on the cold concrete.

Fuck.

The call from Enzo was probably to tell me where the file was hidden. I'd forgotten that he'd still needed to get me that bit of information. It'd take too long to power up my phone and shoot off a text, and there was no way I was risking a call.

My gaze darted across the room, looking for tells. I'd broken into enough places now to know what to look for. Artwork that was slightly askew, scratches on the floor from where furniture was frequently slid out, and walls that were dirtier in areas from being touched often. Or the tried-and-true false bottom drawers. Given that the office had such a flimsy security system, the Russians probably hadn't gone to great lengths to hide these files—so the desk it was.

Well-worn leather gloves slipped over my fingers like a second skin. I pulled on the drawer, testing to see if it was locked. Wood scraping on wood echoed through the room, making me cringe. Why did men always have ancient office furniture? I yanked the drawer open the rest of the way, taking the rip-the-Band-Aid-off approach.

Yellow file folders hung neatly, and I scanned their labels to see if, by some miracle, there would be one labeled *Important Shit*.

My shoulders sagged as I read through the titles. Of course there wasn't. That would be too easy. I placed one of my hands on the outer bottom of the drawer while using the other to push all the files aside and knocked.

No false bottom.

The other proved to be as useless, pissing me off even more than I'd already been about doing this damn job. There weren't any other viable hiding spots. The walls were bare, nothing to cover up a wall safe. Or hell, just hide a fucking folder behind. The only furniture in the room was the desk and two metal folding chairs that sat in front of it. Honestly, it looked like they didn't spend any time here.

Worry settled in my gut, causing me to gnaw on my lip. I needed to execute this heist tonight, or I'd have hell to pay with my uncle. My attention landed once more on the desk. It had to be there.

My knees hit the concrete, and I worked to position my five-six frame to check the underside of the desk. Relief flooded my body as my fingers met a rigid folder.

A muffled sound sent nerves shooting down my spine. "You've got to fucking be kidding me," I whispered as a voice got closer.

I had seconds to decide whether to make a break for the window or settle in and see if they'd leave. The decision was made for me when the office door opened. My breath hitched at the sound of a man's deep tenor.

"I don't fucking care. He's going to do what he wants anyway. Tell him that day's fine. It's not like I want to even go through with the arrangement anyway. Hey, I just got in the office." There was a pause for whatever the person on the other line said. "Tell them I'm fuckin' the blonde in the bathroom. We can't be too obvious with our moves, or they'll be on us in a second."

Who the hell was in here?

My fingers wrapped around the grip of my Sig, dragging it from the bag I'd housed it in. Killing the guy wasn't an option; it'd be too much of a hassle for me. Plus, I'd already left one body behind in my wake.

But the end of a barrel had a way of motivating people. I repositioned so I was balanced on the balls of my feet rather than sitting on my ass, vulnerable. My heart rate spiked when powerful legs came into view.

"Yeah, he said it'd be under the des..." He paused his conversation when my barrel brushed the family jewels. Figured those were precious enough to him. He'd think twice before making a stupid move.

My voice came out cold and calculated. "Tell him you

have to go. Calmly. And keep your hands up where I can see them," I instructed.

The deep tone of his voice was so delicious it pissed me off. "Sorry, yeah, I'm still here. I'll see you in a minute." His words were clipped, but he didn't raise an alarm.

"Slide the chair out and don't make any sudden movements."

He grunted in annoyance but followed instructions. "Do you have fucking hollow points pointed at my balls?" he asked, irritation dripping from his tone.

I duck-walked out far enough to make eye contact. My brows dropped in confusion at the sight of the surly Irishman in front of me.

Caleb Callahan?

I blanked my face, not wanting him to read the surprise in my reaction. Now wasn't the time to work through why he was in here.

"Of course. Who's dumb enough not to use hollow points?"

"Who's dumb enough to break into the Bratva's offices?" he threw back, his eyes dipping down to where the hem of my dress had ridden up when I stood.

The dress had been too tight for underwear, so literally all that stood between my bare pussy and him was a layer of cheap spandex. Heat from his gaze sent my heart rate soaring, and he arched a dark brow at me, as if he could sense the reaction.

"Seems I could ask you the same question, Caleb," I responded, keeping the barrel trained on his junk. Shock flashed in his emerald eyes. Glee snaked through me at his reaction. He hadn't expected me to know who he was. "Lie on the ground, facedown," I instructed, needing to get out of there ASAP.

His mouth turned down into a snarl, giving me images of what it would be like to trade blows with the handsome mobster. I'd heard about how he fought in the underground fight rings, and the idea of going toe to toe with him, any of them, was thrilling.

His fingers twitched, the cogs turning—surely working through how he could overpower me. I tapped his junk to remind him of why he should listen before inching back and putting space between us so I could leap out of grabbing range. He tracked my movement, his mouth pulling down at the corners. I rolled my eyes when he shifted to the balls of his feet. Men always assumed I was bluffing.

"Just do as you're told. I'm a damn good shot and have a soul that makes the devil look like a saint. I won't have a problem shooting you," I promised, mentally calculating how long I'd been in here already. Caleb wasn't the only threat I had to be aware of.

Something in my tone convinced him because he slowly lowered himself to the floor, arms spread out wide.

"I hope you have a good plan, little girl, because when I catch you, there'll be hell to pay," he promised as I dropped over the top of his back, my knees bracketing his waist. I tried to ignore the fact that if I lowered a few inches, my clit would be pressed against his powerful back.

"Hands," I demanded, ignoring his threats. There was no way we would see each other again. His shoulders tensed the moment the hard plastic touched his wrists.

"Who fucking keeps zip ties on them?" he asked in disbelief.

The new position caused his cuffed hands to brush my upper thigh when I leaned forward. "I always keep them on hand for moments like this," I whispered in his ear, savoring the heat of his body.

"Fuck," he said under his breath, the word drenched in anger and...lust? "How did you even get in here? No one knows about this office."

"Oh, Caleb, a woman never reveals her secrets," I said,

reaching behind me and grabbing his pant leg, using the expensive fabric to pull his ankle to his wrist.

"Seriously? You're going to hogtie me?" he snarled, bucking his hips up to unseat me. He stilled when he felt the barrel pressed to the back of his head.

"Be a good boy and lie here, and I'll be out of your hair in a moment," I bit out.

Caleb turned his head. He had to press his cheek to the dirty floor in order to glare up at me. "You'll fucking pay for this."

There was no stopping the cocky smile forming on my face. "It's cute that you think that. You don't know who I am, do you?" I taunted, knowing full well my face was covered and there was only a sliver of light coming in from the windows.

He raked his eyes over me, and the smirk that appeared caused my gut to tighten in anticipation. It was so primal that my subconscious begged me to run.

"*Macushla*, you've made quite the impression tonight. I'll remember you, and when I find you, it'll be my turn to hogtie you, eh? That pretty olive skin of yours will be so fun to mark up. I bet you'll scream so pretty for me," he snarled, the green of his eyes now practically black.

Thank God for the ski mask, because I could feel my cheeks flush. I was going to need a cold shower after this exchange. I didn't know whether his words were sexual or homicidal. Ironically, they turned me on just the same.

"We'll see, Caleb. But for now, do as you're told and stay." I attempted to sound haughty and unfazed when I answered, but my words sounded breathy, causing his eyes to flare.

I looped the strap of my bag over my shoulder, stepping across his massive frame and making my way toward the windows.

"Wait? Where the fuck are you going?" he called out.

The window groaned as I heaved it up, air tickling my

heated skin while bringing in the scents and sounds of the city below.

"You didn't think I would chance walking back through the club, did you?" I asked over my shoulder as my toes touched the small ledge.

"We're three fucking stories up. Get your ass back in here and use the door like a sane person."

The slight edge of panic in his voice caused me to look over at him—I was surprised to hear any. He wriggled around, attempting to loosen his bonds, but when his eyes met mine, I swore I saw concern.

"What about tonight has led you to believe I'm sane? Don't worry. I've done this plenty of times." I paused. "And if you get caught, just tell people you're into kinky sex." I winked before stepping out into the muggy night, closing the window behind me.

My eyes widened when, through the glass, I saw that he'd already gotten a hand undone and was working on the other. I'd left them loose on purpose, but damn, he was quick. I scurried along the ledge at an impressive pace before leaping onto the nearest fire escape and scrambling down, wincing as I leaped from one platform to another.

Let the knees absorb the shock. Yeah, right. Falling still hurt like a bitch. A roar sounded from above, but I didn't chance taking a peek.

"I will find you, *macushla*." His voice carried over the sounds of the city. "And when I do, I will wring that pretty throat of yours."

The hair on the back of my neck stood on end with the amount of conviction he put behind his words.

FIVE
SCAR

"FAMILY" FUCKING SUCKS

RAIN CLOUDS SWATHED the city in darkness, sending tourists scrambling for refuge before the storm broke free. A sigh escaped my lips, fogging up the town car's window and obscuring my view. This weather was eerily appropriate for my frame of mind.

Dark and ominous.

There was something incredibly demoralizing about being capable of killing a person over a hundred different ways but still bowing your head like an obedient bitch to your deranged uncle. Honestly, it *almost* deflated my self-confidence, which would be a shame, because that was the only thing keeping me from falling into a crippling depression, thanks to my sunshine-filled past. Or at least that's what the therapist had said to me before I'd flipped her off and told her to suck my dick.

Not that I didn't *want* to kill the fucker, but he'd put fail-safes in place to ensure that if anything suspicious happened, every member of the Romano Mafia would be on my ass. Dominick had made it clear. If anything were to happen to him, I should be the first person they look for. *Rich coming from a loathed crime boss.*

Sure, the Four Families had a peace treaty, but it was bull-shit. At the height of New York's crime wave, the four leading factions made a cease-fire alliance with each other. Too much heat was being brought down on them by the feds, and their rivalry was killing them—literally.

So, territory lines were drawn, and the Four Families were created. Everyone was supposed to go on their merry way and operate in peace. Keep their noses out of each other's business. But that was well over thirty years ago, and they were all conniving bastards, cloaked in proclamations of peace while holding knives to one another's backs. Just waiting for someone to land a blow and start the inevitable bloodbath.

The Italian Mafia, the Irish Mob, the Russian Bratva, and the Japanese Yakuza all operating in beautiful harmony?

Fucking bullshit.

The indistinct murmur from the moving divider drew my attention. I rolled my eyes when the driver lowered it less than an inch. Like a fucking divider would save him.

Stab one guy on staff, and suddenly no one trusts you.

Technically, I'd stabbed two. The first one no one knew about, though. I'd been twenty-one when one of Dominick's capos decided that I should cater to all of Dominick's men. Julius tried to take something I was unwilling to give. He was the first man I'd killed. Up until that point, all I'd done was train with weapons and complete heist jobs that had never ended in violence.

The dark interior of the car slipped away, morphing into the memory of blood-soaked carpet. My mind perfectly recre-ated the metallic scent. Julius lay on the once-cream flooring, staring up with wide eyes. Shock. That was the expression on his face when I drove the letter opener between his ribs, sinking it home into the muscle that pumped his life force. I'd thrust it home when his greedy fingers were busy undoing the button of my jeans.

My chest felt too tight, like my lungs wouldn't expand and feed my body the oxygen it needed. It happened every time I thought about that day.

"We're here, Ms. Romano. It's 354 West 22nd Street."

"Don't call me that," I shot back, pushing open the car door.

My panic had subsided at the sound of the driver's timid voice. It was barely above a whisper, thick with the undercurrent of fear. His unease reminded me that the girl who'd once been kept in this home was gone.

She'd been too sweet, innocent…trusting.

Weak.

Julius's death was my rebirth. The moment I'd shed my old self and embraced the ever-present desire for darkness and violence. Now I didn't disguise my brokenness. I embodied my sharp edges and fucked-up view on life. Fucking who I wanted and killing who fucked me over. One day, I'd drag my uncle and every Romano to hell with me.

Anche nella morte.

I grimaced at the sight of the arched black doors of the brownstone. Their gothic knockers taunted me. Years had passed since I'd stepped foot in this house. It'd been almost as long since I'd seen Dominick in person. Enzo had acted as a liaison for years. I schooled my features into an unreadable mask, all too cognizant of the green light on the camera in the upper corner.

"Here we fucking go."

My uncle's house manager rushed forward as the door opened. A sneer popped up on her aged face when she realized it was me. Silvia wasn't the only one pissed. Hatred thrummed through me. When I was a kid, the bitch made me watch her dump untouched food into the garbage while I sat there, clutching my stomach. Guess she never considered I'd grow up to have more affluence and money than her.

Or maybe she assumed I wouldn't survive to be an adult —fair assumption.

My shoulder slammed into hers, sending her stumbling back against the doorframe. She slapped a palm over her mouth, and the edges of my mouth pulled up in a sneer. The *help* wasn't allowed to be heard in this household, and Silvia had worked here long enough to know the consequences. Her eyes burned into my back, but I didn't bother acknowledging her. The snub would do far more damage to her ego than any words.

The french doors to the office stood open, displaying Dominick's hunched form frantically scribbling. My fingers itched to grab the Sig holstered by my ribcage and put two in his head. But it would be a death wish, and as much as I liked playing chicken with Death, I wasn't ready to meet him just yet. The fact that the mafioso let me near him with a weapon was a show of power, another way for him to rub in my face that he had me on a leash.

I'd bet money I wouldn't be allowed near him with a fucking pencil if he knew about the assassinations and hits. I resisted the grin that threatened to appear.

He would've thrown me in a dark pit if he had learned about that skill. Julius was my first kill and my first coverup job, and it had been a bitch. Even with my shoddy job, Dominick still had never uncovered that it was me who'd killed the capo.

Now I hired cleaners when I needed that particular skill set, because dissolving a body was a fucking skill.

I couldn't wait to unleash the chaos that simmered beneath the surface. As soon as I figured out a viable plan for getting out from under the don's thumb while still keeping my head, I'd carve out his heart.

My ass hit the hard cushion of the armchair facing him. The coppery tang of blood filled my mouth as I bit my tongue to keep quiet like he preferred. It physically pained me to sit there in submission, but after enough broken bones, I'd learned my lesson.

Patience was an action as much as it was a virtue.

The sound of the front door closing broke me from my thoughts, reminding me that my back was exposed. Not that it made a difference here. I was in danger regardless of where I sat while in Romano territory. The screen of my smartwatch lit up, revealing the video feed of the hallway. Being at the top had made Dominick cocky. It had taken me all of two seconds to tap into his security feed.

Enzo's large frame strode past the camera. His dark hair was neatly trimmed, and I didn't need the camera to know he was in a suit that hugged every muscle in his body. He knew he was handsome and never missed an opportunity to high-light that. I waited to see whether others followed behind the underboss, but no one appeared. A momentary chill flooded me. My most dangerous jobs came from meetings where only these two knew the details.

Heavy footfalls drew closer, and I tugged the cuff of my blouse over my watch. My uncle wouldn't notice me looking at it, but Enzo would. He was almost as observant as I was. Or he had been. He'd gotten a big fuckin' head in the last few years, since he was being groomed to take over.

"Enzo, if everything is in order, then shut the doors for this meeting," Dominick said, not bothering to look up.

"Of course, boss."

The closing click felt like the hammering of a gavel on my sentencing. Dominick's eyes popped up and latched on to me. I nonchalantly raised my chin a little higher.

Silence continued to grow between us. It was a fun game he liked to play. *See how long I can ignore Scarletta before she fucks up, and I can punish her.* I'd lost a lot when I was younger, but now I was the queen of the icy stare. My shoulders dropped, and I settled into the chair, making a show of getting comfortable and setting my expression into a mask of indifference. I'd perfected my social chameleon act, becoming whomever I needed in any given situation.

The slight flaring of his nostrils revealed how pissed he was that I wasn't showing him anything. A nervous cough from Enzo shattered the spell.

"Where's the folder from last night?" Dominick sneered, running a hand over his trimmed facial hair as he assessed me.

A thunk sounded in the room as the manila folder hit his desk. His greedy hands snatched it up, eager to get the contents. "What the fuck is this?" His skin broke out in blotchy spots. In my peripheral, Enzo stiffened at his boss's commanding bark.

"That, Dominick, is a flash drive," I responded coolly, crossing my linen-covered legs.

"Don't get smart with me, Scarletta. Where the fuck are the papers that are supposed to be inside?"

Jesus, how was this imbecile still in charge? The treaty made these fuckers lazy. They assumed they were untouchable, ignoring the murmurs of unrest that traveled through the criminal underground. All it would take was the right person to upend them all. Someone who knew the right strings to pull and palms to grease.

I picked off a nonexistent piece of lint, willing myself not to react with violence.

"Whatever papers you're looking for are probably loaded onto that," I answered.

He was about to have another fit when Enzo stepped in. "She's right, boss. We probably just need to plug it into a computer to get what we need." His placating tone worked on Dominick but managed to have the opposite effect on me.

"Did you look at this?" Pudgy fingers waved the drive around like he was flagging someone down.

I rolled my eyes at his antics. "Why would I, Dominick? What am I going to do with whatever's on that?"

The lie fell seamlessly from my tongue.

I'd done more than look at it. I'd crafted a whole false packet of information to give Dominick instead of what was really on the drive. Last night, curiosity had seared through my veins the entire way back to my apartment. Turned out, Mr. Callahan was attempting to steal information about *himself*. I hadn't had time to do a deep dive into what all was on there, but I'd quickly decided I didn't want Dominick to have it.

Information was invaluable in this world, and I had a feeling having the file could come in handy.

"Good. And I assume everything went fine? No one saw you there?" Dominick asked, his beady eyes roving over my face.

Green eyes that burned with passion flashed in my mind, but I kept the memory from showing on my face. "Of course everything went fine. You haven't heard any chatter, have you?" I challenged.

It wasn't because of the kindness in my heart that I'd loosely tied up the Irish mobster. Blackmail was a form of currency, and I made a habit of having as much as I could on as many people as I could. I might not have known *why* Caleb Callahan was in that office, but I knew he shouldn't have been. I couldn't leverage that information if he'd been caught.

My uncle made his way to the bar cart, pouring a generous glass of whiskey. I was surprised the tumbler didn't break with how tightly he gripped it.

"Now, to discuss the other reason you're here today." He paused. "Those fuckin' *stronzos* assume they can muscle in on our territory? They aren't going to know what hit 'em when I'm done with them. Think they can bargain with me? Me!" he barked. The crazed expression on his face made me think he might've finally lost his mind. And I didn't have a clue what the fuck he was going on about.

The desk chair groaned in protest as he slammed back

down. At one time, he might've been handsome, but he'd let himself go. Why work to look good when you could bribe women—or threaten them?

"Right…" I said, gaining a dirty stare from Enzo for the way I drew out the *R* sound. "What does that have to do with me?"

"I've decided your cousin will be getting married. And *all* family will be at the announcement of her engagement," he said.

Okay? Weird subject change.

I hated that word. Family. It was a load of bullshit, but I knew better than to voice my opinion on that. Dominick was particular when it came to how society viewed his *family*, and unfortunately, I was included in his delusion.

"Of course. Who is he, by the way?" I asked. I didn't give a shit, but I wanted to leave already. Honestly, this meeting could have been an email.

"Caleb Callahan."

Thank God my uncle had never offered me a drink, or I'd have spit it across his desk at that very moment.

"Wait. As in Caleb Callahan from the Irish Mob? Why the fuck is Adriana marrying him? Don't you have a peace treaty with them?" I ask, my voice going up an octave.

Enzo growled from beside me, reaching for the glass of whiskey Dominick poured him. "Disloyal fuck *was* part of the Irish Mob. But he left and formed a new criminal organization with two other bastards. The Syndicate. That's what the assholes call themselves." His voice dripped with disdain. "It's made up of the second sons from the three families. They all left their organizations to form their own. That's what is supposed to be on that file. Information on their plans," Enzo said.

Well, fuck me. The only man who'd ever almost caught me was about to marry my bitch of a cousin, and I was going to have to attend. Honestly, I'd assumed I'd avoid the man for the rest of my life. Now the three of them together made sense. They weren't drinking buddies. They were criminal partners. A million questions turned in my brain, but I stayed quiet. Listening was my best tool at the moment.

"He's their little ringleader. Those sons of bitches are trying to strong-arm their way in on our territory," Dominick spit out, his meaty fist slamming on his desk. "And I can't kill the fuckers because their families all think they'll make their way back into the fold. So now my *principessa* has to marry that Irish *stronzo* so we can form an alliance and keep them from fucking me over." I wanted to roll my eyes at his dramatics. My cousin was a snarky bitch, and if he wanted to inflict pain and suffering on the Syndicate, she was the perfect person for the job. That nasally voice and self-centered attitude would make anyone want to swallow a bullet.

"And you're sure you need me there?" The question slipped out before I could stop it. I'd avoided family gatherings for years. Specifically, since the last wedding Dominick had thrown for a daughter.

"Don't be a smart-ass, Scarletta. I taught you better than that. *Famiglia* over everything. I won't have you fucking this up. You're to attend and stay out of the way."

I wanted to point out that it was easy to stay out of the way if I wasn't there, but I bit my tongue.

A ring disrupted the growing tension.

"What? Fine, give me a sec." Dominick blocked the phone speaker like it would drown out his bitching. "Enzo, set her up with the details we have for this weekend and get the fuck out of my office."

When those words left his lips, I was out the door, making a beeline for the street before he decided he needed something more. Before the memories crept through my mental blockade.

"Scarletta, wait. We need to go over the details."

"What's there to go over, Enzo? I'll show up and play

happy Romano *famiglia* member, despite all the looks from people wanting to fight me or fuck me."

I didn't make it more than a few feet before his hand wrapped around my shoulder, pulling me to a stop. My eyes narrowed at the thick fingers digging into my skin, my fingers itching for my gun.

"I might've known you my whole life, Enzo. But touch me like this again, and I'll have no problem taking your fingers from you," I bit out.

Worry flashed across his face as he snatched his hand back like I'd burned him. "Scarletta, don't be like this. Talk to me."

Wow. Was he fucking serious?

"What the fuck does 'don't be like this' mean, Enzo?" I spit out, my anger building.

It'd been a while since I'd really looked at Enzo. I avoided him like the plague. Clearly, the boy I'd once known was now very much a man. He was like the criminal Clark Kent. Suave, clean-shaven, strong jawline. Everything a woman wanted.

His coffee-colored eyes sparked with interest when I stared a little too long, mistaking my attention for desire, but that emotion hadn't been there in years.

"Scarletta, you know I didn't have a choice." His fingertips came up to brush my face right as reality crashed into me like a freight train.

A sound that should have come from a hissing cat escaped as I retreated back. "Fuck you, Enzo. That's the line you want to go with? That you didn't have a choice in marrying my cousin while you were dating me?" I stepped into his space, no longer able to contain my rage. "Did you have a choice when you came over and fucked me before leaving the fucking wedding invitation on your pillow for me to find? You didn't even have the fucking balls to break the news to me."

He looked away, a pink tinge of shame crawling up his neck. Pathetic. He couldn't even look me in the eye.

"Did you have a choice when you asked me to continue fucking you behind your new wife's back?" I asked, practically shouting now, as years of frustration exploded from me.

His head whipped toward me, a hand coming up to cover my mouth while he checked that no one heard the confession.

Fuck that.

I rammed a fist into his gut, catching his shoulders when he doubled over in pain.

"I would've taken a bullet for you, Enzo. That's how much I fucking loved you. So, thanks for showing me how fucking pathetic you are," I whispered in his ear before kneeing him in the jaw and letting him crumple to the floor.

I was a fucked-up version of Cinderella.

One who'd never known the love of her father and didn't get rescued by a fairy godmother or Prince Charming. And if Prince Charming showed up now, I would probably eat him.

SIX

CALEB

WOMEN IN SKI MASKS WILL FUCK UP YOUR PLANS.

I FUCKING HATED PEOPLE.

So naturally, New York would be where I was forced to live. Fuck, I needed a cabin in the woods and a warm pussy to thrust into. A lithe body flashed in my mind, ratcheting my irritation up another notch. That damn woman had imprinted herself on my psyche. Try as I might, I couldn't shake the memory of her. And even more frustrating? I couldn't find her. A week had passed since the incident at the club. I'd managed to get out of the hogtie she'd placed me in before getting caught, but she'd run off with the fucking folder.

Who the fuck did she work for?

That question kept swirling around in my head. That, and why she'd chosen not to make my restraints too tight. She'd known my name, and I assumed she knew I wasn't supposed to be in that room. So she'd done that as what? A favor? Or maybe I was giving her more credit than she deserved. My inner turmoil caused me to push open the doors harder than I intended, sending them slamming into the wall. I grimaced, knowing the drywall would be fucked now.

"Kenji, are we all set?" I growled out the instant I entered our office, glancing at the mess I'd made. The sounds of furious typing filled the space. Kenji insisted on buying equipment with the loudest haptic feedback possible.

"Wow. Good-fucking-morning to you too, sunshine. Glad to see you took some happiness up the ass this morning."

"And I'm going to shove my foot up your ass if you don't tell me what's happening. Did you track down the woman?"

That got his attention. I loved him like a brother, but saying we were opposites wasn't going far enough. What we did have in common was that we were damn good at our jobs. And Kenji's job was getting information from people. Usually painfully.

He swiveled his chair to face me. Gone was the playful grin he usually carried. "None of my contacts know anything about her. Or at least they aren't fessing up to it. Of course, I haven't taken the hands-on approach yet with any of the family members." He let out a sadistic chuckle. He hated the families, his in particular.

Who'd blame him?

Attempted murder was a family pastime for them, and not the fun kind. The attempts were on each other.

"Wait till they see all the fun plans I have for them," he mumbled, lost in his thoughts.

"Kenji, those plans have to wait for the right timing. Don't forget that," I replied, mulling over the fact that we were no closer to knowing who the woman was or who she'd given the file to.

He waved a hand in dismissal, turning back to his monitor. "In other news, I tracked down a guest list. *Los Muertos* was invited to your shindig, but who knows if any of those fuckers will come. Sergio usually keeps to himself. I bet his asshole of a son is probably jizzing himself over the invite, though." Kenji chuckled. "He's always trying to ride the dick of whoever can get him more power. Fucker dresses like an idiot too."

I nodded my head in agreement. "He dresses like he

wants to be Dominick's son instead of Sergio's. And the Mafia asshole probably wishes the same thing." My head fell into my hands as I groaned. "Fuck. I *know* Dominick wishes the same thing."

Silence hung in the air as Kenji and I both avoided the elephant in the room—my engagement to Dominick's daughter.

I changed the subject, needing to talk about anything else. "We find the supply warehouse for the other two?" Anticipation prickled at my skin. We had all of these carefully laid plans, but they hinged on everything lining up just so.

No unexpected surprises. Like a woman in a ski mask.

"Well," he dragged out the word, and my stomach hit my feet as I braced for the bad news, "we know for sure the location, but Niko doesn't agree with my idea and wants to rig the warehouse with C-4. Which sounds boring when we could run up in there and cut fuckers down." He mimicked guns with his fingers.

Relief flooded my veins. Kenji's news wasn't actually bad news. "Imagine that. Niko has a logical solution to our problem, and you have a bloodthirsty one." I plopped down in the leather office chair, unbuttoning my sleeves and rolling them up my forearms. The word *fuck* taunted me from my knuckles, causing me to shake my head. We all had it—Kenji, Nikolay, and me.

"Fuck you."

Exactly the type of first tattoo ragey, punk-ass teenage boys would get. We were eighteen when we'd gotten them. The same year we became brothers through spilled blood. We'd gotten a lot more ink since then, and we'd spilled a lot more blood.

The three of us never should've become close. We were from three different factions, and even with the peace treaty, the Four Families weren't actually allies. We had hated each other at the beginning of high school, determined to fuck each other over. Of course, infatuation with a girl was the linchpin that had brought us together. Then she became the pawn our fathers had dangled above our heads. They thought that by breaking the girl, they'd break our bond. Instead, the fire forged us into something stronger.

Now we'd be the Four Families' demise.

Kenji's smooth voice pulled me from my walk down memory lane. "Our fuckin' fathers and brothers were invited to your little party too."

I let out a disgruntled huff.

"It's really too bad we have to keep them around. All of them in one place…seems like the perfect setting for mass murder," I said, scratching at the stubble on my chin. "But unfortunately, that's not an option. We need them where they are. Plus, they won't show up. They'll probably send pawns to come observe."

I didn't think any of the crime leaders were smart. They just had no one to challenge them. But that was all about to change, and the assholes weren't ready.

SICKLY SWEET VANILLA coated the air, mixing with so many aerosol hair products that it surprised me NOAA hadn't barged in here to shut us down. Clothing was strewn everywhere, and makeup products stained the pristine white bedding of the room they'd taken over.

This was hell on earth.

I shook my head at the mess my grown-ass cousins had caused. They were so damned spoiled that they never considered having fucking respect for other people's things.

"No, Milania, you can't wear that to my party. Daddy already gave you an engagement party. You're not wearing white to mine," Adriana whined.

I suppressed a groan while my head hit the back of the armchair. Here we went again. Another asinine fight that was completely unnecessary. I should've told her that if she was smart, she'd wear black as a sign of mourning. But my cousin was too self-centered to see this wedding for what it was. All that mattered to her was a big rock and the title of tying down the biggest man whore in Manhattan.

"Adriana, that rule only applies to weddings. I can wear whatever the fuck I want, and this dress hugs my ass the way my *husband* likes." Milania's eyes cut over to me in a taunting sneer. "Where'd you get your dress, Scarletta? The bargain bin at Bergdorf Goodman?"

The two of them laughed, as if they'd made the funniest joke in the world, oblivious to the fact that they'd proved how out of touch with reality they were.

"Wow. What a burn."

My voice was so monotone I could've replaced Ben Stein in the Clear Eyes commercials. I didn't want to be in there. When I'd arrived, Enzo had popped up out of nowhere, a deep black and blue bruise marring his jaw. The sight made me smile so wide my cheeks hurt. I didn't even care that he'd looked at me like he'd kill me. But now I wished he'd taken me out in the foyer instead of telling me I needed to make sure my cousins were ready. All they'd done was argue over dresses for the last fifteen minutes. I needed to get out of here before I ruined the engagement by blowing a hole in Adriana's head so I wouldn't have to hear her awful voice.

Champagne bubbles tickled my nose as I downed the liquid. Maybe if I got drunk, I'd like my cousins better. Not likely, though.

"Has no one taught you to sip champagne? You guzzle that like barn animals raised you." My back stiffened at the venom dripping from the newcomer's tone.

Damn, I hadn't even heard her come in.

Giana Romano, ex-wife of my dead sperm donor. I hated her almost as much as I hated her brother. A bitter smile appeared on my face before I made my way to the door she was blocking. There was no way I was staying in this room if she was going to be in here.

"No, I didn't learn anything from barn animals. But my friends on the corner taught me how to deep-throat a champagne bottle. That's usually my preferred method of drinking bubbly," I replied, fighting to keep my composure as she turned every shade of red imaginable. It was a shame she'd shot her face up with so much Botox that it didn't move. I'd have loved to watch her eyes widen and her brows furrow in anger.

"What man wants to wed a whore?" she spat back.

"Hmm," I mused, looking down at her empty left finger. "Is that why you're still unwed?" I asked, shouldering past her before she retaliated. I'd pay for those little comments later, but I didn't give a shit at the moment. Giana had a bite with her bark, but I was a tough bitch.

Music drifted through the penthouse Dominick had rented out for the event. He wouldn't invite people to his own home, but he still wanted this to feel like a true family dinner. Complete with an enormous table for us all to sit at while we pretended we didn't want to stab each other. Ironically, this event wasn't just family. The guest list was a curated selection of politicians and businessmen. Anyone Dominick felt should be present for the announcement of Caleb and Adriana's union.

There was power in witnesses and deals. The mafioso wanted to ensure enough money and favors were exchanged to keep this engagement between the Italians and the Syndicate from falling apart. The Mafia took part in a lot of white-collar crimes here in New York. Dominick had his dirty fingers in a lot of pies. The Irish operated the same way, at a slightly lower level. But Caleb had been their cash cow when it came to business deals before he'd cut out to play his own game, so it would be interesting to see where these allegiances fell.

As much as it pained me to admit, Dominick wasn't completely stupid. He knew those boys needed this alliance as much as he did. Backing from him would help sway some of these people to stick with Caleb and cut ties with the Mob. On the surface, this was a *you scratch my back, and I scratch yours* agreement.

But I knew Dominick had far more sinister plans in the

works. It was why he'd paid for the folder I'd retrieved from Neon Nights. The one that Caleb had tried to steal back. Did he know who'd paid for the intel? That it was his new daddy-in-law looking to screw them over?

My musings were cut short when I entered the main portion of the penthouse. It was furnished to accommodate events such as this. Seating areas were thoughtfully placed around the room for those who wanted to sit and chat, but there were generous open spaces for mingling and rubbing elbows.

Men in tailored suits were busy kissing each other's asses. Instantly, I marked out the ones who were carrying weapons. I didn't bother doing that with the women. They landed their blows with cutting words and nasty looks instead of bullets.

I scanned the room until I found what I was looking for.

Oh, thank God.

The real beauty of the room was the open bar tucked into the corner. Tonight would require something stronger than champagne to get me through it. I crossed the room like a woman on a mission.

"Can I get a shot of vodka?" I asked, tapping the glass bar top. "And none of that watered-down garbage. Give me something so strong it might induce alcohol poisoning. Do you think needing to get my stomach pumped qualifies as a reasonable excuse for leaving this shit party?" I grumbled.

A young kid, probably barely old enough to pour alcohol, stood there staring at me. He blinked a few times, like his brain was trying to confirm he'd heard me correctly. A smirk crept up my face at the thought.

"Well?" I asked expectantly.

He glanced from side to side before ducking behind the bar and popping up with an unassuming bottle clutched in his hands.

"This is the stuff you want, then," he said with a conspira-torial smile. Anything in a plastic bottle was bound to be strong enough to strip paint. It would taste like shit, but as long as it did the job, I was game.

"I'll take one with you, yeah?" he said.

Obviously, he'd meant it as a rhetorical question because two shot glasses appeared. He poured us both a generous double, using his chin to signal me to grab mine for a toast.

"To beautiful women."

Holding back my eye roll at his flirtation attempt was physically painful. But rather than shoving the glass down his esophagus, I played nice, throwing back the liquid. My throat felt like it was on fire, and the smell of the shot alone singed my nose hairs.

Damn, this could wake you up from a coma.

I slammed the glass on the bar top, ready to leave. "Thanks for the good shit. Now I need to go locate a dick." The moment the words left my lips, I pointed my finger at him. "I didn't mean that the way it sounded, and no, I don't want yours."

I turned to go find an inconspicuous corner to hide in while I searched for Caleb so I could avoid him. But I ran into a brick wall before I made it more than a few inches.

A warm bergamot and whiskey-scented brick wall.

Large hands landed on my exposed shoulders to steady me.

"Whoa, where are you off to so quickly that you can't watch where you're going?"

"To fuck your mo—" The rest of my retort died on my lips when I looked up. Tingles erupted in all the areas his rough fingers touched. I took in the full glory of the Russian Boogeyman himself, Nikolay Volkov.

Fuck, he was delicious.

My lids fluttered closed as I attempted to rein in my reactions, because I was a mess of conflicting emotions. Subconsciously I wanted to run or curl up in the fetal position. Then there was the hussy in me who wanted to ask if he would speak directly into my pussy with that luscious rumble. But a bucket of ice water was dumped on my libido—really, it was more like a cold-ish splash because my nipples were still hard enough to cut glass—when I realized the other two might not be far behind. And I did not want to see Caleb again.

But the man had me boxed in, and it didn't look like he would let me go anytime soon.

EIGHT
NIKO

A DEVIL IN A SATIN DRESS

SHE HAD TO BE UNHINGED. The beautiful ones usually were. And I was pretty sure she'd been about to say she was on her way to fuck my mom.

Fuck. She was gorgeous up close.

I'd been admiring her, watching the way her throat moved while downing the liquid. How her hair brushed the top of her ass with her head tipped back. But I couldn't have prepared for what I would witness when she turned around. Her brunette locks were a halo of soft waves framing her heart-shaped face. Full lips turned up in a sneer, begging to be bitten, but her eyes? They were haunting. Icy in both color and the lack of warmth they held.

Yet they set me on fire.

This damned penthouse was filled with haughty women and corporate asshole men, plus the lackeys the Four Families had sent to figure out what the hell Dominick was doing with us. We were supposed to solidify an alliance with the Italians tonight . Another piece of our puzzle accomplished. The other three families wouldn't touch us. No one wanted to kill off their spare heir. They all foolishly thought we'd come crawling back like prodigal sons. This union was to keep Dominick in line until the rest of our plans were laid out.

Of course, the Mafia don insisted on making the engagement party an event. So here I was, in a rented-out penthouse filled with beige furniture that looked uncomfortable and shit alcohol. The only interesting thing was her. She'd clearly been trying to go somewhere when she bumped into me, and it took every ounce of my willpower to peel my fingers away from her soft skin.

I still hadn't moved out of her way.

It was as if my shoes were cemented to the floor. Her glacial eyes traveled down my body, lit with fight, which was not the usual reaction I received.

"Cat got your tongue?" I asked, intrigued by the flash of defiance in her eyes.

Even women who wanted me acted demure and apprehensive. None of them ever *sneered* at me while making me feel like they might attempt to slap me. Her hand tightened slightly, reminding me of my reflex for holding a weapon. A vision of her with a knife to my throat while I sank my cock into her warm cunt flashed in my mind, making my dick twitch.

If only there were such a woman.

Most only craved the *idea* of chasing me down. If they even found the courage to approach me. Rarely were any of them willing to follow through with the act, especially when they learned of the way I preferred to fuck. Kenji and Caleb got most of the women. Kenji, with his easygoing facade, and Caleb, with his public reputation and impressive net worth.

"Never mind, spitfire. Run back to the dick you entertain," I scoffed when she still hadn't responded. But to my surprise, she moved closer. Our bodies nearly touched as she stepped into my space, craning her neck to hold the stare-off.

I broke first.

The temptation to study the delicate column of her throat

was too much. A growl slipped out against my will as I pictured how pretty she would look with my fingerprints marking her.

"Wanna wrap your hand around it?" she purred, causing my eyes to snap back to hers as I mentally checked that my jaw hadn't gone slack at her words.

Had I said my thoughts aloud?

That's when I saw it. She wasn't unhinged—well, maybe a little—this woman was self-assured. And it was doing things to my balls because I loved to tame a brat but rarely got the chance. My legs shifted apart slightly, widening my stance to accommodate the way my dick was reacting.

She needed to run off so I could focus on something other than how amazing her tits looked in the V of her satin dress and how I'd love to run my tongue across them.

"What's that supposed to mean?" I snapped, giving her the same look I gave the men I was sent to collect, hoping it would scare her away. Instead, her pink tongue swiped along her plump bottom lip, pulling it between her teeth. Like she wanted to devour me.

"Touchy, touchy." She trailed a fingertip over my chest, shocking me when she circled my nipple before pinching it. "You looked like you wanted to choke me, big boy. Did I take your drink? Because I didn't know."

My voice came out huskier than intended when I replied. "They serve watered-down shit here."

A smile bloomed on her face. One so large I felt the corners of my own mouth pulling up. "Nah. He served me the real shit. Want a shot?" she asked, pointing over her shoulder with her thumb.

It was as if we were in our own bubble, too consumed with one another even to notice others approaching.

"Niko. What the fuck is taking so long? We gotta go around and check—" Kenji paused beside me, and I didn't need to look at him to know that his eyes had widened with interest. "I'm sorry, miss. Is my asshole friend here bothering you?"

Jealousy, an emotion I wasn't used to, thrummed through my veins as Kenji took her hand in his. Of course the fucker didn't shake it or kiss it. No, the asshole went full cockblock and bit the top of her hand. Based on how her eyes widened and she seemed to choke back a moan, I fully expected to lose her interest now that he was here. For some reason, I desperately didn't want her to dismiss me. I'd share her with Kenji —with either of my brothers—but we found most women weren't as open to that idea.

I was ready to retreat and leave them when her attention swiveled back to me.

"He's not bothering me at all. Big boy here was about to take a shot with me. Right?"

Before I could answer, Caleb walked up, and I swore her whole body tensed. The brazen woman I'd been speaking to for the last few minutes disappeared. She untucked her hair, letting it fall like a curtain, and avoided eye contact, staring at the patch of flooring in front of her.

Maybe they'd fucked before?

"Well, it was nice to meet you, but I have to go mingle now," she commented, trying to push past the wall of bodies we'd formed.

"Wait," Kenji pleaded. "You never gave me your name or your number. How am I supposed to invite you to the after-party?"

I wanted to be pissed at him, but truthfully, I was grateful he remembered to ask. Because he was right. She'd never given her name, and I wanted to know what to moan while I beat one out in the shower tonight. But the resigned sigh she let out caused my hackles to rise.

She didn't want to give her name. I wasn't the only one who noticed the reaction. Kenji's eyes narrowed, and his happy-go-lucky smile morphed into his predatorial one. We'd made it as far in this life as we had because we listened to our guts. Her reaction might have been nothing, but we wouldn't take the chance that we were wrong.

Caleb's menacing tone cut through the tension. "Name. Now. Unless there's a reason you haven't given it," he said, cocking a brow expectantly. Caleb was even more untrusting than I was, so she'd better have a good reason, or he'd be hauling her ass out of her for questioning.

"Of course there's a reason," she snapped, finally lifting her eyes to meet his. "I know you're used to every woman throwing themselves at you, but here's a little life lesson. We don't *have* to give you our names. We could just tell you to go fuck yourself." Her tongue swiped across her bottom lip, the movement drawing our attention, but it wasn't meant to seduce. She was attempting to work through something in her head. Now I was confident she was hiding something.

"Scarletta Romano," she finally answered. Confusion and disbelief were evident on all three of our faces, gaining us an eye roll from her. "Yes, as in the Romano family hosting this party. He's my uncle. Now, I have something I need to attend to. Have a lovely engagement, Caleb."

She didn't wait for a response, just booked it out of there like her perky ass was on fire.

"Well, fuck me," I whispered.

NINE
CALEB

I COULDN'T REMOVE my eyes from the retreating woman as she weaved through the party guests. "She brought up the engagement. No one knows about that. So how did little miss Scarletta find out?" I commented, sipping on the whiskey the bartender had dropped off.

"Girls talk about shit." From the corner of my eye, I caught Kenji's shrug. Clearly, he wasn't having feelings of suspicion surrounding the beautiful woman.

"But have you ever heard of Dominick having a niece? Because I sure as hell haven't," Niko questioned, pulling out his phone to run a search.

I gave my head a slow shake while never letting her out of my line of sight. We knew all the major players and the women in their lives, but I didn't know her.

"Well, I'll be damned. She is a Romano." Niko let out a humorless laugh. "I can't figure out how exactly. Looks like Dominick took her in as a baby and raised her, according to this news article. It's the only thing I can find that mentions the two names together. But sure as shit, he says in here that she's his niece."

"Why the fuck have we never heard of her, then?" Kenji

chimed in, pulling out a blunt. He preferred weed to booze. His eyes also tracked her as she politely declined advances from assholes. My fist clenched as a man went to trail his hand down her arm. She danced away at the last minute, a faux smile plastered on her face. The one she gave him was too *sweet* compared to how she'd basically bared her teeth at us.

I preferred the version we got. It was at least genuine.

"She's a defiant little thing," I mused, thinking about her attitude toward me demanding her name. There was something so familiar about her, but no way would I forget a face like hers. She was gorgeous with her toffee-colored hair framing a heart-shaped face, full lips that were painted blood red, and those eyes like crystalline water. I had only ever seen a few women with…

Hair rose on the back of my neck. The prickle of recognition I'd felt earlier was now a maelstrom of electric shocks.

"Fuck."

Amber liquid sloshed everywhere as I slammed the glass down, taking off after the woman who'd been haunting me every night.

"Do me a favor and keep Dominick from looking for me," I called over my shoulder.

"Where are you off to?" Kenji asked as I moved toward where I'd last seen a satin emerald dress.

"I'm going to go talk to Miss Romano about the dangers of taking things that don't belong to her."

Both of my brothers laughed. "Oh, shit. I love a good game of chase. Dibs on questioning her. I have so many fun ideas," Kenji said.

For her sake, she had better hope that wasn't needed. But if she was who I thought she was, then I couldn't wait to mar her olive skin and return the favor of being tied up. I smiled at the idea of inflicting violence. I didn't really give a fuck that she hadn't realized she was stealing from me.

She was going to be paying for her sins.

Excitement simmered in my veins. The energy caused me to shrug off business acquaintances I'd normally make time for. But at this moment, I was a hunter after my prey.

She made her way toward the bathroom, probably hoping to hide out until dinner.

Too bad that plan wouldn't work.

I rounded the corner to a shadowy hallway that was more like a hidden alcove. A hint of something warm and sensual hit my nose as she shook her honeyed hair back over her toned shoulders. There was a tightness to them that told me she suspected she wasn't alone. In the next moment, she dashed into the powder room, attempting to throw the door closed.

She was fast, but I was faster.

"What the fuc…" She glared at my dress shoe jammed between the door and the frame.

"You and I need to have a little chat, Miss *Romano*." Even to my ears, my tone was menacing, but she didn't flinch away as I'd expected. Instead, she took an exasperated breath, like I was nothing more than an annoying pest.

"Look, if you need to pee, I'm sure there's more than just this bathroom. In fact, go use the one where your *fiancée* is getting ready. Congrats, by the way, she's a real peach," she said, patting my chest condescendingly before attempting to push me out of the way. But there was no way in hell I'd let her out of my sight without some answers.

Namely, where the fuck was my folder?

A satisfying thud from her head hitting the marble-covered wall reverberated through the small powder room as I pushed us inside, locking the door behind me. The flutter of her pulse under my palm brought a smile to my face.

"What the hell?" she called out as my other hand trapped her wrists above her. "Don't you think this is inappropriate behavior for someone who's about to be engaged to another Romano?"

Her knee came up to ram me in the dick, but I blocked the blow, pinning her hips with mine.

"Do you remember what I said I'd do when I found you, thief?" My voice dripped with disdain as I tightened my grip on her throat. "I want to watch tears streak down your face as I choke you."

She paled, and panic flashed across her face, but it was gone in a second. In its wake was a fiery mask of defiance. Her eyes narrowed as she pushed into my grasp, adding pressure to her windpipe.

"I'm not sure your cock is big enough to choke me, Callahan. It feels a bit…lacking." Her words were a harsh rasp, but they made me aware of how close our bodies were.

Smart-ass bitch.

My stomach curdled with rage at her flippant response. But it didn't prevent the spike of lust from coursing through me as her body wriggled beneath mine. I didn't have time to play with her, though the way her nipples strained against her satin dress suggested she might like how I played. It was too bad that I considered anyone standing in my way an enemy.

No matter how gorgeous the face or great the tits.

"As much as I'd love for you to wrap those lips around my cock, I don't fuck Romano bitches," I snarled. "But maybe, if you're a good girl and answer my questions, I'll kill you quickly. Snap your neck instead of strangling you," I whispered in her ear, savoring how my breath caused her skin to pebble.

Or maybe it was my words.

"Wow. I want to say I feel sorry for your soon-to-be wife. But since you didn't deny the small cock, she's probably better off if you don't fuck—"

Her smart-ass comment ended in a coughing fit as I

pushed into the soft flesh of her throat while yanking her hand down to cup my hardening length. Pride coursed through me at the slight flare of her nostrils when she felt my *small dick.* I'd never denied the fact that I was a sick fuck. But Miss Scarletta seemed to be her own version of fucked-up, if her blown-out pupils and the way her chest rose and fell were anything to go by.

Ten out of ten chance that her underwear was soaked.

Now I got the appeal of hate sex.

These emotions coursing through me heightened every sense. The feel of her skin was like silk under my calloused fingertips, and the warmth of her scent was so heady in the room that I wanted to bury my nose in her hair. Every fiber of my being wanted to slam my cock into her cunt. The slapping of flesh would almost be as satisfying as hearing her sobs.

I didn't have to like her to want to fuck her. Maybe I'd make her an exception to the whole *no fucking any of Dominick's family* rule. In fact, hating her made the idea more appealing. I wanted to use her like the slut I was sure she was. But there wasn't time for that.

She was only useful for one thing at the moment.

"Now, now, Scarletta, enough talk about how much you want me. This is how it's going to work. I'll ask a question, and you're going to answer." Her throat bobbed as she swallowed. "Without the smart remarks. Otherwise, I'll cut off your air. Nod your head if you understand," I stated.

If looks could kill, she'd have murdered me three times over at this point. But she couldn't hide the fact that there was lust mixed in with her anger. We were both warring with the internal battle. Was mine as evident on my face as hers was?

Her curt nod spurred me on.

"Who are you? And who do you work for?" I asked.

Niko had already checked her out, but I wanted the damning evidence from her own mouth. The question of whether she took the folder was on the tip of my tongue, but I didn't want to give information away yet.

The way she rolled her eyes in annoyance pissed me off, as if I'd asked the stupidest question in existence.

"I've already told you. Scarletta Romano. Dominick Romano's niece. Why would I give you a false name when I have to sit through a torturous dinner with you? And of all the people to falsely associate myself with, you think I'd pick your new daddy-in-law? Fuck. I want nothing to do with him, but here we are."

She mumbled the last part of her statement so quietly that I almost missed it. Something in the way she spoke about Dominick reminded me of the same way I spoke about my Da.

"Who. Sent. You?" I bit out, fighting against my desire to cut off her air supply.

"Who do you think, asshole?" she snarled back.

Sweat beaded up along my forehead. Fuck. I didn't know what was on that folder, but it couldn't have been anything too damning. *But* if Dominick knew I was in that office that night... that could fuck us. He might decide just to take us out instead of forming a plan with the intel on the folder.

We hadn't come heavily armed tonight since we were playing along with this alliance.

"Does he know I was there that night?" I asked, my voice coming out as a growl. Anger and desperation seeped into each word, and I increased the pressure on her throat.

Her icy blue eyes met mine. Sincerity and fear showed in them, but I was pretty positive the fear wasn't because of me.

"I didn't tell him I saw you that night. It would've been my ass if he'd found out I was almost caught." She shifted, biting her lip when she brushed against my hardening length. "How 'bout we call this a truce and go on our merry fucking way? Yeah?" she asked in a hopeful tone. Her tongue poked out, swiping across her lip while she eagerly searched my face for a response.

I turned her words over in my mind while studying her. She was an anomaly—a risk—but she might be what we needed. Unfortunately for her.

Kenji, Niko, and I had talents that made us scary mother-fuckers. Being a conniving bastard was my gift. My ability to figure out how to make any situation into a favorable deal was how I'd made the Mob so much money.

A crossroads demon in the flesh, and Scarletta was about to sell her soul to the Syndicate.

My hand moved from her throat to her jaw, and I leaned so close my lips brushed hers, our breaths mingling with each word. "Oh, Scarletta. This is how it's going to play out. You owe me a favor of my choice, with no questions asked when I come to collect. And you'll follow through all the way. No fighting me."

Her lids fluttered closed in defeat. "And why the fuck would I do that, asshole?" she asked as she thrashed in my hands, trying to rip away from my hold. But there was little she could do against my muscled frame.

She was a butterfly pinned to a board, powerless in her fight as I ripped her wings off.

"Because if you don't, I'll make sure your uncle knows about your fuck-up. And I'm guessing I'm the one with the resources to get him to believe my version of events," I responded cockily.

Her snarl was all the confirmation I needed. Excitement at the thought of her reaction when she discovered the full extent of my newly formed plan snaked through my veins. She'd hate every single moment of it. And I took no greater pleasure than knowing I was fucking over the Romano family and the bitch who'd stolen from me.

"Should've taken a picture of your ass tied up," she grumbled, no longer fighting against me.

"That a deal?" I asked, running my nose along her cheek the way a lover might, savoring how she vibrated with anger. She turned her face so our mouths were once again pressed against each other.

"Fine. Deal, fucker," she responded with vitriol instead of defeat. Her fire licked at my skin.

Pain radiated from my bottom lip. The bitch bit me, but I'd be damned if I let her get the better of me. She probably expected me to pull away, not press every inch of my body flush with hers. The soft gasp was the perfect opportunity for me to shove my tongue in, letting the tang coat both of our mouths.

The sounds of the party disappeared, replaced by our labored breathing. But the soft moan she let slip was like a douse of cold water. My body wanted to stay plastered against hers—actually, I wanted to sit her on the counter and sink balls-deep in her—but my mind reminded me that she was everything I hated.

Romano bitch.

"Sealed in blood," she spat when I pulled far enough away to see her face. Anger flared in her eyes, but her olive skin was almost pale, aside from the flush on her cheeks. A tendril of her brunette waves had sprung free from behind her ears, and without permission, my hand came up and tucked it back in place.

What the hell is wrong with my body?

Before she could mistake the gesture for kindness, I shoved her toward the door, needing to get out of this confined space before I did something stupid like actually kissing her.

Because what we'd done wasn't a kiss…

"Let's go. You'll be sitting next to me at dinner."

It was comical how quickly her head whipped around to look at me.

"Like fuck I will. You're sitting next to my uncle and your goons."

I moved into her personal space again, ignoring the inner voice asking why we needed to be so close. "You're my bitch at the moment. Are you not as smart as you look, Scarletta? Because I thought you'd have gotten the picture by now. I own your ass." The corners of my mouth curled upward at her snarl.

Her hands landed on her hips, drawing my eyes to her figure. She looked like she'd been sewn into her dress by the way it hugged her so perfectly. I'd been so distracted earlier that I hadn't really taken in her body.

"Is that your favor, then? You want me to sit with you at dinner? Because if not"—she turned, yanking the door open and darting out of reach—"go fuck yourself."

TEN
SCAR

GOD, his hands were the size of dinner plates, and their warmth seeped through my skin like a brand. A shiver ran through me, and I wasn't sure if it was from disgust or excitement. I'd almost made it out of his reach, but these damn heels I'd worn made me slower than usual.

"No. This isn't my favor." Hot breath fanned across the back of my neck before he spun me around to face him. "But you're still going to do what I say, because unless you have a way of overpowering me," he paused, eyeing me condescendingly, "you can't do shit to stop me from sitting your ass where I want," Caleb stated, jutting his chin and crossing his arms over his muscled chest. "And something tells me you don't want to cause a scene in front of your uncle."

Smug bastard.

The hard steel nestled against my thigh tempted me to show Caleb exactly the type of *scene* I was capable of causing. But that would mean revealing too many of my secrets to way too many people. It was the same reason I hadn't fought against him in the bathroom. At the time, it seemed like the lesser of the two evils, but now that I had some ominous *favor* hanging over my head, I wondered if maybe I should've gone with option A: Leaving the bloodied body of a former Irish Mob member on the tiled floor.

"Lead the way," I stated, flipping him off as he walked past. "Wait." I grabbed Caleb's arm, halting him before we left the cover of the secluded hallway. "This isn't a sexual favor, right? Because I'm not paid pussy."

His laugh surprised me. I hadn't thought the dick knew how to do that. This whole time, he'd been an angry ass. Hadn't even bothered being gentle with me. And I didn't want to explore why that was a turn-on.

"Do I look like I pay for pussy? And I'd rather let my dick freeze off than stick it in a Romano cunt," he said, taking out his phone and shooting off a text before pulling me behind him like a naughty child. The volume increased as we entered the dining room. Scents of spices and comfort food lingered in the air, making my stomach growl in anticipation.

"What?" I snapped at Caleb's questioning glance. "It smells good, and I'm fucking hungry."

He blinked at me like my admission surprised him, which I supposed was possible. Most socialite women were on crazy regimens to maintain unrealistic and unhealthy body standards. Meanwhile, I regularly polished off lobster tortellini by myself and lifted heavy shit so I'd be strong enough to take on a man.

The room was fuller than when I'd made my break for the powder room. I'd counted thirty or so people, with some familiar faces from members of the Four Families spread out along the table. None of them were very high up in the ranks, though. Probably sent to investigate what this gathering was about.

Dominick stood at the head of the table, his head thrown back as he laughed at something a man in a well-tailored charcoal gray suit with pinstripes had said. A mess of blond hair was artfully styled back. Dominick looked sloppy compared to the mystery man whose back was to us. I couldn't tell who he was from my angle, but something nagged at the back of my brain, telling me I knew him. I was so distracted that I hadn't noticed Caleb had led us to the seats to the left of Dominick's.

"I can't sit here," I hissed through my teeth, careful not to draw my uncle's attention. Caleb pulled out a chair next to him, completely ignoring my protests.

He arched an eyebrow when I still hadn't moved. "Why not? You're family, right? Besides, I don't give a damn what Dominick says. I'll sit next to him, and you're next to me. Now, ass in the chair, Romano."

Something warm and moist ran up the column of my neck, and my hand reached for the hidden blade, ready to sink it into the gut of whoever stood behind me, until a smooth voice whispered in my ear.

"Cheer up. You get to be next to me too."

I turned to face Kenji, a manic gleam in his chocolate eyes. I knew that expression, the borderline unhinged excitement that coursed through one's body. Mine always came before inflicting violence. I had an inkling Kenji's might be the same.

Would I find myself at the end of his blade tonight?

A shudder racked through my body. Excitement was not the correct response to that line of thinking, but the man was a walking sexual awakening of all the things I didn't know I was into until seeing him. Kenji had a nose ring and a subtle face tattoo on his temple that followed the hairline of his effortlessly messy inky hair. It read *Insane* and was done in gothic lettering.

That's not concerning at all.

Then there was the not-so-subtle throat tattoo. It looked like it was the lower half of an *oni* mask. The reds and blacks were beautifully vibrant against his skin. I had to resist running the tip of my finger along its lines.

My cheeks heated further when Niko walked up to join us. He stood so close to my shoulder that we were practically touching. My bathroom encounter with Caleb hadn't given me a chance to analyze what had possessed me to act the way I had around Niko. I wasn't sexually shy, but flirting with these three men was not good for my health. Literally anyone else would be a less complicated fuck.

Except maybe Enzo.

A flurry of goose bumps broke out over my skin when Niko leaned forward, running the tip of his tongue along the shell of my ear.

What the hell is with these men licking me? And why the fuck do I want it to happen again, maybe just a little farther south...

"Take the shot. You're going to need it," the Russian whispered, breaking my horny daydream.

My nose wrinkled in confusion until a small silver flask was pushed into my hand. I eyed it for a moment, debating the wisdom in drinking something from these men. This night was already going to hell. Being drugged might be a plus at this point. Cool metal met my lips as I took a swig of the mystery contents.

I bit back my cough, and a delicious burn trickled down my throat. Vodka.

What a sight we must be. Me with my back to the table, surrounded by men who looked like they fucked people up for shits and giggles. It pissed me off how these three made me feel unbalanced, out of control. And honestly, they needed a taste of their own medicine.

Liquid trickled out of the corner of my mouth, and I used my thumb to wipe it up. I made a show of swirling my tongue around the digit while keeping my sights locked on Niko, who still hadn't stepped out of my personal space.

Where my eyes were so light they were borderline silver, Niko's were the color of ocean water. Stormy and dangerous, with death creeping below the surface if you weren't careful. His lips parted slightly at the wet *pop* sound my mouth created when I pulled my thumb out. A soft moan came from

Kenji, but what made the whole act worthwhile was the angry "fuck" Caleb whispered.

Our little bubble of sexual tension and hate was shattered with the boom of my uncle's voice. "Ladies and gentlemen, thank you for joining me tonight. Please, let's sit and have some dinner." The faux friendliness in his face dropped the second he looked over to where I stood.

"What the fuck are you doing over here, Scarletta?" he growled out.

Asshole.

I opened my mouth to answer, but Caleb beat me to it.

"I asked her to sit here. If you want to tear into someone, try me, Dominick," he responded, his tone holding a lethal edge. My eyes bounced between the two men engaged in a silent showdown.

For fuck's sake, this was ridiculous.

My patience for this night was wearing thin. I plopped down in the vacant chair, pulling Kenji down between Niko and me. The move earned me a glare from Enzo, who'd shown up across the table, along with both of my cunt cousins, who were sending me death threats with their eyes.

Great, this was going to be *so* much fun.

A chuckle came from beside me. "You're real popular around here, aren't you?" Kenji asked.

"I'm the family favorite." I feigned innocence while flipping off Adriana and Milania.

My breath hitched when a hand I was becoming far too familiar with landed on the upper part of my thigh. The slit in my dress left a sliver of skin unprotected by the silky fabric, and, of course, those calloused fingers managed to find it. I bit back a moan from the rush of pleasure and pain as Caleb squeezed hard enough to leave a mark.

"Behave yourself, Scar," Caleb said, not bothering to look at me as he gave the command like I was a fucking dog.

Enough conversations were happening that no one else heard his instruction.

I was never out of control around my uncle and his lackeys, but this man pulled at my composure, tempting me to unleash the creature I kept contained.

"I'm not doing anything, Callahan. Now move your fucking hand," I bit out under my breath. Hard eyes turned toward me. His gaze was so piercing that I swore I could see flames licking up the walls of his irises.

"I want to join in on the fun," Kenji snickered, placing his hand on my other thigh.

Instinct kicked in when he came within centimeters of grazing my sheathed knife, and I wrenched his thumb back. His surprised hiss halted my movement before I broke it.

"Sorry," I said sheepishly, not sure how I would explain away this one. So I went with a version of the truth. "I don't react well to being touched."

I flicked my gaze up so I could read the expression on his face. But other than his eyebrow ticking up slightly, it was blank. Kenji assessed me like my secrets were written on my skin. Ironically, they were when you undressed me. But he wouldn't be doing that anytime soon.

I meant ever—he wouldn't do that ever…

His honeyed voice didn't hold a hint of anger when he responded. "Don't worry about it. But you should probably pay attention to the conversation. I have a feeling it's going to be good."

He winked, interlacing our fingers and setting them on his lap. I didn't know what to make of the exchange, but it was clear I wouldn't be getting my hand back for the time being. And Caleb still had a death grip on my thigh. Asshole was probably going to use it like a choke collar, squeezing the shit out of it every time I did something that displeased him. All that was missing was Niko's touch. I found my gaze drifting toward him, and sure as shit, oceanic eyes were watching me.

The weirdest vision popped into my mind of him draping his arm across the back of Kenji's chair so he could place his hand on the back of my neck.

But the daydream was broken when the man who'd been speaking to my uncle earlier suddenly appeared, taking a seat to the right of the Mafia don—a spot that Enzo would normally occupy. My shoulders stiffened as he looked up. His handsome but harsh features were, in fact, familiar. I didn't know him personally, but I sure as shit knew *who* he was.

"Caleb, since we're going to be in business together, I'd like to introduce you to a new associate of mine. But I'm not sure *she* needs to be present for this conversation," Dominick said, spittle flying through the air.

Hazel eyes moved my way, and the man's head tilted slightly, like he was inspecting something interesting. "She's quite beautiful. I don't see the harm in her staying. In my experience, most successful men enjoy having something *delightful* to look at during business transactions." His words slid over my body, feeling tainted and wrong, but I kept all of those thoughts out of my expression. Instead, I offered him a soft, demure smile, suppressing the need to run my blade across his throat.

Dominick let out an irritated huff but didn't protest further. "Yes, well, in that case. Caleb, this is Maxim Petrov. A new partner of mi—"

Maxim cut in. "Dominick, let's be clear. I am not your partner. I am your new employer." His attention moved from Dominick to Caleb, who was the picture of calm, minus the hand he had hidden. That one was white-knuckled against my thigh. "And since you are soon to be in alliance with Dominick here, that makes you my employee as well. No?" Maxim asked, his tone purposefully taunting.

The rest of the party faded away, choked out by the growing lethal tension at the head of the table as Caleb stared Maxim down.

"Yes, well, let's get on with why we're here tonight, and then we can discuss this over cigars in the lounge. And without ladies in the room. Or Scarletta," Dominick commented.

An eyebrow hit my hairline at the underhanded comment. "Your daughter's fiancé has been close to my pussy enough times to know I'm a lady," I mumbled, earning a choked laugh from Kenji as I sipped from my water goblet. I shouldn't have had those shots of vodka, because they had me feeling bold tonight.

Caleb's hand tightened on my thigh, his knuckles practically white, but I swore I saw a hint of a smirk on his face.

Dominick stood, champagne flute and a butter knife clasped in his hands. "Before we get to tonight's dinner, I have an announcement I'd like to make." The faux smile he'd plastered on annoyed me. He looked out over his guests as if they were adoring fans, not a pack of hungry hyenas vying for whatever scraps he'd send their way.

None of them were loyal. They'd align themselves with whomever guaranteed them a piece of the pie.

Dominick peered at Caleb, his grin morphing into something sinister. But the Irishman seemed at ease. The tension from moments ago was gone. Or at least he played it off that way, lounging back in his chair like he owned the place, fingers pulling at the loose thread on the tablecloth. My eyes fluttered closed for a moment when he started caressing my thigh with his thumb.

He's trying to kill me. Get me offed for being seduced by my cousin's fiancé.

Fuck. He's supposed to marry her.

Suddenly, the heat from his hand was gone as he stood. "I'll take it from here, Dominick." Confusion colored my uncle's face. But he didn't like to seem like he wasn't in control, so he played it off as a planned exchange. Motioning for Caleb to take it away as he sat back in his seat and glared as if the younger man was shit on his shoe.

"Most of you here know me, but for those few who don't, I'm Caleb Callahan," he said, his deep voice easily carrying across the space.

Pompous ass would figure people knew who he was.

"My brothers and I have recently branched off and started our own…company." He paused for the chorus of chuckles, giving the table a charming smile—a stark contrast to the man who'd had me pinned against a wall not twenty minutes ago. "And this dinner is to celebrate the joining of families."

Soft clapping erupted from the table from everyone but the members of the Four.

Adriana was practically beaming, and she sat so straight I'd have sworn there was a stick shoved up her ass, preventing her from slouching. Anger at her reaction turned in my stomach, which pissed me off even more.

Why the hell would I be upset about her marrying this jackass?

In the next moment, I was yanked to my feet. An oomph fell from my lips as my body crashed into Caleb's, my hand coming up to brace against his hard chest. Before I could remove it, he interlocked our fingers and pinned them in place. Panic swept through me when his arm banded around my back, coming to rest on my hip, the touch searing.

He continued to address the crowd as I stood there, intimately plastered to his side, while my family all shot daggers at me.

"My *wife*, Scarletta Romano, and I are so excited to finally announce our union."

My heart beat so loud in my ears that I barely heard Enzo shush my cousins' cries of outrage. Throwing a flashbang into the crowded room would have caused less disruption than his announcement.

What the actual fuck was going on?

Caleb's lush lips slammed down on mine, his tongue demanding entry as it swiped along the seam. This wasn't a kiss —it was a claiming. A warning to keep my fucking mouth shut.

You owe me a favor of my choice, with no questions asked when I come to collect. And you'll follow through all the way. No fighting me.

His words from earlier tonight played on a loop in my head.

"I should've gone with option A and murdered you," I whispered against him, feeling him give me a smug smile.

"Watch your tone, wife. I'll bend you over this table and teach you a lesson in manners in front of our guests."

I snapped my gaze to his. Chaos lurked in his eyes. It didn't frighten me…it excited me.

"Please do. I'll be sure and yell Niko and Kenji's names real loud," I snarled back, savoring how his nostrils flared. "You picked the wrong bitch if you wanted someone submissive, *husband.*"

I swallowed thickly as he tore his gaze from me and signaled to the other two before addressing the table again. "Please, enjoy your dinner. Unfortunately, we have somewhere else we need to be," Caleb announced, pushing me into Kenji's waiting grasp.

Across the table, Enzo's and my uncle's eyes burned with anger, but neither of them said a word. It would look bad for them if they revealed that they didn't know what the fuck was happening.

"Yes, they have somewhere else to be tonight," my uncle spat. "Please, enjoy the food. I'll be right back after I see them out."

The threat in his words caused me to wince.

Fuck. I was in for some bodily pain when he got to me.

ELEVEN
KENJI

I WOULDN'T REFUSE A FUCK IF SHE WANTED ONE...

SHE WAS PISSED with a capital *P*.

I mean, I understood. Up until we created the Syndicate, my entire life had been dictated by others, and I'd hated every second of it. Countless times, I'd considered taking the heads of my family members and the other Yakuza bosses. But they were like fucking rodents. More would just replace the ones I'd eliminate.

The solution to that problem required a different approach.

I watched the way Scarletta's body posture changed when her uncle mentioned walking us out. She reminded me of a predator ready to strike, but I swore I saw a flash of fear when he looked over at her.

"Want to explain to me what the fuck is going on, Callahan?" Dominick spewed when we'd moved far enough away from the party. He ran a hand over his trimmed facial hair, a typical tell for feeling out of control. "And you." His attention shifted to Scar. "Fucking slut of a girl," he growled as he moved to strike her.

Before it could land, Niko's giant hand wrapped around his wrist. "I suggest you don't touch her. Ever," Niko said, his words vibrating with barely contained rage, his chest rising and falling rapidly.

Niko's grip was so tight that Dominick's hand was nearly white. The idiot was lucky he still had a hand. He'd been seconds away from learning to live with a stump. I was normally fast with my weapon, but the speed at which I'd removed my katana from its sheath when he went to slap her surprised even me. The way her body had braced for impact told me everything I needed to know. This wasn't a first-time thing.

"Scarletta, come stand by Kenji so Nikolay can release your uncle," Caleb stated in a bored tone, as if he were calm and indifferent. But I knew better. The ticking in his jaw and flush of color at the back of his neck said he was teetering on the edge of losing his shit.

Scar's nostrils flared at the command, but she followed the instruction, discreetly flipping him off as she moved toward me. I chuckled at her antics. She didn't enjoy being ordered around. She might've been quiet and obedient during the dinner, but she was like a panther lying in wait.

It was hard to imagine something as beautiful as her being violent. Her thick hair was the color of caramel and hung in soft waves barely past her shoulders. She looked prim and proper in her satin dress and heels. But her eyes? I recognized the hard edge they held. Violence shone in her irises, like an ice storm of rage every time she looked at any of us.

God, watching her and Caleb battle was going to be fun. Because they would. I'd heard about how she made him lie on the floor while she hogtied him—barrel of a gun pointed at his balls. I thought I'd pulled a muscle I'd laughed so hard, and I hadn't stopped giving him shit for it since.

I wouldn't be surprised if he returned the favor to his new wife. Asshole claimed he wanted nothing to do with the woman romantically.

Hell, I didn't either, but I wouldn't refuse a fuck if she wanted one.

My musings were interrupted by Caleb's harsh tone. "Dominick, you speak to my wife like that again, and I'll take it as a personal slight." He stalked closer to the don, pressing in on his chest. Caleb had a good six inches on the man. "And if you *ever* raise a hand to her, you'll be fed through a tube for the rest of your life."

He couldn't threaten to kill him, not yet anyway. So the promise of irreparable damage would have to do.

I didn't bother paying attention to Dominick's response. No, I was too entranced by the beauty whose body radiated nervous energy during the exchange. I glanced down at her heeled feet.

She can't be comfortable in those.

Or maybe I was just a selfish bastard and wanted her close. A leather bench spanned the entry wall behind us, and without a second thought, I plopped down, yanking her onto my lap and smirking at the yelp that slipped from her plump lips. Her eyes were blazing with irritation.

I leaned forward and practically purred in her ear.

"Now, now. Be a good girl. Didn't you hear? We own you now, Scar Romano."

Her breath hitched right before she called me a mother-fucker under her breath, causing my smile to widen and my cock to stiffen. Caleb cleared his throat from where he stood in front of us. We'd been brothers long enough that I could hear all his unspoken words.

They were something like: *Quit acting like a fucking child, Kenji. Why do you have her in your lap? I'm about as fun as a cactus in an asshole.*

Okay, the last part was all me.

I looked up at my friend and winked as I slid my hand under the slit of her dress, caressing her silky skin. I felt her tremble. Our bodies were so close I could feel the heat rolling off her, but I didn't take my eyes off Caleb. I loved the way his jaw ticked at my antics. I lived to fuck with Caleb, and I had a few scars from when I'd pushed him a bit too far. Niko gave me the slightest of headshakes, but he secretly loved my shit-stirring. He'd never said that, but I could tell.

"What happened to the union with my beautiful daughter?" Dominick asked, rubbing his wrist, which already had a purple hue. "It's the perfect deal for both of us. You will have access to the dowry she comes with, and I want to be treated as a partner in your dealings," he added when he hadn't received the response he was looking for.

"No," Caleb stated. The rest of his response was interrupted by Dominick's fist hitting the penthouse door, the slam echoing through the entry.

"No? What more do you want? Milania too?" Dominick yelled, causing his underboss, Enzo, to stiffen, his hand moving toward his firearm.

Yeah, that's what we wanted. Both of your idiot daughters.

I apparently didn't keep that thought to myself because Enzo sent a glare my way. Red crept up his neck, peeking out over his collar when he spotted my hand on Scar's upper thigh. A possessive look crossed his face.

Interesting. Was this the girlfriend he dumped for Dominick's daughter?

To fuck with him, I leaned forward and sucked on the tender flesh behind her ear. My free hand came up to rest high on her ribs, my thumb gracing the curve of her breast.

"You're going to give me a hickey," she hissed, but she didn't make an effort to shake me off, and I nipped at her lobe.

Enzo broke, speaking out of turn. "Get the fuck up, Scarletta. You're acting like a whore sitting on that *stronzo's* lap. And what the fuck are you wearing?" he bit out.

Niko's fists tightened at his sides, and he glanced at Caleb. But he was too busy staring holes into the cocky fucker.

"If you want to tell a woman what to do, go tell your own fucking wife, Enzo." Caleb canted his head toward Scar. "She can wear whatever the fuck she wants. One, because that's her fucking prerogative, and two, I know my dick is good enough to keep her coming and coming *and coming*…back to me every time."

Enzo practically vibrated with rage. Caleb turned his attention back to Dominick. "We have plenty of money. Keep your daughters and their dowries. Scar will do," Caleb replied.

"And we don't need more than one woman," I added, savoring the unhinged expression on Enzo.

"And what the fuck am I getting in exchange for her?" Dominick practically spat out the words. I didn't know why he hated his niece. None of us had even known he had one before tonight.

There were a lot of questions surrounding the spitfire. A mystery waiting to be solved.

My eyes fell back on her as Dominick yelled about compensation and disrespect for denying him. But I tuned him out, focusing on her. Other than the outburst she'd had a few moments ago, she'd been quiet. Most would assume that meant she was like the other women in our world—submissive. But it was a ploy. I watched as the pulse in her neck beat wildly, and I didn't think it was from fear.

I doubted her uncle even knew how perceptive his niece was. Scar seemed happy to let those around her underestimate her. Maybe Caleb *should* have agreed to let her leave the room, because she was collecting all the bits of information she could to prepare for her escape.

God, did I love a challenge.

Once more, I found the shell of her ear. "I'll find you, Scar." Her back stiffened. "I see the wheels turning in that pretty little head. You can try to run…hide. But I'll hunt you down."

She turned to face me, and her piercing eyes felt like they were staring into my soul. She didn't appear to be the least bit intimidated. My pulse jumped for a second, and my confidence slipped slightly. There was definitely more to this woman than we knew. My instincts screamed that she was a fellow predator. Her face broke out in a cocky grin, like I had said my thoughts aloud.

"Scarletta. You have not been given over yet. I need details of my compensation," barked Dominick.

Instantly, a mask came down over the woman I'd just seen.

"Yes, Scarletta. Why don't you stand up until we have properly paid for you? But good to know you're so *willing* to cooperate," Caleb drawled.

She peered at him, mimicking the bored expression he did so well, before getting up and walking toward him. The tension between the two was palpable, but it wasn't all anger. Lust charged the space between them.

Even in heels, she had to stand on her toes to reach Caleb's ear. "If you want me to sit on your lap, Caleb, ask me like a good boy," she whispered, only loud enough for her words to reach Niko and me as well.

The ghost of a smile pulled at Caleb's lips, but he squashed it almost as quickly as it appeared. "Deal is the same, Dominick. I'm still marrying your blood. Why does it matter if it's a daughter or a niece?" he asked.

Scar's throat did a nervous bob at the question. But Dominick? He smiled for the first time since Caleb had dropped his bomb on him.

The don laughed and grabbed for the door handle. "You're so right. The deal is good if you're marrying my blood. Please, enjoy your new wife, and we will be in touch to discuss business. No?" His attention moved to Scar, who looked like a caged animal. "Scarletta, don't forget your place."

It was clearly a threat. But I wasn't sure whether he was talking about her place as a wife or her place as whatever the fuck she did for him.

TWELVE
SCAR

DID HE MOAN WHEN I STABBED HIM?

"GET IN, *PRINCIPESSA*," Caleb bit out.

"Oh, look at that. I've moved up from Romano bitch," I responded tightly. Tonight had not gone anything like it was supposed to. The plan was to hide out in a corner, chug champagne, chow down on a free meal, and then Uber my way home. All while not making contact with a certain Irishman and his *brothers*. Oh, and hopefully, piss off my cousin enough that she begged daddy dearest to uninvite me to the wedding.

But no.

Instead, I was being pushed into the back of a bulletproof SUV with three psychos who thought they owned me now. Caleb should've gone with my cousin as his wife, because I wouldn't be sticking around for long. Still, a sour taste lingered in my mouth at the thought of them together. As much as I didn't want him, I didn't want her to have him, either.

That slam to the head in the bathroom had obviously done some damage because why the fuck would I care about that?

Black fabric hit me in the face, interrupting my internal meltdown.

"Put that over your head. You don't get to see where we're

taking you. And don't fuckin' cry, either. I hate women's tears," Caleb said, glaring at me through the rearview mirror as Kenji opened the passenger door and slid in.

How ironic.

Until his comment, I hadn't considered that a normal reaction to essentially being kidnapped would be tears. Because truthfully, my initial instinct was to wrap the blindfold in my hands around Kenji's throat and use the moment of surprise as an opportunity to grab his Glock and put a forty-five-caliber hole in Caleb's head. But that would jeopardize my freedom. The element of surprise only gave someone a few extra seconds. I could probably take out my new husband in that time, but it would still leave me with two pissed-off men in an underground parking garage.

Might as well put the bullet in my own brain.

Survival hinged on knowing when to act on instinct and when to sit back and observe. So I tightened the black fabric behind my head, cutting off my sight.

The hair along my arms stood on end when the back passenger door opened. Even through the covering, Niko's cologne tickled my nose with its masculine scent. The desire to curl into his hulking form pissed me off.

"Is your blindfold on?" Caleb barked out as the vehicle roared to life.

"You tell me, Callahan. You're the one who can fucking see."

Kenji cackled, and there was even a slight rumble of amusement from Nikolay, but nothing but silence from the asshole Irishman. He was probably trying to set me on fire with the power of his pissed-off thoughts.

"See, this is why I have a car with a trunk and a loud sound system when I pick up marks," Nikolay added casually, like we were talking about the fucking weather, not hostage transportation.

I flipped them off, biting back a remark about how my

marks usually drove themselves to where they'd unknowingly be killed. Why work harder when I could work smarter?

Interesting that they'd decided to keep my hands free. What was stopping me from yanking the cloth off?

Apprehension bloomed in my mind, my senses seeming to heighten. I kept my breathing even and the worry out of my voice, pretending I hadn't noticed the shift in the air.

"What about my shit? I'm going to need my things, my clothes—"

Tires screeched as the vehicle shot forward before making a sharp right. The erratic movement sent me slamming into a hard chest. What felt like steel bands wrapped around me.

"What the fuck, Callahan? Do you even know how to fucking drive?" I yelled out, trying to wriggle free from Nikolay's grasp. When his grip didn't loosen, my stomach dropped to my feet. "You can let me go now, Nikolay," I said tightly, hyperaware of the rustling sound coming from Kenji's seat and the way Niko had pinned my arms to my side.

"Sorry, love, but he can't do that. I need you still for this next part," Kenji said, now close enough to touch.

There was a pinprick sensation at the upper part of my arm. He'd dosed me with something, and it was fucking potent based on how quickly my muscles relaxed. Moving my body was like trying to swim through syrup. Unconsciousness threatened to pull me under. On pure instinct, I managed to grab the blade sheathed on my thigh, despite Nikolay's tight hold.

Right before the world turned black, I drove my blade into the fleshy part of his massive thigh. I'd only had enough energy to barely puncture the surface of his skin, but it still brought a smile to my face.

The last thing I remembered before darkness called me home was the vibrations of his chest as he let out a deep groan. It sounded more like he was getting a blowjob than a stabbing.

Fuck.

The scent of fresh plastic itched my nose as memories shifted through my mind in a muddled mess. Pounding behind my eyes intensified the closer I got to breaching the surface of consciousness. A ragged moan echoed in the distance, slamming the final piece of the puzzle into place.

Caleb, Kenji, and Niko.

The moan was mine, and those three assholes had ruined my night of free booze and food. I mentally took stock of my body. Besides the bitch of a headache and feeling like I had been hit by a truck, everything seemed to be still attached. Including my clothes, based on the feel of soft satin against my skin.

Unlike what was shown in movies, chloroform actually took closer to fifteen minutes to knock someone out. And your victim had to be actively inhaling the poison for it to work, making it a shit method for kidnapping someone. But say you decided to shoot someone up with Rohypnol while a tank of a human held them still…*that* would fucking work.

After a few seconds of complete silence, I bit the bullet and opened my eyes.

"Motherfucking Russian," I muttered, my lids slamming shut again. The light from the buzzing fluorescent bulb felt like an icepick was being jammed through my eye socket.

A chuckle came from the corner of the room. Or I thought one had. I was still adjusting to being awake.

"Wow. What a mouth."

"Yeah, and your mom loves it," I spat back, testing how tight my wrists were bound to the arms of the chair they'd placed me in. Based on the sultry, smooth tone, I assumed it was Kenji in the room with me. Plus, this was his field of expertise.

Rough fingers dung into my jaw, forcing my head up. I peeled my eyelids back open; it took them a minute to adjust.

I was greeted with a toned chest adorned with hauntingly beautiful traditional Yakuza ink. Kenji was like a human tapestry, and I wanted to drink every part of him in.

Too bad the body belonged to an asshole who'd kidnapped me.

"I'm so glad you're up. I was worried I'd never get to have fun with you." Dark eyes felt like they were siphoning my soul, and his smile was downright sinister. The playfulness from earlier was gone. "I bet you bleed so lovely," he said.

Heat licked across my skin.

Right below my clavicle was the telltale tingle of a sharp blade slicing skin. Blood beaded up along the cut before a tattooed thumb smeared the red liquid across my chest. Anticipation sang in my veins at the sight of Kenji wrapping his mouth around the digit, licking it clean. For some un-fuck-ing-explainable reason, the whole act was incredibly erotic to me.

God, I had issues.

"Want to play a little game with me?" he asked, voice dripping with ill intentions as he lorded over me.

I ignored the moisture pooling at my core. "Like what? Clue?" I canted my head, pulling my lips into a sneer. His slight flinch only made it wider. "That's easy. The bitch killed him in the torture room with a chair leg," I answered sweetly, trying to take in my surroundings.

It looked like they were holding me in a basement of some sort. The brick walls were painted over. At one time, they'd probably been white, but now they were dulled by time and dust. The space felt like a storage closet, with its singular fluorescent light buzzing above and the lack of windows or furniture. There was a hint of must in the air, but the pungent odor of plastic overtook it. That smell probably originated from the tarp my wooden chair sat on top of.

The absence of a drain and the stinging scent of bleach helped put me at ease.

They didn't kill in this room.

But they did watch. A camera mounted up in the top corner caught my eye. Someone had taped over the green light to try to hide it better, but it'd been the first thing I spotted.

Kenji let out a genuine laugh, my attention flicking back to him. It was a fifty-fifty shot at him laughing or hitting me. I'd seen him work once. That was how I knew he wasn't taking this seriously. A big fucking blessing for me because he was a scary fucker when at work.

Chocolate irises traveled down my body, the ring of color disappearing little by little the longer he looked. Did he get this excited over every victim strapped to a chair? Or was this something special for me?

"I've never had a woman use talk of murder as foreplay, but I like it," he said, his tongue swiping across his lips.

"Then you haven't had a real woman," I threw back, tracking his movement as he paced before squatting in front of me, twirling a blade between his fingers. The position made it so that I was looking down at him slightly, and images of that black head of hair between my thighs had my pussy clenching.

Fucked up. I was 100 percent fucked up.

"What's so funny?" he asked, pointing out the laugh I hadn't realized I had released.

My teeth sank into the meatiness of my bottom lip while I contemplated whether I should tell him the truth.

What the hell? These might be my last minutes alive. I should go out living my truth. Because if these fuckers didn't kill me, my uncle would. I'd seen his face at the party. He thought I was in on tonight's events. Thought that I'd betrayed him.

I could hear him now.

"Disgraceful fucking bitch. Bastard daughter to a betrayer. I always knew you'd end up the same."

I shook off Dominick's callous whispers, trying to regain focus. "Apparently, being kidnapped makes me horny because I'm imagining your tongue buried in my pussy." I leaned as far forward as my restraints would allow. "Let me out, and let's play, Kenji."

His nostrils flared.

Suddenly he was standing over me, caging me in with his body and forcing me to crane my neck to look up at him. Painfully slow, he lowered his face, stopping when we were less than an inch away.

"Who did you give the folder to?"

Copper wafted in the air, and pain radiated from my lip as he bit it—hard—before smashing our mouths together. Weed and the metallic taste of blood coated my tongue as we fought for dominance. When he yanked away, his chest was heaving, and I was so turned on that I squirmed in my chair, trying to find some release. Kenji caught the movement and wrenched my thighs apart.

"Answer me, Scar." He punctuated each word with the tightening of his grip on my thighs before running his tongue up the side of my face, demonstrating how talented he was with that particular appendage. Lust fogged my mind, and I wanted so badly to palm his growing bulge.

Focus. I needed to focus.

"I already fucking told Caleb. Dominick sent me to collect the file." I huffed in irritation, even if it was sexual irritation.The heat that had radiated from his skin was suddenly absent, and the stagnant air grew thick with tension. His glare was chilling as he stood a few feet away, inked arms crossed over his chiseled chest.

This relationship between their two organizations was *very* cloak and dagger, and now I was smack dab in the middle of it.

Ironically, they thought I was a helpless maiden, not the hidden player.

He spoke again, anger oozing from his tone. "Where's he keeping it? And has he looked at it already?"

"What's in it for me?" I bit back, regretting my remark when his face morphed into something sinister.

"Tell me what I want to know, or I'll send you back to your uncle."

Fuck him.

My eyes slammed shut, as if that would block out the reality of my situation. Bodily harm I could've endured, but Kenji's threat was one of the few that would get me talking. Because if Dominick got ahold of me, he wouldn't kill me. He'd drag out my misery.

A resigned sigh escaped my lungs, but when I looked up from the patch of concrete I'd been staring down, Kenji's face was twisted in pain, and his eyes were sealed shut.

THIRTEEN
KENJI
TRAUMA-BONDING

THE SHUTTERED LOOK of fear that flashed across her delicate face at the mention of sending her back to her uncle had emotions I thought I'd buried ripping through me. The dingy walls of the supply closet dropped away for a brief moment, morphing into the memory of concrete walls covered in grime. Acid stung my throat. The smell of bile was so overwhelming, it was as if I was still there.

Trapped in that warehouse surrounded by bodies. Back to the night we found where our fathers had sent Jessica. It was our fault she was dead. Panic clawed at my mind, and I fought to catch my breath and avoid being dragged under.

The irony wasn't lost on me that I'd just threated to send another woman to her demise. Guilt churned in my gut.

My eyes popped back open, and she was intently watching me—studying me. Anyone else, I'd have said they'd missed my moment of desperation. But I had the impression that Scar rarely missed anything. The four of us had that in common.

She might have a talent for masking her emotions, but the violence stirring at her core shone through those icy blue eyes. It was the only genuine reaction she'd shown besides lust. I'd bet my left nut there hadn't been a single moment while she'd been strapped to this chair that she was intimidated. Fuck, I doubted she'd even been nervous.

Not until I said we'd send her back to Dominick.

My skin itched at the idea of threatening to deliver her back to the Romanos.

Maybe instead of making her an enemy, we make her an ally.

I was only one head of the Cerberus, though. My brothers would have to agree to the deal too.

"What was the plan you landed on for escaping?" I asked, my curiosity getting the better of me.

A tingle ran down my spine at the way she slowly dragged her gaze over to me, a calculated expression firmly in place. It was borderline creepy how she cocked her head to the side while the corners of her lips drew up ever so slightly. The blood I'd smeared on her chest glistened under the light, and the shadows cast from that sole bulb danced along her skin, making her appear unhinged. Fuck if it didn't make my dick hard.

"What makes you think I have one?" Her voice was devoid of any emotion. The passionate woman from a moment ago was gone, her prior panic neatly tucked away.

I stepped closer, nudging her thighs apart with my knee. "You're not losing your shit while strapped to a chair. After being drugged in the back of an SUV by three massive men who could do *whatever* they wanted to you," I said, digging into my front pocket.

Black seeped into the blue of her irises, and I didn't think she realized her tongue swiped across her lips like she was savoring the finest ambrosia.

Her nipples pebbled at the flick of my switchblade. I loved the way her breath hitched when the metal touched her leg. "In fact, if I remember correctly, a moment ago, you asked me to lick your sloppy cunt," I said, running the tip of my knife up her exposed thigh and studying her face to see if she'd flinch as it sliced her supple skin. The only reaction she gave was a slight shift in her chair, but she couldn't hide how her pulse quickened the higher I ran my blade.

"Trying to get relief? You've got to be a little fucked in the head to get turned on at a time like this," I taunted, entranced by the crimson droplets running down the inside of her thigh.

Her eyes darted to my hard-on, and she raised a manicured brow. I chuckled at how she'd expressed so much without speaking.

"I've only met two others before you that are the same kind of fucked-up. We trauma-bond over the shit our families put us through. You'd fit in well with us, Scar." I untucked the joint from behind my ear and lit it, taking a long drag before letting the smoke caress her face. "We could play whenever you want if you stay with us," I murmured against her cheek.

Her moan echoed off the walls.

Fuck.

The comment was meant to entice *her*, but the moment the words were out, I realized how badly I wanted to keep her. To play with her.

To break her.

"Tell me what I want to know, Scar, so I can keep you," I whispered, pulling the lobe of her ear between my teeth while dragging the knife closer to her center, being careful not to pierce but still exerting enough pressure that red scratches marred her.

I dropped between her thighs, inhaling her intoxicating scent. Blood, sweat, and her wet fucking pussy. I craved bottling that shit up and wearing it like a cologne.

Pressing my tongue flat against her skin, I reveled in the hitching of her breath. Saltiness infused with the metallic taste of her blood exploded in my mouth. I didn't bother suppressing a moan as I lapped up what had leaked down her inner thigh. Her hands clenched and unclenched where they were tied. I had to restrain myself from cutting them free so they could tug on my hair. Her hips thrust forward, attempting to get my attention where she craved it.

"Kenji, please," she breathed out, her head dropping back and rolling from side to side.

The desperation in her plea was music to my ear. I wanted to see what other noises I could drag from her pliant body. Two people didn't have to like each other to fuck each other. And I made a point to enjoy pleasures while I was still breathing. Unfortunately, fucking the beauty wasn't the most important thing at the moment.

My tongue was teasing the edges of her lace underwear—my nose essentially in her pussy—when Caleb stormed into the room with Niko on his heels. I'd barely scrambled out of the way before he caged her in with his body. His anger was palpable, yet she remained unfazed, those glacial eyes burning with challenge.

"You drugged me and tied me up, Callahan. Bitch move," she spat, her words laced with poison.

"What was in that fucking file?" he seethed, gripping her chin so tightly her teeth were probably cutting into her gums. His volume ticked up a notch, bordering on yelling when she didn't answer.

"What did the file say, you Romano bitch?"

Her eyes hardened, and she yanked her face out of his grasp. Baring bloody teeth.

Idiot.

With that one word, he bolstered her defiance. Now she didn't fucking care what he was talking about. She'd push back solely on the principle of fucking him over. Even at the expense of her life. How did I know this? Because the dumb motherfucker was the exact same.

"Shit," Niko whispered from beside me.

"Yup." I let the *P* pop as I leaned against the dust-covered wall. "We're going to be here awhile now."

Her voice shook with fury when she answered. "I thought

you had all the answers you needed, Callahan. I already fulfilled our deal." She leaned as far forward as the zip ties allowed. Their noses practically touched as she spat her response. "You wanted a wife? Here I fucking am. Should've thought about what you'd use your one *favor* on." She leaned back, putting on a facade of calm and collected, but I saw the ticking of her jaw.

"You don't want to fuck with me, Scar. If you don't know what was in that file, then where the fuck is it?" he asked, folding his arms across his chest in a way that was usually intimidating, but she didn't seem to give a damn.

"Little one, we aren't actually planning on keeping an alliance with Dominick. And he's clearly planning on fucking us. We just want to know what he knows about us," Niko said.

It surprised me that he'd spoken at all. Usually, he was just the retrieval man.

Two sets of eyes snapped to where the deep rumble originated from beside me. Uneasiness prickled over my skin at the calculated look on Scar's face as she stared at Niko. I didn't miss how her gaze briefly dropped to his injured thigh before refocusing on his face when she couldn't spot a bandage on his jean-clad legs.

"What the hell was that, Niko?" Caleb asked, clearly pissed off.

"Your threats were getting us nowhere. Thought she should hear what it is we're after. Maybe she'd be more willing to help," he said, shrugging a massive shoulder. The rigidness of his spine told me he wasn't sure whether his gamble would work.

Caleb looked like he was unraveling, pulling at his auburn hair in distress. "Yeah? And what if the bitch tells her uncle? Huh? That's what we need."

Scar watched the interaction, soaking it in like a sponge.

Her body relaxed, and she crossed a silky leg over the

other. "Little one is insulting. You've just packaged it with a pretty bow instead of going with bitch," Scar responded, her eyes narrowing on Niko. He stiffened at the accusation. She was right. He hadn't meant it affectionately. He'd hoped the sweet words would get her to open up.

"And why is it I should give you what you want? To avoid being tortured?" she asked, shaking her head in disbelief.

I couldn't help but chime in on the fun little conversation. "Generally speaking, the threat of physical pain is plenty motivation to speak up." She tracked my every move as I approached, halting when I was shoulder-to-shoulder with Caleb. "But you seem completely unfazed. Why is that, *little one*?"

"Because I'm a masochist," she sneered.

Caleb's composure broke. He fisted a hand in her hair, a knife to her throat. Crimson droplets trickled down her olive column, falling between her breasts and joining the blood from earlier.

"Where the fuck is Dominick keeping the file?" he bit out.

The two studied one another, the air growing thick with hostility. Everyone was hyperaware of the ledge we were teetering on.

I moved closer, unsure of what Caleb would do. "Answers, little one." I waved off the ass-chewing she was about to unleash. "Yeah, yeah. You don't like the name. Tough shit. I like it, and so does the big guy. And you're strapped to a chair, which automatically makes it so you don't get a say on shit."

She literally snarled when I leaned over and booped her nose. By now, Niko had joined, and the three of us were lording over her, determined to pry the answers we needed free.

She frowned, gnawing on her lip, looking at us as if she were facing an impossible decision. "Do you plan on killing him?" For the first time since I'd met her, she sounded small, unsure of herself.

I followed my intuition and went with the truth.

"We're going to gut him, Scar." I brought my finger to her breastbone, running it down to her navel, painting her skin with her blood and drinking in the way her breath shuddered. "Split him down the middle and pull his entrails out. Use them as bait for the sharks when we dump the bastard in the water. That was always the plan."

"Fuck. Kenji, don't tell her shit like that," Caleb barked, throwing a right hook at my face. I laughed as it connected, busting my lip, before delivering a jab to his ribs. This was how it was between us—a volatile dance of aggression and brotherly love.

He assumed my crazed remarks would be why she clammed up and didn't say shit. But I noted how her eyes chilled at the images my words painted in her equally fucked-up head.

"I want to hold the knife," she stated.

Caleb's head whirled back to her, while Niko arched a brow in surprise, mumbling about nature making her most deadly things beautiful.

Steely determination shone on her face. She held her head high, looking like a queen and not a captive. "We have a common goal. I want Dominick dead, and based on that lovely description, so do you. So how about a deal? We team up for this endeavor, and then, when the asshole is gone, you three let me go on my merry way."

Caleb eyed her suspiciously, working through whether there was any way for her to screw us over. His hesitance gained him an eye roll from her.

"Look, I have inside information about the Mafia. I *know* I can help put Dominick in a grave. Hell, you can record me saying that so you have leverage." Her face soured when Caleb still hadn't responded. "I'm backed into a fucking corner, okay? If you send me back to him, my fate is worse than death. He thinks I was in on your little plan tonight. You're my best fucking option, Callahan, so don't be an idiot. Go with the win-win." The tone of her voice was strained. Desperate. I flicked my eyes to Caleb, reading the lines of his body.

Caleb considered his options for a long moment, not that we really had any. As much as he hated her, he'd never send her back. What happened with Jessica haunted us all. He wouldn't willingly send a woman to her death. Not again.

"And I never gave him the file…" she said, a hint of irritation in her tone, like she hadn't wanted to reveal that tidbit of information.

Caleb's hands landed on the arms of the chair, caging her in. "What do you mean?" he asked, his tone one of surprise. I studied her, looking for signs of deception, but she looked… resigned.

She sighed, drumming her fingers on the wood. "I saw you three together that night. Before we met in the office, and I thought it was strange that you'd all be together." Her eyes pinged between the three of us before landing back on Caleb. "So when I saw you in the office going for the same file Dominick wanted, I decided I'd keep it for myself. Seemed it might be useful," she said, shrugging a shoulder like she hadn't told us she'd willingly *stolen* for the don.

Woman had some fucking balls.

"What did you give him, then?" Niko asked, his eyebrows pinched in confusion. A sly smile appeared on her face, like she was about to reveal a secret. Which, I guessed she was.

"*Idiota* didn't even fucking know what was on the file. Just paid some random rat for a 'file on the Syndicate.'" She rolled her eyes, clearly not impressed with Dominick. "So I made some shit up."

Caleb blinked his eyes like his brain was short-circuiting.

"So he doesn't know anything?" he asked slowly as she shook her head. "Fine. You've got a deal, Roma—"

"Don't call me that. You can call me Scar," she interrupted.

"Whatever. You've got a deal. But know this: if you fuck us over, your uncle's version of *punishment* will be fucking child's play compared to what we will do to you. Bring her up."

He turned and stalked out the door.

FOURTEEN
NIKO

"GRAB ME THE FIRST AID SHIT."

When I first saw her, she was all fire and fight. Hell, when Caleb claimed her as his wife, she took it in stride but not lying down. My cock twitched, remembering the sinful words she'd spoken against his mouth.

"I'll be sure and yell Niko and Kenji's names real loud."

Logically, I knew she'd said it to taunt him, but my dick didn't get the message, and he was ready to make that statement a reality. When I really knew she was so much more than what she showed the world was when she was around Dominick. Her uncle was an idiot, missing what was right in front of him. Hell, he treated her the same way our fathers treated us.

Dismissively.

If his head wasn't shoved so far up his ass, he'd see how she watched his every move, categorizing and calculating her next comment or reaction. Vitriol for him oozed from her pores, but there was also the acrid tinge of fear every time her uncle addressed her.

Dominick underestimated a lot of things, including us, but I had a feeling his biggest miscalculation was not recognizing the threat clothed in an emerald satin dress. I raked up and down her figure as we walked into our apartment. My hackles rose thinking about the exchange at the party. He'd given us Scar *too* easily, and it made me wary.

Protecting a woman was a trait ingrained in my soul. I'd grown up doing so for my sisters until my father had dragged them away, but with Scar I was torn. Every fiber of my being wanted to treat her the same, but my brain screamed that she held secrets.

Ones that could harm my brothers.

Fuck, the woman was ready to endure torture in order to spite Caleb. Bodily pain wasn't her motivator, and that was extremely unusual for...anyone. A twinge of discomfort radiated from my thigh, reminding me of how she'd stabbed me right before blacking out. She'd barely broken the surface, but the way a blade was in her hand the instant she felt Kenji sink the needle into her arm screamed that she was familiar with the weapon.

Caleb had told us about their very first encounter. We'd thought it was pure luck that she'd gotten the drop on him the night they met. Chalked up the loose bindings to her not knowing what she was doing. But I now thought the beautiful woman was far more capable than we'd originally given her credit for. Ending the don's life was why she'd struck the deal with us, and it *felt* like she was telling the truth, but she was such an anomaly. I knew I needed to keep a close eye on her.

She scanned the room, something she'd done every time I'd seen her. The woman was probably mapping out every escape possible.

Too bad there were none.

Our penthouse was on a private floor above our club. The only way in or out was through our secure elevator, which required a keycard to open and operate. There were also men posted at all the building's exits. If she wanted to go somewhere, she'd need one of us to accompany her.

She padded across the polished concrete floors on silent feet, following Caleb into our kitchen.

"You better have some food in this fucking place because not only did you roofie me and then tie me to a chair, but the worst part? You didn't let me eat the lobster ravioli."

I shook my head at her complaint, hiding my smile with my hand. Of course she was more pissed about not being fed than being drugged and interrogated. Now that she had my attention, she wouldn't be able to shake it. Obsession was what I did best. Taking in everything about a person and figuring out what made them tick—what they would do next. People wondered why I could always find my mark. It was because I crawled inside the person's mind.

The problem with her? I wasn't sure I'd be able to detach.

Cold seeped through my shirt from the metal I beam I leaned against, grounding me. Caleb walked straight to the bar cart, pouring himself a *generous* glass of cognac.

"It is a fucking *kitchen*," Caleb said between clenched teeth, missing the middle finger she threw his way. "God, I'm married to an idiot who can't even fucking feed herself," he mumbled, causing me to chuckle at how badly he was in denial. His face looked pained as he closed his eyes, attempting to regain some semblance of control of the situation. He was supposed to bring home a betrothed whose daddy we'd kill before the wedding. And the bitch would've stayed in the apartment below us.

Give her a guard and call it good. That was the plan.

Instead, he'd announced to a room full of essential business associates that Scar was his fucking *wife*, and we'd have to keep up the charade until all our plans were in place. Fuck, we were in for an *interesting* time. Caleb and Scar did not get along because they were exactly alike—full of fire and fight, unwilling to kneel to the other.

Then there was Kenji. He liked to dirty up every innocent and shiny thing he came across, so he'd try his damnedest to get her to bite at his advances. According to him, too much societal perfection made him uneasy. A reminder of the expectations of his family. It's why the role of interrogator suited him so well. He found release in carving imperfections into someone's flesh. The beauty in violence.

She might be his match, though, because I didn't think she was as innocent as her posh exterior tried to convey. *She might be perfect, though.*

I ignored the thought and focused on tracking her as she made her way to our commercial-size fridge. She didn't have to worry about whether we had food. All three of us had massive appetites. But her brows furrowed when she peered inside.

Did we not have anything she liked?

My gut turned at the thought, both because the idea of her not having something she liked upset me and because *that* reaction disturbed me.

"You don't have anything…microwavable?" she asked, shifting uncomfortably on the balls of her feet.

"For God's sake," Caleb groaned.

Before I thought better of it, I strode toward her, nudging her out of the way. "Do you not know how to cook, little one?" I asked. She might hate the name, but I didn't give a fuck. Compared to me, she was small, and my tongue seemed to like the way the term rolled off it.

Vulnerability shone in her eyes for a second before she scowled.

"So what if I don't?" Her hands landed on her hips, causing the material of her dress to shift and reveal blood trickling down her thigh. The crimson droplets ensnared me. I barely caught her arguing about how we lived in New York and no one cooked since there were more places to eat than toilets to shit in. A shriek echoed through the kitchen as I lifted her, setting her ass down on the massive soapstone island and ripping her dress to the side.

My body relaxed when I realized the cut was superficial and probably resulted from Kenji's playing. A knot unraveled in my gut.

Shit. That's concerning. Obsession had already sunk her talons in deep.

"Kenji, grab me the first aid shit," I barked.

I had to kneel to be at eye level with the gash. Being this close to her pussy and not leaning forward to pull her bundle of nerves between my teeth was a herculean feat. The thought alone had my balls tightening.

"It's nothing. Don't worry about it. Kenji was being a tease and licking up my blood to try to get me to squeal," she said, shrugging her shoulders and attempting to push her dress back into place, as if the comment was completely normal.

Someone should have a talk with my body because the fucker was acting without permission. Or maybe Scar was a witch, and she'd hexed me. Because there was no way I should've leaned forward and cleaned up her thigh with my tongue.

She tasted divine, and I longed to lap up more than her blood. I glanced up at her. Scar's head was tipped back, lips slightly parted, and she white-knuckled the counter like she was restraining herself from pulling my face to where she really wanted me.

Or maybe those were all wishful thoughts on my part.

A chuckle boomed from behind me. "Here you go, brother. Antiseptic might be better at cleaning up her wound than your saliva," Kenji joked, handing over the pad.

"You clean up all your hostages that way?" she asked, her words coming out breathy.

I hitched an eyebrow at her smart-ass comment. She didn't enjoy feeling out of control and covered up her discomfort with her sass.

"No, not all hostages." My fingers swiped the alcohol over the cut, smiling at how she winced. "Only my brother's wife," I stated, standing up after placing a bandage on her skin.

She gawked at me. Her mouth opened and closed several times, but no smart-ass remarks came out.

"You broke her, brother." Kenji's hand slapped my back as he chuckled. "Wait till she hears about how we like to share."

"Kenji," Caleb barked. He'd been leaning against the wall observing, but apparently that bit of information was the breaking point of his composure.

Her head snapped back and forth between the three of us as my hands landed on either side of her body, caging her in.

"Look at me, little one." That got her attention. "You'll sit here while I cook something to feed you. Got it? And try not to fight with Caleb too much," I instructed, turning to start the burner. I needed to find something to do with my hands before I ended up sinking my fingers into her pussy and watching her writhe on my island.

FIFTEEN
CALEB

FUCK. I HAVE A WIFE.

THE MINUTE the elevator doors opened to our penthouse apartment I'd tossed my suit coat onto the nearest piece of furniture and hunted down a drink. Honestly, I'd needed about five drinks and to fuck something up—or someone. My feet had carried me to our kitchen while I'd dragged my hands over my face in frustration.

I hadn't even heard her behind me until she'd asked about food. It pissed me off that my first reaction was concern that she hadn't eaten. Then, as if my resolve wasn't already being tested, her tanned flesh had taunted me as Niko *kneeled* between her thighs, his saliva leaving a glistening trail on her skin. The scene had been fucking erotic and only made my irritation flare higher.

Now Kenji was piling a selection of meats and cheeses on the countertop for her to choose from.

Of course he liked her.

The scent of sauteed garlic and onions wafted in the air from where Niko stood at the range, preparing her dinner like she was fucking family. I guess that was exactly what I'd made her when I'd announced her as my wife. I still couldn't wrap my head around why *that* word had slipped out. I'd meant to call her my fiancée, and then we'd keep the same plan as we had for Adriana.

"My wife."

I closed my eyes again, trying to rein in my conflicted feelings. "We need to talk about rules and how this will go," I gritted out.

"Of course my new jailers have rules," she responded, rolling her eyes.

"Rule one, no leaving the building without one of us accompanying you," I said, making my way back to the bar cart because I needed the entire bottle of cognac to deal with this shit. "In fact, don't do anything without telling us first."

"I am not a fucking toy to be yanked around, Callahan." She leaped off the counter and prowled forward, stopping when we were only inches apart. "Let's cut the bullshit. I don't have time to play games. You aren't going to move me in here, ignore me for weeks, and ice me out. I won't wallow and try to gain your attention. So tell me the fucking plan, because I have better shit to do."

My fucking molars were going to crack under the pressure of how tightly I had my jaw clenched. This woman thought she was calling the shots? She choked out a breath as I wrapped my fingers around her throat. My grip was notably softer than I'd grant anyone else who spoke to me the way she did. This was more along the lines of the pressure I'd use while fucking someone.

Her throat bobbed as she swallowed, and images of her swallowing my cock filled my mind. I scowled and pushed away the thought, trying to focus on the defiant woman in my grasp. I smiled at the fluttering of her pulse. I didn't want to admit it, but her demeanor was so damn cold that I couldn't get a read on her other than her hate for me.

But the thumping of her vein under my thumb didn't lie.

My dick hardened because I didn't think fear was causing

her reaction. No sane person *glared* at me while my hand was wrapped around their throat. No one but her.

I leaned in so my lips were against her ear. "Scar, I'll make you sit and wait for as long as I fucking want. Be a good girl and learn that lesson early." My cold smile faded at the distinct pressure of a knife's edge. I peeked down to find a switchblade at my balls.

Where the fuck had she gotten that?

"I make my own rules, Caleb. Be a good boy and learn that lesson early," she parroted back.

Smart-ass bitch. This woman didn't know who she was dealing with. We weren't to be messed with—I wasn't to be messed with.

"Don't inflate your worth, Scar," I spewed out cruelly, my anger flaring further at being challenged. The blue of her eyes seemed to deepen, and the look of determination and loathing had me hesitating.

"Caleb." Niko's deep tenor pulled me from my spiral. "We can use her help with our plans, and our goals align. We all want the don dead."

I took in calming breaths, forcing my fingers to loosen around her delicate throat. "How do we know she actually means that and isn't playing us?" Even as I said them, the words tasted like ash. Anyone who'd spent even a second with her and Dominick would know that the two hated one another. But I still didn't trust the woman.

In my soul, I *knew* she was more than she let on.

Scar's head was cocked to the side, eyes slightly narrowed, analyzing me the way I did to others. It felt like I was being dissected—studied. It had me feeling exposed.

The blade's pressure disappeared, but even as I lowered my arm, she didn't move away.

"I know my worth, Callahan. Now, as the big guy over there pointed out, we have the same goal. So fill me the fuck in, or I'll walk my ass out the door."

She stepped away, her eyes never leaving mine as she hopped back onto our island.

Kenji piped up. Honestly, I was surprised he'd stayed quiet for the whole exchange.

"Well, Scar, welcome to the family. You survived your first anger blowup," he said, plopping a mozzarella ball into his mouth. "We're taking over New York. Gonna kill our daddies and your *famiglia* too. Sorry about it."

"Kenji," I hissed, my hands curling into fists.

"What? You heard the lady. She wants to skip over the part where your brooding ass locks her up and doesn't tell her shit. Which I'm all for." His playful tone turned serious. "Besides, we don't have time to fuck around, Caleb. Not now that we know Dominick's gunning for us."

Niko grunted in agreement from where he was cooking.

"Hold on." Scar had her hand up in the air like we were in fucking class. "You're overtaking the Four Families?"

A deep sigh left my lips. As much as the beauty pissed me off, my brothers were right. We didn't have time to waste.

"That's the plan. We'll cripple them and ensure they realize who they now serve."

SIXTEEN
SCAR

I'LL CUT YOUR DICK OFF.

WE DIDN'T DISCUSS their plans after Caleb's tantrum. He let me eat my pasta in peace as I mulled over everything that'd transpired in the last twenty-four hours. Fuck, more like the last eight hours.

Now I was trying, and failing, to ignore how Kenji's slacks hugged his ass as I trailed behind him to my new jail cell. The guest room—thank God I wasn't sharing a bed with Caleb—was located down the hall from the open living and kitchen area.

It better have nice sheets and a robe.

The guys lived in a beautiful modern-industrial apartment above what I figured was their club. I'd done some digging on the three after my little run-in with Caleb. They owned club Hush Money. When they'd let me out of the storage room, we passed what looked like alcohol backstock, and there was music coming from behind a door. But they'd dragged me into the elevator too quickly for me to investigate.

I'd nearly choked on my spit when I walked into their penthouse. There was a wall of floor-to-ceiling windows showing off the city night. Polished concrete floors had cooled my feet as I padded across their living room, taking in the massive charcoal sectional that looked large enough to seat an entire football team. There were exposed brick walls and metal I beams all over. Honestly, whoever their designer was had done an amazing job.

Then there was the kitchen.

I didn't cook, but damn if it didn't make me want to learn. Black soapstone countertops lined the space, and the island was the size of a king-size bed with at least eight stools surrounding it. The commercial-size fridge was so large that Niko looked normal size next to it, which was a feat.

A twinge of affection ran through my gut at the memory of the massive man shoving a bowl of homemade pasta into my hands. It surprised me that he hadn't insisted on spoon-feeding me. The way his fingers had twitched, I got the impression he was tempted. Niko might be the scariest one to look at out of the bunch, but damn, he was secretly the sweetest.

"This one's yours," Kenji said, pushing a set of double doors open.

"Holy shit."

The room was moody. Bedside lamps bathed the room in low, warm light, enhancing the deep green walls so dark they bordered on black. A massive bed faced the room's own set of floor-to-ceiling windows. The city lights shone like a sea of stars on the other side of the glass. I ran the back of my hand along the velvet duvet on my way into the en suite. The black marbled shower, with multiple showerheads, was the space's main attraction.

"I take it you like it, then?" Kenji asked, amusement in his tone.

"I've stayed in worse hostage accommodations."

I winced at the admission. I didn't want to answer questions about the other times I'd found myself at the mercy of men.

If Kenji thought anything about my statement, he didn't point it out. "Let me know if you need anything—and I do mean anything," Kenji commented suggestively from behind me.

"Actually." I turned, taking in his beautiful face and the way he watched my every move. "I need help getting out of my dress."

He moved slowly, like I was a caged animal who might bolt, stopping when we were a hairsbreadth away. "You want *me* to help you out of your dress, Scar?" he asked, hitching a brow. "You sure about that?" Raw lust dripped from his questions.

God, men were arrogant. What did he assume? That I wouldn't be able to keep myself from hopping onto his dick because those deft fingers trailed down my back as he unzipped me?

My pulse ticked faster at the thought. Actually...it was probably a good thing he'd put a shirt back on because I might've done just that.

I pulled my hair over my shoulder, turning to allow him access. "The zipper is a bitch to get undone, and I need a shower after all you three put me through tonight."

"Last night," he commented. "Put you through *last* night. It's one a.m., making it a new day. What do you think we'll put you through today, Scar?" His warm breath tickled over my neck, sending adrenaline shooting down my spine to my core.

Fuck, this man felt like danger and poor decisions. He gripped the back of my neck possessively, his touch scorching my skin like a hot iron as he shoved me forward. I had to catch myself before my face hit the countertop. When my ass pressed against his hardening bulge, the heat transformed into a current of electricity zapping at my skin. Images of us fucking in this position filled my mind, and my chest heaved as I tried to remember how to breathe properly.

"Are you teasing me on purpose, Kenji?" I asked, attempting to sound haughty and unfazed. The complete opposite of what I felt. I was a damn live wire, a current of chaos and lust since the moment Niko had walked up to me at the bar.

This fucking shower better have a detachable showerhead.

"I'd never tease you, Scar," he replied, as the telltale sound of a zipper echoed in the space. The chilled air hitting my exposed spine caused my skin to erupt in goose bumps.

He yanked my dress over my hips, ripping the thin straps.

Every ounce of sexual tension fled my body as satin pooled at my feet. My eyes clamped shut at the shocked gasp Kenji let out at the sight of my body. Shame swirled in my gut at the sensation of his finger tracing over the marks and scars marring my thighs.

"What the fuck, Scar?" My hackles rose at the irritation in his voice. That single question charged the air with intensity.

I'd heard it all before, the disgust over the way my body looked. How ironic that my nickname was a reminder that, like the marks on my skin, I was an unwanted blemish placed upon my family.

"You weren't supposed to do anything more than unzip me, Kenji. If you don't like the way they look, then turn away," I bit out. My fingers twitched against the cool marble as I resisted the urge to cover up.

"Scar, that's not how I meant it."

I looked up into the mirror, ready to chew him out some more, but my breath stalled in my lungs. A choked gasp came out instead at the sight of Caleb sipping on a glass of amber liquid. A demon clothed in a fitted suit. Inked forearms stood in stark contrast to the crisp rolled sleeves of his dress shirt.

He looked at ease with his leg crossed, one over the other. The thick material of his onyx dress pants pulled taut across his muscled thighs. I'd be a fool to think he was relaxed just because he leaned against the door frame. My gaze drifted to his shoulders. He was stiff. His expression was one of cool detachment and fiery rage, all wrapped in a mossy package.

He devoured me.

His attention slowly traveled down my naked body, feeling like a physical touch. I knew what he'd see when his gaze reached my ass. Two heart-shaped cheeks with my pussy barely concealed in black lace peeking out at the bottom. If he ran a fingertip down my center, he'd find the effect he and Kenji had on me.

Up until Kenji'd scoffed at my scars…

I swallowed thickly, arming myself for the barrage of insults I was sure he'd sling at me now that he'd seen my blemished flesh. It didn't matter how much healing you'd done. When accepting your body, there were always bound to be moments where you'd need to rebuild your walls and remind yourself that you were a hot bitch whose worth was determined by more than appearance.

I had a feeling I'd have to do that rebuilding after Caleb said whatever was on the tip of his tongue.

His voice was tight when he finally spoke. "Kenji doesn't give a shit how they look. He cares about who the fuck thought they could touch you like that. So…who the fuck did this to you?" he asked. His voice was deadly calm, but the tendons in his neck flexed.

That hadn't at all been what I'd expected him to say. I turned to face the brooding Irishman, savoring the way his focus shifted to the taut nipples I hadn't bothered covering.

Kenji piped up from beside me. "Yeah, I fucking love scars. Who wants perfection? But I *do* give a shit that those weren't given to you willingly." He gripped my chin, bringing my focus to him. His playful demeanor was nowhere to be found.

Chaos swirled in his eyes, his intensity building with each word. "If they aren't dead, I expect you to tell me, because I'm going to peel off their flesh for laying a finger on you." Rage gathered in his eyes, making it impossible to hold the contact.

I tore my gaze away, focusing on Caleb setting his glass on the counter, stalking me down like a predator. His finger trailed along my flesh, tracing the edge of my breast down to the top of my thong. It dipped below the band ever so slightly before landing on the pink puckered skin of the stab wound from Tokyo.

Fuck, that seemed like a lifetime ago now.

He'd entrapped me like a fly caught in a web, waiting to be devoured by the spider. I was powerless to look away as he drew circles around my scars.

"She's not a fragile flower, Kenji. I'm sure they're either taken care of, or she has a plan for them."

I stood a little taller. I hadn't even realized I was curling in on myself, but Caleb had seen it. I wasn't sure what to do with that realization. Thankfully he spoke again before my mind imploded from his kind gesture.

"How'd this one happen?" he asked, tapping on the newly scarred flesh.

"Knife fight," I answered truthfully, wondering what his reaction would be. Would he believe me?

His eyebrow ticked up in question, but he didn't push the subject. I wished he had pushed instead of asking his next question.

I watched his lips part, the tip of his tongue peeking out to trace along his bottom lip. "What if your husband wanted to undress his wife on their first night together?" he asked cruelly, ending the moment of comradery. His tone kicked on my fight-or-flight response. Fucked up part? I wanted either of those responses to end with me writhing below him.

"Just because you announce I'm your wife, Callahan, doesn't mean I'm actually married to you," I threw back, crossing my arms over my chest in indignation.

I was so locked into our stare-off that I barely noticed

Kenji's laugh as he left the bathroom, mumbling about how we were the same damn person.

My blood chilled when Caleb pulled his eyes from my chest. He looked so smug that my knees wanted to buckle. I had a suspicion of what he'd say before he opened his beautifully arrogant mouth.

"You don't think I'd have someone submit that paperwork right away?" Fabric rubbed against my skin as he stepped into my space, leaning forward to speak into my ear. His hand slithered around my waist, pulling my chest to his.

"Mrs. Callahan, you were mine the moment I saw you again. And I made sure it was official minutes after I announced it to that room." He pulled my lobe into his warm mouth, biting down so it was just short of being painful.

A moan tumbled out before I could catch it, my pussy aching to clench on something more than emptiness.

"And don't ever fucking pull a knife on me again unless you plan on using it, wife," he snarled.

Cold metal burned my hip as he cut both sides of my underwear, letting them join my dress on the floor. Time slowed as he reached down and picked up the scrap of fabric. The corners of his mouth pulled up into a sinister smile as he rubbed a thumb across my arousal.

Everything in me locked up, my body throbbing with lust, and I cursed him in my head as he brought the soaked crotch up to his nose, inhaling deeply. My heartbeat went wild, bordering on out of control as the pad of his tongue ran along the full length of my underwear. His eyes fluttered close in ecstasy. His dick twitched in his pants.

It was so wrong, but so fucking erotic.

Fuck. What would he look like when he climaxed?

"You taste fucking delicious." His eyes turned hard, cruel. My body went rigid. "Here, have a taste." His fingers knotted in my hair, yanking my head back. The other pried my mouth open and shoved the thong inside.

"Get fucking clean and then get some sleep. We've got shit to do," Caleb said, shoving me away as if my body burned him. He grabbed his glass before heading out the bathroom door.

I spit out the fabric, the heat of my anger clawing at my skin. "So we aren't consummating the marriage, then?" I called after him.

Why the fuck had I asked that question?

Did I actually want to have sex with the asshole who'd forced me into marriage? And that wasn't even touching on the other shit, like his infatuation with my throat. He seemed to like to either hold a knife to it or a hand around it.

I bet he'd like his cock shoved down it too.

Caleb paused at the question, his body tensing. When he spoke, his tone was so cold it felt like the temperature had dropped in the room.

"I might've had to marry you, but I don't fuck Romano scum. No matter how sinful you taste. Your family is fuckin' tainted."

I flinched at his words. My feelings were rarely hurt, yet for some unexplainable reason, Caleb managed to chip at my armor. He turned around to face me fully.

"If I want to fuck, I'll find other pussy," he spat.

Insanity. That was the only explanation for what happened next. Because I sure as fuck had no reason to act like a jealous wife to a man I didn't fucking know and shouldn't fucking want.

Like a viper, I whipped my hand out and grabbed Caleb's cock through his dress pants, resisting the desire to tug it free and stroke him. He groaned as I squeezed the delicate package. Delicate and *large* package.

White hot rage had replaced the pity party from seconds before. "You may not want to fuck me, *husband,* but if you stick your dick in another bitch, I'll cut the fuckin' thing off. Which would be a shame because it feels like it's a nice mouthful." I stepped in closer. "You may like sharing, but I won't fucking share you," I snarled, releasing his dick and walking into the shower before he retaliated.

I watched him from under the spray of water. His chest heaved while he balled his fists, his knuckles white. I could practically hear him thinking. He didn't know what to do with me.

Men rarely did.

Without a word, he turned on a heel and stormed out.

"Hope you're good at making yourself come with your hand," I shouted after him, grabbing the massaging shower-head and laughing at the sound of my door slamming closed.

SEVENTEEN
KENJI

A HAND IS A MAN'S BEST FRIEND

A BUZZING NOISE sent me rocketing out of my bed, drenched in sweat, katana in hand, ready to take someone's fucking head from their body. But the red lights I kept on at all times revealed nothing but an empty room. The second time the buzzing went off, I realized it was my phone and not someone coming in to try to assassinate me.

"Fucking psychotic family," I muttered as I grabbed my cell from the bed. Two messages from an unknown number had the hair on my neck standing up. No one had this number. I glanced around my room once more to be sure no one was lurking.

"This is feeling very horror movie or some shit, and I swear if you jump out while I'm reading this message, I'll stab you in the gut and throw you from the roof," I yelled out, waiting for someone to reply, but no one did. Neither Caleb nor Niko would come running down to check on me. One, I could handle myself fine. But the bigger reason was that my sleep was normally plagued with nightmares and flashbacks. Niko had a nasty scar across his abdomen from running to my aid. Thank God for his quick reflexes, but I still felt like shit every time I saw the fucker without a shirt on.

Vibrations alerted me to another text, pulling me from my thoughts.

UNKNOWN:

Hey, tell Callahan that I need some fucking underwear.

UNKNOWN:

Well, I need clothes and shit in general. And when are we going to get to the killing?

UNKNOWN:

Also, sorry if I woke you up.

A goofy smile spread across my face the moment my brain figured out who was texting me. My fingers flew across the screen as I responded. The dark emotions from moments ago were forgotten.

ME:

Little one, how did you get this number? And are you telling me this because you don't think Caleb will listen if it comes from you?

ME:

Honestly, you probably should've asked the big guy to tell Caleb.

UNKNOWN:

Have you seen how tight that man's pants are? Those fucking thighs of his take up every inch of fabric. How the fuck was I supposed to get my hand in there to steal his phone? You just leave yours lying around.

UNKNOWN:

Bad habit, by the way.

Her message caught me by surprise, and I laughed out loud. The woman was hilarious when she wasn't busy shutting people out. But I knew the effects of fucked-up families when I saw them. Her attitude around her uncle was survival mode. My breath quickened at the thought of what might've happened to her.

Did her uncle make her fight her cousins to determine who was *worthy* of eating that day like my father had? I wanted to bust into the asshole's home and run my blade through his chest. But I couldn't. Plus, I barely knew the woman. I might like pussy, but I knew I wouldn't jeopardize our goals over this one.

ME:

I have noticed his thighs. Want me to send
you a picture of him in briefs?

UNKNOWN:

Are you going to tell Caleb or not? Because I
would really rather avoid the asshole, or I'm
going to have to hold another weapon to his
junk.

I smiled at the memory of Caleb's pale face when he realized she had a blade poised at the family jewels. He should commission a stab-proof cup since she was always gunning for his junk.

ME:

Fine. I'll arrange it. Anything else you need?
A picture of my thighs? Those are nice too.

UNKNOWN:

I'm sure they are. Night, Kenji. XX

My head hit the pillow. I was too restless. I needed a release if I was going to fall back to sleep. The way I *wanted* to release the tension wasn't an option. Not even a full minute had passed since I'd sworn off her pussy, and I was already thinking about it. I'd been so fucking close to shoving my tongue into it while she was strapped to a chair. So close to swirling my tongue around her bundle of nerves before biting down.

A groan left my lips as I recalled how those fuckable lips of hers had asked me to eat out her dripping cunt. My balls tightened, and my underwear felt like it was strangling my now-hard cock. In seconds, I was out of bed, the cold of the concrete floor doing little to cool my heated flesh.

"Where the fuck are you?" I mumbled, digging through the pile of random shit in my closet. Now that I didn't live in a home where minimalism was demanded, my room looked like an upscale thrift store. A visual cacophony of shit I loved, like the vintage guitars that hung on my wall beside a Book of Mormon marquee sign I'd stolen. Or my collection of traditional Japanese *Noh* masks displayed above my bed.

My fingers wrapped around what I'd been searching for. Giving it a few rough pulls to untangle it from whatever other shit was in the pile in my walk-in closet, I practically ran back to my bed, checking the angle of my phone as I set it up on the tripod.

The mattress slumped underneath my weight as I leaped back into it, making sure to stay in the frame. Scar better appreciate the production levels going into this, the red lights, and the tripod. *Shit, I needed music to add some ambiance to the hand fucking I was about to do.*

As soon as I pressed play, my dick was out, twitching at the thought of the breathy moans she'd made when I ran my tongue along the cut on her thigh. The metallic tang still lingered.

I gripped my heavy shaft, rubbing my thumb against the ridge of my head while my other hand snaked down to cup my balls, imagining it was hers. The action pulled a moan from me, and my dick somehow managed to get harder as I envisioned her perky nipples glistening with my saliva. My thumb swiped the precum beading up at the tip, spreading it over my shaft as I made a few languid pulls, looking directly into the camera.

"Scar, here's a gift for you. Material for when you use your fingers to fuck that leaking cunt of yours," I said to my phone.

She'd definitely know I was thinking of her while I jacked off after getting this. I pumped my cock faster, my head rolling back, envisioning her warm mouth wrapped around me. What would she think when she got the video?

"Are you going to bury your fingers into that wet pussy while imagining me pumping my cock in and out the way I'm pumping into my hand?"

Labored breathing mixed with the sensual sounds from Chase Atlantic. I increased my pace, shamelessly moaning and saying her name. The thick head of my cock moved through my clenched fists. My eyes connected with the camera as I spit on my hand, lubing it up before switching hands.

"I need that wet cunt of yours to come drip down my cock, Scar. It'd be so much better than my spit." My eyes fluttered closed with pleasure, hand stroking base to tip, going faster and harder with every pull.

"Fuck, Scar. I want to fill you up and watch my cum leak out before shoving it back in," I breathed out, my movements becoming erratic and desperate. Thrusting into the tight grip of my fist faster and harder. Pretending it was Scar I was slamming into as she moaned my name. My balls drew up in anticipation. The image of her bouncing on my dick sent me over the edge.

"Ugh, fuck. Scar, I'm going to come."

Thick, warm liquid hit my hand and abs, my body shuddering with each spurt of cum. I peeled my eyes open again, staring down my phone like it was her icy eyes I was looking into as I dragged a finger through my mess, bringing the digit to my mouth and licking it off.

"Will you come clean me up next time, Scar?"

EIGHTEEN

SCAR

DICK VIDEOS ARE ONLY GOOD IF THEY MOAN YOUR NAME.

MY EYES FLEW OPEN, and it took my mind a second to catch up with where I was. The blackout shade submerged the room in darkness. I owned nice mattresses in all of my homes, but this bed rivaled them. Or maybe it was the sheets.

Or that the three fuckers had kept me up past three a.m. They'd plagued my dreams and made it impossible to fall asleep.

At some point, someone had dropped off a shirt to wear to sleep and my clutch. Even left a charger for my phone, which was good because it had died after texting Kenji. My money was on Niko being the good Samaritan. I hadn't been around them long, but he was clearly the mother hen of the group. Which meant he was also the most ruthless if you fucked with those under his protection. He might be kind to me now, but I had no doubt he'd put a fucking bullet in my brain if I threatened his brothers. Questions about how the three of them became so close swirled in my mind as I climbed out from the middle of the bed.

I'd only ever been close to one man, and that had fucking backfired epically. Ryan was now my sole friend, and we only spoke every few months. But we'd connected on a soul level and didn't need daily communication. It was a relationship that transcended space and time. Plus, she didn't have a dick.

Dicks were trouble.

I'd bleed for her. It was why I'd given her a burner with my personal number. No one had that. A direct line to Cain—the merc for hire who was known for the ability to get to anyone.

Of course, Ryan only knew me as Scarletta Romano, niece to Dominick Romano and the bastard daughter of Anthony Russo. I'd never shared with her that the infamous assassin and I were one and the same. She had her suspicions, though. Friendships, when you were a criminal, had different rules. We didn't share our every secret. Being a good friend meant not having an issue with secrets being kept from you.

Mine could get her killed. She'd become a target for anyone looking to unseat Cain. I laughed thinking about it because Ryan would probably shoot them in the head before they even got close. *La Brujita de Los Muertos* had twitchy fingers and didn't give a shit about asking questions.

The cold from the tiled bathroom floor pulled me back to reality. My secrets would be hard to keep around these men. I'd have to figure out what I was going to do soon. I wasn't even a fucking Romano. At least not by blood. My sperm donor had shot his load into my mother while he was married to the devil, Giana Romano.

It got him killed. My literal saving grace was that my mother was a random stripper he'd assaulted, so Giana *graciously* allowed Dominick to keep me.

"Remember, Scarletta. I blessed you with life. How is it you'll atone for your father's sins?"

In this world, family and loyalty were everything. Someone had to pay Anthony's penance. My whole life had been atoning for sins that weren't my own, and I was at my wit's end.

The bathroom mirror revealed the dark shadows that

rimmed my eyes. Their light blue seemed to make the bags stand out even more.

Maybe it was time to make a deal with demons and give up atonement. I ran my finger along the thin line below my clavicle. There was a strange longing for the cut to scar. First time I'd ever wanted a mark to remain.

For so long, I'd planned my escape from my uncle and his empire. Killing him was a fantasy I hadn't truly believed would happen. But now…maybe that life wasn't what I really wanted. Maybe what I craved at my core was to tear apart the man who'd stolen my freedom.

The idea of him writhing in pain as his entrails fell to the floor filled me with sick pleasure. I longed to hold the blade that would seal his fate. Carve my rejection of repentance into Dominick's skin before plunging the blade into his gut and twisting.

No, I didn't want to disappear.

I wanted to seat myself atop his throne like a blasphemous goddess and make him watch as every man he commanded bowed at my feet. I'd help my new husband and his brothers in their quest to take over the city. Not out of loyalty to them, but out of pure, unadulterated rage for the hand Dominick had dealt me.

He could have loved me as his own—the way Sergio had done with Ryan—but instead, I'd felt the sting of a belt and the twinging pain of hunger.

I straightened my back, renewed with purpose. I'd have to be careful. There were a lot of skeletons in my closet, and not all of them I wanted revealed to the new men in my life. I'd have to tread lightly when determining what to reveal and what to keep shrouded in secrecy.

I moved back into the bedroom to check the time on my phone. My lock screen read one p.m., but what caught my attention was the notification that Kenji had sent me a final message with what looked like an attachment.

Holy shit. That's a dick.

I slammed down on the volume buttons as Kenji's moan came through the speaker. He was spread out on his bed, bathed in red light. His hand was wrapped around his cock, twisting up and down. The sight had me squirming where I sat at the edge of my bed. Blood rushed in my ears, my nipples pebbling when my name fell from his lips. Lust pooled between my legs as he stroked his hard length.

His eyes were hooded when he looked into the camera.

"Scar, here's a gift for you. Material for you when you use your fingers to fuck that leaking cunt of yours."

Each gasp and moan from his lips ratcheted my desire higher and higher. I hadn't moved since pressing play, too entranced by the way he fucked his hand while saying filthy things for *me*. I craved to replace his hand with my own.

I couldn't take it anymore. My hand trailed down my body, swiping through my arousal before pushing inside. My moan synced with one of Kenji's, giving the illusion that we were actively fucking. I circled my wet fingers against my clit, knowing I'd be able to make myself come faster that way. My fucked-up goal was to come with video Kenji.

"Fuck, Scar. I want to fill you up and watch my cum leak out before shoving it back in."

My jaw dropped at the confession. My brain painted the image of Kenji's fingers shoving his hot release back into my well-fucked pussy, and that was all it took to take me over.

But if I thought that part of the video was the *pièce de résistance*, it didn't hold a candle to the full body aftershock I got when I watched him drag his cum-coated finger up to his mouth and lick it off.

"Fuck," I moaned out as the video cut out.

Silence mixed with my labored breathing. My body was flushed with post-orgasm bliss. That was so much better than a dick pic. Men should *only* send vocal jerkoff videos like that.

Indecision racked my brain. What the hell did you say back to *that*?

Thanks for the masturbation material. Your dick looked great.

I chuckled, because that was exactly the thing to say back to Kenji. I shot off the text before making my way into the main part of the apartment. It didn't seem like anyone was around, but I wasn't entirely sure. I padded across the space in nothing but an oversized silk button-up. A rumble from my stomach echoed through the quiet apartment. Disappointment settled in my gut because I didn't fucking know how to cook. The idea of delivery flitted through my mind for a second, but it would be a bitch to get it up to the penthouse.

"Fuck me in the ass," I grumbled as I yanked the fridge door open, knowing there wouldn't be anything I could just pop into the microwave.

"Is that really where you want to start?"

A startled yelp slipped past my lips, and I chucked the closest object at the deep voice. It just so happened that the object was pinot grigio. The Russian giant didn't flinch as he caught the wine bottle against his chiseled chest with a single hand. Damn, he could probably throw me around with ease. Suddenly my mouth was dry as a fucking desert.

Who was still shirtless in the middle of the afternoon?

"You aren't wearing any pants. Arguably, that's worse than no shirt," he said, amusement in his tone.

It took my lust-filled brain a second to figure out that I'd said my quiet thoughts out loud. My cheeks flushed as he stepped into my space, gently pushing me away from the fridge.

"Hungry, little one?" he asked, not waiting for an answer before gathering an armful of ingredients, his skin pulling taut over his muscled back. Tattoos rippled with each move he made in a mesmerizing dance. What did they look like when he fucked?

I shook my head, trying to clear the lust that was still present from Kenji's video earlier.

"Kenji and Caleb have already left the apartment, so you're stuck with me this afternoon. Least I can do is feed you," Niko said.

The smile he threw me over his shoulder was breathtaking. It looked so carefree. It was borderline innocent, which was the complete opposite of his body. Covered in tattoos and chiseled muscles—a woman's wet dream.

"Can I help you?"

I surprised myself with the question because what I wanted to say was, "Eat me out?" But something about how excited he was to shove nutrients down my throat, and not his cock, was strangely endearing. I'd never felt these feelings for my Uber Eats drivers. Maybe the secret was in the man actually turning on a burner.

"Sure. Start by cracking these," he said, handing me a carton of eggs.

I fished for answers while cracking the eggs into a metal bowl. I'd seen enough Food Network to know how to do this part. "You got stuck babysitting me while the other two..."

He drew out a cutting board and large knife, skillfully starting in on the bell pepper and onions he'd pulled out. He moved with such precision. Clearly the meal he'd made last night wasn't a fluke situation. Niko really could cook.

"Caleb is out at a business meeting. Some of the people who were at the engagement party have reached out." He moved to the range, placing a large skillet on the front burner before coating it in olive oil. His eyes moved toward me periodically, checking up on what I was doing. "Money is power, and we have a lot of New York's elite in our pocket."

I perked up at the tidbit of information. That was something I could work with. "If you get me a list, I can dig up *helpful* information. Create it, too," I said nonchalantly, carrying the bowl of eggs to Niko. The shirt I wore rode up my thighs when I hopped up on the counter next to where he worked. The kitchen lights reflected off the faint pale lines of my scars.

His gaze flicked to them briefly, but he didn't comment. Instead, he grabbed a whisk and went to work on the bowl I'd brought him.

"You talking about blackmail?" he asked, his tone neutral, lightly dancing around the topic. A reminder that while he was easy to be around, he didn't trust me.

"Yeah, I mean blackmail," I said with a chuckle, mesmerized by the quick flicks of his wrist as he broke up the yokes. "Who taught you to cook?" I asked, deciding to navigate us into easier conversation topics. Or so I thought, but his body tensed and his words were tight when he replied.

"My mother taught me." He poured the mixture into the heated skillet, not looking at me as he worked with confidence. "She taught me and my sisters."

His jaw ticked, as if he hadn't meant to mention the part about his siblings. A pang of sadness hit me. It wasn't necessarily that I wanted siblings. The worry I'd have for them in this life would drive me to the point of insanity. But there'd been so many moments I'd longed for someone to be by my side, supporting me.

"How do they feel about you leaving the Bratva?"

"I have no clue. They're back in Saint Petersburg. I haven't spoken to any of them in over ten years," he responded, removing the skillet from the heat to flip the omelet with an expert jerk.

My focus was fixated on his movements, so it took a moment for his words to register. I may not have had any family, but even I knew it was a long time to not speak to them.

"Why so long?"

As soon as the words slipped out, I wished I could shove them back in. An angry sneer streaked across his face as he slid his creation off onto a plate, perfectly folding it over.

"Sorry, that's not any of my business," I mumbled, holding my hands up in surrender.

The lines between his brows softened at my tone, giving me the impression that the look hadn't been meant for me. "My father forbade any communication with them." He shrugged his massive shoulders.

His hands landed on the counter, caging me in. Heat radiating from his bare chest. My finger had a mind of its own. It came up and traced the Cyrillic tattoo on his chest. The air between us crackled with tension.

"What does it mean?" My words were barely above a whisper.

"Blood decides nothing," he responded, pulling a fork loaded with omelet up to my mouth. His pupils dilated as my lips wrapped around the prongs. Flavor exploded in my mouth, and my lids dropped closed, a moan slipping out.

"That is the best fucking thing I've eaten in my life," I responded, my eyes fluttering open.

He studied me for a moment. "You really don't know how to cook?" he asked, placing the fork back on the counter.

Normally I'd bristle at the question because there was so much to unpack with my answer, but something about Niko was disarming, and he'd shared something vulnerable with me.

"Nope." I popped the *P* while wiping down the counter to stay busy, uncomfortable at the admission I'd made. "Dominick didn't like to feed me as a kid. Knowing how to cook would've made it hard to keep me hungry."

An uncomfortable silence grew between us as he stared at me. His attention was so acute it practically burned.

"He really didn't feed you? Or let you learn?" Niko asked. His tone was devoid of emotion, but the deadly swirling sea was back in his eyes. His gaze was so intense that it was hard to hold. It was like he wanted to claw inside my body and pull out my secrets.

And I found myself wanting to let him.

All I could manage was a small shake of my head. My normally smart mouth was at a loss for words. His free hand came up and threaded in my hair, right at the base of my scalp, and he moved even closer into my circle. He pushed between my thighs, his bare skin brushing against my silk-covered nipples, causing them to pebble.

"You'll never go hungry while you're in my care."

Heat curled in my core at the word *care*. No one had ever cared for me before, and suddenly it was the only thing in the world I wanted.

My tongue popped out, swiping along my bottom lip. The orgasm I'd given myself not ten minutes before clearly hadn't been enough to quell my need.

"What if food isn't what I'm hungry for?" I asked, barely above a whisper, not sure what he'd do. I was technically Caleb's wife, but he didn't seem to care when his brothers touched me. Something had simmered in Caleb's eyes last night, but I wouldn't have categorized it as jealousy.

Niko's oceanic eyes widened, his nostrils flaring, as the grip on my hair tightened.

"What do you want me to fill your mouth with then, little one?" he asked, gripping my waist, pulling me off the counter, and pushing me to my knees. His tone was sweet, but his actions were commanding—the two sides of his personality warring for dominance.

He was both.

But my guess was that he thought he had to choose between the two. I saw the struggle painted on his face.

My hands curled around the waistband of his sweats as I peered up at him through my lashes. "You can call me your dirty slut and shove your cock down my throat *and* still cook for me and tuck me into bed," I said, yanking down his gray sweats till they banded around his muscular thighs. My brain had a goddamn aneurysm at the sight of him.

Thick Slavic style lettering covered each thigh, bracketing his already erect cock. Saliva started pooling in my mouth as my fingers wrapped around him, giving a languid pull and drawing out a ragged moan from both of us.

Precum beaded at the head of his cock. My thumb swiped over the liquid before dragging it over his shaft. Images of Kenji fucking his hand sprouted in my mind, sending another wave of desire shooting to my core.

"You can be both hard and soft with me, Niko." I leaned forward and drew a ball into my mouth. My heart beat loud in my ears as I sucked, hollowing out my cheeks.

"Oh, fuck," he uttered as I released him, dragging my mouth up to swirl the tip of his cock with my tongue, flicking the velvety-soft skin. His words were like a prayer on his lips.

Yet I was the one on my knees in worship.

NINETEEN
NIKO

"BE MY GOOD LITTLE WHORE..."

WAS this what it was like to have a lobotomy?

Because my brain was short-circuiting, my synapses running haywire. I had to *tell* myself to breathe. Straight up moaned the word *inhale*, which, of course, Scar took as a request, and she sucked down more of my length. Her mouth was so sinfully good I swore I could fucking see sounds.

This hadn't been my intention when I'd offered to cook for her. How the fuck had we gone from me wanting to tear off Dominick's limbs for not feeding her to my hand buried in her brunette locks while she fucking tickled her esophagus with my cock?

My fingers twisted in her hair, angling her face so I could watch how she took me. The tears collecting along her lashes spilled over as she gagged on my cock, her throat constricting around the head like a vise grip. Fuck, she was a sight to see. Her blue eyes peering up at me through dark lashes, with those pouty lips of hers stretched thin around my dick. I was going to nut from the sight alone.

I spread my feet apart, giving her more room to work. Fire seared up my balls at the wet sound she made when she took me to the back of her throat as I worked my cock in and out of her mouth. She let her saliva slide down the shaft, the lubrication glistening under the kitchen lights. A soft hand wrapped around my cock, syncing to the rhythm of her mouth.

It was too much. If I let her go on any longer, I'd come in her mouth. Or maybe I'd paint that pretty face of hers with my release.

"Be my good little whore and get on the fuckin' counter."

I winced at the words. They sounded too harsh and gruff. I'd never felt self-conscious about how I liked to fuck before, but of course, this woman had already wormed her way into my psyche, and my brain didn't want to drive her away with our inability to be soft in bed.

But she scrambled onto the island like her ass was on fire. Her very bare ass.

"Why the hell are you not wearing underwear?" I asked, stepping between her spread thighs and running a finger over her slick pussy, pulling a moan from her. "Was this always your plan? You came in here ready to get your cunt fucked?"

She shook her head like she was already lost to the lust. "Caleb cut them off last night," she replied breathlessly. I paused at the mention of his name. We'd all talked last night after she'd gone to sleep. He was furious to be working with another Romano, but we'd all agreed it was the best option we had. Kenji filled us in on his hunch about her hating her family as deeply as we did ours. And Caleb knew better than to question Kenji's gut on these matters. Where my obsession drove me to learn every little thing about a person, Kenji was a human lie detector with an uncanny ability to read people.

As much as the little nugget of information she dropped moments ago pissed me off, it confirmed Kenji's suspicion. Her revenge-filled vendetta against Dominick wasn't for show. But the most important topic of that conversation was that Caleb had no problem with either of us fucking his new wife. Well, those weren't his exact words. But I was taking the fact that he hadn't said, *Don't fuck my wife,* after watching me lick the blood off her thigh and letting Kenji unzip her dress and see her tits as a green light.

Ask for forgiveness and all that shit.

I reached forward and tore open the shirt I'd brought her while she showered. The pinging of buttons hitting the hard surface was muffled by Scar's gasp as my fingers pinched her nipples.

"Niko, please," she moaned, lying flat, her feet propped up on the counter, fully exposing her glossy cunt to me. "The showerhead is great, but fuck, do I want to be filled."

Her head popped back up, and she stared me down with a look so intense I was frozen in place. "You better stretch me with that thick fucking cock of yours, Niko. Because I swear if you're just fucking with me right now, I will lose my shit, and you'll end up with a second stab wound."

The rough pads of my fingertips dug into her jaw. I loved the little noise of surprise she let out at the move.

"I'm going to make that dirty fucking mouth of yours clean up the mess you make on my cock after I'm done using you." I dug two fingers into her warm heat with my free hand, reveling in the way I made her eyes roll back at the intrusion. "So. Fucking. Wet." I punctuated each word with a thrust.

There was no way I could hold off being inside her any longer. Her moans echoed off the walls, the soundtrack to my madness. Fuck, I wanted a recording of her sounds of pleasure so I could play it whenever I wanted.

"Open," I barked, tracing her lips with the fingers I'd just used to fuck her.

She obeyed without question, swirling her tongue around the digits like she had my cock. I was half delusional at this point. Completely consumed by lust for this woman. I leaned down and pulled a nipple into my mouth, sucking hard while pinching the other.

Her moans of pleasure spurred me on as I plunged my

fingers deep inside her, her breathy *holy shit* music to my ears. Her pussy got wetter and wetter with each deep push and twist, her lungs confused about whether they should be inhaling or exhaling.

Her eyes fluttered open. She was so beautiful when overtaken by lust that I couldn't hold back. I slammed my mouth to hers. I never kissed women. It always felt too intimate for fucking. But Scar's pouty pink lips taunted me.

Our tongues slid past one another in a sensual dance. I couldn't take it anymore. I ached to be inside her. To coat her with my cum.

She shrieked as I palmed each ass cheek, yanking her off the counter and sinking her onto my cock without warning. I stumbled. Not because of her weight but because she felt so fucking fantastic that I wanted to drop to my knees. It took me a second to realize that the animalistic growl I heard was coming from me.

"Show me what you got, big boy. I thought you wanted to provide a mess for me to clean up." Her teeth dug into my neck, and I felt her smile around my flesh when my dick jumped at the pain she'd inflicted.

I flipped us around, slamming her body against the fridge, taking a stiff peak into my mouth when the cold caused her back to arch.

"Next time, bite me fucking harder, little one."

She moaned loudly as I ran my tongue up the center of her chest before claiming her mouth and biting hard enough to draw blood.

"All you fucking assholes love to make me bleed," she said against me, grinding her clit into my lower abs. "But how about one of you make me fucking come?"

I withdrew my cock, laughing at how she'd called me an asshole before I drove back into her relentlessly. If she wanted to be fucked, I'd grant her that wish.

"I want you so fucking sore, Scar, that with every move

you make, you think about how you let someone other than your husband fuck this delicious pussy," I said, drinking in her yells as I pinched her clit between my fingers while driving into her, groaning at how she dug her fingers into my shoulders and her heels into my ass.

"Faster," she breathed.

Her body met mine stroke for stroke. It was like she wanted me to crawl inside her.

Her eyes popped open. The blue had almost completely disappeared. My body shuddered at the look of desperate, hungry *need* she gave me. She looked at me as if I was the only one who could fulfill her desires.

Shit.

Fucking her had been a bad idea. My infatuation was too deep already. I knew better. These fixations of mine had to be treated carefully, or I'd fall headfirst into an obsession. And even though I was fucking Scar, she wasn't mine to keep. I thought I could let her suck my dick, and then I'd return the favor. Release some tension. I'd known I was gaslighting myself when I said having a taste would help get her out of my system.

Fucking lie.

"His fucking loss if he doesn't want to have me," she whispered, licking her lips as she searched my face.

Have her. That's what I fucking wanted.

I wanted to possess her and be possessed by her.

Our lips came together once more, but this melding felt different. Her tongue slid over mine in a tangled mess, and a sense of desperation sent us over the edge into oblivion.

Fuck. I was obsessed with my brother's wife.

TWENTY
SCAR

WHAT WOULD MY THERAPIST SAY?

WHOEVER INVENTED the IUD deserved a kiss on the mouth. Because I had let a six-five giant of a man—who'd held me still while his brother *drugged me*—come inside me while he fucked me against a fridge. And if that wasn't deranged enough behavior, I'd then dropped to my knees to suck our combined cum off his thick cock before he made me lap up what I'd leaked on the floor.

The smooth texture of the silk pillowcase cooled my heated cheeks as I vividly recalled the words he'd spoken to me.

Be a good little whore and clean up the messes you've made.

I could still feel the ghost tugging of my hair as he directed my mouth where he wanted it on his thigh, leaving a glossy trail over his tattoos.

Fuck. I needed to restart therapy. Actually, if something was wrong with what we'd done, I'd rather live in denial than give it up. Because sex with him was invigorating. Too bad the aftermath was turning out to be shit.

When I sank to my knees in the kitchen to give Niko a blow job, it had been partly out of frustration. Kenji's tease of a video had only added to the pent-up emotions Caleb had given me the night before, and I wanted to make him pay for the way he'd made me feel.

It was as if he'd stolen me away, only to place me in a corner to be forgotten. Like a bird with clipped wings that had been put in a cage.

And I'd wanted to test whether he truly didn't give a shit about sharing me. Not because I felt Caleb cared about the sanctity of this marriage. He'd forged the fucking license, for God's sake. He just didn't seem like the type of man who liked being denied, and for as many times as he said he didn't want to fuck me, I'd felt that hard dick of his during our argument.

Giving Niko a blow job was supposed to drive a wedge between them or get a reaction. Anything other than stirring up these weird butterflies inside. After we both saw stars, he completely shut me out.

I'd had plenty of one-night stands and hookups before. Usually, I *wanted* to come and get the hell out. But this time, I felt…sad when Niko didn't want to lock me away in his room. Honestly, I wasn't sure what it was I was feeling.

He'd cooked me a fresh omelet. Even added extra salt, which I hadn't realized he'd noticed I liked from the last time he fed me. If it didn't taste like an ocean shit on it, I wasn't eating it. But he said as few words to me as possible the whole time. It didn't feel like he was trying to ghost me. It was more like he was trying to get some space between us. Brick himself off from me.

That was a day and a half ago.

I'd holed up in my room, only leaving to grab something to eat. Niko might've been avoiding me, but he'd made sure there was something in the fridge for me to heat up in the microwave. Whatever the three of them were busy doing, they didn't include me, and it was pissing me off.

"Ugh. You're literally a killer. How did you manage to catch feelings after one fuck?" I mumbled into the down pillow. *Feelings* seemed too strong a word to describe what I was experiencing for the big guy. What did it say about me that I wanted to set a man's balls on fire for smiling at me, but then put a man's balls in my mouth for kidnapping me? And feeding me.

I'll take she needs help *for five hundred, Alex.*

Maybe I was so starved for any type of affection that the second someone was kind-ish to me, I folded like a damn chair. Enzo had really fucked me up on the relationship front.

I'd retreated to my room as soon as I finished shoveling egg in my mouth; the silence had been too much for me to stand. But all I'd accomplished since was throwing a pity party. Literally, under my blankets.

Well, and tapping their phones and emails. Kenji's number wasn't the only thing I'd taken from his phone.

Today I'd start doing shit, even if they weren't including me. But first, I needed clothes. I'd been living in dropped-off borrowed shirts. And almost as important as clothing, I needed some of my shit. Laptop, burners, and cash. Most of that was held at my safe houses, but I still wanted to have something on hand in case I couldn't get to one of those right away.

I'd staked out what their security looked like. There didn't seem to be any interior cameras, which was a good thing for me. The only visible way in was through the elevator, which required a key card. They should've hired someone better to do their security system because the thing with keycard systems was that they could be hacked.

I was tired of sitting on my ass. If they didn't want to give me any information, I'd find it myself. The fact that Enzo hadn't tried to reach out made me nervous. There was no way in hell my uncle would let the stunt the boys pulled go unpunished. Even if he couldn't touch them, I'd still suffer the consequences.

Unease turned in my gut at the thought as my hand wrapped around the lever of my door, easing it open.

Silent hinges were a thief's wet dream, and this apartment had ones that were as quiet as church mice. Across from my room, two more sets of double doors lined the hall. My guess was that they must be the guys' bedrooms, but there weren't any clues telling me whose they might be. I also wondered why the third bedroom in this hall was a guestroom. I gnawed at my bottom lip, debating which room to try first.

I decided to go with the one closest to mine, so if someone came back, I could quickly get the hell out of Dodge. I wiggled the handle, surprised to find it was unlocked. Before I even moved far enough into the room to get a look at it, I knew who it belonged to. The scent wrapped around me like a hug. A hug that was meant to strangle me—spicy and rich. If I thought my room was impressive, Caleb's was flat-out exquisite.

Shit, maybe I should ask to share a bedroom.

The entry opened up into a room that was painted charcoal gray from floor to ceiling. The wall his bed sat against looked like some type of dark stone, and his bed was cognac-colored leather with black bedding that looked so soft I wanted to drop face-first in its pillowy goodness. But what really took my breath was the giant art prints he had hanging around the room. Black and white paintings of the mug shots of New York's more notorious gangsters.

I tiptoed my way through his space, careful not to disturb anything. Caleb felt like the type of man to notice when someone had been in his room. The nightstands were bare other than a journal and a frame. Gingerly, I lifted the frame, curious about what Caleb would have deemed important enough to display. The corners of my mouth inched upward at a gangly looking Caleb with his lanky arms wrapped around the shoulders of a pubescent Kenji and Niko. Niko was smaller than he was currently, but still massive compared to the other two. And Kenji looked so…bare without all the artwork on his skin.

My smile slipped when I noticed that it wasn't just the boys in the photo. Somehow, I'd missed the slight girl standing in front of them, arms wrapped around Caleb's waist. I frowned at the spike of jealousy that shot through me. All four looked so happy. I couldn't help but wonder who she was and why Caleb had chosen to frame a photo that included her. There were memories etched into this photo. Memories I wasn't entitled to but found myself still wanting to know.

A throat cleared behind me.

I reacted purely on instinct, crouching and moving my hand to my hip, but I didn't have my gun or my knife.

"There a reason you broke into my room?" Caleb asked. His tone was neutral, but his eyes narrowed on the frame still clutched in my hand.

"You can hardly call it a break-in when I literally opened the door." I rolled my eyes, pretending my heart wasn't still in my throat as I stood. "Who is she?" I asked as he plucked it from my fingers, setting it back on the nightstand. His proximity sent electric shocks coursing through my body.

Jealousy clenched in my gut as he looked at the photo with affection before sliding his piercing gaze toward me. "Don't worry about who she is. It's you I'm married to, right?"

The attitude in his tone pissed me off. It was dismissive and bitter—he didn't want to be married to me. And, logically, I didn't want to be married to him either, but logic didn't counteract the bitter taste of rejection coating my tongue.

I shook my head, trying to clear the feeling of being unwanted from my mind. "I was coming to look for you." I said, gesturing with my hand to the oversized shirt swallowing me whole, making the half-truth believable. "I need clothes to wear. Kenji was supposed to tell you I needed my shit."

Caleb's nose wrinkled at my statement. I couldn't get a read on the emotion that flashed across his face.

Also, why the fuck was I holding my tongue about the fact that Kenji had sent me a video of him fucking his hand like it was me? Or that I'd fucked Niko? That was supposed to be the whole point of that little escapade. Yet here I was, standing in his room, with nothing on but another man's shirt, avoiding the topic.

My therapist would say I avoided telling him because I was still reeling from the rejection. I felt Niko pulling away, and I didn't want to experience yet another person telling me with their actions that I was unworthy.

Fuck.

Therapy was the worst decision if you were determined to sit in denial and disassociation.

Caleb stepped closer, stripping off his suit jacket and tossing it on the bed. "You're already wearing something, Scar. Are you being greedy and want a shirt from all of us?" he asked, moving so close I had to crane my neck to keep our eyes locked.

My mouth had a mind of its own. Because what I was trying to say was *No. I don't want to wear your fucking shirt.* But what came out was, "Maybe I do want a piece of all three of you, Caleb."

What. The. Fuck?

Caleb's brow ticked up ever so slightly, like he was as shocked as I was that I'd admitted that little tidbit. So, of course, I had to remedy my mistake.

"I also want to try heroin, but some shit is so toxic it should be avoided no matter how fun it looks," I said, letting my eyes pointedly drop to his crotch for a second so there was no mistaking what I was referring to. "Now, who the fuck is taking me to my apartment to grab clothes?"

Steam was practically coming out of his ears. Hopefully they had good dental insurance, because with the way he was clenching his jaw, he was going to need replacement molars. He turned without a word and stalked out his door, calling over his shoulder, "Get your ass out here so we can go get your shit."

The smile I had fell when I remembered my bare legs.

"What the fuck am I supposed to wear to get there? I don't have pants." My panicked question was met with silence. "Caleb, I don't fucking have underwear either," I yelled after him.

TWENTY-ONE

SCAR

THAT'S RIGHT, BITCH. I HAVE $$ TOO.

I'D PROBABLY SLEEP like the dead tonight.

Because feeling emotions was fucking exhausting. I didn't know how people did it. Today I'd felt rejection, anger, and jealousy—all within a few hours of each other. Well, I wasn't 100 percent sure I was jealous. Maybe envious was the better word for what I'd experienced when Caleb had dragged me into Kenji's room and rummaged through the random clothes he kept in there that his hookups had left behind. I could've made myself a closet from all the shit in that drawer of his dresser.

The city passed by the window of Caleb's SUV. Walking would've been faster, but the bulletproof surround made me feel safer than being out in the open.

"Where you taking me, Callahan?" I asked as he pulled into the entrance of a parking garage of a high-end department store.

"You said you needed clothes, so I'm taking you shopping," he answered, as if my question was ridiculous. His eyes flicked to me as he pulled up to the valet booth. "It's not like I can have my wife walking around in *that*." The green of his eyes wasn't visible in the low light of the garage. Instead, he peered at me through two inky pools.

I tensed under his scrutiny, which was ridiculous. *He* was the reason I looked like this. The tiny biker shorts were the most normal-looking piece of clothing I could find, and I'd had to steal one of Kenji's graphic tees to wear on top because everything else showed my nipples.

"Well, no shit," I bit out. "But I meant I wanted you to take me to my apartment for clothes, asshole. I have other shit I need to get."

He said nothing more as he exited the car, handing over the keys to the parking attendant. The fabric of his tailored suit hugged his muscled body like a second skin. Irritation spiked in my veins as he left me to trail behind like a damn dog. The ass hadn't even opened my door for me.

I jogged to catch up, interlacing our fingers. His hand was warm and calloused, and I ignored how well mine seemed to fit in his.

"What the hell, Scar?" he asked, looking at our interlocked hands with disdain.

We had to look like such an odd match standing there. Him in his expensive suit and loafers and me looking like a homeless hooker.

"Ashamed of your *wife*, Callahan?" I started walking toward the private entrance of the high-end boutique, C'est La Vie, tugging him along. "Come on. You wanted to take me shopping? Then let's go fucking shopping."

The store was beautiful, with its pearl-white walls and opulent chandeliers. Fresh floral arrangements were dotted around the space, filling the air with their fresh scent. The two women standing at the counter in the middle of the shop halted their conversation when they heard the tinkle of a bell. The pause in their chatter left only the sounds of smooth jazz echoing in the space.

Caleb must have booked an appointment, because there

was no one else in the normally busy store. He strode forward with purpose, leaving me behind as I trailed my fingers along the racks of fine clothing.

"We're here to see Megan," he announced.

The two women gawked at Caleb. The blond one's back was going to hurt by the end of the day with how aggressively she arched it. She was basically presenting her tits on a silver platter to him. Both attendants looked to be in their early twenties and *obviously* eager to bag a wealthy man. I rolled my eyes at their bright smiles and doe eyes, continuing to gather up items I wanted.

"Mr. Callahan, we're so glad to have you in our store today. Who is it that you're shopping for?" Blondie leaned forward, resting her heart-shaped face on her palm. The position gave Caleb an eyeful of the cleavage tucked behind her black button-up. "Or maybe you're preemptively buying for someone who catches your eye." She giggled at her attempt at flirtation.

Gag me.

I moved closer, observing how Caleb would react to the advances. His smile was charming, but there wasn't the same heat in his eyes as when he watched me. Or maybe that was all wishful thinking on my part. He glanced over to where I stood slightly behind the ladies, his eyes turning cold and challenging before he ripped them away.

"Does who I'm shopping for change the *service* I receive?" he asked, making the question sound dirty and explicit.

The asshole was toying with me.

The girl's mouth fell open, like she hadn't actually expected her flirtation to result in anything. "Oh, I'm happy to help you with *whatever* you need, Mr. Callahan."

My position let me see how she hit her coworker's leg in excitement under the counter. Poor girl thought she was about to get lucky. I rolled my eyes, pulling out my phone and typing out a message. I'd let them have their fun a few minutes longer. It wasn't like they knew he was taken. The asshole had yet to say anything, and they'd both been so struck by his hot ass that they still hadn't noticed my presence.

"I'm going to need a dressing room because I'll need to see the clothes on to know if I like them or not," he drawled out.

If he liked them? Fuck that. All he got to do was slide his credit card across the counter and load my bags.

"Oh, of course, Mr. Callahan. And I'd be happy to model the items for you. We even have a selection of lingerie."

The clacking of heels on marble cut off whatever Caleb was going to respond with. "Mikayla," an angry voice barked out. "If you're so eager to get Mr. Callahan some lingerie he'd like, then I suggest you ask his *wife* for her sizes. This is no way to treat one of our best clients."

Two sets of eyes snapped to where I stood behind them, widening when they saw the petite woman with the harsh bun giving them a disapproving stare. The one girl at least had the decency to look away in shame, but Mikayla glared at me, smirking when she looked me up and down. Apparently she found me lacking.

"So sorry, Megan. Mr. Callahan never mentioned her, and I've been *very* helpful to him," blondie said in a sickly sweet voice before turning back to Caleb. "Mr. Callahan, I can still model the clothing if you'd like. It might be hard to tell the garments' full potential without her hair and makeup done."

My mouth literally fell open at the dig. Any sympathy I had for her went out the fucking window. The dumb bitch was picking a fight with the wrong person.

Megan's wine-colored lips turned down into a disapproving line. "He's not the client I'm referring to, Mikayla," she said, taking the items from me as we moved toward the counter. "Ms. Scarletta is the one who regularly shops here."

I gave Caleb a blinding smile when he looked at me in confusion.

That's right, asshole. I've got money too.

He'd been quiet this whole time, his eyes pinging back and forth like he was watching a damn tennis match. The smirk on his face suggested he liked being fought over.

I moved in front of him, giving the women my back as I stood on my tippy toes to whisper in his ear. "Your little game is going to cost you, Caleb. I hope your bank account is bigger than your dick."

I looked over my shoulder at Mikayla, motioning toward the pile. "You can start bagging those up for us. Oh, and by the way, those dark roots of yours are far more distracting than my fresh face."

Rough fingers gripped my chin, pulling my attention away from the woman.

"Don't like women talking to me, *macushla?*" His tongue poked out and swiped across his bottom lip. "There's no limit on my card, but I want you to try on the lingerie for me. Now."

Warm lips pressed against mine, devouring me as if there wasn't an audience at my back.

"I'm the only woman who gets to model for you, Callahan," I bit out between kisses. The deep rumble of his chest caused my nipples to harden.

He was playing me. Riling me up to get a reaction.

And I was powerless to stop it.

The clearing of a throat broke our lustful exchange. "I have a room already for you two. If you'll please follow me," Megan said while walking us toward a dressing room. I could practically hear the smile in her voice.

I didn't know whether her amusement was for the way Caleb and I had just kissed like horny teenagers or the look of loathing that Mikayla was sending my way as she wrapped my items.

Megan flashed me a smile as she held the door open for us, quirking an eyebrow behind Caleb's back and giving me a look that said I was a lucky bitch.

"I've already dropped off some of my favorite pieces. Take your time. No one will bother you," she said, pulling the door closed behind her.

Caleb's eyes grew darker and hungrier the moment she stepped out of the room. His gaze was sexual and raw. The hair on the back of my neck stood on end as he stalked me down, my back hitting one of the three mirrors in the room. His hands landed on my hips, giving the shorts a rough tug.

"Here, let me help you out of these," he said against my neck, his breath like a warm caress against my skin.

I gasped when the cool air hit my breasts as he tugged the baggy shirt over my head, leaving me completely naked. His eyes widened at the sight, but he didn't say a word or attempt to touch me. I stood there like a mannequin waiting to be dressed, and it pissed me off.

He turned to the pile Megan had left and began to rifle through it.

"Why is it that I've never seen you before?" he asked over his shoulder. "Adriana, Milania, Giana. I've seen all three of them numerous times." He turned back around, a pair of blood red silk panties in his hand. "You, I've never seen."

He knocked my hand away when I reached for the garment before getting down on a knee in front of me. My mouth went dry as he instructed me to step into the thong, trailing his fingers up the outer part of my legs as he pulled the fabric up over my hips.

The garment was so small it barely covered my pussy. The temptation was apparently too much because he leaned forward and kissed my silk-clad mound. My core clenched at the intimate gesture as blood rushed in my ears, my nipples tightening. Everything he did made my mind hazy with lust. The control that normally came so easily for me winked out of existence the moment I was in the vicinity of any of these three men.

"Fucking tease," I bit out when he stood, giving me a cocky grin before it fell away and was replaced by his intimidating stare.

"Answer the question, Scar." He placed his hands on either side of the wall, trapping me between them. Caleb acted as if he was unfazed, but the bulge straining against his dress slacks suggested otherwise.

"I get a question of my own then," I said.

His jaw popped. He didn't like the thought of giving me answers, but he knew it was the only way I'd cooperate. The fact that he was even asking me outright meant he'd exhausted all his information outlets.

"Fine," he said through clenched teeth.

I knew he had to hate the smug smile I was giving him. "Dominick hates me, and I hate him. I don't attend anything I'm not forced to," I answered with a shrug, trying to make light of all the nuances that existed in my relationship with Dominick.

"My turn. Why are you three going after your fathers?" I asked.

His face flickered between lust and loathing. So the usual way he looked at me. He gnawed on his bottom lip, clearly conflicted about giving up the answer.

"The girl in the photo. Her name was Jessica."

My brows wrinkled in confusion at the change in subject, but before I could ask what she had to do with anything, he continued on.

"Niko, Kenji, and I didn't hold the same importance as our older brothers. We were sent off to public high school, tasked with keeping a presence among the young men who'd eventually join the ranks." He ran his hand through his hair as he stared off, lost in his memories. "That's where we met

Jessica, and all four of us got close. Closer than we should have been for rivals."

He whispered the last part, his eyes shadowing over with emotion.

I knew the look. The one you made when you worked through all your past choices and wondered what the outcomes would have been if you'd done something differently.

"Then what happened?" I asked, placing a hand on his chest, trying to pull him back.

I was taken aback by the openness shining in his eyes when he turned to face me. My heart clenched at how he tucked a stray hair behind my ear, the touch tender. He'd shown this side before—these hints of the man under the shield he placed between himself and the world.

The moment was charged with vulnerability, and I was afraid that if I breathed, I might ruin it. His throat bobbed as he swallowed, a nervous gesture I'd yet to see him do.

"Our fathers arranged for her to be kidnapped and sold." His voice was thick with emotion, and he couldn't look me in the eye as he spoke the words. "They figured she was the reason the three of us had gotten so close, and without her in the picture, we would go back to hating one another."

He let out a humorless chuckle. Anger churned in my gut at the disgusting actions of their sperm donors. Those men didn't deserve the title of father.

"You three were in love with her…" I whispered. My hand had a mind of its own because it traveled up and cupped Caleb's face, offering him a semblance of comfort. He snapped his attention to me at the touch but didn't pull away.

"We were infatuated with her. Cared for her, but we didn't love her. We only had love for her since she was the initial catalyst for our found family." He covered my hand with his own, holding it in place as he stepped even closer to me. "But her fate weighs on us. It was our fault she got killed," he said.

The guilt he carried for actions that were not his own resonated with me. My entire life was this rollercoaster of coping with the hand I'd been dealt and how much of it was my own fault.

"No. It's not your fault. You can't carry that burden. You can choose to exact her revenge and bring her justice, but your fucked-up sperm donors were responsible. Not three boys," I said, a fierceness to my voice that took us both by surprise.

Needing to change the mood, I snaked my hand down to his belt, pulling it loose. He stiffened at the gesture but didn't move to stop me as I unbuttoned his pants, slipping my hand inside and palming his thick erection.

I smiled at the way it jumped when my fingers wrapped around it. We definitely had to buy the underwear, because I knew there was now a dark spot on the front from where moisture was pooling. I didn't break our stare-off as I brought my hand up to my mouth and spit on it. His nostrils flared when I gripped him with my wet hand and gave him a rough tug, pulling a moan from his sinful lips. His forehead hit mine as he rocked against my grip, and I watched his hooded eyes as pleasure rolled through him.

"Why did you marry me?" I asked, rolling my thumb other the top of the thick head of his cock, savoring the full-body shudder it caused.

That hadn't been a question I'd meant to ask, but the words slipped out. His eyes fluttered open. My heart seized at the look he gave me, but he shut it down almost immediately.

"You're hotter than his daughter," he said with a shrug, wrapping his hand around mine and pumping his cock faster. "And that was more than one question. Fucking get me off so we can go. It's the least you can do since I'm buying you all this shit."

He was lying. There was more to his decision, but his

closed-off expression told me I wouldn't get anything further from him.

"Fuck you, Callahan. Get yourself off," I hissed, pulling my hand away so I could cross my arms over my chest.

His eyes glowed with challenge as he continued to pump his cock, now glistening with precum and my saliva. "Fine," he responded, pulling his hand off the wall and shoving it down the front of my underwear.

I moaned his name as his thick finger ran through my arousal. My hands found the wall for support as he rubbed my slick clit, swirling the bundle of nerves with the rough pad of his finger.

"You're so fucking wet for me, *wife*. Say my name louder so they know I'm bringing your pussy pleasure."

I didn't even care that he was ordering me around like a plaything. I was too lost in lust at the sight of his hips pumping into his hand as he fucked me with his fingers.

Good on him for the coordination and timing.

"Your pussy is leaking everywhere. You're going to leave this room as my messy little whore." His filthy words mixed with the wet sounds of his hands. "Pinch your fucking nipples, Scar," he ordered between labored breaths.

I brought my hands up and played with my nipples, watching the way he jerked off furiously. I was so fucking turned on, I couldn't help but add a finger of my own to where he was pumping them in and out of my pussy.

"Dammit, Scar," he groaned, slamming his lips to mine. "Why do you have to be so fucking hot?"

He pulled away from my mouth and yanked the front of my underwear open, stretching the elastic as he brushed my clit with the tip of his cock. I gasped as warm, thick cum hit my pussy, dripping down my slit and gathering in the crotch of the panties.

I couldn't pull my gaze away from the way his hand was squeezing out every bit of his release into the silk fabric.

I didn't know what the hell these men had done to me, because instead of being disgusted, pleasure rolled through my body at the erotic exchange we'd just shared.

"You're going to be coated in my cum the rest of the day. Understand?" he asked, his green eyes arrogantly staring me down as he tucked himself back inside his slacks while I stood there with his cum leaking down my leg. "And just so you know, the three of us tell each other everything. Niko says your mouth is like a gift from the devil."

He leaned forward and whispered in my ear. "I'll have to tell them that you love to be coated in cum too."

Holy shit. I was fucked.

TWENTY-TWO

SCAR

AM I INTO THIS? SHIT, I THINK I AM...

"MS. SCARLETTA. Nice to see you this evening." My doorman's eyes darted to Caleb for half a second before settling back on me. "You have a guest, I see. Will you require parking validation?"

Parking validation. Code word for *do I need to take this fucker out?*

I was tempted to say yes so I could get some space from Caleb. The air between us had been charged since we'd walked out of the dressing room. Megan had brought me some joggers and a cute tank top to wear over the underwear that was drenched in Caleb's release.

When she left, I checked for cameras in the room, because the sly grin she gave me told me she knew exactly what we'd done. Turned out she did, but not because of cameras. It was because I *had* moaned his name so loudly they all knew he was fucking my pussy with his fingers.

Caleb had given me an evil smirk when I walked out to them all staring at me. If he'd thought I'd leave that dressing room with my head held in shame, he had another thing coming.

"If you flirt with my husband again, I'll rip out your

tongue," I'd said to Mikayla when she continued to "acciden-tally" touch his arm.

"She means that literally," Caleb had added on, looking at me with something that looked an awful lot like pride.

"And if you don't push off their advances, I'll cut off your balls."

He'd smiled at that.

The drive to my apartment had been tense, and I'd nearly sprinted inside when the car came to a stop.

"Hey Henry. No, thank you. He's rich enough to cover the parking," I responded, throwing him a wink.

Henry wasn't just a doorman who sat behind the pretty terrazzo stone desk in the lobby. He was head of security for my building. Literally mine. I'd bought a whole fucking building so I could employ my own security team to watch over me.

I knew there'd come a time when my uncle deemed that I knew too much or was no longer of use. I didn't want anyone to know what protection I could afford. So we spoke in code and kept everything discreet.

All of the security staff were instructed when they were hired to treat each resident as a high-profile client. Communi-cation, payment, and everything business-related was run through my security company, Leslie George Security.

If you knew the right questions to ask, that was how clients got a hold of Cain.

Ryan had a similar setup with Lotería, her club in Tucson. Legal business on paper, but not so legal business when you dug around. She ran guns with hers. I sold mercenary services.

I led Caleb into one of the elevators, pressing the button for the thirtieth floor.

The second he crossed the threshold, he backed me into a corner, caging me in with his body. His inked hands landed on either side of my head, kicking my pulse into overdrive with his proximity, reminding me that we'd done something similar to this only an hour before. But this time, his eyes didn't hold lust.

"Don't play games, Romano. You won't like the results of fucking with me," he said, a low rumble in his chest. Heat pooled between my thighs, and I kept my eyes locked on him, trying to hide my reaction to the intimacy of our position. I was still on edge from our earlier exchange since only one of us had gotten off.

Actually, I probably would like the results of fucking you…

Thank God my mouth decided to keep that little thought to itself. There was something invigorating about going toe to toe with Caleb. Sure, he called me a bitch, but he never dismissed me.

"I have absolutely no clue what you're talking about, Callahan," I drawled out, attempting to sound bored with the whole exchange.

His mouth dipped closer to my ear. Mint with a hint of whiskey tickled my nose when he spoke. "You have that look in your eyes that says you're planning some shit. We're going to get your shit, and that's fucking it. Don't try to pull whatever is going on in that pretty head of yours."

He poked at my temple before dragging his finger down my cheek. And because I was losing my damn mind, when it neared my lips, I turned and bit it. In true asshole fashion, he shoved it in my mouth. The air crackled with tension as I swirled my tongue around the digit.

His eyes bored into mine, and I felt the hairs on my arms rise with the intensity of his attention. I wanted to roll my eyes back into my head with how hot the masculine groan he let out was. It didn't matter that I'd heard it before. It was just as hot every time.

I respectfully—but firmly—disagreed with anyone who felt being on your knees in front of a man was a position of weakness. I'd argue that someone with that opinion had never had a dick in their mouth before, because on my knees was when I was my most powerful.

Fuck, after the dressing room incident earlier, I now wanted to see what I could get Caleb to do when I had his cock in my mouth.

The clearing of a throat broke our moment. My cheeks flamed at the wet plopping noise that came from Caleb pulling out his finger. It was so damn loud in the silent elevator. Thankfully, with Caleb's muscled frame almost completely covering me, I could barely be seen by the person who'd entered the elevator.

"There you go, man. The whores are fun to fuck. Just be careful she doesn't try to take anything." The newcomer hit Caleb's shoulder while letting out a laugh like they were best fucking friends. "Mind if I give her a go when you're d—"

Faster than my brain could process, Caleb hit the emergency stop button on the panel and had the man pinned to the wall by his throat, the barrel of his gun shoved between the guy's quivering lips.

"What the fuck did you just say about my wife?" Caleb bit out.

Warmth pooled in my belly at the term.

The man's muffled cries were indiscernible as he clawed at Caleb's hand hard enough to draw blood, but the Irishman didn't even flinch. I could tell by how still he was holding himself that he was barely holding back from pulling the trigger. Naturally, it was the hottest thing I'd ever seen.

"Caleb."

Locked into his rage, he didn't respond. It happened to me when I was taking out particularly heinous people, and unless I distracted him, he'd kill the pitiful-looking man.

"Sweetheart," I said tentatively. I thought maybe the term of affection from me would shock him out of his anger, but he didn't even register that I'd spoken. Ignoring the blubbering idiot and the fresh scent of urine, I moved closer, trailing my hand up his chest. I physically had to pull his attention to me. The green of his irises was completely gone. Instead, chaos and violence shone in the inky depths of his eyes.

"I'm not going to say he didn't mean anything by that comment. Obviously, based on his receding hairline, he can't get laid, so he pays for that shit. But you can't kill him here, because if you kill him in this elevator, it's going to be a bitch to get clean."

That comment earned me a slight grin.

"That's your concern? Not the outright murder? And I have people for that, Scar," Caleb responded. I had to hold back my *so do I* comment, but I was just happy that some of the murderous rage had subsided.

A sly grin spread across my face. He was probably shocked that I wasn't cowering in a corner at his actions. That was what most women would be doing. Actually, Caleb didn't seem to be surprised by most of my reactions. When he'd seen my scars, there was this moment of connection between the two of us. He knew I didn't want sympathy or even attention over them.

I pressed closer. "I'd pull the trigger if you asked me to, and I'm pretty good at ditching a body too." Confusion flicked across his face. He didn't know whether I was serious or fucking with him to distract him from why he was so irate. I didn't offer any clues as to what the correct answer was.

"What's your proposal? That we let him go?" Caleb snarled at the suggestion, and it made me laugh. He was like a toddler having his favorite toy taken away.

It wasn't lost on me that we were having a conversation while a middle-aged man sobbed with a pistol shoved between his lips.

"Hold on. We let him go, but we get his name and address. I'm going to do some digging, and we can decide whether we need to revisit our friend here in an easier-to-clean space." I turned to address the guy. His ruddy cheeks were streaked with tears and snot. He'd spoken some bold words for someone who was unremarkably average.

"For your sake, I hope you're just sleazy and not into some awful shit. If so, I can convince him not to kill you. But if I look you up and don't like what I find, I'll be the one to cut off your balls before letting my husband have his way with you."

The man whimpered at my words, and I already knew I'd be seeing him again. In the next moment, Caleb roughly searched for the man's wallet, stashing the whole thing in his suit pocket before restarting the elevator.

"You're extremely lucky my wife had a clear head tonight, or yours would've painted these walls. I might not kill you in here, but you don't get to fucking speak to her like you did." Shrieks filled the small space as Caleb drove his knife into the hollow of the man's collarbone.

The doors opened with a soft ding, and Caleb turned to exit, letting the dude collapse onto the dirty floor.

"Fucking crazy bastard. I'll have you arrested," he said between ragged breaths.

I whipped around, warm blood coating my thumb as I pressed it into the wound, dragging out more yells. "You aren't going to call or report anyone. Believe me when I say I can find out *anything* about you. And I have a feeling your days are numbered." I wiped the crimson liquid off on his white shirt, mentally noting that I needed to call my cleaners to get out here ASAP. "Sleep tight. We'll see you soon," I called over my shoulder.

When I exited the elevator, Caleb stared me down as he leaned against the hall wall. His suit pants were tight, drawing my eyes to the bulge at his crotch. The rage had shifted into something that looked an awful lot like hunger.

I moved past him, opening the door to my apartment. All the hairs on my arms stood on end at the feeling of being stalked. It was nearly pitch black in the space. The only light was coming from the windows in my living room. Hot breath fanned across the back of my neck, causing my skin to break out in goose bumps.

Caleb's deep tenor shot straight to my pussy.

"I want you to run."

I moaned as his teeth latched on to my flesh.

"I'm too worked up. First the dressing room, and now this. I need an outlet. Since you didn't let me kill him, I'm going to give you a five-second head start, and then I'm going to come after you, Scar," he said against my neck, his hands digging into my hips as his cock hardened against my ass.

"One." *Bite.* "Two." *Bite.* "Three."

He'd short-circuited my brain with the nibbling on my neck because it didn't even register at first that he was counting down. My head start was practically nonexistent. But I knew this apartment like the back of my hand. I pushed off him, taking off down the small hallway to my left. My lungs burned with how fast I sprinted toward my bedroom. I needed to get to my closet and my go bag before Caleb looked too closely.

This little game of his was actually going to be very helpful. Problem was, I was so fucking turned on by the idea of being chased by him.

I careened around a corner, listening for any sign of where Caleb was.

"Ready or not, here I come, *wife.*"

My heart rate kicked up higher at the sound of thudding feet. The man was fucking running like he was out for blood.

I slipped behind the door. The moment his hulking form burst through, I launched myself onto his back. I attempted to wrap my arm around his throat as my legs locked around his muscled waist, but I couldn't lock in the choke. The position made it so that my pussy was pressed against his muscled back, and the friction of it rubbing against my clit had me moaning.

Caleb froze at the sound, but it only lasted for a split second before he slammed us against a wall. My back took the brunt of the blow. The weight of his body sent the air whooshing from my lungs, and my hold loosened enough for him to pry me off his back. There were no words exchanged, just our combined labored breaths. Of course, since we were both fucked in the head, we had massive grins on our faces as we attempted to beat the shit out of one another.

In the back of my mind, I wondered whether this was all a test. I'd given up quite a few hints about myself over the last twenty-four hours. I should have known that if anyone pieced them together, it would be Caleb Callahan. I broke out of his grasp, but he sent me sprawling on my bed. I was face-down in my blankets when his heavy body landed on top of me. He grunted when my elbow rammed into his ribs, giving me enough space to scramble from beneath him and stand on the mattress. The cocky asshole hadn't anticipated the right hook I threw at his face, sending his head snapping to the side. He slowly turned his face back toward me, his pink tongue prodding the split in his lip.

His bloody smile was so sinister it sent my blood spiking, but not in fear. I was 100 percent turned on.

"Oh, little one, that was not the right move."

He lunged, aiming for my legs, but the mattress threw him off, and I jumped off the bed, keeping it between us.

"Don't run from me, Scar," he yelled after me as I dashed into my en suite, with him only steps behind me. A hand wrapped around my ponytail, yanking on the hair until my head was dropped back against his shoulder. Warmth radiated from his chest, seeping into my back as his wet tongue ran along my collarbone before he sank his teeth into the crook of my neck.

"I thought you didn't want me," I taunted, rubbing my ass against his hard cock and trying to hold back a moan as he nuzzled my throat with his nose. "Didn't want to fuck a Romano bitch," I added through labored breathing.

Telling him I wasn't a true Romano was on the tip of my tongue, but I couldn't get the words out for whatever reason. It pissed me off that he'd decided not to like me from the start. Like everyone else, I was a burden from the beginning. Never even given a chance.

No. I didn't owe him anything.

"I never said I didn't want you, Scar. I said I wasn't going to stick my cock in you." A chill ran down my spine as he breathed into my ear. His palm pressed against my clit through my pants. "How does my cum feel against your sloppy cunt?" he asked, letting out a low chuckle as I writhed against his hand, moaning and strung out on how deliciously dirty everything with him was.

Fuck.

"You like being chased? Does the idea of me roughly fucking you turn you on?"

I nodded. Need fogged my mind, and I pushed back against his hard cock, grinding as his free hand wrapped around my throat, pressing slightly against the sides, giving me a head rush.

"Want me to take care of this greedy pussy of yours, Scar? Huh? Do you want me to make you gush all over my fucking hand like my dirty little slut?" he growled in my ear, his rhythm picking up speed.

"Yes. Fuck, make me come, Caleb. Least you could fucking do," I hissed out.

"Fuck," he whispered as I writhed against the hand he still had pressed to my clit from the outside of my joggers. "That's my good little slut. Dry hump my fucking hand. Can you feel my cum rubbing into your pussy? I want you covered in my scent," he said, teeth grazing the sensitive skin of my shoulders.

"My. Fucking. Wife."

Panting breaths filled the room as he continued to whisper filthy things in my ear. I was too far gone to even register what he was saying. My orgasm built and built, pleasure finally erupting from my center when he pinched my nipple through my tank, sending an orgasm rushing through me. I cried out his name so loudly that my neighbors were bound to hear.

Heat swept across my skin, bringing with it a numb bliss.

Holy shit. I just humped his hand until I came.

My knees threatened to give out as my core clenched around nothing.

"Fuck, you're beautiful when you come. Let this whole fucking building know who you belong to." He flipped me around, pressing me against the wall and pushing his tongue between my lips, his cock straining against his pants.

City lights filtered in through the window above my claw-foot tub, bathing Caleb in enough light for me to make out his features. He was devastatingly beautiful, an incubus in human flesh.

He wrapped his hand around my ponytail as his tongue slid over mine in a messy tangle. Even though he'd just made me come, desire pulsed through me. My pussy was still wet and aching for him.

But when he pulled away, I saw it.

This moment had changed nothing. I wasn't good enough for him to fuck.

What really pissed me off was that regardless of how I *wanted* to feel, the twinge of sadness and shame was still there.

"You're still not going to fuck me, huh?" I couldn't hold back the vulnerability in my tone.

He looked taken aback for a moment. Like he didn't think I'd ask the question. His mouth opened and closed a few times, confusion painted on his face.

"Scar—" Whatever he was going to say was cut off by the

ringing of his phone, and I used the distraction to slip under his arm and dash off to my closet. I needed space from him.

"You deal with your own blue balls," I mumbled.

The call was the perfect opportunity for me to grab the bag with the packed hidden compartment and throw some other shit inside before he came in to play jailer.

"Grab your shit fast. I'm dropping you off at the apartment. I have shit to do," he called out before walking away. The events from earlier today were forgotten. The wall between us had been rebuilt, but it was admittedly not as stable as before.

At least not on my end.

And that was what worried me.

TWENTY-THREE
NIKO

THREESOME...THAT'S THE TITLE.

ANGRY STEPS STORMED across the living room. Scar practically ran through the kitchen, making a beeline for her room, a duffel bag slung over her shoulder and mumbling about dumbass men who didn't give her dick.

Just the word *dick* falling from her lips had my own twitching at the memory of what we'd done on the kitchen counter. I'd been keeping my distance, but the longer I was around her, caring for her, the tighter the strings tying me to her got.

"Clearly, that went well," Kenji commented from where he was perched on one of the island stools, pulling me from my thoughts.

"Seems so. And where the hell is Caleb?" I pulled out my phone as I asked the question, checking to see if he'd sent us a text about it. Sure enough, there was a message about him sending Scar up while he prepared for the meeting we were supposed to have in a few hours.

Indecision racked through my body, my fingers twitching with the need to go to her.

"Come on," Kenji said, standing. "You look like you're

itching for a hit, so let's go check on our girl." He turned and started for her room, not bothering to see if I'd follow.

Our girl.

The words sounded so right when he said them.

Her door was slightly ajar, and there was the faint sound of running water mixed with music coming from her bathroom.

"Oh look, we're right on time," Kenji said, stripping off his shirt and unbuttoning the black Dickies he'd been wearing.

Most thought I was the quiet, respectful one of the three of us, and maybe there was some truth to that assessment, but not when it came to Scar. If she was naked in the shower with her door propped open, I wasn't wasting that fucking opportunity.

"Your ass is so fucking white, Kenji," I commented, stripping out of my clothes.

"How the fuck can you even tell? It's fucking tattooed," he said, attempting to get a glimpse of it.

The action had me chuckling. "You still have skin poking through your ink, dumbass."

I pushed past him into the steam-filled bathroom. The sight of Scar's naked body through the fogged-up glass had my cock hard. It didn't matter that I could barely make out her curves. I moved toward the opening of the doorless shower.

My mouth went dry the moment I laid eyes on her. She had two fingers buried in her pussy, moving them in and out at a leisurely pace, like she was working herself up. Her other hand held the removable showerhead flush to her clit. Droplets of water cascaded down her skin from the rainfall head above, taunting me as they rolled down the curves of her breasts.

Kenji's shoulder brushed my arm as he came to stand beside me, equally entranced with the sex goddess bringing herself to an orgasm. His tattooed hand wrapped around his cock, matching the pace of her fingering herself.

Her face began to morph, her panting picking up. She was close to coming, and as much as I wanted to see her orgasm, it wasn't going to be because of a fucking massaging shower-head. At least not without my dick or Kenji's buried inside her too.

The stream of water hit my chest as I walked in, snatching the showerhead from her hand and pushing her back against the cold tiles.

I swallowed her surprised gasp, fucking her mouth with my tongue like I had with my cock only a few short days ago. "I don't want you coming unless it's because one of us brought you to salvation. Understand, Scar?" I asked in a menacing tone against her lips.

Her eyes narrowed on me. "What the fuck are you doing in here, Niko?"

"And Kenji," he threw in from behind me.

Her body went rigid at the sound of his voice, and I chuckled as she nearly broke her neck to look for him. Her icy eyes met mine again, wide with surprise and interest.

"You two are just, like, fine with seeing each other's cocks?" she asked, her words coming out breathy.

I moved over as Kenji joined us, tangling his hand in her wet locks and pulling her into a kiss. I didn't bother backing up to give them room. Kenji and I had shared women before. This wasn't new for us, but based on the question, two men would be new for her.

I loved that Scar was proud of her sexual experience, but fuck, was there something hot about knowing this would be her first threesome.

"Yeah, babe. We're fine seeing each other's cocks, and I plan on sucking on your clit while Niko fucks you." He leaned forward, speaking against her swollen lips. "Sometimes my mouth even touches his thick cock. I've given it a lick a time or two."

Pleasure snaked across my skin at the mention of the memories, and precum beaded up at my tip. The lust coursing through me made me restless, and I yanked Scar forward, turning her body to sandwich her between us. My cock nestled between her ass cheeks as Kenji crowded her front. The feeling of her body against mine was a mind-altering experience. Electricity ran down my spine to my balls. Her skin dented under my fingertips as I reached down and kneaded her ass.

"We're going to fuck you until your legs quiver, Scar." I spoke against the shell of her ear before nipping at the sensitive skin below her lobe while Kenji leaned forward and swirled his tongue around her pert nipple. He looked up at me, and we silently communicated, our movements along her body like a coordinated dance.

I ran my teeth along the curve of her throat, biting down hard as he shoved two fingers into her pussy. A strangled yell burst from her mouth, and her head fell back, hitting my chest. Kenji dropped to his knees, leaning forward and sucking on her clit. Her body bucked, and the sounds of her pleasure bounced off the marble.

Her body was out of her control.

Our marionette.

"You taste so fucking good, Scar. I knew I'd be addicted. I want to bury my tongue in your pussy every day until I die," Kenji said, his eyes swirling with lust as he fisted his cock. "You need to have a taste, Niko."

I reached down from behind, running two fingers through her wetness, scissoring them around her clit before plunging them into her cunt and coating them with her pleasure. My skin was practically on fire with how feverish she made me feel.

Lust ratcheted higher and higher with every devilish sound that sprang from her lips.

"Is he right, *solntse? Do* you taste fucking divine?" I asked as I slipped my soaked fingers into my mouth.

Fuck.

"Fuck me. Both of you. Please." She whimpered, her body practically vibrating with anticipation. "Or are you like Caleb? Won't fuck a *Romano bitch*, but you're fine using me like a whore?" she asked, looking over her shoulder at me. Her tone was bitter and angry, a stark change from the breathy moans from a moment ago.

The vulnerability in her eyes tore at my blackened heart. Even this confident woman had tender areas she kept shielded under her fierce persona. She wanted to belong. Wanted to be cared for.

Possessiveness thrummed in my veins.

She was mine. Ours.

Even if Caleb was too dumb to see it right now. Still chained to the idea that women wouldn't survive the harshness of being with us in this world. But Scar was already doing that without our fucking help. And if it was her last name keeping Caleb at bay, that was fucking ironic, seeing as how we'd built our found family on the principle of hating our blood-related families. It could be the same case for her.

"Scar." My voice was breathless as she pressed her ass against my cock, my hands landing on her hips to still her movements so I could fucking think. "I'm going to use you like a whore, but that's because you're *my* pretty little whore. Caleb's a fucking idiot who needs to pull his head out of his ass," I said, picking her up and dropping her ass onto the shower bench. "We're going to fuck your pussy raw now."

Kenji nodded his head in agreement. "I hope you're ready, little one, because I've been fucking *waiting* to sink into this delicious cunt of yours since the moment I saw you staring down Niko at the party," he said, gripping her chin and tilting her head toward him while I nudged her thighs apart with my muscled frame.

"Fuck," I whispered as I watched Kenji hold her jaw and spit in her mouth, then thrust his tongue inside. She whimpered at the action and squirmed on the bench, moving her dripping pussy toward my face.

Tile bit into my skin, but I didn't care. "I may not be religious, but I'll sink to my knees for my *solntse*. Anytime," I said, thrilled with the prospect of tasting her on my tongue.

Kenji chuckled at my admission, running his tongue along the slope of her neck. "We give our tithe to the temple of your pussy," he said with a snicker.

She growled out curse words in Italian when I slid my nose up her inner thigh, nipping at the skin as I made my way toward where she wanted my attention.

"Open your legs, little one," Kenji ordered, a half smile overtaking his face.

Without hesitation, her legs fell open, revealing her glistening cunt. Her pink pussy was so pretty—and ready to have my tongue buried in it.

"Grab his cock, Scar. You're going to pump Kenji while I eat this pretty pussy of yours. If you stop, I stop. Understand?" I asked with a bark in my tone.

Her body stiffened at the order, her spine straightening.

"Answer me, Scar," I demanded, slapping her pussy at her disobedience. The wet slap was only hard enough to grab her attention, but her breath hitched, and goose bumps erupted over her skin.

She liked that shit.

Kenji chuckled at her reaction, but his breath hitched when her hand snaked out and gripped the base of his shaft, giving it a rough tug.

"Yes," she finally replied. Her body tensed as I ran my finger through her wetness and plunged two inside while Kenji rolled a pebbled nipple between the pads of his fingers.

Her crystal blue eyes swiveled to Kenji. "I think your thick cock looks prettier with my hand wrapped around it, Kenji," she taunted. "This is mine. No more bitches get to fuck this cock. It's either your hand or me. That's it. Understand?" she asked with a growl.

His body practically melted under her tone.

He liked her in charge of him.

"Yes, ma'am. My body is fucking yours, Scar," he said with a thrill, pumping in and out of her hold. I was momentarily hypnotized by the sight of his tip thrusting through her clenched fist. She looked at both of us with hunger in her eyes. I'd never felt more wanted by a woman.

Caleb was an idiot.

"Niko, shouldn't your tongue be fucking me right now?" she asked, breaking my lust-filled trance.

My gaze snapped to hers, my hand latching around her throat. "The attitude isn't cute, Scar. You might be able to tell Kenji what to do, but that's not how it works with me." I stood, my cock jumping at the uptick in her pulse under my fingers. "Your hand better not stop, *solntse*."

"What does that mean? *Solntse*? You've called me that more than once now," she said, her chest heaving—nipples hard.

There was a skip in my heartbeat at her question. The term of endearment had accidentally come out earlier, but now I couldn't stop it. I hadn't anticipated her asking me what it meant, and now my tongue felt too thick for my mouth as I tried to answer.

What would she think when I told her the meaning?

"It means 'my sun' in Russian," I replied, watching the emotions ebb and flow over her beautiful face, feeling the way her throat bobbed as she swallowed. Her pink tongue poked out and swiped across her bottom lip.

Kenji leaned in, pressing his face against her wet hair. "Are you going to shine for him while he fucks you, Scar?"

His words caused her eyes to morph from tender to lustful, and she nodded, the honeyed strands clinging to her body.

I reached down with my free hand, putting my thumb on the hood of her clit and moving in slow circles. Her shudders were sexy as hell, and I thought I'd come from her noises alone. Every nerve ending in my body was firing. I felt so alive as I watched her writhe against my hand, hers still pumping Kenji's shaft.

Each time she called out my name, the obsession grew. There was no way she'd be able to get away now that I'd accepted the bond the fates decided to tie between her and me. I'd care for her until someone put me in the grave, and then I'd search the underworld to find her.

She threw her head back, letting out a frustrated yell as I sank a single finger in, only going to the first knuckle before removing it completely.

I chuckled, gripping my cock and giving it two rough tugs before burying myself as deep into her pussy as I could, practically crawling inside. One of her hands groped my back, raking her nails down the taut flesh and leaving a burning trail in their wake. She was so fucking perfect. So vicious, yet so willing to please.

A ragged groan fell from Kenji, syncing with my own as I roughly pumped in and out. My hand intertwined with her damp hair as we devoured each other, our tongues sliding against one another in a tangled mess.

The fuck was dirty and fast and so fucking amazing. There was no way I could control my orgasm with how her pussy strangled my cock, and the symphony of wet slapping noises and pleasured cries echoed off the marbled walls.

Scar flung her head back as her orgasm ripped through her seconds after my own. Hot streams of cum filled her as her pussy clenched around me in spasms.

"Fuck, it's so hot to watch him fill you up, little one," Kenji groaned out, sounding close himself.

He deserves to feel how perfect her pussy is too.

I reached out and stilled her hand. Her eyes homed in on where my large palm gripped Kenji. Even if her hand acted as a barrier, my fingertips still grazed the velvety soft skin of his dick, and I watched how her chest rose and fell a little faster.

"Is the sight of my hand on Kenji's cock going to send you into another orgasm?" I asked, leisurely drawing our joined hands up and down his shaft.

"Fuck." The word sounded like a plea on Kenji's lips.

"That's right, brother. You're going to fuck our little cum slut." I pulled out of her warm heat. "You look so pretty leaking my cum from your used cunt," I said, watching the sticky white substance trail down her perfectly marred thighs.

She watched with fascination before locking on to Kenji, who looked like he was on another planet he was so turned on. A sinful twinkle in her eye had my balls tightening like they hadn't emptied inside her moments ago.

"Kenji, be a good boy and get on your fucking knees. I want you to push Niko's cum back where it belongs before you add your own," she ordered.

Holy fuck. This woman.

He scrambled over so fast he nearly tripped over himself. I expected him to use his fingers to shove it back into her waiting pussy, but instead, he collected it with his tongue. My brain had a meltdown at the sight, and my heart was palpitating.

I'd never thought about how I'd feel watching another man lap up my release as it leaked out of a pussy, but I knew right then I wanted to see this again and again and again.

Fuck.

"This what you wanted, little one? To see my tongue coated in yours and Niko's cum? You both taste fucking divine." He leaned forward and pressed his tongue flat against her flesh, dragging it from her asshole to her clit before latching on to the bundle of nerves.

Her whole body shuddered as she cried out his name, plunging her hand into his black hair. She was still lost in pleasure when Kenji stood and drove himself into her. Milky white liquid seeped from where they were now connected, and my cock jumped at the sight.

"Who would have thought my favorite lubrication would be Niko's cum," Kenji said as he increased his pace. Their flesh slapped against each other as Scar bucked her hips off the bench, using her hands to brace herself as she met him stroke for stroke.

I moved closer, the spray of water pelting me in the back, and I stood beside where they were fucking. "What do you need, *solntse*?" I asked, leaning over and pulling her nipple between my teeth.

"My clit. Touch my clit, Niko."

I reached down and swirled the sensitive nerve endings. The way she called out my name had me feeling invincible.

"Why is it so hot to feel Niko's hand brush my cock every time I drive into your fucking gorgeous pussy?" Kenji asked. "Fuck, I'm going to come."

Without thinking, I reached around and cupped Kenji's balls from behind while keeping my fingers on her clit. He cried out, stilling his movements as he emptied inside her.

"Me, too. Niko, don't stop," Scar added in.

They both let out a strangled *fuck*.

"We're doing that shit again," Scar said, looking positively worn out with pleasure.

I didn't know if she would say the same thing when she found out we were still going to leave her behind for tonight's meeting.

"SHE'S FUCKING HUSTLING PEOPLE."

CALEB WALKED around the club office looking like someone had pissed on his dinner—or had given him blue balls. Seeing as how he'd been out with Scar earlier and *didn't* fuck her, I was guessing the second option was why he was throwing a fit.

Meanwhile, Niko and I were on fucking cloud nine after the shit we'd done in her shower. That memory was going to be burned into my brain until I died.

"Three, two, one…" I muttered while scrolling through social media and waiting for Caleb to bitch about the brunette goddess for the fiftieth time in an hour. Right on cue, he stormed over, gripping a glass of something amber.

"Damn, she's really got you worked up. Is that a wrinkle I see?" Caleb instantly looked down, mumbling curse words under his breath and raking his hand through his already messed-up hair.

"Honestly, I'd be pissed too if I were you. She let you coat her thong in cum, *walked around* with them like that, let you *chase her,* and you didn't fuck her?" I asked, in total shock at what a fucking idiot he was.

Shards of glass rained down on me as he threw a glass

above where I was lying on the floor. I laughed at how out of sorts Caleb was. He'd already shattered one glass when we told him how we'd fucked her against the marbled bench.

Fuck.

I could still taste her and Niko on my tongue. We'd shared women before, and had no qualms about getting close, but fuck, that was the first time I'd done that. The breaking of another lowball pulled my attention back to Caleb.

He was used to always being in control. Measured reactions, thoughtful answers, quiet violence. His anger was the only emotion he had trouble locking down, but those outbursts only solidified his reputation. Even as the second son, Caleb was still widely respected and feared in the Mob. He was used to people following his direction to a T, and if they didn't, he killed them.

Then came a fierce brunette with piercing eyes and a mind that seemed to be calculating the demise of anyone who stood in her way. And we were walking dangerously close to standing in her way. I didn't for a fucking second think that she was actually being compliant. Sitting up in our tower like a good little prisoner?

No, that woman was plotting.

"Caleb, she's not a prisoner." Niko's words echoed my inner thoughts.

Ironically, she'd thrown a glass at our heads, too, when we told her she couldn't come to the meeting with us. The look of betrayal was like a stab to the gut—a stark difference to the affectionate gazes from moments before.

"We need to decide what the fuck we're going to do with her. If we involve her, we can't half-ass that shit. There can't be distractions or loose ends while we execute our plans. So we either bring her in or let her go," Niko said, finality in his voice.

From the outside looking in, you'd think he'd be the one with an anger issue. The Russian was built like a brick shit-house with almost as much ink as me, but he was a big softy on the inside. And once he'd decided to keep you, the fucker wasn't letting go.

I had a feeling Scar would fall into that category soon, if she wasn't already. The thing with Niko was that he had to stick to one-night stands or risk hyper-fixating on them. There was no way he could have done what we just did and *not* gotten obsessed.

Caleb groaned, plopping down on the leather couch. "Fuck. Can we trust her?" He chugged half of the fresh glass he'd poured. "She didn't bat a fucking eye at the fact that I had a handgun shoved between the fucker's lips. Not a yell. She didn't cower in the corner crying. She fucking walked up to me and told me I could kill him somewhere easier to clean." He lifted his head from where he was cradling it in his hands. "Bringing her in means trusting her."

"Is it smart to bring her into this? Like, we're not having a fucking picnic. It's one thing not to freak out around a gun, but it's a completely different thing to handle a gun." I pointed out. Her scars popped into my mind, and my gut twisted at the thought of her in danger.

Caleb waved a hand dismissively. "I'm not concerned about how capable she is. She can handle it. I'd bet my life on her having a shit ton of secrets we don't know about, and half of them are about how fucking capable she really is."

I raised my hands in surrender, my mouth pulling up into a smirk. She'd fucking love to hear that Caleb felt she was capable. But knowing those two, she wouldn't know how to take the compliment *if* the fucker figured out how to even give her one.

"We won't know whether we can trust her or whether she's capable until we let her prove herself. She's our enemy's niece, but there's clearly no love lost between the two. He fucking tried to hit her," Niko growled out from where he was cleaning his Glock. It was a ritual he did every time something was on his mind. If I were to guess, I would say we all had the same thing on our minds.

Caleb sneered at the mention of the exchange with Dominick. "Yeah, and I'm going to remove the fucker's hand for that offense."

My eyebrow raised at his admission. I knew he didn't hate her as much as he claimed to. If the fucker pulled his head out of his ass, he could actually *enjoy* his wife.

I piped up from where I was lying on the floor, legs propped up on the wall. "Her uncle clearly doesn't like her, and she obviously hates him. She's all for gutting him. Literally. So why the fuck does she stick around?"

The question had been burning in the back of my mind since the engagement party. There was something we were missing. It was rare that there were people we didn't know. We spent years planning and learning every in and out of the Four Families. Of course, we had the least amount of intelligence on the Italians since none of us were in that organization. But we'd learned the players and gained allies on the inside—ones who were still feeding us intel. But none of them had ever mentioned Scar.

So who the fuck was she?

"Did we find out anything about her?" I asked, my inner turmoil spilling over.

An exhausted sigh left Caleb. "No. All I know is that she's Dominick's *niece*." He used air quotes around the term. "Which I don't know how the fuck that's possible. Not unless Giana had a kid and has kept it secret this whole time."

"If that's true, Dominick's sister is an even bigger bitch than we thought. You didn't see the glare she cut Scar when you announced her as your wife. I thought I'd have to jump in front of a bullet for you two," Niko added, moving over to the armchair with a glass of vodka in his hand.

Caleb's dark eyebrows wrinkled as he stared out the panoramic window, deep in thought. "That doesn't *feel* right.

Giana's a bitch, but even more than that, she's a conniving narcissist like her brother. If Scar were her daughter, she'd be manipulating her for her benefit fucking left and right. And Scar lived with him until eighteen and then moved out." His attention whipped back toward us. "Oh, here's some irony for you. Apparently, when she's not being a thief, she has a successful security firm for the very wealthy. She's the owner and CEO of Leslie George Security. Which that name doesn't make sen—"

Laughter erupted from my chest, getting me strange looks from my brothers. "Clever fucking girl," I said, shaking my head as I sat up. "I think I'm going to propose when I see her."

"She's already *my* wife, asshole."

I ignored his possessive tone, pushing on with my explanation. "*George Leslie* is the godfather of 1920s New York bank robbers. The man was never caught. He's who inspired the movie Ocean's Eleven. He'd use blueprints to map out ahead of time where he would pull off his heists. Never used a firearm to pull off a robbery."

Niko grinned at the revelation. "She's fucking hustling people."

Caleb's hand curled and uncurled from where it rested on the arm of the sofa, and I was slightly concerned his mouth might permanently be stuck in a tight line.

"Listen, Caleb, I think we work with her. Clearly, she's been able to survive in this world. Sure, she's got secrets, but she could be an asset. Then you can divorce her, and we'll never have to see her again," Niko said.

I couldn't tell whether my feelings were coloring my judgment, but I swore Niko's voice hitched a bit when he mentioned being done with her. But he was right. We knew nothing about Scar, and we had other goals that were more important than pussy. Even for a pussy lover like me.

A deep sigh came from Caleb's chest. "All right. Since this

is a fucking democracy, what's everyone's vote? We bring her in and trust her? Or keep her locked in the fuckin' apartment?" he asked, pinching the bridge of his nose.

I chuckled, thinking back to when we were in high school and I told him his nose was too perfect and he wouldn't get chicks looking that way.

He let me punch him, even though he knew what I said was bullshit. Caleb could always tell when I needed to release the tension building inside.

High school was when my need to ruin perfection first started. My father demanded excellence. He wanted the Jirocho clan to be the strongest of all the Yakuza clans, including those back in Japan. He felt the only way to achieve greatness was to be perfect in every aspect.

"Kenji, it's your duty to tell our father you are the one who messed up. You aren't important. I am. You can afford the beatings."

I couldn't wait to run the blade of my katana through my brother's chest. But not before giving him a matching injury for every one he'd forced me to endure.

"Kenji." Caleb's voice pulled my attention back to the present. "What's your vote?"

"Let's test her. An initiation of sorts." I shrugged. Equally excited and nervous about putting her in harm's way. "I say we start off with letting her peek behind the curtain, but let's keep the important shit to ourselves until we think we can trust her. Fuck, we may never decide to tell her all our plans," I answered, my gut turning at the thought of not fully committing her to our group.

"That works." Caleb pushed up from his seat, walking over to the large desk in the center of the room. "Kenji, take her with you when you visit the fights. Let her get a look at the underbelly of the city. We don't know what the fuck her uncle had her doing besides sneaking around in a ski mask and fucking schmucking it up with the elite. She probably doesn't have a fucking clue."

Niko snickered. "Fuck off, Caleb. You were just telling us how she almost got you in a chokehold. None of us thinks she's as innocent or aloof as the other women we've been around," he teased. His eyes darted to Caleb meaningfully.

The fucker pouted like a petulant child, but he couldn't fully cover up the smirk. Caleb liked that she was full of fire and fight.

He may not have wanted to admit it, but she was his twin flame. All talks of Scar halted when Caleb's phone went off.

"The Bulgarians are on their way," he stated, staring at the illuminated screen before locking eyes with us. "If we want to control the drug drop, we need them to side with us."

My gut tightened. All of our plans teetered on the small organizations agreeing to our coup. If they didn't, there was no fucking way we could pull this off.

The leader of the Bulgarian crime organization had been murdered two years prior. He was a nasty bastard and enjoyed women who were unwilling and way too young. I'd have done it myself if Cain hadn't gotten to him—at least that was the rumor.

But the problem was that we didn't know who was leading the group now or what would convince them to join us. It was why we'd locked Scar upstairs. We needed this meeting to go off without a hitch, because it was the current linchpin.

TWENTY-FIVE

SCAR

ALWAYS BRING A BAT TO THE PARTY.

THOSE FUCKERS HAD LOCKED me in my room.

Well, it was one fucker in particular, but the other two went along with it, even after we'd had the most amazing sex of my life. They might have had amazing cocks, but fuck, they were dicks.

I don't know. Paint your fucking toenails or some shit.

That was Caleb's suggestion when I asked what the fuck he expected me to do while they were gone. It pissed me off that they didn't trust me to go with them.

Then again, I didn't trust them.

But I might have to show them how fucking capable I really was so I didn't get left out in the cold again next time.

The ding of the elevator drew my attention, my heartbeat ticking up a notch. The tendons of my fingers flexed as I adjusted my grip on my partner in crime for the night. The sound of my angry steps bounced off the polished concrete floors.

"Ma'am. Ma'am. You can't bring that in the club."

I ignored the bouncer, pushing through the throng of people. A hand clasped around my shoulder.

"Ma'am, you can't bring a metal bat into the club."

I spun on my heels, staring down the giant manning the door to the posh club as I broke his hold, pulling his thumb back almost to the point of breaking it. He let out a shrill scream, which was honestly disappointing. I thought he'd handle pain better. My mouth curled up in a cruel smirk when he flinched under my gaze. "I own the fucking club now. I'll walk in with whatever the fuck I want," I said, loud and angry.

The confusion that crossed his face confirmed what I'd thought. Caleb was keeping this union a secret. But if that asshole thought I would roll over and come to heel whenever he barked an order...well, he was in for a rude awakening. I didn't even wait for the man to understand what I meant. I just melted into the crowd.

"Of course it's stunning," I grumbled when I walked into the club's heart. Hush Money was more of a trendy speakeasy. The 1920s style was a throwback to the glory days of the Art Deco era in New York.

Black and gold adorned every surface. Velvet booths lined the room so patrons could rest while taking a break from dancing on the massive black marble dance floor. Hundreds of chandeliers hung at various heights, creating a sexy ambiance with their golden hue bouncing off every shiny surface. I found myself smiling when I recognized the artwork. Giant black and white murals depicting the mugshots of famous New York criminals were painted on various walls, re-creations of the art in Caleb's bedroom.

"Damn," I said under my breath as I moved farther into the club. I'd studied the blueprints of the place, but my research didn't do its beauty justice.

The buzz of conversation bled into the sensual sounds of The Weeknd's "House of Balloons/Glass Table Girls." A wave of déjà vu rolled over me as I made my way down the dimly lit hallway to another club's office. I was in this mess because of a situation eerily similar to this one.

Low murmurs sounded from behind the door. A door that only had a lock on the handle.

Fuckin' amateurs, I swear.

A loud thud sounded in the room as I shoved the door open and it hit the wall. "Evening, gentlemen," I said nonchalantly, walking in with my bat casually thrown over my shoulder, ignoring the handguns pointed my way. Caleb leveled a gaze at me. His stare was violent and dangerous. I should have been terrified as he slowly drifted over my body with his mossy eyes; instead, my excitement increased tenfold.

The corners of my lips curled up.

A nasally voice came from one of the chairs in front of Caleb's desk. "Well, Caleb, this is a nice surprise. Beautiful, why don't you come to sit on my lap while we finish discussing business?"

My skin crawled at the demand, but I didn't look at the man who'd spoken—continuing my stare-off with Caleb while tracking the other two in my periphery as they stood along the back wall, flanking him. All three of them looked ready to throttle me. Their glares intensified the longer I stood there. You could cut the tension with a knife.

Pudgy fingers bit into my bicep, drawing my attention to the man twice my age sitting in front of Caleb's desk. His greasy graying hair was combed over, not doing a damned thing to hide his receding hairline. Beady eyes the color of dirt glared at me, a look of disdain plastered across his ugly mug. Cheap cologne itched my nose, and even in an ill-fitting suit, I saw how out of shape he was.

"Don't be fucking rude, girl," he barked, his grip tightening. "When a man says you're beautiful, thank them. You can give me a blow job to make up for your poor manners." His laughter caused him to miss the low growl coming from Niko.

Within seconds, the barrel of my Sig was flush with his

pocked skin. I smiled as the color drained from his face, leaving him ashen. Sweat beaded up along his wrinkled forehead when he realized I wasn't being reprimanded or thrown on the floor.

"What the fuck is the meaning of this, Caleb?" His tone was panicked and higher than it had been a few seconds ago. Satisfaction thrummed in my veins. The three boys earned back some brownie points by standing there silently. It was clear that they didn't want to, though. The shoulders of all three were practically in their ears, and Kenji's hand was resting on the hilt of his katana, while the other two had their guns pulled.

This was a test.

They wanted to see what the fuck I was doing here and whether I was about to lose my nerve and turn into a sniveling pile of nerves. Or whether I would fuck up their meeting.

"What? Don't like a bitch with a backbone? That's a shame because that's what you got. See, if I'm rude, it was because you fucking deserved it." I moved in front of him, giving the boys my back as I perched my ass on the desk. "I'm not rude. You're upset that you weren't able to assert dominance over me. But just because I don't have a dick doesn't mean I'll get on my knees to suck yours." I leaned forward, digging the gun barrel deeper so it'd leave an imprint. "I owe you nothing. Not my name. Not my attention. And sure as fuck not my politeness," I bit out.

Men like him preyed on women who'd been told "don't be a bitch." That term had been used to shrink women for so long that some still believed the lie.

Be a bitch. Eat the ones who want to prey on you.

The man's partner sat in the chair, watching the entire exchange, not making a move to intervene. The asshole in front of me was visibly shaking in fear and anger, fueled by the coke I was sure he'd snorted earlier in the evening based on how blown his pupils were and the powder still clinging to his sorry excuse for a mustache.

"You—"

"Ivan. I'd be *very* careful with what you're about to call my wife." The rumble of anger in Caleb's voice sent heat shooting down my spine and settling between my thighs.

"Wife?" Ivan asked, his confusion clear as his gaze bounced between Caleb and me.

I waved my hand in dismissal of his question. "It's a new development, but that's not what we need to discuss, Ivan." I crossed one leg over the other, slightly bouncing my heeled foot as I spoke. "Here's how this is going to work. You're going to place your hand on the desk, and I'll ask you some questions. If I don't like your answer, I'll slam this metal bat down on your fingers. Got it?" I asked.

A laugh spilled from his lips as he looked toward Caleb for a clue as to what was going on.

"Scar, come stand back here and shut the fuck up or leave the fucking room. We have a meeting with Ivan, and you're interrupting the information he's giving us." He bit out the words.

Irritation burned deep inside, fanning the flames of my anger. I wasn't some fucking plaything to be taken out only when they wanted. I had a fucking life, and this shit was what I did best.

There wasn't any patience left in my body, so unless one of these assholes physically carried me out of the room, these walls would be painted with blood tonight. Ignoring Caleb's command, I stood and rounded Ivan's chair.

"Ivan, you do a lot of work with the cartel, right? You might know my friend, Ryan Hernandez." His head shook, his eyebrows furrowing in confusion. "No? Maybe you know Ryan's street name then." I leaned down and whispered it in his ear, keeping my eyes locked with Caleb's. The minute the name hit Ivan's ears, a physical shudder took over his body, bringing a smile to my face.

"Yeah. I thought that would be the case. Well, see, the techniques Ryan uses during…interrogation? Some of them came from me. Like this one."

The next second, I had my Sig pressed to his knee, and I pulled the trigger. Screams of agony echoed throughout the room. Hopefully the music would be loud enough to drown out the noise because Ivan wasn't the only one being loud. All three guys were yelling out either profanities or questions like, *"What the fuck was that?"* But I didn't move my attention from the man slumped over in the chair, attempting to hold together his ruined knee.

"How you feelin', Ivan?" I asked. He had no response other than shrieks of pain that faded when he passed out from the pain.

Kenji moved toward me with his hands lifted in the air like I was a wounded animal. They thought I'd lost my mind, when really, they were getting a glance at the real me.

I turned the gun on him when he got too close.

"Scar, sweetheart. Amateur move. Now he can't answer any questions. This is why we left you at the apartment," Kenji said, his condescending tone grating on my nerves. To think I'd let him stick his dick in me.

"Niko, get her the fuck out of here as we try to salvage this shit show." Caleb's voice trembled with rage when he spoke.

I dropped the bat, drawing a second pistol from where it had been hidden under my black blazer and pointing it at Niko's shoulder. I didn't want to kill the hot asshole, but I wouldn't hesitate to shoot.

"Or you three can pull your heads out of your asses and learn a thing or two tonight," I gritted out, nodding toward the man who'd sat quietly during this exchange. "I was 98 percent sure that Ivan was a mouthpiece for the Bulgarians, but I needed that last shred of proof. In any organization I know of, the lackeys have their boss's dick rammed so far down their throats that they do shit like throw themselves in front of a bullet for them. Yet he didn't move a fuckin' muscle as his *boss* got his knee blown out."

Dull brown eyes stared into mine. A hint of a smirk crept up onto his face. I'd have loved to see the look of shock and confusion on the other three, but I didn't want to risk taking my attention off the *real* Mob boss.

"Smart woman. But maybe I just hate my boss." His thick accent rumbled with amusement.

I heard Kenji whisper what sounded like *oh shit.*

Caleb's laptop had been comically easy to hack into, and the information for this meeting was right there on his calendar. My interest piqued when it said they were meeting with the Bulgarians. I'd done a job for them a few years prior. Killed their boss so the son could take over. Of course, I wasn't supposed to know the son had hired the hit. It was the reason for tonight's dramatics.

All I had to do was essentially hot-wire the elevator, which was something I could do in my fucking sleep at this point. No one should ever do anything less than biometric scanners —or iris scanners, if possible, because an eyeball was a bitch to dig out.

I tucked one gun back into my waistband. "Gregori Ivanov. Head of the Bulgarian crime syndicate, currently the main supplier of coke and MDMA for the Russians. But you double dip and supply to the Yakuza too," I commented, walking back over to perch myself on the desk.

Gregori was young. His inky hair hung in loose curls down to about his ears. Thick eyebrows and a hooked nose framed muddy-colored eyes. His strong jaw was peppered in a five o'clock shadow. He wore an expensive suit, looking perfectly at ease as he lounged back, arm draped over the back of the chair.

"When did you get married?" he asked, amusement in his

tone as he trailed his eyes down my body, lingering on the black lace bodysuit I wore. "And can it be annulled? Because it's hard to find a bloodthirsty woman like you." He peered over my shoulder at Caleb. "Not everyone is man enough to recognize the power in having a murderous woman by their side."

I opened my mouth to answer but found myself being hauled backward across the top of the desk and into Caleb's lap. His hands were like a brand against my waist, searing my skin. He buried his face in the side of my neck. Shivers of pleasure rolled through my body as he sucked and licked at the sensitive skin.

"No, it can't be annulled, and as you can tell, she likes being my wife just fine," Caleb growled out, his voice vibrating against my throat.

Had I been moaning?

His next words were whispered in my ear, his hot breath heating the skin still wet from his saliva. "We're going to have a long talk about you barging in here, but if you keep writhing against my dick like that, I'm going to bend you over this desk." The hardening length twitched under my ass, sending more moisture pooling between my thighs.

The clearing of a throat pulled me from the haze of lust. Gregori's eyes twinkled with amusement as he winked at me. Caleb caught it and stiffened against my back, while Niko pressed forward, wrapping a large hand around his throat.

"I suggest you quit making moves toward our woman if you'd like to stay alive longer than your father did," Kenji said, his tone dark and menacing.

Instead of cowering in fear, Gregori's smile grew, and his eyes pinged over all four of us before coming to rest on me, an eyebrow quirked.

"Choo, choo," I said, my lips pulled up in a cheeky grin when Caleb choked from behind me. Gregori busted out in laughter. Clearly, Niko hadn't had an overly tight hold on his throat.

They should do their research, because if they had, they would've known that Gregori had a longtime partner. It was a big part of why he'd had his father taken out. The bastard threatened to have his son's lover killed.

"Don't worry, gentlemen. She's all yours. My husband wouldn't appreciate it if I brought her home," Gregori said, watching each man stiffen in surprise. "Now, what is it that you want?" His tone switched, going into full business mode.

Caleb considered his question for a moment, determining his options for answering. There was only one: the truth. Gregori wouldn't respond to anything other than that. If the Syndicate wanted to wage war, they needed loyalty, not coerced soldiers who would turn traitor when a better offer came.

"We want a partnership. We plan on taking over New York and need those who want to see the current Four fall," Caleb said.

Gregori looked intrigued yet suspicious—the playfulness long gone. "That's quite the goal," he said cautiously.

I glanced up at Caleb. His expression was calm and indifferent, but his grip on my thigh tightened, his knuckles whitening. He looked down at me, studying my face.

Realization dawned on me. Caleb didn't know whether he could say what he needed to in front of me. My heart sank to my feet, disappointment burning in my gut, until he gripped the bottom of my chin, pulling my attention back toward him.

"I'm taking a risk here, Scar. Don't make me kill you by fucking me over." Caleb's deep eyes were piercing, a swirl of vulnerability and hope. He wanted to be able to trust me.

I dry swallowed and found myself nodding. Was it obvious that I desperately wanted these three to trust me, to bring me into the fold?

"Good girl," he whispered, his soft lips meeting mine,

tongue prodding at the seam of my lips. The kiss was intimate but only lasted a moment.

"We plan to blow up the Bratva and Yakuza," Caleb stated nonchalantly.

Wow. That was one way to get a meeting going.

Gregori blinked back in surprise. Whatever he'd thought Caleb would say, it wasn't that. Hell, I hadn't predicted that, either.

"You're going to blow them up?" he questioned, fingers drumming on the arm of the chair. "You know I sell them drugs, not explosives."

Niko chimed in from where he once again stood, flanking Caleb. "We've got the explosives covered. We need you to get them to the warehouse we rigged with explosives when we give you the go-ahead."

"Because the heads of those organizations always come to check the new product," Gregori responded, understanding in his tone as he shifted to lean forward in his chair. "And what do I get for my cooperation?"

"You get control of the drug trade in the city. The percentage breakdown will be seventy-thirty." Gregori nearly choked on Caleb's answer.

"All of the city?" His expression was one of surprise. All they were currently allowed was to sell to the Four Families, and they got a fraction of what the shit sold for on the streets.

Fingers trailed up and down my black pants. The touch was gentle, like he wasn't aware he was doing it. For whatever reason, that idea caused my heart to squeeze. I gripped Caleb's hand in mine, interlinking our fingers. There was no way to focus while he drew those lazy circles on my thigh, reminding me of the circles he made with those same fingers on my clit.

"Except around schools," I said, uncaring about what the three men thought about it.

"That includes the high schools," Kenji added.

My head snapped to him in surprise. That was more generous than I'd even hoped for.

Gregori nodded in agreement. His expression was excited. Clearly, he was happy with any deal other than the one they currently had.

Caleb relaxed. The stiffness I'd been too distracted to detect melted away. "Good. Continue your business as usual. No one but your most trusted knows about our deal. Understand?"

"Of course. Business as usual until you tell me otherwise." Gregori pushed up from his seat and extended a hand to Niko before doing the same for Kenji and Caleb.

"Mrs. Callahan." He held his hand out to me last, a gesture normally left for the person in the position of power. I quirked an eyebrow at his decision, and he laughed. "These three are lucky to have a partner as competent as you are. Is the cleaning fee still the same?"

His question confused me at first before understanding hit me like a freight train. He'd figured out I was involved with his father's hit. Clients got an invoice labeled *cleaning fee*.

Words lodged in my throat, and I bit down on my cheek, giving him nothing but a slight uptick of my lip. He straightened; an easy smile snapped into place, as if the interaction hadn't even happened.

"Boys, mind getting rid of this one for me? He's been a pain in my ass since I had my father killed," he asked over his shoulder before walking out the door and shutting it behind him without a second glance at Ivan's prone body.

Kenji clapped his hands together. "I'd say that went well."

TWENTY-SIX

KENJI

ORDER ME AROUND, BABY

THREE DAYS HAD PASSED since the night down in the office. We'd all been trying to navigate living and working together. Caleb was pissed that Scar had managed to hot-wire her way out of the apartment, but the glaring flaw in our security couldn't be ignored. So he'd hired her to change it out. Along with all the other areas she felt needed upgrading.

The three of us watched her like fucking creeps as she lay in the elevator with her tiny shorts and oversized T-shirt and soldered wires together. There was a rotating donation of men's shirts that made their way onto her bed when she wasn't in there. The room was starting to look more like her own. Caleb had a desk delivered and two additional monitors hooked up so she could work out of the apartment.

Jealousy had briefly zinged through me when she'd walked in to find his gift. She'd looked at Caleb with an emotion I hadn't seen from her up to that point—affection. The jealousy lasted only a second because I wanted her to look at Caleb like that. Niko too. But more importantly, I wanted her to look at *me* like that. And I was hoping the time we'd get together that night would provide that opportunity.

Niko had a retrieval job tonight, and Caleb was staying to

keep watch over the club, so it was going to be Scar and me making the rounds. I crept into the apartment, keeping as quiet as possible. Scar was probably snooping around, trying to figure out as much as she could about us. Or maybe she was putting bleach in our body wash. But the place was silent. Apprehension crept up my spine when I called out her name and she didn't answer.

The kitchen and living room were empty. I knocked on her door. Nothing. I rushed in with my katana drawn. Blue eyes popped up from behind a laptop screen, and a Sig pointed at me. She set the gun back down after she registered who I was, pulling off the silver headphones covering her ears.

"Hey, Kenji, what's up?" she asked, her tone light and chipper, as if she hadn't been ready to blow a hole in someone.

I leaned against the wall, taking in her setup. Two laptops, headphones, a phone, a gun, and a sixteen ounce sugar-free Red Bull.

"Come on. We're going to your initiation," I said, turning to leave for my own room on the other side of the apartment.

"Wait, what do you mean by that? Kenji." The pattering of bare feet trailed after me. Her hand grasped my shoulder. "Kenji, what the fuck does that mean?"

I turned to face her, gripping her chin between my thumb and forefinger. "That means, little one, that you are going to need to dress for action. We're going to the fighting rings tonight."

Her sculpted brows dipped in confusion for a second before she broke out in a wide grin. "Give me five minutes." She skipped off to her room. I wasn't entirely sure what response I'd expected, but it hadn't been that level of cheeriness.

She didn't need the full five. By the time I'd made it to the living room, she was already coming out, hair pulled up in a ponytail and black leggings that hugged her ass in a way that made me want to bury my face between her cheeks. There was also a black backpack strapped to her back, but I was too distracted by her ribbed burgundy sports bra to ask about what she was bringing with her.

"Where's your shirt?" The question was out before I could think better of it.

"Excuse me?" She narrowed her gaze on me. "Kenji, you walk around with a fucking katana and your chest spattered with blood, and I don't say shit. If I want to walk around with my tits and ass out, I can." She crossed her arms against her chest in indignation. She was fucking intimidating, I'd give her that. But she was also hot as fuck while scolding me. Honestly, I liked the idea of her pushing me around.

"We're taking my bike. You're probably going to want something more than just your sports bra."

She stalked in close, our chests touching. "How about you take care of yourself, Kenji?" she said, her voice dripping with snark.

I leaned forward, licking the seam of her lips and using her surprise as the opportunity to suck on her tongue. Her little gasps sent electric shocks straight to my balls.

"I have been taking care of myself, Scar. Remember my video? I'm waiting for you to come to do it for me," I said against her mouth before pulling away and walking into the elevator.

TWENTY-SEVEN
SCAR

"PLASTER THAT PUSSY TO THE BACK OF MY ASS CHEEKS..."

INITIATION. Hopefully, theirs was more pleasant than the one my uncle had put me through. My entire childhood had been an initiation. I was fifteen when I met Enzo. His dad was a capo in the organization, and he'd started bringing Enzo around so he could become immersed in the life. Luca pitied me, so he'd suggested to Dominick that it would be good for me to train and learn.

Why waste a resource, Dominick? You have the girl; you should use her. Teach her to be useful, bring her into the fold. She can train with Enzo. It will be good. She can protect the girls later.

One day after training, Luca pulled me aside and told me that if I wanted to survive, I should do myself the favor and become a weapon. Use the fact that I was underestimated as a strength. I never got to ask him why he bothered to care. He died in a job gone wrong later that year. That was when Enzo and I really became close. We were each other's emotional support—a friendship that blossomed into first love and then first backstabbing.

"Here, little one. We don't want that pretty face getting fucked up if we eat shit," Kenji said, shoving a sleek black full-face helmet into my hands.

He looked delicious standing in front of a matching matte black Ducati with red accents on its wheels. The gray sweatpants he was wearing hung low on his trim hips, and I really wished he'd lift up his graphic T-shirt a bit so I could drool over the defined V I knew he had. I'd gotten a peek earlier when he'd sheathed his katana.

"Can you not handle her?" I indicated to the bike with my chin, stepping closer to the pair. "Because if you can't, I sure as fuck can."

Our bodies were inches apart, and the parking garage faded away. There'd always been an easy banter with Kenji. He drew out my daredevil side. We both wanted to fall into chaos, revving each other higher and higher. Getting on a bike that went as fast as this one did was probably a death wish waiting to happen, but I couldn't seem to care.

"Oh, babe, I can handle her just fine. In fact, I could handle her and fuck you with my fingers if I wanted to," he answered, his eyes dipping toward where I was licking my lips at his proposal. But then he turned, swinging a leg over the beauty. "Too bad we've got places to be. So put the helmet on and plaster that pussy to the back of my ass cheeks."

Laughter spilled from my lips. Kenji might be broken as fuck—weren't we all?—but damn if the cheerful facade bullshit he fed to people wasn't funny.

It's what made him dangerous.

The easy smile and jokes caused people to let their guard down. Before they knew it, they'd look down to find his blade through their chest and an insane grin on his face. What concerned me was that I liked both sides of the fucker.

My chest barely brushed his when he pulled out of the spot, taking the corner of the garage at a breakneck speed. I squealed in excitement, my adrenaline spiking and making me feel alive. I flipped the visor down right as he pulled out into city traffic, weaving through the taxis and cars.

Kenji had a special holster mounted to the side of his bike

that held his katana, allowing me to plaster my body against him. My thighs were practically molded to his, and they were going to be sore as fuck after this ride with the way I had to keep them flexed to grip on.

I had my own bike. In fact, I had this very same Ducati, but there was something about riding with Kenji that was a completely different experience. Every single nerve ending was alive as we cut across lanes of traffic at reckless speeds. Blood pounded in my ears, and my cheeks hurt from how big I was smiling. Buildings were a blur as we made our way through the city. I had a feeling I knew where we were going. It was a part of Brooklyn I was pretty familiar with. These boys probably thought I didn't know shit about the underbelly of the criminal world, but I had my claws deep in that part of our world.

Remaining anonymous and lurking in the shadows had a lot of advantages. But I was well known when I stepped into certain circles. Or cages. That was how Ryan and I had met —in the illegal fight circuit. I was working a job out in Arizona, and my mark was supposed to be at a fight night held by *Los Muertos*. The only way in was to enter the bracket.

My interest was piqued when in the fight before mine, a petite woman with ink-black hair and beautiful tanned skin stepped into the cage. She was maybe five foot two, but she was built like someone who knew what she was doing. But that wasn't what convinced me that she knew what the fuck she was doing. It was the bloodthirsty glare and the way she paced the octagon.

A caged predator.

That was what her body language screamed. It was the same way I looked before a fight.

I was in my mid-twenties at the time, so I'd already pulled some big jobs and had money of my own. I'd bet a hundred grand on her that night, and I didn't just bet that she'd win, either. I bet it'd be by KO. The bitch still jokes that I owe her half my winnings.

She didn't realize it was all set up in an account for her for when she was finally ready to get out from under that fucker Mario. All thoughts of my arms dealer friend ended when Kenji cut the engine in front of a decrepit-looking building.

"Damn, woman. I don't think I ever want to ride that bike without you." He turned toward me, his fingers brushing my chin as he helped take my helmet off. We wore matching grins, the electricity of the ride still coursing through our systems.

"How about next time I drive, and you can plaster your dick against my ass cheeks?" I asked playfully, but my pussy fluttered when his gaze darkened and he stepped closer, leaning forward to whisper in my ear.

"I'd *love* to do things with my dick and your ass."

My brain short-circuited at his words as lust washed over me. The moment he took in my face, he chuckled and tugged on my hand, leading us toward the brick building. Glass crunched underfoot, and muffled voices hit my ears. Kenji looked over his shoulder at me, his eyes raking over my body but not in a sexual way. He was gauging my reaction to walking into an unlit abandoned building in the middle of a sketchy neighborhood at night.

He wasn't going to find fear. Hell, he wasn't even going to find concern.

I'd let him see the Scar this part of the criminal under-world knew. Fuck, I was excited to see their reactions to learning how fucking intertwined I really was. There was something so satisfying about watching men show their whole asses as they dug themselves into holes with their mansplaining.

Ryan dealt with it all the time since people mistook her for a dude with her name. It was why she welcomed the nick-name *Brujita de Los Muertos*. It let men know a woman was coming for their fucking balls. I got similar reactions right before I pulled out a knife and sliced their throats, oftentimes only a few hours after I had let them wine and dine me.

"Stick close to me, okay? This is a rough crowd you're going to be around." His eyes dipped to my sports bra, and he groaned. "And for the love of all things sinful, if anyone asks if you belong to someone, you fucking do. Got it? You belong to me, and I'll carve their eyes out for looking."

My nipples hardened at the possessive growl in his voice as he gave me the warning. I couldn't even muster up anger at being claimed because it was so hot.

"Yours, huh? I thought I was married to your brother," I sassed, needing to regain some control, and having Kenji pissed would be easier to handle than having him look at me like he was going to fuck me against the graffiti and grime-covered walls. But the comment had the opposite reaction.

"Oh, babe, he wants the best for his wife. Who do you think sent you with me tonight? Caleb is *very* in favor of you being taken care of," he said, leaning to speak in my ear again, his breath causing my skin to break out in goose bumps. "Even if being taken care of means letting you have a dick for every hole to make sure you're feeling *full*."

My cheeks flamed as images of all three of them surrounding me as I writhed in pleasure flashed in my mind. I was so entranced in the fantasy that I barely registered that Kenji was tugging me along behind him. The fog of lust was broken, though, when we approached a metal door.

I smiled at the sight of the rust-covered entrance.

It looked like a piece of shit, but that was all by design. A new, shiny-looking door would have drawn too much attention, and a bouncer would have too. So security for this place was all done remotely until you got inside.

I glanced to the upper corner of the alcove we'd stepped into; the camera was tucked up in the corner inconspicuously.

"What are we doing here?" I asked as we waited to be

buzzed in, anticipation and trepidation making my skin feel too tight. The curiosity in my tone was genuine, though I was well acquainted with this particular spot. Kenji didn't look at me when he answered, keeping his eyes trained on the door. His shoulders were pulled back, but his limbs were loose. Ready to strike.

"Initiation. We decided to give you a leash. See if you hang yourself or not."

My hackles rose at the insinuation, but I kept my reaction in check, resisting the urge to clench my fists or stab him.

"This place holds fights. They make big money for the Mob, and we're going to get them to partner with us instead."

I raised a brow at that.

"Smart. Get the smaller organizations to switch who they work under," I said. These smaller organizations and gangs were more valuable than they even realized. Not separately, but all together? Yeah, that would get the Syndicate enough power to overtake their daddies.

"What do you know about who runs this?" I asked, curious about how much he knew and what the plan was.

Before he got a chance to answer, there was a clicking noise, and the door popped open, revealing a set of metal stairs that led below ground into the heart of the real operation. An operation I was very familiar with.

Well, this will be fun.

TWENTY-EIGHT
KENJI

IT'S HARD TO FIGHT WITH A HARD DICK.

SHE WAS SO FUCKING hard to get a read on. She was obviously curious as to what we were doing here, but she was also relaxed. I was a pro at reading people—it was what made me so good at torture. Knowing how far to push, when to let off, and when a fucker wouldn't say shit regardless of what I did. Those were the tough bastards.

Scar was in that category.

"Stay close. They have the creepiest fucking tunnel to get into the place," I commented, lacing our fingers as we started down the cemented tunnel. The entrance felt like you were walking into your death. Which, I guess, some were. The tunnel resembled a bomb shelter with its rounded ceiling.

All she gave me was a grunt of agreement. I wanted to peek at her and see how she was taking it, but I couldn't see shit. Red rope lights that ran along the pathway only illuminated the path enough to see the next step in front of you. Stale air permeated the space, and a low murmur came from somewhere farther down the path.

Honestly, it felt like a scene out of a horror film, but that was by design. Sent the random pedestrians who strayed too far off the straight and narrow packing as soon as they experienced the creep factor. Then, for the psychos like myself, the feeling crawling up my spine wasn't fear but excitement. A thrill of danger lurking around the corner. But tonight my brain was nagging me that Scar might not feel the same way.

A single bulb hung in front of a door that matched the one we'd come through, but this one had a cutout about six feet off the floor. The hollow sound of metal being knocked on echoed through the tunnel as I rapped on the door. The cutout opened, and a pair of black eyes stared back, looking us over. The bouncer's gaze narrowed on Scar for a brief moment before flicking back to me. Whatever the emotion that crossed his face was when he looked at her happened too quickly for me to analyze, but it put me on edge.

"Password?" he asked with a gruff Eastern European accent.

"We're here to see your boss." This time I did catch the irritation in his eyes when I barked out the demand.

"He doesn't take visitors without appointment. Fuck off."

I opened my mouth to speak before he closed the window, but Scar beat me to it.

"He does if you fight. No?" she asked, her voice sure. *How the fuck did she know how this worked? Had Dominick or Enzo brought her here before?*

The bouncer was silent for a beat. The two were locked in a stare-off, and it felt like they were silently communicating. The hair on the back of my neck stood on end, because this woman managed to get more and more interesting by the second.

Without another word, the window shut.

"Fuck," I cursed under my breath, ready to bang on the door again, but it swung open, showing off the goliath who manned the entrance. Fucker was at least two-ninety and six foot three. A dark mop of curly hair was pulled up in a messy bun, and his throat was as tatted as mine.

I gave him a smile that made him shift uncomfortably. I

might be slighter than him, but people always recognized the desire for violence that shone in my eyes.

"Which one of you is fighting?" he asked in earnest. It surprised me that he actually considered Scar a viable contender. There wasn't an ounce of sarcasm or general assholery in his tone.

"We should do a WWE tag team version," she answered back, a smile playing on her lips.

Fuck no.

The last thing I needed was to be worried about her in the ring next to me.

"I'm fighting, and we're going to do it now," I demanded, shifting my body so it covered Scar's, because the bouncer was still looking at her, and I didn't like it. The switch in position didn't stop him from tilting his head to look past me.

What the actual fuck was happening?

His gaze didn't seem sexual or hostile, but it still unsettled me. Bringing her might have been a bad idea.

"All right. Go to the cage. I'll let them know," he replied, stepping out of the way to let us pass. Scar's body collided with me as I yanked her arm to pull her close. She shot me a glare but otherwise didn't complain about the show of possessiveness.

The roar of a crowd went from a murmur to deafening levels. Shouts rang out from all around as bodies were packed together, enraptured by the bloodbath happening in the cage. Two dudes were going at it. The copper tang of blood mixed with perspiration and weed. Money was being exchanged left and right. Everyone was buying booze or drugs or betting on a fight.

Peppered throughout the crowd were more bouncers like the one at the door, all of them massive to keep patrons in check. The bulges on their hips let everyone know they were packing.

My grip around Scar's shoulders tightened as I tucked her farther into the crook of my arm, snarling at men who dared get too close. The women were as fucking bad. One slapped her ass so hard I could hear it over all the chaos. It gained her a growl from me but a wink from Scar.

We finally pushed through to the corner of the ring right as the fighter in red got his opponent in a *kimura*. The fucker didn't let go when he tapped, though, and the ref had to come pry him off.

Underground fights were a different level of brutality.

Hot breath hit the shell of my ear. "Have you watched him fight before?" Scar's question took me by surprise, so I didn't answer right away, and she pushed on. "Zabit. He's the top dog here. And the fucker is good. Really good. You probably have a better chance if you keep the fight on your feet. The guy's been doing combative Sambo since the fuckin' womb."

Now I was really taken aback. I knew that shit because tonight had been planned for months. Scar was the only new addition. We assumed bringing her along wouldn't cause too much of an issue since all she had to do was sit in the corner and look pretty. But here she was with intel and suggestions on their number one fighter. The question popped out before I could stop it.

"How do you know that?" I asked with more hostility than I intended.

She bristled at my tone, her shoulders stiffening and indecision clouding her face. But it cleared as quickly. "There's a lot of shit I know, Kenji. I'm a fucking asset if we can learn to trust each other."

I opened my mouth to ask what the hell she meant, but she stopped me with a raised hand. "We aren't there yet, so don't ask, but I'll give you this as a sign of good faith. Zabit has a bum left leg. Injured it a few fights ago and needs surgery, but the fucker is stubborn and doesn't want to take the time off. Some well-placed leg kicks are going to have him hurt. And for the love of God, don't give the man your back. He'll choke you out before you know what the hell is happening."

I didn't know about the knee, and I'd been watching the dude for months, so how the fuck did she know? As if she could see the indecision, she called one of the dudes taking fight bets over.

"Hey, twenty grand on the new guy." She indicated to me with her head.

I was taken aback by her confidence in me since there was no way she knew whether I could fight. "Caleb isn't going to appreciate you betting his money without asking," I teased.

She whipped her head toward me, anger licking at her irises. "I have my own fucking money, asshole. I don't need him spending money on me."

God, I loved her temper and willingness to throw down. It made my dick hard, which was less than ideal right before I stripped down into some tight-ass shorts.

I stepped into her space, bending low to speak into her ear. "No, but you're going to let us fucking spend whatever the fuck we want on you, little one."

The fight announcer broke the tension between us with his announcement of the next fight.

My fight.

"You stay here and look sexy cheering me on," I said, pulling off my sweats. Her eyes zeroed in on my cock, and she subconsciously licked her lips. "You can suck me off after, Scar. But right now, I need you to sit your hot ass down in that chair and don't fucking move. And if someone bothers you, stab them. Run it right through their fucking heart. Don't even ask questions," I said, pushing my katana into her hands.

I didn't wait for a response as I grabbed the back of my collar and pulled off my shirt. The hitch of her breath when she saw my body was the best fucking prefight pump-up I could have asked for, and without thinking, I grabbed the back of her head and slammed our lips together. I wanted to make out like we were horny teenagers, but the crowd was chanting *new blood*.

"We're fucking after the fight, Scar."

TWENTY-NINE

SCAR

HEAD KICKS MAKE ME WET. SO DOES
PUNCHING MEN IN THE FACE...

THE *ONI* ON his back moved like it was alive as he gracefully stepped into the cage. A ripple of nerves shot through me the moment the gate closed. These fights were bare knuckles and brutal. Zabit was a bad motherfucker too. There was a reason he'd been at the top for as long as he had been.

Kenji was playing this visit off like it was random and sporadic, but I'd bet my damn life those three had this all planned. Hopefully that meant Kenji had been practicing stuffing takedowns because he would need it against his opponent. The bum knee bit wasn't common knowledge, and I'd have to make it up to Zabit later, but honestly, it was the fucker's fault for not going and having that shit taken care of.

No one said shit to me as I moved closer to the cage and leaned against the perimeter of the mat to corner for Kenji. He hadn't asked me, but he didn't know I'd trained for years, either. The roar of the crowd faded into the background as my focus homed in on him.

He was gorgeous and covered in ink. Both legs were fully sleeved in tattoos. It was an interesting dichotomy between the two. One leg was fully done in the traditional Japanese style. Two koi fish took up the majority of the real estate on his toned left thigh, and then the other was a patchwork of American tradition. His art was the story of his two halves.

The perfection and tradition versus the chaos and passion.

"Ladies and gentlemen, we have a change in tonight's main card. New meat is entering the cage to take on…the champ, Zabit Mayhem."

The announcer's voice carried over the crowd, echoing off the cement walls of this inner chamber of a room. The air was hazy with all the smoke from blunts and cigarettes. I always thought it was a major fire hazard since we were underground without a window or door in sight, but criminals and degenerates didn't give a shit about fire safety.

Kenji bounced on his toes, looking loose and relaxed. Like he'd done this before. And I hoped to God he had because he was going to need every advantage he could get against the current champ. It was one thing to practice a combat sport. It was another thing entirely to have experience in the cage in a full-fledged fight. Even sparring wasn't a true example of what it was like to be in the throes of a brawl with another person who wanted to fucking break you.

From the corner of my eye, I caught movement in the crowd. The champ was making his way toward the cage. The corners of my mouth turned up when I saw Zabit. He'd cut his hair recently, but it hadn't done much to make him look less boyish. He hated when I told him it was fine that he looked like a baby since he was one at only twenty-two. I was tempted to tell Kenji to call him a baby, but it probably wouldn't garner the same reaction as when I said it to Zabit during training.

I gnawed at my lip, watching the stare-down between the two fighters in the center of the mat. How mad was Kenji going to be when he found out I knew everyone here? There hadn't been a lot of time to play twenty questions when we showed up here. And I might like the guy, but that didn't mean I *trusted* the guy. The more I thought about it, the more comfortable I was with my decision to keep Kenji in the dark. He should know by now that you survive in this life by keeping secrets close to the chest.

I'd share shit with the guys. But on *my* time.

The bouncer, Umar, had almost blown it when he saw me at the door. Luckily, Kenji had been standing slightly in front of me, so he didn't see me give the man a small headshake. And the damn vault of a door I'd installed for Magomed's fight venue covered the shit poker face the bouncer had.

That's how I'd come to train with Zabit. I made a deal with Magomed. I'd do his security setup if he taught me how to fight properly. That had been years ago now.

The Four Families *ruled* the city, but a whole underbelly operated under their own rule and regime. This fight operation was an example of that. The Dagestanis took root in this part years ago, and with their fighting prowess, it only made sense that they'd run illegal fight nights. Magomed made fucking bank with his fighters. He had to give a cut of their profits to the Mob since this was technically on their turf, but the Irish were cocky, and they assumed the Dagestanis weren't making all that much.

The Callahans assumed their boxing fights owned the fight market. But who the fuck wanted to watch boxing when you could watch someone choke a fucker out?

Cornering Kenji felt a bit like a betrayal to my training partner, but Zabit would get over it. What was going to be interesting was when we met with Magomed. I pushed all those thoughts out of my mind to focus on Kenji.

He quirked a dark brow when he walked toward me.

"I'm cornering you. Now focus. He's got a fucking gas tank, so don't tire yourself out. He can go the distance if he has to. But he usually doesn't, because he catches guys in a takedown and then mauls them. He favors the double leg, so you fucking stuff those. I hope your ground game is good. If you have a stand-up game, that's even better, but the fucker is good at that too," I said, attempting to info dump as much as I could before the ref called them to the middle.

Kenji's face was so comical I wished I'd gotten a picture. He looked at me as if I had grown a second head. The ref called out before he got a chance to ask me how I knew all this.

"Gentlemen, to the center and touch hands."

His face shut down, flipping from confused to a ruthless killer. The difference was so stark that it sent my heart racing. Something about the look he'd given me made me less nervous for him and more concerned for Zabit.

A ding rang out, signifying the start of the round, and everything disappeared other than these two predators circling each other. They felt each other out, throwing feints and testing their reach and reaction. Zabit got tired of waiting and threw a jab, but Kenji blocked it without a problem and sent one of his own. The move was a cover for the leg kick he was gearing up to throw. A giant grin spread across my face when it landed. Apparently, Kenji threw hard fucking kicks, because red bloomed across Zabit's shin almost immediately.

The two circled again. The change put Kenji's face in my eyesight right as Zabit made it through his defense and landed a punch to his jaw. My breath stuttered in my lungs. He *should* be able to take that hit with no problem, but it didn't stop my nerves from crawling up my throat. The nerves turned into a simmering heat when his tongue swiped across the bloodied lip and he smiled. Crimson liquid leaked from a cut above his brow, but he looked *hungry*. He loved the violence, the same way I did. Seeing him bloodthirsty was turning me on, which was wildly inappropriate for his corner man.

Zabit threw out his own leg kick when his next combination was defended.

"Check the fuckin' kicks, Kenji," I yelled out, my face

practically in the cage. There was a slight stutter in Zabit's movements.

He knows I'm here now.

The crowd went wild as the two exchanged a flurry of punches and kicks, neither one really making much ground. They were an even fucking match, which meant Kenji was fucking good.

"He's going for a double leg," I yelled out so loud my throat felt hot with the effort. My voice was probably going to be shot after this.

I could spot Zabit's setup instantly. He'd taught me everything I knew, and I ended up on my fucking back enough times from his takedowns that I was an expert on it.

Kenji must have heard me, because I watched the next moments happen in what felt like slow motion. He adjusted his stance, loading up his hips to power his next move. A cocky smile showed up on Kenji's face as Zabit angled down and rushed forward right as Kenji threw his kick.

Dropped.

Zabit hit the mat with a thud that sounded like a gunshot.

KO from a fucking head kick.

I was losing my shit over it in excitement. The top of the cage bit into my stomach as I launched myself over, shouting *let's fucking go,* like a maniac. Lips slammed on mine, and copper flooded my tastebuds as Kenji shoved his tongue inside. They slid past each other in a tangle of passion, our teeth knocking as we fought for dominance. It was like we were trying to consume one another. Bloody hands wrapped in my hair, and he touched my forehead with his.

"You fucking gem of a woman." His mouth found mine again. The onslaught of his kisses made me dizzy. "You're so much more than you let on, aren't you?" he asked as he was tugged off the cage to stand in the middle for the winning announcement.

"And new, Kenji the Reaper Jirocho."

It was a fitting fucking name for him.

The second the announcement was over, Zabit gunned his way to me. "Hey, what the fuck are you doing?" he asked jokingly. But the bragging I had ready for him went out the window when Kenji shoved him against the metal of the cage.

"Watch the way you fucking talk to her because I was being nice in there. I'll permanently put you in the ground if you disrespect her," he whispered menacingly, red tinged spit landing on the fighter's chest.

Horrification would've been the appropriate reaction to Kenji's outburst, but instead my leggings were fucking soaked by the show of possessiveness and aggression.

Zabit's hands came up in surrender at the threat. "Hey, man, no disrespect. And no offense, but if I disrespected Scar, she'd put me in the ground herself. She wouldn't need you to do it for her."

Kenji's hold on him loosened, and he shot me a questioning glance. Zabit chuckled at the exchange.

"That answers my next question. She hasn't shown you her takedowns yet. Since she snitched inside info on me, here's some on her: she's shit at getting out of heel hooks," Zabit said, amusement in his eyes.

"Hey." It was true, but damn, he didn't need to say anything, especially with what was about to happen next. My eyes cut to Kenji, who still stood there wearing a look of confusion.

The announcer's voice boomed over the chatter once more. "Ladies and gentlemen, it's a special night indeed. Not only does your new champion already have to defend his title, but he gets to do it against a familiar face. Don't let the fact that she's a woman fool you. She's a killer."

Understanding followed by horror spread to Kenji's face. If he wasn't already red and sweaty from the fight, I was sure that announcement would've done the trick.

"No," he stated firmly, his head shaking.

"No?" I asked, fixing my hair into a tight braid that landed slightly past my shoulders. "Don't you want to meet with Magomed? We both have to fight for that to happen."

Color faded from his face, and his throat bobbed, as if swallowing was difficult. My heart fluttered while a fire raged in my veins. Sure, it was sweet that he cared, but I wasn't a fragile fucking flower.

"That's how this works here. If you want to meet the boss, you have to fight. That night." I walked up the steps of the cage. "Hit me like you mean it, Kenji. Where's the man who had the balls slice my skin and then lap it up?"

Fire and chaos.

The reaction he'd denied me a moment ago flashed in his eyes. The tendons in his neck flexed as he stretched his muscles from side to side, beginning to bounce in place. The crowd roared at the obvious change in demeanor. They'd probably been scared they'd get denied a bloodbath.

We made our way to the center as the announcer ordered.

"You want me to make you bleed, little one?" He looked impossibly arrogant, and it caused moisture to pool at my core. Blood whooshed in my ears, drowning out the crowd. My sole focus was on the man in front of me.

A demon personified, with his blood-spattered body and split lip leaking crimson that I longed to lap up the same way he had with the cut on my thigh.

I leveled a gaze in his direction as we touched hands, mine not yet torn and bruised.

"I want you to make me *feel*, Kenji."

My words struck a nerve with him. He understood what I meant. The rush of violence was something no drug could recreate, and I had a feeling violence with Kenji was about to become my favorite high.

Before I could move to my corner, his hand wrapped around my throat, and his lips pressed against mine as he spoke. Heat licked at the areas he touched, sizzling like a hot poker.

"Mine. You're mine, Scar."

Pain radiated from the spot he'd sunk his teeth into while a jolt of electric pleasure shot straight to my clit. The crowd went wild at the violently sexual energy coursing in the ring.

"You know," I called out as I backed into my corner, "I'm pretty sure they have videos like this where the winner fucks the loser in the ring after," I said, bouncing on my toes.

A cheeky grin appeared on his face. "You want me to fuck you here in front of everyone, Scar?"

"Bold of you to assume it's not going to be me who fucks you," I threw back right as *fight* was called out.

We circled one another, each throwing out feints. I'd have to wait him out, look for the opening, and then strike hard and fast. He had a longer reach and was bigger than me in height and weight. I flung a leg out, connecting with his thigh in the same spot I saw Zabit connect with earlier. He let out an audible grunt at the hit, and I smirked at his flash of surprise.

I loved when they underestimated me.

I caught his right hook when I made my way to his inside. I could feel the bruise that would bloom there, but the risk paid off, and I landed a hit to the gut, dancing away before he could catch me with anything else.

"You're playing with fire, little one," he taunted as his leg snapped out, aimed for my head in the same move he'd dropped Zabit with. This one caught my forearm as I blocked it, hitting me so hard my teeth rattled in my head.

It didn't matter that the kick hurt like a bitch. I could feel the goofy smile on my face. It was the same one Kenji gave me when I landed an uppercut to his jaw. His cut from earlier opened up even more.

"You're so hot covered in blood, Kenji," I said, licking my lips as he walked me down.

"Are you going to lick it off me?" he asked while circling around, looking for a chink in my armor.

"Oh, I'm going to lick something."

The minute the words were out, I knew they were a mistake, because steely determination settled over his face. I had given him the motivation to end this fight quickly. Kenji rushed forward for a takedown. My forearms dug into his shoulders in an attempt to sprawl, but he was like a wild animal, and his arms reached out and grabbed a hold of the back of my thighs and yanked me forward.

The movement left me with no other choice than to wrap my legs around his waist. He rushed forward, pinning me against the cage. His breath fanned across my face. "I am so fucking turned on right now, Scar. Where the fuck was a woman like you hiding?"

He didn't give me a chance to answer as he slammed his lips on mine, diving his tongue inside. Claiming me in front of the crowd of people. His hands kneaded my ass as he flipped us around so his back was to the cage. Our kisses were as brutal as our fight, tongues lashing out as we nipped and bit. I was so lost in lust that I barely felt the two taps he gave my ass.

I didn't even fucking care that he'd thrown the fight. Nothing mattered other than this man.

THIRTY

KENJI

I'LL SINK TO MY KNEES FOR HER LIKE A
GOOD BOY...

SHE WAS A GODDAMNED ENIGMA.

When we'd gotten here, I wasn't sure why she seemed so comfortable around the fights. I would never have fucking guessed that she trained *with* the Dagestani. A shiver of excitement shot down my spine, straight to my balls.

It was a good thing my sweatpants were back on, because otherwise, everyone would get an eyeful of my cock, free of charge.

My eyes cut to her. There'd never been a woman I wanted to be thrown around by. But this violent Italian?

"Your dick's getting hard, Kenji. Imagining my tits?" she asked without meeting my eyes.

I leaned over, not wanting the two men we were following down a low-lit hall to hear me. "No, I'm thinking about sinking to my knees and lapping up that cunt like a good fucking boy," I whispered, my hand shooting out to steady her as she lost her balance.

Fighting and fucking went hand in hand, and I was pissed that we had this meeting because I wanted to be balls-deep in her so badly. The fantasy was broken when the office door was pulled open.

Stay on track, Kenji. You can rail her after.

She pushed in front of me, walking in like she was familiar with the space. And after what happened in the ring, it was clear she was.

"Scar, there are other ways of getting Zabit to get his knee fixed that don't include you fucking me out of a shit ton of cash."

I bristled at Magomed's words. We needed him to agree to our plan. Otherwise, we'd be fucked. Pissing him off by taking his money wasn't a good start to this potential partnership. But as I came to stand beside Scar, I noticed his eyes twinkled with what looked like affection. Which, of course, had my mood doing a one-eighty. I no longer wanted to work with the fucker; skewering the man sounded like a better idea.

Scar plopped onto the worn leather sofa that faced the desk, tucking her feet under her as she made herself comfortable. A stark contrast to the way I made sure to stay standing in case they decided to attack.

"If I recall, I suggested he get that fixed months ago. Yet here we are, and the idiot is still fighting on it. You're lucky I was cornering his opponent," she responded, wagging a finger at Magomed as if he were a petulant child and not a notoriously vicious crime lord.

Toffee-colored eyes cut over to me with the mention of the fight. The warmth they held for Scar leeched out when we made contact. He was probably used to that stare making men cower.

"Yes." The word was wrapped in suspicion. "I was told you wanted a meeting," he said, his attention back on Scar.

"*I* wanted the meeting." The words came out harsher than intended as my fists clenched at my sides. Thankfully, the pain of broken skin stretching over my knuckles cleared my mind. I needed to remember that a positive outcome was essential.

He tensed at my reply, his knuckles whitening as he folded his hands like he was restraining himself from retaliating against my tone. With a sigh, he leaned back in his chair, feigning being comfortable, but the tension in his shoulders told a different story.

"Well, you have one now. What is it you want?"

"He wants to know how you'd like to be under a new regime," Scar answered for me.

A vicious glee radiated from Magomed's eyes. He liked the idea of not answering to the Irish pricks that controlled this area. His head swung to me, interest burning in his face. A jagged scar cut from his eyebrow down to the corner of his mouth, and his nose was flat, clearly having been broken before. One look at his blocked ears let anyone know he'd been in many brawls over the course of his life. His steepled hands hit the desk as he leaned in close.

"So, the rumors are true. The spare heirs have committed treason against their own blood." A dry laugh followed his words.

"Кровь ничего не решает," I spat out. His thick brows hit his hairline in surprise at the Russian I'd spoken.

Scar untucked her legs as he and I stared one another down. Her movements were so graceful that she reminded me of a lynx as her muscles bunched in preparation for an attack. Flutters erupted in my stomach when her body turned to face Magomed. Her intentions were clear—it was my back she had. He let out an amused huff at her silent declaration, his lips peeling back into an ever-so-slight grin.

Bringing her was turning out even better than we'd planned. I wasn't sure the Dagestani would have partnered with us otherwise.

"Blood decides nothing," he translated, savoring the phrase in his mouth like something delicious. "Seems we are all bastards here, no?"

Scar's body stiffened.

"We're interested *if* the perks are there," he said, lounging back in his seat. His voice was devoid of emotion, but my vantage point let me see how his knee had begun bouncing below his desk. The nervous jitter told me he wanted this deal to work out.

"We're going to cripple the Four, take everything from them. Starting with their money. We want you to stop giving the Mob their cut," I responded.

"And when they come demanding their money? What do I do then, huh? Will you be the one here to take their bat to the hand for disobedience?" he sneered, the words clearly a recount of prior experience.

But that wasn't my fucking problem.

"Our plans will already be in motion by that time." I slammed my palms down on the top of his desk, causing him to twitch at the sudden movement. "Hear this, Magomed. We are offering this partnership once. If you don't want in, I don't really give a fuck. It will just be more heads for me to take from their shoulders."

All three men paled at the expression painted across my face. The chilling cold of not giving a shit about the sanctity of life. No one should depend on my moral compass, because it didn't function properly.

Beads of sweat collected along his hairline, and his throat bobbed, but he managed to tear his attention from me and direct it toward Scar, who'd been quietly observing the exchange. Nothing in her body language clued me into what was swirling in that beautiful mind of hers.

"Were you given these same terms?"

Are you with them against your will? That was what he was really trying to ask. Fucked up part was that was a correct interpretation of her situation, but it still made my hackles rise. I didn't want her to be with us because she'd been forced to. I wanted her to be here with me because she wanted to be.

Air stalled in my lungs as I waited for her response.

"I'm the new Mrs. Caleb Callahan," she said, tilting her head in a move that felt predatory.

The fight club owner barked out a laugh. "Does he still have a dick?"

"Barely. He is missing a ball," she replied, smirking before her face turned serious again. "No more games. Are you going to join or not? You get control of this territory, and your cut will go from fifty percent to seventy."

His dismissive scoff and wave had me seeing red. Shouts rang out when the tip of my katana pierced his cotton T-shirt, the white fibers soaking up the blood leaking from his chest.

"Take the seventy, or I'll take your tongue for disrespecting her," I bit out as he lifted his hands in surrender.

"We'll take it. And there was no disrespect. Scar is family, and she knows it. If she's giving you three her loyalty, then we will too. But don't make the same fucking mistakes the Four are doing and disrespect *us*," he said, his eyes hardening.

Our stare-down lasted only a few tense moments, but nothing in his posture suggested he was lying.

"We won't. You will be well taken care of. This information doesn't leave this room. Got it?"

THIRTY-ONE
SCAR

GRAVEL AND GLASS CRUNCHED UNDERFOOT. We'd gone out the back way from the office, and the muggy night air was a balm to my lungs. Supposedly they force-circulated fresh air through the underground arena, but that concrete coffin made the city smog taste like crisp mountain pine oxygen in comparison.

I opened my mouth to ask where we were going next, but the words never left. The familiar *pop, pop* of a gun echoed off the bricked alley walls. A guttural yell tore from Kenji, stopping me in my tracks. Time slowed as a mist of blood and fabric particles exploded from his arm. The world grew muffled. The only sound was the rushing of blood in my ears and my sharp inhale. As quickly as it began, time then flew forward.

"Fuck. Get on," he called out, throwing his leg over the bike as it roared to life. Crimson droplets kissed the gravel, forming pools. The sight kicked me into action. I ripped my backpack off, digging for my Sig as the volume of the world grew tenfold. My hand wrapped around the rough grip. The weight of a gun felt natural and transformed my emotions from uneasy to a feeling of control.

"Get the fuck on, Scar." He barked out the command like an order, but his words were drenched in worry. I got the impression the concern wasn't for himself. The same reason he wasn't chasing after these assholes. He didn't want to risk me getting injured. My leg slid over his sinewy thighs. The heat of his chest seared into mine as I settled in front of him—the position awkward but necessary.

"What the hell?" he asked.

The pounding of soles intertwined with angry shouts drew closer. Trepidation flooded my system like the bursting of a dam. And it wasn't the barrage of bullets that caused the reaction—it was the language of the shouts. Instinct hijacked my body, force-feeding my limbs the proper instructions of how to send back my own shots.

The recoil sent jolts of satisfaction coursing up my arm. A pained shout told me I'd hit my mark. Horror or regret were never the emotions that ran through my mind after a kill. Not even after my first one. I felt nothing but satisfaction knowing whoever had shot at us was lying there, his lungs gurgling for air as blood seeped into the earth, watering it.

Cursing the land with the blood of my enemies, like the Curse of Cain.

"Fucking go, Kenji. I can't shoot if I'm facing the other way," I said, firing off two more rounds down the dark alley.

His chest rumbled with laughter as the tires squealed, the back end of the bike fishtailing as it tried to gain purchase on the pavement. Moments like this were when I was aware of how fucked in the head I was. Because it wasn't fear running through my system. It was excitement. I lived for the thrill. Kenji seemed to feel the same way because his bulge hardened under me as we weaved through the traffic at breakneck speeds, bullets flying by until we were far enough away. Only a few layers of fabric separated us, and I squirmed slightly, seeing if I could get more contact where I really wanted it.

The bike wasn't designed for the passenger to straddle the

driver, but we made it work as we rode back to the penthouse. When it was clear that no one was following after us, I tucked in close, moving my head to the side so Kenji would be able to see over my shoulder. The fabric of his shirt rubbed against my skin, and the rumble of the bike between my legs sent shivers through my body. Of course being shot at had made my libido skyrocket rather than plummet.

Kenji pulled into his spot right in front of the private elevator. His labored breathing became apparent when he cut the engine, reminding me that he'd been hit. Worry clawed at my lungs, and I scrambled off the bike, my hand gently wrapping around his injured arm.

"Off the bike, Kenji, so I can take care of this arm," I said, unwrapping the blood-soaked fabric. He must've torn off some of his shirt while I'd been busy grabbing my gun. I peeked up at him when he'd yet to answer. His helmet was still on, but the visor had been lifted. Espresso eyes stared back at me, his brows slightly pinched. I couldn't place the expression on his face, which made my heartbeat kick up in a panic.

"Are you in pain? Stupid question. You've been shot. Grazes hurt like a bitch." I grabbed the bottom of his helmet and lifted it off. "Here, I'll help you with this." My words came out more rushed than I intended because I was feeling out of control, and he wasn't giving any feedback.

"You really care?"

His question took me off guard.

"What are you talking about?" I asked, instantly placing the back of my hand on his forehead. It was clammy, but nothing crazy, and he hadn't lost that much blood.

"I mean," he took my hand in his, "you really do care about whether I'm okay or not."

I was still completely at a loss for what he was talking about. Of course I cared about the fact that he'd gotten shot, and I told him as much. A giant grin spread across his face.

"Get the fuck off the bike, Kenji. I don't know what the hell is wrong with you, but I'm getting you upstairs because I think you're in shock." I tugged on his good arm, helping him off the bike. The moment he was standing in front of me, his mouth pressed to mine, his hand tangling in my hair. This kiss was different from the others. This one wrapped around my heart and refused to release it.

"No one, other than Caleb and Niko, has ever cared about me when I've been injured," he whispered. Now I recognized the emotion that had flitted across his face. It was the same one that now dripped from his tone—awe.

I froze, the adrenaline dump hitting me hard.

I avoided emotions in general, so I didn't know what to do with someone else's emotions. My life had been spent on autopilot. When one task was accomplished, I'd quickly fill it with another, all to push back the fragility that clawed at my soul. Stopping to acknowledge that I *felt* meant turning off the numb coursing through me. My mask had been on so long that I didn't know who I was beneath it or how I would cope with the consequences of removing it.

Calloused fingers caressed my tear-stained cheeks.

When had I started crying?

My eyes focused on the painfully handsome face in front of me. The look of understanding was so evident, it was as if I'd said the words aloud.

"It's okay to let someone in. I used to think I had to do this alone too, that stuffing my emotion would save me from the pain of love and loss. But it doesn't. You can only flip that switch for so long before the pressure of all you've shoved away explodes." His thumbs were featherlight as they rubbed across my face. "I was surprised that you would care for me after the way we started out. Let me care for you too."

It wasn't a question, and he didn't seem to care whether I answered either, because he pulled me into the elevator and tucked me into his side.

Two sets of eyes were on us the moment the doors opened, and it only took a second for them to register how pale Kenji's face was and the blood that had once again begun dripping down his arm.

"I need a first aid kit and whatever shit you have for sewing stitches," I said, my voice not quite its normal calm when I dealt with similar situations.

There was the sound of bare feet striking the concrete floor as Niko's hulking form burst into action, disappearing into the kitchen.

Rage trembled in Caleb's voice when he spoke. "What the hell happened? Are you okay?"

He appeared in front of me faster than I thought possible, smashing my body to his. Ink adorned his wide chest: "Blood defines nothing." The same phrase Kenji quoted in the meeting. Caleb leaned forward, his intense eyes drilling into me as his hands ran over my body.

"Did Magomed do this to you?" he asked. His words were sharp and angry, but hidden underneath was concern. His pouty lips were pulled downward, his brows pinching in worry.

Caleb's presence was so all-consuming that I hadn't realized that Niko had pulled Kenji over to the sectional and had begun tending to the wound until Kenji let out a sharp inhale.

The noise helped clear my mind enough to answer before Caleb began making assumptions and went off, guns blazing in the wrong direction.

"No, it wasn't Magomed," I responded as I watched Niko work.

"We don't know that," Kenji said. I could hear the doubt in his words.

Caleb's body was literally vibrating with anger. My heart

beat faster at the tic in his jaw and the tightening of his fists on my biceps. The man was murdering someone tonight, and if I didn't shed some light on this situation quickly, it might be my friends.

The heat from his bare chest warmed my chilled skin as I stepped closer into his space. I had to crane my neck to maintain eye contact. He leveled a gaze that had my adrenaline and desire increasing. It drifted down, taking in my peaked nipples. Of course I was attracted to how violent and dangerous he was.

"I know Magomed. He wouldn't have attacked us, and if he were going to, he'd have done it in his office. This attack wasn't him."

Silence hung heavy in the room, making my skin crawl. The low murmur from the club below was the only sign that this moment hadn't been frozen in time.

I broke the connection between us, looking off into the distance and debating about whether I should tell them what I knew. An exhausted sigh left my lips. I'd been on my own for so long that it was difficult to relinquish some control to others. They may not react the way I wanted, or they might think I was lying, and then I'd end up at the mercy of their wrath. But standing around wondering whether either of those would be the outcome wasn't going to do shit.

"I know who attacked us," I said. My voice was quiet but firm.

The impossibly arrogant expression Caleb typically had was replaced with something more closely resembling a confused little boy. But it disappeared pretty damn quickly. Replaced by a cold, cruel expression, like he was ready to burn down all of New York.

"Scar," he tilted my face up to him, "you're ours, and we protect each other in this family. I can't do that if I don't know who I'm going to fucking murder for shooting at my wife." There was a cruel flicker in his eyes. No doubt men withered under this glare, just as they did mine. My spine stiffened, each vertebra stacking one on top of the next until it was as straight as a rod. Caleb didn't scare me. He excited me.

"Well, you don't have to worry about at least one of them." Caleb's attention flicked to the couch, where Kenji was being tended to. "Our girl there took one out," Kenji said, wincing as Niko cleaned the graze.

"They were speaking Italian," I said while moving to plop down in the velvety softness of the couch. Angry footsteps chased after me.

"What the fuck was Dominick thinking? We made the deal with him to keep him off our backs," Niko said as he wrapped gauze around the upper part of Kenji's bicep.

The scent of bourbon and musk enveloped me, making my head feel light. Desire speared through me at the sight of Caleb's low-hanging gray sweatpants.

Fuck me.

Gray sweatpants and dickprints were to women what tits were to men. Instant insanity the minute they're put in our faces, and I was not immune to their enticing pull. Especially the one that Caleb was rocking right now.

Kenji's chuckle broke the spell. "Caleb, she can't concentrate with you hanging your dick in her face like that."

Caleb glanced down at the comment, as if barely noticing how closely pressed our bodies were.

"But her mouth does feel wonderful working up and down a cock. The way she flicks her tongue over your shaft..." Niko hummed in approval over the memory of his cock buried in my throat.

His words had my cheeks heating and my heart beating in my ears. The *thump-thump* practically synced to the music drifting up from the floors. How had we gone from talking over who'd shot at us to how proficient at sucking cock I was?

Caleb's eyes flared with desire, his soft tongue swiping across his lower lip. My brain splintered under the idea of that tongue buried between my legs. Would he do it right here, with an audience? Would they all want to flick their tongues over my flesh? Using their mouths to work me into a frenzy?

The heady scent of lust swirled in the room, making it hard to breathe. Hard to think about anything other than falling into one another's arms, but a single chime from my phone shattered the moment.

Blood leeched from my face at the sound. There was only one reason *that* phone would be going off. I frantically dug into my backpack, searching for the seam marking the hidden compartment. My fingers wrapped around the burner, and I tried to steady my breath before I answered. There was no need to look at who the caller was. There was only one person who had this number, and I didn't want her to know she had me rattled.

"Ryan. I've missed hearing that sexy voice of yours," I responded, ignoring the growls that erupted from the men around me.

I had to angle the phone out of reach when Caleb lunged for it. He grunted when I shoved my foot in the crease of his hip and thigh, dangerously close to kicking him in the balls. The look I leveled him was meant to confirm that his family jewels were at risk if he went for the burner again. I rolled my eyes at the loathing sneer plastered to his face.

No dick was more important that Ryan. Even if the dick was attached to any of the three sinfully hot men I had no doubt knew how to show me nirvana over and over and over again.

Ryan's sensual Hispanic accent refocused my attention. "Scar, I have a favor to ask. But we need to meet at one of your places."

The lack of distress in her tone helped loosen the grip of fear around my heart, but the fact that she needed to meet at my safe house was concerning. That meant her club was compromised. My gaze flicked to the guys, their attention stifling. There was no way they'd let me walk into the other room to finish this conversation, and they sure as fuck were going to drill me on this when I hung up.

I shut my eyes, gnawing my lip at the decision I needed to make, but Ryan was worth it. The question now was, would these three let me help her, or would I be dissolving bodies in Caleb's tub?

I pulled the phone away as I let out a resigned sigh. I guess these three were about to become acquainted with my secrets.

"Anything for you, Ryan. But I have a bit of an asshole men problem at the moment."

THIRTY-TWO
CALEB

TINGLES SPREAD across my skin and anger flooded my system the moment she murmured another man's name with affection in her tone.

Her affection should be ours alone.

I burned feverishly hot—out of my fucking mind with delusion. I knew the thought was completely irrational, but I didn't give a fuck.

Her heel dug into the flesh of my thigh, threatening to deliver a punishing blow to my balls if I made another attempt for her phone. I glanced over to Niko, projecting my thought without words and without drawing her attention to our intentions. I wanted to talk to this fucking *Ryan* person and let him know he better savor his last days because we would be coming to kill him very soon.

Why the fuck did she have a burner phone buried in her bag?

Her eyes flicked up toward me, causing her to look at me through her black lashes. Her plump lips pulled up at the corners into a sly grin. Clearly, they were speaking about me, and I'd had enough of the secrets.

I yanked on her delicate ankle. The move sent her sliding

down the couch, her back flat on the seat cushion. I shoved myself between her open thighs, keeping a hold on her ankle. She shuddered, her breath ragged with excitement as my hand wrapped around her elegant throat.

Clearly, it was my favorite handhold because we always seemed to end up in this position—her heartbeat fluttering under my calloused palm. Her throat bobbed as she swallowed. She wasn't concerned that I held power over her every breath. In fact, her stare was carnal and sexual. She lay there, unmoving, but her abdomen was flexed, her muscles bunched like she was waiting to attack.

She'd *let* me take power over her, and I had the sinking suspicion it was because she loved the thought of wrestling it back from me.

Caring for someone meant having a weakness. I already had two I would die for, but I knew they could handle this life. And as I stared down at this beautiful anomaly who'd matched me in every way since the moment I met her, it dawned on me that she could handle it too.

My irritation increased tenfold. "Tell your little friend you need to go because your husband is going to stuff his cock down your throat."

The comment ignited the air, crackling with sexually charged energy. Her chest heaved, and her eyes were now as black as the barrel of a gun, electricity jolting across our bodies.

"Do you need me to look into what's happening? I'm guessing the club is compromised if you need to meet at my place," she responded. It took me a moment to realize that she was talking to the fucker on the other end of the line.

Her eyes drilled into mine. A flicker of defiance intertwined with excitement sparkled in them. She knew she would be punished for this little episode as soon as she hung up. The only reason I'd allowed her to continue the conversation was because there was no fucking way she'd tell us what was happening if I forced her to end the call.

I'd appreciated how my brothers let me take the lead on this, but it was clear they were just as pissed off.

"I'll text you with the details. You know where to go. I'll meet you there."

The moment she flipped the phone closed, it was as if all the oxygen was sucked from the room. We teetered on the edge of madness, waiting on bated breath to see who'd move first.

Her breath hitched when I slid my hand down her inner thigh, pressing my fingers against her pussy. It was as if I'd been doused in accelerant and her pleasured gasp was the flick of a match that set me on fire. She grew wetter, soaking through her leggings with each circle of my thumb on her clit.

"Who told you that you could speak to another man, *wife*?"

I punctuated the question by slamming my fingers inside her, uncaring that the spandex prevented them from going in more than a few centimeters. She choked on air with her inhale at the intrusion. I didn't give a fuck. She deserved to feel the rough rub of the fabric in her dripping cunt and the unsatisfying feeling of my fingers only barely fucking her.

"Fuck you, Caleb. I can speak to whoever I want," she bit out. Her words were strained as she thrashed against my hands, trying to force more length into her heat.

A groan of pleasure came from the direction of Kenji and Niko. I'd bet a million fucking dollars that they would both have their dicks in their hands in a matter of minutes. She wouldn't be the first woman we'd shared, but I knew she'd be the last.

"Kenji, let's look at these sexy fucking tits."

He practically tripped over himself, scrambling over to where she writhed on the sofa. His hands grasped the sports bra, yanking the offending fabric up, exposing her teardrop breasts. The sight of him pinching her nipples, rolling the pebbled peaks between his fingers, sent a shot of lust through my balls, tearing a moan free.

Niko appeared on the other side of her, running the tip of his nose up the slope of her breast and following it with the pad of his tongue, sucking on the sensitive skin as he mimicked Kenji's ministrations.

"Who the fuck was on the phone? And what did they want?" I asked, digging the palm of my hand against her clit as her arousal coated my fingers through her leggings. Fuck, I wanted to bury my face between her thighs and lick her, asshole to clit, before feasting on her. Tasting the remnants left on her thong the other night hadn't been enough, but she wasn't going to receive pleasure until she'd served her punishment.

The idea of our cocks halfway down her throat almost had me blowing my load prematurely. My hand stilled, and she whimpered at the loss.

I curled my mouth in a smile when she glared at me through slitted eyes.

"My friend Ryan needs information and asked to meet at my safe house in Tucson tomorrow."

Jesus fuck. That hadn't been what I'd expected her to say. Frustration churned in my gut because it was clear this needed to be a more in-depth conversation, but my balls were throbbing far too badly to stop what I'd started with her. I didn't bother to hide the disdain in my eyes as I raked my gaze over her body, letting her think the emotion was directed at her. But the tic of her brow left me feeling exposed and raw. As if she could see through the sneer into the growing ball of affection for her.

The connection we had was electric—too intense to pretend it didn't exist. And I wasn't alone in that feeling.

Saliva glistened on her tits from where my brothers were

laving her skin. Niko was sucking hard enough not only to pull gasps but mark her as his.

As ours.

Her cocky grin pissed me off, taunting my warring emotions. I wouldn't allow her to unnerve me. I was in charge, and she'd kneel at my feet. My fingers wrapped around the back of her neck, pulling her up and slamming my lips to hers, thrusting my tongue in her mouth. Our tongues slid past each other like we were fucking. The angle had her back awkwardly arched as I leaned over her, practically lying on top of her, but I didn't give a fuck if she was comfortable or not.

I pulled back, roughly running my thumb across her bottom lip as I spoke. "I'm going to fuck your smart mouth now. Got it?"

Her glacial eyes flared with heat, carnal need flashing in them.

"Oh, husband. Having a cock in my mouth puts me in a position of power." Her eyes drifted toward Kenji and Niko, who both had their dicks fisted in their hands. "You should try it sometime. There are enough cocks to go around."

A loud groan fell from Kenji.

The reaction made Scar bite her lips in interest. My hand gripped her shoulder, shoving her down on the floor so she was kneeling at my feet, her sinful mouth in line with my throbbing cock. Hands that weren't mine tugged at the waistband of my sweats, ripping them down my legs to where they caught on my thighs. My erection hung in her face, and she licked her lips at the sight, making eye contact as she leaned forward and lapped up the precum glistening on my tip.

There were no rational thoughts left in my brain. I was a shell of need and lust, with every nerve ending firing off sensations of arousal.

"Open your fucking mouth, Scar." She followed the

command. "That's a good fucking girl. I'm going to coat that throat in cum."

The moment she sucked around my shaft, I knew I was in trouble. The blood thumping in my ears competed with the wet sounds of her mouth going up and down in long, slow strokes. Pleasure spread through my body as she worked my thick dick in and out of her mouth. Her hand ran up my thigh, grabbing my heavy balls and rolling them around in her palm.

"Fuck. Just like that."

"Ugh. Listening to her choke on your cock is the hottest shit," Kenji commented as he fisted his shaft, fucking his hand.

Niko nodded in agreement, his hand wrapped around his own cock while he watched Scar on her knees through hooded eyes.

She moaned around my cock as she took in the sight of the other two. The sound spurred my hips on. She matched my punishing pace, her eyes locking in on me through her lashes.

"Fuck me," I groaned out as I came, filling her mouth. My legs threatened to give out from the intensity of my orgasm. "You're not going to swallow until I tell you."

The string she'd wrapped around my heart pulled tighter. I wanted to crawl inside her, body, mind, and soul, and never leave. Bury myself so deep she couldn't leave even if she wanted. She looked up at me, mischief shining in her eyes as her throat bobbed.

"You fucking brat," I said, shaking my head. Before I knew what was happening, she slammed into me, knocking me on my ass as her hand grasped my jaw. She pried my mouth open and spit my release into my mouth, then shoved her tongue inside.

"Like the way you taste?" she asked against my lips.

I was too stunned to speak. I should have seen it coming, though. She'd been *too* obedient.

"Let's take care of this dripping pussy. On the couch. Now," Niko barked out, coming to stand next to me. I chuckled at his demanding tone. I'd forgotten what a commanding fucker he was when it came to sex. She whimpered as she scrambled back onto the cushion.

Niko's large hands yanked off her legging like they offended him. "Spread your thighs. Show us that pretty pussy," he instructed.

My cock jumped as she followed his instruction. Her pink pussy was the sexiest thing I'd ever seen.

"Fuck, you're wet," he said, pressing his thick fingers to her pussy. "Kenji, on your knees in front of her."

She moaned at the sight of Kenji crawling between her thighs at Niko's command. This was their dynamic.

Niko led and Kenji followed.

The chaos and the control.

Kenji ran his tongue through her wetness, swirling it over her clit and drawing out a ragged moan from her.

"I'm going to fuck that tight pussy of yours while Kenji fucks your throat. Understand, Scar?" Niko asked, gripping her jaw so she had to pay attention. He reached down and lifted her up, carrying her over the chaise part of our sectional and positioning her so her head hung over the edge while her pussy was in perfect position for his cock to drive in and out of it.

Kenji moved in front of her, rubbing his thick tip across her lips, smearing his precum. The two men looked at each other and filled her at the same time, pulling a straggled groan from her.

She'd just drained my balls, but I was already hardening again.

"Fuck, Scar. You're never getting away," Kenji moaned out, watching his cock disappear down her throat.

Niko's shaft glistened with her arousal as the two pumped

in and out, seeming to work in sync. The room was a symphony of pleasure.

"You look so fucking perfect, Scar. You're taking their cocks so fucking well, babe. Our good little whore," I praised, working my hand up and down my shaft, matching their pace.

Time didn't seem to exist. It felt like we'd been going forever and not long enough all at the same time. A surreal state of pleasure.

"Fuck, I'm going to come," Niko called out, his body doing a full shudder as he filled her with cum. Kenji found his own release moments after.

I pumped my hand faster and faster as I walked over to where Niko was still buried in her pussy, cum leaking out around his shaft. The sight pushed me over the edge, and my own hot, sticky cum hit her pussy, sliding down her slit toward her ass.

She propped up on her elbow, her chest heaving, pupils blown. "Kenji, be a good boy and clean me up?" she challenged.

Niko and I stepped out of the way to let him through, and he dropped down to his knees, a devilish smile on his face. Kenji pressed the flat of his tongue to her thigh, lapping up the combined release from Niko and me, then moving to lap up her slit.

"Fuck. We're completely fucked," I said to Niko, who nodded in agreement.

If I hadn't already made her my wife, I'd be getting on my knees and proposing right that fucking moment.

It was time to execute our plans, because I wasn't going to lose this woman to her fucking uncle or our fathers.

Sleep had eluded me for hours.

Niko had fed us all after our couch escapade. The images of Niko's cock sliding between her glistening pussy lips mocked me. Why the fuck was I avoiding having sex with her? It was clear she was nothing like her asshole uncle, and try as I might to hate her, the emotion had morphed into something else entirely.

I longed for her heated glares and silky touches. The way her quick tongue would verbally lash out. Her brain was so fucking sharp, like another blade in her arsenal. I rubbed at my chest, the spot where a knot seemed to be forming every time I thought about her.

Silky sheets went flying as I kicked them off, launching myself out of my bed to go to hers. With each step, my heart beat faster. What would she say when I showed up in her room alone?

Did her emotions mimic my own?

Or was hate all that coursed through her veins?

Her door opened without a sound, the city lights barely casting enough light into the room to make out the silhouette of her bed. I swallowed thickly as I crept closer to her sleeping form. Honeyed waves splayed across her pillow, her face a beautiful mask of calm—not a single worry marred her features.

I reached out and trailed the tip of my finger along her face.

"Fuck," I hissed as she latched onto my wrist and yanked me forward. My free hand slammed against the headboard to keep me from crushing her.

"Caleb?" she asked, her voice raspy from sleep.

"Yes, it's me." I responded, our faces so close her minty breath caressed my skin. "Now could you get the fucking barrel of your gun off the underside of my chin, please?"

It was fucking hot that she had such quick reflexes, even coming out of the dead of sleep. She glanced at her hand, as if she hadn't even known she'd drawn the firearm. Maybe she hadn't.

"Sorry. It's a habit," she replied, tucking her Sig back under her pillow as she sat up, forcing me to pull away despite only wanting to get closer. The sheet pooled in her lap, revealing the crimson bra she'd worn to sleep. She looked positively sinful in the tiny lace cups that barely came up high enough to cover her nipples. Nipples that hardened under my scrutiny.

"Stop staring at my tits, Caleb, and tell me why you broke into my room."

I dragged my eyes up to her light cerulean ones. "You can hardly call it a break-in when I literally opened the door," I said.

The corners of her plump lips pulled up into a bright smile as she let out a bark of laughter.

"Well, I guess I can't argue against my own line, huh?" she asked, amusement dancing in her eyes. The hate that usually painted her pretty face was missing, and hope skipped in my heart.

"Caleb?"

Her voice was breathy as I cupped her face gently, leaning in and pulling her bottom lip between mine. The wet plop it made when I released it was like a gunshot at the races, sending us into a frenzied make-out session, our lips and tongues devouring each other. She was everything I could ever want. Ever need.

The delicious burn of her hands pulling at my hair sent eclectic pulses straight to my cock as she broke away and sank her teeth into the tender flesh of my throat.

"What are you doing in here, Caleb?" she asked, laving at the spot she'd just nipped.

The words caught in my throat.

She leaned back at my hesitation, a frown pulling down her brows. There was no way for me to resist smoothing away the lines with my thumb and pressing a chaste kiss to her lips.

"I'm a dumbass, Scar. I've always held on to the belief that I couldn't love a woman because women can't handle this life. That I would lose someone again because of that." Her eyes widened when I said *love*, but I continued, choosing not to think too deeply about my word choice. "You've always been fierce and capable, and it fucked me up that the only woman who could soothe my fears shares the same last name with a man I hate. But I don't give a fuck what your last name is. You're fucking mine, and I'm yours, if you'll have me." I held my breath as I watched her, looking for a sign of what she was thinking.

She searched my face, gnawing on her bottom lip.

"Last name was," she replied, satisfaction shining in her eyes.

"What?"

Her soft hands cupped my jaw. "You don't care what my last name *was*. Because I'm now a Callahan."

I watched as she licked her lips, making my stomach clench.

Those words shattered my brain function, making me lose control until she was pinned below my body. My lips slammed onto hers. Her soft lips moved against mine, their sensual caress making me feel like I was drunk on my favorite whiskey. All the emotions we hadn't said aloud flowed between us with each kiss.

"I wanted to fuck you nice and slow, wife, but I don't think I can do that," I growled out, ripping off the rest of the sheet and groaning when I spotted the blood-red silk thong she wore. The one she'd let me fill with my cum.

"On all fours, wife. I want to eat this pussy from behind."

I chuckled darkly as she moaned out *fuck*, scrambling into the position I wanted her in. The globes of her ass had my cock rock hard. She yelped when my hand cracked across her perfect flesh before rubbing the sting away. Her body shook with anticipation as I pulled the silky fabric down her thighs, blowing cool air on her dripping pussy.

It was only by an act of God that I was able to resist leaning forward and burying my tongue inside, but I wanted her on fucking pins and needles.

"Don't you fucking move, Scar," I ordered, landing another hit to her ass cheek as I pulled out my phone and started music.

"Damn, Caleb. Pulling out all the stops."

"I want the first time your husband sinks his cock into that sinful pussy of yours to be a good one," I answered, pulling off my boxers. My erection bobbed and swayed as I moved toward her glistening pussy. "Look how fucking wet you are for me. Do you want me to fuck this tight cunt, wife?" I asked, brushing the head of my cock through her slit to her clit.

"Holy shit."

"That's not an answer, Scar." A loud crack sounded in the room, red blooming across her ass cheek. "Tell me," I demanded.

"Yes. I want you to fuck my tight cunt." She looked over her shoulder at me, defiance shining in her eyes. "Fuck me hard enough that it's your name I yell out. I have a few to choose from."

I swiped my hand across my face, attempting to hide my smile. I fucking loved that she gave me shit. Challenged me. It reminded me that she had the balls to survive this world. She could put any fucking man in his place. He'd probably thank her for stepping on his throat.

I would.

"Open these fucking legs wider," I demanded, slapping the inside of her thighs and pulling a yelp from her. I dove in, latching on to her pussy, swirling my tongue around her clit.

Her moan was so fucking sexy, and I smiled against her

flesh when my name fell from her mouth. The sound spurred me on, and I pulled her ass cheeks apart. I started at her clit and ran my tongue up to her asshole, ignoring the way she tensed as I swirled my tongue around it.

My head buzzed with lust as she pushed back ever so slightly. "My wife likes to have her asshole eaten," I teased, not waiting for her to answer as I pushed her chest flat onto the bed. "I can't wait another fucking moment, Scar. I need my cock buried in you now."

"Who's that asshole that prev—"

I drove so deep inside her that her quip ended in a strangled cry. Her pussy gripped my dick.

Fuck, it felt so good. I might never leave.

The next thrust was even deeper and harder, and her ass cheeks bounced with the impact. Our grunts and moans intertwined with the sensual sounds of the music I'd put on—skin slapping against skin.

I'd never felt more alive than when I was with her.

"We're so fucking good together, baby. This pussy was designed for me," I said, slamming into her so hard my balls bounced off her clit. "My. Fucking. Wife. *Say it.*"

She panted in pleasure, beads of sweat pulling at the small of her back as she met me stroke for stroke. "You're my fucking husband. I own you." She cried out. "Fuck, I love the way your balls slap my pussy," she said, reaching down and rubbing her clit, her pussy getting even wetter around my cock.

The dark goddess below me held me in a choke hold. There was no way I would survive without her. She was a drug in my veins.

Her breath and the pace of her fingers on her clit increased. She was getting closer. We both were. I picked up my tempo, my thighs burning with the exertion. Our cries rose to a crescendo.

"Fuck, I'm coming, Caleb," she panted out. I pumped

through the tightening of her pussy on my cock, watching as she writhed and pulsed on the bed, moaning my name.

My power over her body sent me over my own edge. My mind went blank with blinding pleasure as I emptied into her, coating her with my cum.

I collapsed on top of her, our slick bodies feverish.

"Holy fuck," she groaned, pushing me off, only to pounce on top of me and kiss up my throat until she reached my mouth. My tongue stroked hers, our heavy breaths mingling.

"You're ours," I whispered against her lips, and sleep pulled me under.

THIRTY-THREE

SCAR

WELL, THIS IS GOING TO BE AWKWARD.

THE ACHES at the back of my throat and pussy were not-so-subtle reminders of our night.

When we left for LaGuardia, expressions of confusion and surprise flickered through all three sets of eyes when I directed our driver to the private entrance and onto the tarmac.

Flying private made it less of a hassle to get the type of work equipment I used through security. There were fewer questions when you owned the jet and the pilots.

But these three had lots of questions for me, and my gut turned at the idea of revealing all of my secrets. There was such an electric connection between the four of us, that the thought of keeping things from them didn't sit right with me.

Especially after last night.

The air was charged as the other three found their seats next to me. I inhaled, holding the oxygen in my lungs, savoring the burning pressure of my body begging me to release the breath.

I might as well pull the pin on a grenade regarding the conversation we were about to have. Death was an expected outcome of my lifestyle. Explaining that I *wasn't* blood-related to Dominick *and* that I was a mercenary who was stockpiling money like a Cuban drug lord was never on my bingo card for life.

The leather squelched as I shifted uncomfortably.

Caleb had selected the seat directly across from me so he could stare into my soul like he was trying to consume me from the inside out. The green of his gaze held the same intensity as when I spit his arousal into his mouth. The same cum he'd instructed me not to swallow.

Technically, I'd followed orders.

Like the way you taste?

The question matched the one he'd asked me when he shoved my soaked thong in my mouth before the asshole sneered at me and told me that he wouldn't fuck a Romano pussy. Until last night, when something snapped between us, and we'd connected. The fucking felt more like a claiming, and my body hummed in approval.

Would the truth sting like a betrayal?

I let out an exhausted sigh, breaking the stare we'd been locked in while I played mental gymnastics over how the next few hours would go. It wasn't a short flight to Arizona. Sneaking out of the penthouse had crossed my mind for two seconds, but once I started looking into the information Ryan had asked about, it was clear this problem was much bigger than the West Coast. Turned out, once again, that Ryan's life and mine were colliding.

I couldn't shake the feeling that change was on the horizon and death was banging at the door of the men I loathed. I only hoped I would be allowed to hold the blade that severed their ties to the land of living.

The dulcet tones of the pilots giving their onboard speech finally ended, submerging the cabin in silence. Caleb's voice was tight, like the string of a bow that had been pulled taut.

"You own a private jet."

"That takes a lot of money to purchase and maintain, little

one. How is it that you can afford that?" Niko asked. The undercurrent of suspicion was like a knife to the gut.

I'd already made my choice when I didn't put bullets in their brains and slink off into the dead of night when they'd kidnapped me. Since then, they'd grown on me, and I didn't think I could do it now. So, it was time to grow some balls and rip off the proverbial Band-Aid. Where the fuck to start, though?

I decided to start with my parentage. It might make the rest of what I was dropping in their laps easier to digest. Or at least make them more willing to try.

"I'm not a Romano by blood or by choice."

A weight that had been pulling me down was suddenly gone. So few people knew the truth about my parentage, and I'd never revealed the Romanos' dirty secret. All the guys' bodies went rigid, their shoulders practically pinned to their ears.

"That's why Dominick attacked. At least, that's my theory. He took your dismissal of his daughter's hand in marriage as a personal slight. You might as well have spit in his face. But the slimy bastard is particular about the wording of deals…"

"And the alliance was for marrying Romano blood," Kenji stated, pulling his katana from his back like an attack was liable to happen while we were in the air. He ran a polishing cloth along the well-maintained blade, his face void of emotion.

Curses fell from both Caleb's and Niko's lips, their attention zoning out as they tried to process the news.

If they thought *that* was a lot to take in, how would they take the next bit of information? "I didn't know how the contract had been written until last night," I stated, tossing manila folders onto the marble table that partitioned the seats. "That's why Dominick agreed to you marrying me. He knew my bloodline was his loophole. It was an ace up his sleeve. A way of backstabbing you three without sullying his reputation."

Niko's head snapped to me, blue eyes darkening, looking like a swirling whirlpool. Chaotic and deadly. "Are you a spy for him?" The accusatory tone hurt as badly as a physical slap. As much as I understood why he'd feel that way, the idea of him being upset with me caused my palms to sweat and my stomach to turn.

"No. I mean, I'm sure at some point he would have recruited me for that task if he failed to kill you…and me. But I've been a pawn since conception," I answered.

"Explain. Now," Caleb ordered as he slammed his gun onto the table, the black a stark contrast to the white marble. A tattooed Y taunted me from where it rested on the trigger. A wildness was painted on his face, and I was acutely aware that he'd never truly shown me how deep his cruelty ran. Every interaction up until this moment had been Caleb showing me kindness.

Last night, he'd laid himself at my feet, and in his mind, this was all a confession to my untrustworthiness.

All three men were angled toward me, their weapons aimed and ready.

I rubbed at my chest and the growing pain where my heart was, but I stood by my decision to keep my secret until now. "If I'd betrayed you and thought you'd find out, I would have slit your throats already," I said, my tone cold and calm despite the heartache.

Niko's mouth went slack while Kenji cackled, the tension in his shoulders easing a bit. But Caleb was a statue, frozen in his position.

"Okay." I sighed. "My father was Anthony Russo. Years ago, an alliance was made between the Russos and the Romanos. Anthony was married to Giana, creating a union between the two most powerful Sicilian descendants' families. But he fucked up and stepped out on the bitch.

Although, I'd imagine that cunt is icy cold and probably eats dicks for fun."

In my periphery, I caught Kenji's physical shiver, and a smile crept up on my face despite the tension filling the cabin.

"Keep talking, Scarletta *Romano*."

I flinched at Caleb's slight. They could probably hear my molars cracking as I held back a retort. It wouldn't help my situation if I laid into him. Clearly, he needed more to thaw the icy wall he'd erected between us again. Fine, I'd blow the fucker to smithereens. But I had better get a good dicking down after I spilled all of my closest-held secrets.

"He raped a stripper. The woman who ended up birthing me." The guys at least had the decency to look uncomfortable.

"What was her name?" Niko asked cautiously, his eyes no longer meeting mine.

Saliva stuck in my throat, making it difficult to swallow down the emotion that clogged it. When I spoke, my words were barely above a whisper, and I looked at my hands as if they were the most interesting things in the world. I didn't feel shame or regret about most things, but this failure haunted me.

"I don't know her name."

The air shifted as if it were sentient—affected by our moods—moving from angry and charged to mournful.

Kenji's warm fingers gripped mine. "You're going to make yourself bleed," he commented, stopping me from picking at my abused cuticles.

"He didn't let you know your mother's name," Caleb said. The words were injected with understanding.

Tears collected along my lash line, threatening to run over the edge and paint my face with salty streaks of shame.

"It's why I taught myself to get good with computers and find information people didn't want out. But she was sold into the sex trade from Russia, and then Dominick got rid of *anything* that could have given me a clue as to who she was."

Niko piped up. "You're Russian?"

I let out a chuckle. I couldn't tell whether his tone was full of excitement or horror. "Don't worry, we aren't related. You can still fuck me." I winked, loving the pink tinge that bloomed on his neck. "All I was ever able to determine was that she was from Dagestan."

A sharp inhale of air came from Kenji. "That's why you know the fighters."

It wasn't a question. They were starting to see the criss-crossed lines that made up my life, and I was about to blow their fucking minds even more.

"Yeah. Magomed hired Cain to take out some asshole stealing children back in his home country. He's not allowed back there, so he needed—"

Caleb cut me off.

"Wait, *you* fucking know Cain? No one can get a hold of them. They're a fucking ghost. So how the fuck did you?" Understanding flashed in his eyes. His thick brows hit his hairline as he leaned forward on his powerful forearms. "You mean to fucking tell me that *you* are the infamous merc for hire?"

THIRTY-FOUR
NIKO

CAIN HAS A PUSSY?

SHE SHRUGGED HER SHOULDERS NONCHALANTLY, as if she were talking about the weather, not the fact that she was one of the criminal world's leading hits for hire. Her kill rate was perfect, probably because word was, she was extremely picky when it came to what jobs she'd take.

My mind whirled, connecting information so quickly that a dull thudding was beginning to form above my eyebrows. I kneaded the area with the pads of my fingers, shutting my eyes so I could reduce all the stimulation happening at this moment. Luckily the cabin lights were dim since we'd hit an early flight and the sounds of her and Caleb's *activities* had kept me up all night.

The fabric of my jeans was suddenly too tight in the crotch as images of my cock glistening with her saliva while she bobbed her head on my shaft threatened to shove what we'd just learned out of my mind.

Ironically, imagining her coated in the blood of another after she'd violently taken their life was equally hot. Cain had a reputation for being ruthless. She ran clean jobs in the sense that there was no evidence as to Cain's true identity, but there were rumors on more than one occasion of the chaos she left strewn in her wake.

It was why it was widely theorized that Cain had to be a man.

"Holy shit," Kenji commented, his eyes lit with excitement, making me chuckle. I knew she was perfect for us. When you had shitty things happen in your life and recognized that one more second on this floating rock wasn't guaranteed, you didn't question whether it was crazy to become infatuated with someone in such a short time. And Scar seemed to be a collage of all of our broken pieces.

Fragmented shards forged together to create something beautiful.

Perfectly imperfect.

"I honestly don't know why everyone assumes Cain is a man anyway. Has no one watched an episode of *Snapped*? Women are fucking ruthless; we push out humans we *grow*, for God's sake."

She huffed, drawing her legging-clad legs up into her chest and resting her chin on top. Her messy bun flopped to the side as she studied Caleb.

The only change in his body had been the shifting of his finger farther from the trigger. He was still holding out. It wasn't that he didn't believe her. It probably wasn't even that he didn't trust her. It was that he didn't know if he wanted to let her in again. There was a flash of vulnerability on his face, but it was gone as fast as it had appeared.

The pounding of my headache revived. Stubborn bastard.

"Okay, go on with your little explanation. What does that have to do with anything?" Caleb asked, his tone frosty and his eyes even colder.

"Dominick doesn't know about my other *occupation*. I don't think he cares enough to keep track of me. Enzo is my handler. He's the one who calls when they have jobs for me. All of them are strictly stealth heist gigs. Like stealing from the Russians." She unfolded her legs, tucking them once again under the table. Her demeanor changed to professional, guarded. The change showed how much she truly had brought down her walls for us in the time we'd been together.

Dainty fingers pushed the top folder forward.

"You've already met the man listed in that file. Turns out Maxim Petrov is the liaison for the Circle. I'm sure you know the Russians are heavily involved with them. But now—"

"Dominick is working with them too," Caleb filled in, flipping through the papers.

Her hair shook on top of her head, her bun flopping, as she affirmed his statement. "Here's where shit gets interesting."

"Oh, because it's not already interesting?" I asked.

She smirked at my comment but continued. "Ryan's little problem is connected. Mario, heir to *Los Muertos*?" She peeked up from where she was shuffling around paperwork in search of something, ensuring we were following. I gave her a slight nod to continue. We were well aware of the little shit stain from the West Coast. "Looks like Mario is trying to team up with Maxim too."

"Why?" Kenji piped up, thumbing at a few of the top papers—grainy photos showing Mario in some type of club auctioning off women. Bile rose in my throat at the sight.

Was that how my father had planned to sell my sisters before I'd intervened and we'd made our deal? The threat he held over me— how he kept them from me.

I pushed the thought out of my mind, focusing on the information Scar was laying out for us. My sisters were safe, and we were doing all we could to keep them that way.

"They've got a successful gun smuggling business. As much as it pisses me off to admit it, the prick is good at arms dealing," Caleb commented.

Scar laughed.

She laughed so hard she snorted, and her hands slapped

over her mouth, pink crawling up her neck. Not even Caleb could hold back a smile at the carefree reaction. She shifted in her seat, clearly a bit embarrassed but trying to play it off. You could drug her, kidnap her, shove your cock down her throat, but it was a snort that would make her uncomfortable.

"He doesn't do the smuggling."

"What do you mean?" Caleb asked. "*Los Muertos* has some of the best clean handguns money can buy. I order from them all the time."

"Majority of the East Coast orders are run through Tucson. *Ryan* is in charge of all operations there. *So*, if you don't believe me, ask about it when we get there."

The confidence in her posture had me second-guessing if we truly knew what we were talking about.

She tipped her head to all the evidence she had spread out across the table. It was an impressive spread of information she'd managed to get her hands on. I wanted to ask about it, but clearly, we had bigger problems to solve. Like why this Ryan person had contacted her.

"Sergio, for years, hasn't wanted anything to do with the skin trade. It's forbidden in his organization. He's good people. You know, for someone who sends the heads of his enemies to their homes in boxes, anyway. He either, one, changed his mind, or two, doesn't know that his little boy is a piece of shit." She ticked off the options on her fingers.

Kenji had been quiet during this time, busy searching through all the paperwork.

"This feels a little like we're on an episode of *Criminal Minds*," I said offhandedly, picking up a file and barely catching the eye roll Caleb gave me. He didn't say shit, though, because the ass loved that show too, and he didn't want me to reveal that we watched them together all the time. Sometimes their analyses hit a little too close to home, and I hoped they weren't spouting true psychology shit on there.

Kenji peeked over the folder.

"Okay, to recap—so I can start drinking—Scar is not blood-related to the Romanos, so our alliance is shit with them, and they already tried to kill us."

"Yup," Scar replied, popping the *P*.

"Dominick's also an idiot and hasn't realized that he literally created a killer who I'm sure is plotting his demise. You also loaded fake information on that file, and this Maxim asshole is who everyone is working for. Oh, and now we're traveling to Arizona because this Ryan person needs this information on Mario, who is *also* working for Maxim?"

With every word out of Kenji's mouth, Caleb's body tensed. But Scar relaxed, reverting back to her position of hugging her knees to her chest.

"And now we need to move up our timeline because Dominick is gunning for us," Caleb added, pinching the bridge of his nose.

"Yeah, that about covers this little session. Now, I could really use a martini and sleep," she said in a chipper tone.

THIRTY-FIVE
SCAR

HE'S CUTE.

"WHY THE FUCK are we going down an alley where it looks like people are regularly murdered?" Kenji asked, carefully traversing across some sketchy-looking debris.

"I suggest you don't touch anything." I pointed out some low-hanging fabric that covered the entrance to my safe house. The corners were coated in something brown that splintered out across the once-white cloth. The rigid edges acted more like cardboard than fabric. There was a fifty-fifty chance that the substance was blood. The distinct smell of urine wafted from puddles lining the worn brick walls.

"This place is disgusting, Scar. Tell us why the fuck we're here and where we're going," Caleb bit out, his agitation growing with each word.

I whirled around to face him. His thick brows popped up in surprise. Their dark color always made his eyes pop, but they stood out even more today since he wore a mossy-colored T-shirt and jeans. I'd never seen them all so casual. Well, other than Kenji, but he had a style all his own. The other two I'd only seen in suits or sweats. Both dangerous to my libido.

It turned out that everything they wore made me want to climb them like trees.

"Then go." I folded my arms across my chest, planting my feet just outside some suspicious goo. "I literally didn't invite you. You all just lorded over me when I told you I was going."

Warm flesh pressed against mine, sending chills down my spine. I had to tilt my head back to continue to glare at the Irishman.

"You think we're going to just leave you alone with *Ryan?*"

The other two boxed me in, staring down at me with sneers on their faces, but I got the impression that the irritation wasn't solely directed at me. Was I being childish by not pointing out that Ryan was a chick? Yeah, I was. But I didn't give a fuck. Men, honestly, caused so many problems in the world with their inflated egos and pissing contests. Served them right to dig themselves into a hole. And I was happy to hand them the shovel.

"Fine."

A buzzing went off on my computers, alerting me of someone approaching. I used to have the sensors way down at the end of the alley, but the damn thing would go off all the time. Now I only had one, and it was right outside the door.

I'd acquired this place a few years ago. There'd been a member of a local MC that would prey on women and men in this neighborhood. The Reapers, as a whole, were a bunch of pieces of shit. Ryan was constantly busy keeping them at bay. Her vigilante justice had started long before we met, but her reputation in Tucson as *La Brujita de Los Muertos* began the night she and I killed that asshole. She gained a nickname on the streets, and I garnered a reputation for not being fucked with. No one bothered my section of this alley. And there sure as hell were no more attacks unless I was holding the blade.

That night we'd been scoping out a good place for me to set up a safe house when a bloodcurdling yell rang out. It had reminded me of the yells I'd make when Dominick beat me before I learned it was better to stay quiet. He got bored faster.

The memory of that night was fragmented. Only flashes of my hands coated in sticky warm blood as his life seeped into the broken pavement remained. Ryan crouched over his limp figure, hissing through her teeth.

"Dile hola a diablo para mi."

"Say hello to the devil for me," I whispered, coming back to the present as I watched my friend step to the doorway and peek up at where she knew my camera would be. Interesting. She'd brought someone with her. A man, if his height and bulk were anything to go by. She must've trusted him if she brought him here. Last I knew, she hadn't even told Sergio about our friendship.

"They're here," I called out, pressing the button to let them into the inner chamber to be scanned. Niko's posture stiffened in the chair, his muscles bunched, ready to pounce. Kenji had taken up residence on my couch the moment we'd walked into the door. All three were relieved to find that the interior wasn't anything like the exterior.

"What is it doing?" Caleb asked, watching the feed, the heat of his body seeping through the cotton cami I wore. New York might be humid, but Arizona's heat was a bitch.

I crossed my arms over my chest, trying to resist the urge to reach down and interlock our fingers as I watched Ryan run her hands down the mystery man's arm after he grabbed her and shoved her behind him for protection, which was laughable really.

Hot breath hit the shell of my ear, startling me because I

hadn't realized I'd zoned out. "You'd hate it if I did that," Caleb stated, his tongue trailing along the sensitive skin before he buried his face in my neck. His trim facial hair sent shivers of pleasure rolling down my spine.

I steeled myself against the reaction, beating back the desire to melt back into his hard body. "What? Protect me?" The moment the question was out, I wished I could shove it back in. Why would I care if he protected me? Fingers roughly gripped my jaw, yanking my head to face him. He leveled a gaze in my direction, the look dripping with honesty. Whatever he was about to tell me, he believed.

"Exactly, little one. You don't want a white knight. You want someone whose soul is as twisted as your own." The thrum of my pulse spiked at the statement. He tipped his head toward the monitor, where Ryan and her man mirrored our position. Or maybe we mirrored theirs. Caleb cut the distance between our bodies in half. My breasts brushed the top ridges of his abs at the new proximity. "You don't want my protection. You want my loyalty. Our loyalty."

The world slowed to a standstill. His words seeped into my psyche and itched at a scratch I'd had since childhood. Because he was right.

"And do I have that? Your loyalty?" I asked, my heart stopping altogether as I waited for his response. Our time together had been short and rife with chaos. Yet it felt oddly perfect, because there was a pull between Caleb and me that was impossible to ignore. Two sides of the same coin. I trusted him because I felt I knew him intimately already. But did he feel the same way?

He opened his mouth to answer, but he never had the chance because the smooth metal door slid open—the scan was complete.

I broke the hold, rushing over to the opening. Thankfully, Caleb hadn't followed me over. Maybe he was afraid I'd insist he answer the interrupted question. My gut churned at the thought that he might not feel loyalty to me. Even with a farce of a marriage, it still stung. I held back a chuckle. I couldn't say I was only faithful to him, seeing as how I was fucking his brothers too. But I knew for sure that wasn't a problem for him. Shifting my line of thinking, I made sure to shut down the emotion on my face. Something I was doing less and less since being around the three men.

Whoever the guy was, he didn't look happy to be here. Knowing Ryan, she probably hadn't told him where she was taking him. Maybe the stiffness in his shoulders was because of that? But there was something in his posture that sent a tingle of apprehension running through me. My attention shifted to my friend, cocking my head as I made sure she wasn't here under duress.

"He's cute," I stated matter-of-factly, rolling my eyes at the growl Caleb let out from behind me. No doubt the other two would've made similar sounds of protest. Thankfully they were situated farther away from the door. I could already imagine the death glares this dude was about to get.

Okay, so fucking Kenji and Niko are cool. Calling a man cute was a problem.

It filled me with a sick sense of joy to know that Caleb didn't like me flirting with other men. Not that you could call my comment flirting. I sounded like I was announcing the time the way I'd said it.

"Come on, follow me. And ignore my pest problem. I keep trying to exterminate them, but they continue to come back like roaches. Or psycho criminals." I mumbled the last part as I led them into the space. The apartment looked like a fucking CB2 advertisement. For practical reasons, the floors were sealed concrete. Cleaning up blood would be a bitch on wood flooring, yet the unhinged portion of my brain had decided ordering a white sofa made sense. I'd literally held a blade to the underside of Kenji's chin when he jumped on it with his Doc Martens still on.

I barely caught the guy's whisper from behind me. "Why do I feel like she means literally when she says 'tried to exterminate'?"

"That's because I did mean literally," I replied. Several incidents flooded my mind, but I decided against giving examples. Until I got the information from the scans back on him, I didn't want him to know the relationship between the three guys and myself. He could be an agent or some shit. If he was, though, he'd be undercover, because Ryan wouldn't have shit to do with him. Whatever I found, I'd pass it on to her too. She'd want to know whose dick she was riding—because I *knew* she was riding that.

Curiosity was painted on her tanned face. Questions were burning on her tongue, and with her smart mouth, there was no way she would be able to hold them in.

"Bringing clients home, Scar? An interesting group here. We've got, what? Yakuza, Bratva, and...Irish Mob?" she asked, canting her head toward where Caleb stood, glaring. What was interesting was the way the guy with her stiffened at the mention of the Mob. His leather cut made it obvious he was an MC member, and his patch said sergeant at arms. Road name Gunner.

I'd thought maybe the reaction was because his girl was in a room full of criminals, but then he locked eyes with Caleb, and the tension in the room reached nuclear levels.

"How did you say you knew these people, Scarletta?"

The tension in my body from the stare-down evaporated, replaced by a burning inferno. The asshole was going to use my full name and a tone that suggested we were barely acquaintances?

Didn't you just say you didn't want the newbie to know your relationship with the guys?

My inner voice could go fuck herself. Right now, I wanted to storm over to him and be a bitch.

"I didn't say, Callahan. Because it's none of your fucking

business. Now, stand there quietly like a good boy. Maybe you'll get a reward." His eyes heated at the command. The push and pull for power between us was like a live wire, and I didn't think I'd ever tire of it. The ticking of his eyebrows told me that the reward he was going to get was teaching me a lesson. One that probably involved his cock down my throat or his fingers shoved in my cunt as he teased the release I would so desperately want. The images caused my nipples to pebble. It was completely the wrong time for such a reaction.

Frustration flooded my body, turning to anger at the irritating sneer he gave me.

"Okay, let's get down to business," I called out, turning away from him and moving toward the table that had stacks of papers and photographs spread out across the wooden top. Ryan and Gunner joined me, and my heart sank at the news I was about to share with my friend. Her heart was large, caring, where I was missing the organ entirely. A cold block of ice occupied where mine should be. She'd thawed it all those years ago, and now three more had seared their way into the glacial appendage.

She stiffened when she met my eyes. Damn, I hadn't been able to hide the pity quickly enough. Those coffee-colored eyes of hers drifted to the table. Her jaw clenched as she absorbed the glossy images. Images I'd wished I could've shielded her from. Although I never understood why she continued to have even an ounce of tolerance for Mario.

"How far does this go back?" Barely contained rage shook in her voice. Gunner pulled her into the crook of his body, his hand falling to her hip as he rubbed comforting circles.

"How did you get all of this?" he asked. Something in his tone struck me as off. It was a combination of horror and awe, but there was something *off*.

Instincts told me to keep the details vague. "I keep tabs on all of my clients. It's a good security measure to have dirty details on people for when they become..." I paused, searching for the right words so he'd understand my subtle threat. I didn't give a damn that he was hot or that he comforted Ryan during this hard time. If I found out he had bad intentions for her, I'd rain down hell. "Difficult to deal with."

"That strategy didn't go well for Epstein."

Kenji's comment caused me to pinch the bridge of my nose to keep from busting out in laughter. If Ryan saw I was comfortable around them, this visit would become a game of twenty questions, and I didn't want her MC friend to know anything about me. About us.

When I opened my eyes, I caught the grin that was pulling at the corners of Ryan's mouth. The twinkle of amusement only lasted a second, but it was there. "As I was trying to say, I keep tabs on all the people I work with or may work with. I've been watching *Los Muertos*, the Jimenez men in particular, for years. That's how I discovered that they had a fellow woman running shit in this toxic paradise that is the criminal world. But I've kept a closer eye on Mario since deciding I liked Ryan. I didn't care for the way he treated her," I explained, locking eyes with Ryan.

Fucking Mario was always coked out of his mind and claiming all the hard work that Ryan did. But that part didn't piss me off as much as the way he whored himself out, all while claiming Ryan was his property. *Muñeca—doll.* His nickname wasn't some cute show of affection. No, it was meant to prove she was nothing more than an object he owned. Sick obsession always lurked in his face when he was around Ryan. It made my skin crawl and every warning bell go off.

Ryan knew it was wrong too, but she figured she could outrun the problem. How ironic. I'd always felt that was a foolish move, yet until I met these men—hell, even at the start of this—I did the same thing. No more. Even if this all fell apart in the end, I'd at least enjoy the affection while it lasted. I shook off the emotion.

"Anyway, some of these go back years. But these," the glossy film stuck to my fingers as I plucked one from the pile, "these are what I could pull from the last few months. This picture was from earlier this month," I said, pushing it across the table.

Her body wrenched forward. Betrayal hit her like a physical blow, and her body reacted. Her skin took on a pale green tinge, a stark difference from the normally tanned flesh.

"Fuck. Can we keep these?" Gunner piped up, drawing my attention. He studied another pile of photos, those being from about two years prior.

Why does he want old photos?

"Of course you can. I have my copies." The words came out harsher than intended as I watched the way the photo shook in Ryan's hand. Emotions rotated across her face, the revelation putting her through a whole spectrum of feelings.

"He's selling skin."

Her anger hung in the air, pressing down on the room uncomfortably before it just shut off. It was a trait we shared, the packing away of emotions so we could handle the task at hand. The skill was a blessing. Some would say it was a curse as well, but you'd have to live long enough to finally face the damage.

My feet shuffled uncomfortably, not ready to inform her of how long her fucked-up frenemy had been selling women.

"Looks like he's been doing it for months. He's trying to get the attention of the Circle. Nasty bunch of assholes, let me tell ya," Caleb commented, beating me to it. We locked eyes, and I swore I saw understanding in those green orbs. He told her so I wouldn't have to. His attention was short-lived, then it swiveled back to Gunner. He'd been watching him ever since he'd stepped into the space. Caleb's body language might be locked up tight, but I'd been around him long enough to pick up on tells. He didn't trust the MC member.

I added to his statement. "Mario will never get it. He's got too many eyes from law enforcement agencies looking at him, but no one's been able to pin him for shit." A dry chuckle left my lips. Fucking FBI didn't do shit, and so fucking many of them were in bed with criminals. Their hands were just as dirty as ours. More so, even, since they were supposed to stand for *justice.* Justice was a farce and better off doled out by your own hand. At least when dirty agents were involved. "If only they would be willing to break a few rules, he would've been taken care of months ago. I mean, look at all the shit I found."

Caleb walked over as I fanned my arm out over the piles and piles of paperwork on Mario and his little gang of scum. The table hid how his hand brushed the side of my thigh as he made his way toward my ass. Ryan and Gunner were too distracted by how he plucked the photo out of the biker's grasp to notice how he slapped my ass. He timed his comment perfectly so that the rumble of his voice concealed the sound of his palm striking my ass. It was soft for Caleb, only hard enough to give a delicious taste of what his hands could do.

"They would never do that. Citizens would freak out if they thought government agencies were spying on them." He laughed at the irony.

We'd decided before they arrived that it would be better if they all stayed low-key. Caleb clearly hadn't included himself in that restriction, but Kenji and Niko were doing their best to sink into the background.

Until now. For the first time since the two arrived, Kenji piped up. "Snowden tried to tell them, and look what happened to him. People don't want to know how trackable and hackable their shit is. Buncha sheep."

He wasn't wrong. I regularly pulled information normal people thought was tucked safely behind their passwords. It was always the name of their first child and their birth year.

Their security was so flimsy that even a government employee would be able to hack in.

"It's why we end up cleaning up this kinda shit," Caleb said, studying Gunner like a puzzle he was trying to solve. Now I was positive I wasn't the only one whose *sketchy shit is happening here* meter was going off. But this was Ryan's man, and I wasn't going to interfere with whatever was happening. She was capable enough to take care of herself.

Her explosion kicked me out of my thoughts. "Fuck the police or the FBI or whoever the fuck it is who's failing at their job." Gunner seemed to flinch at her words, and Caleb zeroed in on the movement like a hawk. Ryan was so upset that she didn't see the suspicious glances at her man. Or maybe she assumed the uneasy expressions on our faces were for an entirely different reason.

"I'm going to kill Mario since they won't. Where is he now? And where the fuck is Sergio in all of this? Why set up the deal with the Skeletons of Society to let all this other shit go down?" she asked, throwing her hands up in frustration while Gunner inspected more of the photographs. He consumed them greedily, his eyes bouncing from one glossy photo to another, reminding me of a kid in a candy shop lusting over the candies he wouldn't be allowed to take home.

Why was he so interested in the older evidence?

THIRTY-SIX

CALEB

AN ARMS DEALER AND A SKETCHY DUDE WALK INTO A SAFE ROOM...

I WAS skeptical when Scar first claimed to be Cain. It was evident she was lethal. I'd known that from the first time we met. When she shoved the barrel of a gun against my junk and threatened to pull the trigger, her hand was steady. Not a single nervous tremor ran through her when she'd crouched at my feet, peering up at me through thick black lashes. Glacial eyes had consumed me as she bossed me around. Then she'd disappeared. Tied me up, leaped out a window, and let the city welcome her into her crowded streets.

I was hooked from that very moment.

Niko wasn't the only one who'd become obsessed with her, it was just that my obsession began as hate, a fight against the overwhelming need to fall into her embrace.

Now we stood in her safe house in Tucson, giving over information to the arms dealer for *Los Muertos* and her sketchy man, whom I was convinced was lying about who he really was. His posture was too tight, and he was too much of a gentleman to be a one-percenter. Ryan probably hadn't noticed because of what a shithead Mario was. The Gunner guy was probably a welcome change.

Scar went over all the information with us before these

two arrived. As soon as it was clear Ryan's favor was intertwined with what was happening in our city, she showed us all she'd dug up. Her capabilities were impressive. She'd really taught herself to be a one-woman show.

The noose around my heart loosened when she did things that proved how capable she was. I needed that reassurance. What happened with Jessica haunted my thoughts and kept me from caring for another woman.

Then Scar came crashing in, constantly proving she didn't need protection.

My attention moved back to Gunner, not wanting to think too much about the growing feelings I was having for Scar.

Something about him felt so familiar.

I roved over his face again, taking in green eyes that matched my own and his impressive mustache.

If he didn't have that, he'd almost look like…

Ice flooded my veins as the pieces clicked together. I did know who this fucker was, and he wasn't a biker. Or he hadn't been when he was in New York making his rounds in the Irish fight rings.

He wasn't looking at me at the moment. He was too consumed by what was on the table, information he hadn't been able to get his greedy hands on because he was shackled by rules, unlike my wife.

I jolted at that thought, my hand tightening where it rested on Scar's ass cheek. That was the first time that I'd *thought of* the word wife. I'd said it, mainly to needle her, but that…that admission hadn't been said aloud.

"Unless Sergio doesn't know about any of this," Gunner spoke up, snatching up another piece of paper. This one was a wire transfer transaction. But the fucker was trying to figure out how to work the system so that this shit would be admissible in court.

"Then where the fuck is he? He hasn't answered any of my messages in days. If he wasn't a part of this, why is he avoiding me?" Ryan asked, pulling my gaze to her. Clearly, she was frustrated by the lack of information as to where her pseudo-dad was.

For years, there'd been the rumble about a girl Mario had brought home like a fucking puppy, forcing his dad to bring her into the family. I'd met Sergio more than once when he'd come to meet with my da and my brother. I liked the fucker. He was a take-no-shit straight-shooter. Mario, on the other hand, was a twisted fucker. "You're the *Los Muertos* arms dealer," I stated, looking over toward Scar. Her cheeks heated under my scrutiny. I resisted the urge to smile at her look of guilt. "So, Ryan doesn't have a dick," I stated, my eyebrow hitting my hairline as I directed the comment at my lovely wife. She knew her lie would lead to a fight between us later tonight, and I had a sneaking suspicion that she'd told the lie for that reason.

I never knew Sergio had made her a part of the cartel. It wasn't common for women to be in the underworld in any other capacity than lying on their backs. Yet here I was in a room with two highly skilled women who not only worked in the criminal world but were dominant in their areas. It was a shame they had to operate under the guise of being men so they would be respected in the ways they deserved.

A chuckle came from Gunner. "No, she doesn't, but you're just finding that out, huh?"

I didn't bother acknowledging him. Instead I gave a nod of agreement to Ryan as I stared her down, trying to decide whether she knew Gunner's true identity. Because if she'd brought a fed into Scar's space to nail her to the wall, she would have problems. I didn't give a shit how much Scar cared about the arms dealer; if Ryan was trying to hurt our girl, I'd strike her down with zero leniency.

But her coffee-colored eyes held nothing but an inferno of rage for the information she'd just learned about Mario and the mess happening in her house under her nose. Whatever

Gunner had done up to this point, it had been convincing, because this woman had no clue she was brushing shoulders with an FBI agent.

Turning, I headed out of the room before I said more than I meant to in front of the two. I needed to confirm my suspicion before I blurted something like that out.

I palmed my phone, dialing a number I hadn't called in months. Anxiety crept up my spine at the fourth ring. Had something happened to him?

"What the hell, man? You know you're not supposed to call me. Are you trying to fuck everything up?" he asked, his thick Irish accent making him sound even angrier than he probably was.

"That the way you speak to your favorite brother?" I asked, a smile pulling at my lips at his huff of frustration. "Listen, Rowan, do you still have that picture of the boxing championship? From three years ago?" I asked.

"The one where I lost to that cunt fucker who ended up being the goddamned law?" Bitterness seeped into the question, making me chuckle. Yup, he hadn't let that go yet.

"Yeah, that would be the one. What was his name again?" I asked, plopping down on a stool at the kitchen island and running my fingers along the cool marble. The neighborhood might be shit, but damn if her apartment wasn't nice. Light colors and lighting made up for the fact that the hideout didn't have any windows to let in natural light. She did have skylights that mimicked can lights, though. They were too small for a body to drop down, and apparently, the glass was bulletproof.

Rowan's gruff rumble refocused me. "Greyson McGregor. Our own fuckin' kin betrayed us." He paused, clearly busy doing something. "It's sent. Why the hell would you risk calling me over this shit?"

A ding indicated the photo had come through, but I didn't risk putting him on speaker so I could look at it. I'd have to wait until we hung up, which would have to be soon if we wanted to keep up the ruse that we hated one another. "I'll tell you when I know more, but I might have just run into the asshole again."

My blood brother practically growled on the other end of the line. "Put a fucking bullet in his brain for me. Not only was he the law, but he fucked up my win streak."

"What win streak, Rowan? I beat you every single time we fought," I reminded him. Warmth swam in my veins as I imagined his face and how he would wave his hand in dismissal. Losses to me didn't count in his eyes.

As if on cue, he responded. "Doesn't count. You know that. Now be careful, and don't fucking call me again, asshole. If Da catches us, then all of this will be for nothing."

I let out a sigh, dropping my head into my hand, suddenly tired. "It's time, Rowan. We have to start making our moves now," I responded, dread and excitement churning in my gut. "I'll see you soon, brother."

Silence.

Then finally, "I can't wait. Will I get to meet that wife of yours? Or is she going away too? You created quite the stir when you denied Dominick's offer of his daughter." There were a million unspoken words in that statement. The words were pleasant, but I heard the irritation under the surface.

Why the fuck didn't you marry his daughter? That was the plan.

I caught myself smiling at the thought of Scar. "You'll get to meet my wife. Make sure you keep your dick in your pants when you meet her, though."

He chuckled, the tension leeching from his voice. "Holy shit. You took a woman hostage, and now you're all in love with her." My back stiffened at the comment. "Knowing how you three work, she's got her hands *full* of dicks. And a mouth if my assumptions are correct," he stated with no judgment in his tone.

He knew the three of us would share women on occasion. The idea of there being a woman that we could all be in a relationship with had been put on hold for years, but Scar seemed to be changing that. Somehow, she'd clawed her way in.

"Okay, I really have to go now before we get caught. I'll be ready when you need me, brother," he answered before the line went dead.

I pulled up the text message with the photo. Staring back at me was one *Gunner*—sans mustache—standing next to me and holding his silver medal.

"First loser and federal scum," I whispered. I'd bet all my money that Greyson McGregor hadn't turned over a new leaf to become a one-percenter. Pushing off the stool, I marched back into the living room space, determined to expose the fucker, but I stopped cold at seeing Scar wiping a tear from her cheek. Red was all I saw. Who the hell upset her?

My feet carried me across the room before I could think through the consequences of embracing her. That move would tip Ryan and Gunner off to our relationship. At the last second, I forced myself to resist wrapping my arms around her and drawing her into my chest. The moment the asshole left, I'd hold her.

THIRTY-SEVEN
SCAR
WELL...SHIT

STRONG ARMS WRAPPED me in a vise grip the second Ryan and Gunner disappeared back down the alley. Caleb's firm chest warmed the side of my face as he pressed me into it. Cedar and soap invaded my senses. His scent comforted me in a way I didn't want to examine. His fingers tipped my chin so that we were staring into one another's eyes.

"What did he say to make you cry?" he asked.

My brows furrowed in confusion at the menace in his tone. Why was he so upset? I pulled back, putting space between our bodies.

"Are you pissed that I was crying? I'm sorry that I'm not always an unfeeling bitch," I said hotly, pissed that he'd caught my moment of weakness. Apparently, a crying Ryan triggered my own feelings.

His lush lips pulled down at the corners, his eyebrows mimicking the movement. Embarrassment heated my cheeks at my outburst, because the confusion on his face made it clear that he wasn't upset because of that.

Rough fingers tucked a stray hair behind my ear. "That's not why I am upset, Scar. I want to know what that ass said to you that made you cry. Did he comment that you were wrong for this lifestyle?" he asked, tone soft. Caring.

"Like being with all three of you?" The question slipped out before I could stop it. And the minute it was out, I wanted to shove the words back into my mouth. It sounded like I was insinuating that all four of us were in some type of relationship.

And we weren't. Were we?

"Stop whatever doubt is running through that brilliant mind of yours. That's not the lifestyle I was referring to. But yes, Scar, you are ours. As in all three of us." The words rang true, sending warmth pooling in my center.

"But back to that asshole. Did he make you feel guilty?" Caleb pressed.

"No, not guilty." I paused, chewing on my bottom lip, wondering whether I should bring up the fact that Gunner *had* made me feel suspicious. "Something about him feels… off."

A squeal slipped when Caleb hauled me up into his arms. Large palms gripped each of my ass cheeks as he dragged me up his front. A jolt of pleasure shot through my core as my pussy brushed over his bulge. The man was fucking hung even when not hard.

My head swam, and my body acted on instinct, my legs instantly wrapping around his middle while my arms circled his neck.

"Stop moaning like that, Scar," he gritted through his teeth. "We need to have a talk, and I'm not going to be able to concentrate if all I can think about is sinking into that warm, messy cunt of yours." He pulled my lobe into his mouth, laving it with his tongue.

Because *that* was going to help calm my libido. It was taking all my willpower not to writhe against the hardened peaks of his abdomen. Although I didn't really have to, because they were rubbing against my clit with each step he took as he carried me toward the couch Kenji was sprawled out across.

Kenji let out a grunt as Caleb deposited me on top of him.

"Hold her for me because I'm two seconds away from fucking her against the closest surface, but I have shit I need to say." Caleb huffed as he adjusted his cock. "Not helping, Scar. Stop staring at my dick like you're going to devour it." His words were gruff, but the undercurrent of desire was clear. It wouldn't take much to push him over the edge.

He must have seen my intentions on my face because he turned his back on me, walking as far away as possible while still within hearing range.

Niko laughed. The man had been uptight the entire time Ryan and Gunner had been around, sitting like an unmovable statue. "We'll fuck you after Caleb tells us what he needs to," Niko said, lounging back in the chair, finally able to relax.

We all turned our attention to Caleb, whose large hand ran over his handsome face. Worry lines crinkled at the corners of his eyes, setting off warning bells in my head. Kenji had the same impression because he lifted me off his lap and sat up.

"Our timeline is being pushed forward now that we know Maxim is involved with Mario. When we get back, we have to take him out. Rowan is already aware," Caleb stated.

"There's no way that Ryan is going to let that stand. She can take Maxim out for us when she takes out Mario," I stated.

The sigh that Caleb let out had me on edge. He knew something I didn't.

"She might want to, but I doubt she'll be able to kill anyone. Even Mario," he admitted, clearly conflicted. "That guy she's with isn't a one-percenter. He's playing one. His name is Greyson McGregor, and he's undercover FBI."

He was telling the truth. I could feel the rightness in my soul. All the little clues clicked together.

"Fuck," I whispered, looking up to meet Caleb's gaze. "He

must have done *something* to convince Ryan otherwise, because she's a smart bitch. There's no fucking way she would bring him here if she had any clue about who he really was."

Shit. Would he arrest her too?

Because there was no way she hadn't already stabbed someone in front of him. She was not a patient person.

Kenji piped up from beside me. "You think the FBI is in on it with Maxim?" he asked. My blood froze in my veins and my heart rate picked up. Sweat beaded up along my hairline at the thought of what this would mean for my friend.

Caleb's eyes locked on mine, the color of a dense forest.

"I'm sure they're in on it, but I don't know if McGregor is. He was pretty straitlaced the last time we met."

What the hell was he talking about? They'd met before today?

I opened my mouth to ask him as much, but he halted me.

"I didn't know for sure until I called my brother when I stepped away," he confessed. His words seemed to suck the air out of the room for the other two. Both leaned forward, concern marring their faces.

Niko practically growled out his question. "Rowan? You called Rowan over that?" he bit out. I tensed at the anger in his tone.

Caleb plopped down in a chair, slinging his arm over the back, his face turning to stone. "Yes, I called him. 'Cause that FBI agent was in New York three years ago, and now he's here going after Mario and Maxim. And all this shit is linked to New York."

"So we strike before everything unravels," Kenji finished. The three of them spoke as one, but I was fucking lost.

"Wait, wait, wait." I held up my hands. "Someone tell me what the fuck is going on. Your brother Rowan? As in the heir to the Irish Mob, Rowan?" Caleb nodded his head in confirmation. "I thought you two hated each other," I said.

A conniving smile smeared his face. "That was by design,"

he said. "We wanted everyone to think we hated each other. Then no one would suspect the two of us were working against our dad."

I dug my palms into my eyes to quell the pounding behind them. "Okay. Someone explain everything to me. From the beginning."

Niko chuckled, his elbows coming to rest on his knees. "We're good, but there's no way we can take over New York on our own. We aren't getting rid of the Four Families altogether, just the current assholes running them. So Rowan and Caleb have spent years convincing their dad that they hate each other."

My eyes bounced to Caleb and then to Kenji. "So are you working with your brother too?" I asked him tentatively.

"Hell no. We're going to gut my family." He pointed the finger at Niko. "His too."

"And you're going to burn Dominick's empire to the fucking ground," Caleb stated, stunning me into silence. "But first, we have a murder to plan." A vicious sneer streaked across his face, violence and danger lurking under the surface of his skin.

For once, I felt at home.

"Dominick is going to kill Maxim Petrov," I said, lifting my head and sending waves of brunette flying backward. "We're going to frame it as Dominick killing Maxim. And then we kill Dominick."

"Oh, is that all?" Caleb mocked, rolling his eyes and taking a gulp of his whiskey.

My jaw ticked. Fighting was foreplay for us. I didn't think there'd ever be a time when we weren't at each other's throats —followed by being in each other's pants. But damn if he wasn't annoying at times.

"Wait, that really is your plan?" he asked, dumbfounded. I resisted punching the fucker. He was a real ass when he wanted to be. Which was essentially always.

"Okay. Let me explain to you how this is going to work." My voice was quiet but deadly. "Maxim is highly egotistical. He likes to think he's big and bad on his own. I looked him up when I saw the pictures of him and Mario together. We can get him to dismiss his security if we stroke his ego the right way."

"And how do you suggest we do that?" Caleb asked, with noticeably less attitude this time.

THIRTY-EIGHT
SCAR

I'D SPENT hours prepping for this damn job.

Holed up in the apartment, figuring out what made Mr. Petrov tick. Turned out my boy Maxim loved to play with things that weren't his. Rich men were usually entitled assholes. Conveniently, I was a married woman who'd already caught his attention.

"Miss, your stop."

I'd gotten so lost in my thoughts that I hadn't realized we'd arrived. I took in the bricked building we were pulled in front of. An onyx canopy with scalloped edges sheltered the iron door of my destination. The heady scent of sauteed garlic wafted into the cab, making my mouth water. I barely got the fifty-dollar bill into the driver's hand before he pulled away, profusely spouting out his thanks. He was probably nervous I'd change my mind on the tip.

The last minutes of daylight caressed my bare shoulders. The silk chemise dipped low in the front, showing off the cleavage I'd dumped a shit ton of shimmer powder on. My entire outfit looked like I was presenting myself as a present. The wide-legged suit pants I wore flattered my ass, but the price I paid was that they'd need to be cut off me after this meal. Caleb wouldn't have an issue with that request, though he *would* hate that I encouraged Maxim to eye fuck my tits. But we needed the whole mood to be set for tonight if we were going to pull this shit off. So unless he was going to let Maxim grab his ass, he could shove it.

Cold metal cooled my clammy hands as I pulled open the door, sunlight glinting against the gold letters. *Morte—Food to Die For.*

I didn't want to admit it, but I loved the play on the name —an Italian restaurant run by the Mafia that catered to the wealthy and morally corrupt. Brilliant. Many had died inside these textured walls, but it wasn't from the food. It was deceivingly inviting with its low lighting and intimate setting. The clicking of my heels sounded against the dark wooden flooring, mixing with the smooth jazz playing over the speakers. The place was empty for weekend dinner service, and there was only a skeleton crew working tonight. I hoped Maxim didn't question that. If he did, I was planning on telling him we'd rented out the space for him. His ego would love it.

By design, the place was long and narrow. The front half was a normal restaurant, though it was almost impossible to get into without an invitation, but the back room was where important business was conducted. You had to know about the hidden dining room since it was walled off and soundproofed. And it was where tonight's job was going down. I pushed through the large double doors made to look like the entrance to a wine cellar, which was pretty spot-on. A large table draped in a white cloth, the top dotted with tea light candles, sat in the far corner of the space. I grimaced slightly at how pristine it looked, knowing tonight's plan would ruin that.

"Can I get a martini, extra dry? Thanks," I called out to one of the hired waiters, taking the opportunity to scan the room. I'd been here a few times with Dominick and Enzo, but never at this table. Usually, it was *me* playing waitress. The alcohol burned my throat, centering my focus while loosening my limbs. My body tingled as fabric brushed my bare back. Hot breath caressed the shell of my ear, and I melted into the chiseled chest.

"What the hell are you wearing? Did you seriously come in lingerie and pants?"

"Evening to you too, husband." I turned to look at the man growling at me, realizing how close his face was to mine. Our lips were only inches apart. I loved the small scar marring his upper lip. The minor imperfections made him hotter. When I glanced back at his eyes, his gaze burned with lust.

"I'm here to do the job you *hired* me for, Caleb. Now, are you capable of keeping your dick in your pants for a night to get this done?" I dragged the tips of my fingers down the center of his black dress shirt, pulling away right before they made it to his growing bulge. "And since you must not see women out of their clothes often, this is a chemise. My lingerie has far less fabric to it," I called over my shoulder, as I walked away, winking at the waiter, who choked at my words.

"Keep your eyes away from her ass or I'll cut them out," Caleb growled, stomping away from me to wait for our guest. If he were any more aggressive with his steps, he'd have the plates bouncing off the tables.

Of course professions of violence turned me on.

I ignored the inconvenience of a soaked thong and focused on the man who appeared in front of me.

"Niko, have I ever told you that you're my favorite?" I asked, dropping into the wooden chair he had pulled out. Tonight's seating arrangements were carefully orchestrated. Head of the table was Dominick's supposed seat. To his right was Caleb's, then mine, and the boys'. Maxim had the seat of honor to Dominick's left, a position with the best line of sight to the door.

Let him have a false sense of protection.

"You tell me every time I have my tongue buried in that pussy of yours," Niko whispered in my ear, causing an eruption of goose bumps along the back of my neck.

"Psh. I bet I eat her pussy way better than you do. She's just saying that so you keep cooking for her," Kenji said, seeming to pop up out of nowhere. He slipped into the chair next to me, stealing it from the Russian giant still at my back. His lips were cold, probably having come from the walk-in freezer in the kitchen.

"Who'd you stuff in the freezer, Kenji?" I asked against his lips, my tone playfully chastising.

Niko scoffed, taking his seat and mumbling about being stuck with bloodthirsty degenerates.

Kenji pulled back, taking my bottom lip with him, releasing it with a pop as he wiggled his eyebrows. The movement drew my attention to a smattering of blood he'd managed to miss when he'd cleaned up before joining us. Luckily Maxim wasn't here yet to witness me wiping it from Kenji's hairline.

"One of Dominick's boys was sniffing around. Guess he's got a waitress he likes to bang. Didn't want him to talk about this secret meeting of ours."

I was about to comment when my phone buzzed in warning. Kenji's playful demeanor melted away and was replaced by that of the silent killer that had grown men shitting their pants. "Showtime, boys. Don't miss me too much," I said, pushing out of my seat to make my way back into the main section of the restaurant where Caleb and Maxim were.

I slowed my pace when I spotted the Russian billionaire, giving myself time to assess him. He was a woman's wet dream personified. Blond hair meant to look effortlessly messy, a fit, trim body that he probably pointed out every second he could, and a panty-melting smile with teeth so white Crest should hire him. He was the definition of poison wrapped up in a pretty present. But all the abs and money in the world couldn't make up for how fucked up he was when it came to how he treated people.

My heeled feet carried me toward his bodyguards. Nausea crept up my throat as I reached a hand out to the billionaire sex trafficker. The thought of him touching me made me want to vomit all over his Gucci loafers, but I pushed the reaction down.

"Mr. Petrov. Nice to see you again," I said, my tone light and sweet.

A large hand wrapped around my bicep in a bruising grip, and I cut a glare to the bodyguard.

"I suggest moving your hand. And next time, get some fucking consent," I sneered at the man lording over me, his bald head practically glowing under the lights. Based on the direction his nose was shifted, I'd guess the ogre had been in his share of fights, and I wasn't sure if they made him uglier or better looking.

"Feisty little one, aren't you?" Maxim said, placing a placating hand on his bodyguard before extending his other toward me. Over his shoulder, I caught the rapid rise and fall of Caleb's chest and the daggers he shot at the meathead who'd put his hands on me.

I willed Caleb to keep his reaction under wraps. Tonight, he was supposed to treat me the way Maxim treated women. Like property. Nothing more than a hole to fuck or skin to sell. And I had to be the submissive wife, ready to suck a cock on command.

Otherwise, the bodyguard would have been missing a limb for touching me the way he had.

"Caleb, this wife of yours truly is a beauty. I can see why you chose her," Maxim commented.

God, I love being talked about like I'm not in the fucking room.

Bile coated my tongue at the sight of Maxim's smile. It was too wide for his face, predatorial in a way that turned my stomach. Mario's face flashed in my mind. I'd always felt the same way about him too. It was no wonder these two fuckers had teamed up.

I'd been so lost in thought that I didn't catch Caleb moving until his fingers bit into my waist as he pulled me flush to his side. A silent declaration of ownership. One that, a few short weeks ago, I'd have stabbed him in the groin for. Now I relished his possessiveness because I knew it ran both ways. I'd still stab him if he pissed me off, just somewhere that wouldn't hinder his ability to drive his cock into me.

"She's definitely a catch. We're working on her sass outside of the bedroom," Caleb commented.

I wrapped my arm around his back, gazing at him like a doting wife while pinching the skin above his ass cheeks as hard as possible. Fuck him and his taut body. It would've hurt more if he had some fat to grab on to. Caleb's jaw ticked at my assault, both of us fighting to keep on the proverbial masks we wore tonight.

Maxim's contemplative hum had me turning my attention back to him. "Is that what you do, Scarletta? You're a house-wife?" he asked, amber eyes locking on to the slight movement of Caleb's thumb brushing along the curve of my breast, heating with lust and envy. Tingles ran up my spine when Maxim pulled my hand to his lips, but they had nothing to do with attraction. My instinct screamed that danger was near, but my entire life had been spent living in danger and learning to take the fucking hearts of those who tried to make an enemy of me. Maxim would be another name on my list.

The billionaire paused at the smile I gave him.

Shit. Too much deranged killer in that one.

His own subconscious probably picked up on the shift in energy.

"Shall we sit at our table while we wait for Dominick?"

Caleb asked, using his hand to direct me back to the others while keeping his body between Maxim and me.

"Oh, he didn't tell you? He won't be meeting with us tonight. He said it would be a good opportunity for us to get acquainted," Maxim said from behind me.

Thank God my back was to the men, because there was no hiding the bloodthirsty smile that pulled at my lips. Hacking text messages was such a handy skill. Made it much easier to plan dinner murders.

THIRTY-NINE
CALEB

SPIT IN MY MOUTH

SHE WAS BRILLIANT.

Her ability to morph into any role was a wonder to watch work. She'd clocked Maxim from a mile away. The prick wanted things that weren't his, and tonight it was her. The entire night, she'd been playing him, a perfectly timed comment here, a sensual smile there. Every time she leaned forward, her shirt dipped low, giving him an eyeful of her cleavage, but not enough to show the pert nipples I knew were hidden under the silk.

Crescent-shaped marks were probably permanently indented in my palms because, as much as I loved the view, I wanted to carve out Maxim's eyes for every look he took. Smug bastard didn't bother to hide that he was ogling another man's wife.

"Boys, should we retire to the lounge for an after-dinner drink?" Scar asked, slurring her words as if she were drunk. She trailed a finger down my chest, eyeing me like she'd like to ride my cock right here. That part wasn't an act. We'd been caressing each other all night, and my dick was about to burst out of my pants. Knowing what we were about to do to Maxim just made it harder.

"Are you going to join us, Maxim?" she asked, resting her head on my shoulder, her hair fanning across my chest, reminding me of how she looked when I fucked her. "We have so much *fun* in there together." She leaned forward, crooking her finger in a come hither motion, and Maxim complied without question.

I glanced toward his bodyguards. Their postures relaxed about thirty minutes into the dinner, which had been filled with false laughter and superficial topics. But it had served its purpose, making them drop their shields.

"There aren't any cameras in there," she whispered.

His tongue swiped across his bottom lip at the wink she gave him, and fury raged in my veins. Kenji's whole body was rigid, and he'd been uncharacteristically quiet the entire time. Niko was always the silent one, adding a comment here and there, but tonight he'd been chatty. Entertaining Maxim on talks of St. Petersburg and the Bratva. "I'd love to join you, love," Maxim answered before addressing the two goons at his back. "You two stay here. Order yourselves something."

A smile threatened to creep up on my face, but I bit it back.

The lounge was a smoking parlor, dark and intimate. Wood paneling covered every inch of the space, low lighting shedding only enough light to see the person seated in the leather club chair across from you. And Scar had been correct. This room didn't have cameras or mics, and it was soundproof.

I sat down in the tufted chair, pulling Scar into my lap. Hooking my ankles around hers, I pulled her legs apart, my thumbs coming to rest in the crease of her thighs. She stiffened for a split second before melting into the touch. Putty in my hands.

I tugged on her lobe with my teeth, savoring the hitch in her breath. "Your pussy is radiating heat, wife. How fucking wet are you right now knowing what you're about to do?"

She ground her ass against my cock, not bothering to be subtle about her movements.

"She is quite the specimen, Caleb. Have you considered sharing her?" Maxim asked, practically drooling over the show he was getting. His slimy voice itched at my skin, and my grip tightened on Scar.

"Scar honey, why don't you get us some drinks?" I asked, locking eyes with Maxim as I ran my tongue up the column of her throat, lapping up the salty flavor of her skin.

She rose obediently, and the loud snap of my hand slapping her ass echoed in the small space. Her head flicked toward me so quickly that I was surprised she didn't crack her neck. I choked down my laugh before she added me to her list of people she was killing tonight.

"Drink of choice tonight, gentlemen?" she asked as she sauntered over to the drink cart, adding an extra sway to her hips. She looked at Maxim expectantly, a perfectly manicured eyebrow quirked.

"Let's do tequila. That's the kick I've been on lately. A new business partner of mine has a club in Tucson that serves the best tequila," he responded.

The hairs on the back of my neck stood on end. Was his attention on Scar purely out of lust, or had shit happened on the West Coast, and he'd found out we had a contact there? If the comment made Scar nervous, she didn't show it. Her black nails wrapped around the neck of a bottle of tequila shaped like a human heart.

I watched in rapt fascination as she straddled Niko. Lust thrummed through my veins as she lifted up on her knees, the black fabric of her pants pulling taut across her ass cheeks. Her thumb and forefinger came up and parted Niko's lips, tilting his head back slightly.

"In that case, a Spanish toast is only fitting. *Arriba, abajo, al centro y pa' dentro,*" she said, lifting the bottle up and down before bringing it center and taking a pull.

My pulse sped up, and my dick hardened as she spat the liquid into his waiting mouth. Niko's large hands grabbed her thighs hard enough to bruise, his tattooed fingers grazing the edge of her perky ass. She dipped down, pulling Niko's bottom lip into her mouth.

"Fuck, bite me harder," my brother groaned against her.

She apparently complied, because as she moved to stand behind Kenji, Niko looked up. The look on his face resembled that of post-orgasm bliss, and his lips were stained with blood. He swiped across the wound and stared at the liquid in awe before cutting his gaze to the woman who'd caused it.

"Kenji." She dragged out his name, gripping his hair and yanking his head back hard. "Be a good boy and open your mouth."

She barely got the command out, and his mouth was open and waiting. The smile on her face was pure seduction, demanding we all get on our knees and worship her. I was glued to her every move. Pouty lips wrapped around the morbid-looking bottle as she took another drink of the liquid before setting it on the floor, her now-free hand wrapped around Kenji's throat, drawing a moan that ran straight to my balls. The devil was a woman with glacial eyes that glowed under the dim light. Dangerously persuasive and violently sexual. She dared me to look away as she trickled clear liquid into Kenji's mouth.

"Holy shit. I can't wait to yell your name when we fuck, baby." Kenji's comment distracted her from me, bringing about a sense of loss.

Her grip tightened as she licked away the droplets that had missed his mouth. "What if my hand is so tight around your throat there's not enough air to yell?" she asked, sounding sinister as she increased the pressure. The inhale he took told me she'd been choking him.

"Baby, I'd thank you for death by your hands." Lust clung to Kenji's words.

An arrogant chuckle came from where Maxim sat next to me. This whole act of seduction was supposed to be for him, but at some point, it had become a treat for us. I hadn't bothered looking to see if he was watching. I didn't want to ruin the moment with the blinding rage I knew I'd feel if I saw that fucker with a hard-on.

She appeared at my side, and I took my time trailing my eyes up her body.

We studied one another for a beat. Her eyes were so haunting you couldn't help but fall into their icy depths, welcoming the suffocation from her attention.

I didn't give her a verbal response. Instead, I settled into my chair, tilting my head back with parted lips as an open invitation. My eyes fluttered shut as her fingers dragged along my arm as she came to stand behind me. Warm breath hit the shell of my ear, making my balls jump.

"I'm going to greatly enjoy this," she whispered, roughly nipping at my lobe.

The burning taste of tequila hit my tongue, and her hands trailed down my chest before caressing my thighs. I nearly choked when her hand squeezed my cock. I needed more of her.

"You're quite generous with your wife there, Caleb. Does she *service* your guests too?" His question charged the air, tainting the moment. Scar stiffened, a slight tremor running through her body.

Her throat bobbed as she swallowed, waiting for my answer.

"Of course. It's not like I married her because I care for her," I commented, swiveling my head to watch Maxim's greedy gaze consume her as if she were nothing but a piece of meat. The words felt like ash on my tongue when I looked back at her. Pain lurched in her eyes, my words cutting her deep and drawing out buried emotions.

I curled my fists to resist smoothing her worries and

kissing away the pain, reassuring her that the words I'd said for Maxim's benefit were nothing but lies. She'd clawed her way into my heart, ripping away the safety net I'd kept around it, and she'd demanded I acknowledge the powerful connection we had.

We all had.

The sultry sway to her hips was gone as she walked toward Maxim, replaced with the lethal strut of a woman stalking down her prey. "Close your eyes, Mr. Petrov," she instructed.

My heart beat faster, roaring in my ears, when he yanked her onto his lap, practically crashing their bodies together. She wasn't quick enough to hide the look of disgust that flashed across her face as his hands wrapped around her waist and slammed her onto his crotch.

"I want you here in my lap so you can feel the cock your husband is going to let fuck you."

Violent rage roared in my veins when he looked over with a cocky smile. She'd better act fast, or I'd say fuck the plan and beat his skull in with my bare fists. I'd relish the feel of hot blood coating my skin as the life drained from his eyes.

"Eyes closed, Maxim," she bit out, her words losing the sweet facade she'd held all night. She gripped his jaw so tight it must have hurt, but Maxim liked her attempt at aggression. Well, he thought it was an attempt. All worry leeched from my body when his lids fluttered closed, and a violent smile bloomed on Scar's face.

The pale flesh of his throat was exposed when she forced his head back. His Adam's apple bobbed when she leaned in to whisper in his ear.

"We're going to have so much fun," she said, pulling a blade from her waistband and sliding it across his throat. Blood spurted from the wound, coating her hands and chest. His eyes flew open in shock.

"You'll regret this," he choked out as his throat continued to gurgle, his ashen skin a stark contrast to her tanned flesh.

Scar slid from his lap, peering down at him in disgust. "See, I don't think we will. The men you work for aren't as untouchable as they think. And the minions you have planted in my city? I'm fucking coming for them," she seethed, dropping her face closer to his. "We know about your friends at the FBI too. Their hands aren't as clean as they want the public to think, huh?"

Maxim's face twisted in rage, but the life in his eyes was already dimming. Nothing but a gurgled groan escaped his garish lips.

I'd thought love was bullshit, but this woman had all three of us by the fuckin' balls, and the feelings swirling in my heart no longer felt like lust alone.

FORTY
SCAR

EVERYTHING IS GOING TO HELL...

WORRY SHOT up my spine when my burner vibrated in my pocket. Caleb's eyes caught my own in the rearview mirror, his smoldering with tension in the darkness.

"Don't worry," I said, digging the phone out of my blood-crusted pants. I should have brought a change, but I hadn't planned on being in Maxim's fucking lap when I slit his throat. "It's the burner I use when Ryan calls." Caleb's and Kenji's shoulders relaxed at the knowledge that it wasn't my uncle calling.

Earlier today, I'd looped the video feed from a few weeks ago. There wasn't any trace of us being there tonight, and the staff was all hired out—people loyal to the Syndicate. Maxim and his bodyguards were piled in the walk-in freezer, and I had my cleaners scrubbing blood from the oak plank flooring of the lounge.

But fear still crept up my spine, and sweat beaded along the back of my neck. I'd given this number to her years ago, and she'd never once used it. Now this was the second call in a short span of time. "Ryan. What's wrong?" Three sets of eyes landed on me at the note of panic in my voice.

The masculine tone startled me, and I instantly set the

phone to speaker, not wanting to have to repeat the conversation for the guys later.

"Not Ryan. But she's in trouble," Gunner said.

My breath hitched at the news. She had to be in some deep shit if he needed to call me for backup. And what the fuck did he want me to do from New York? I listened, and all that kept me grounded was my training because I wanted to go ballistic at what I heard.

"What do you need from me? I'll help however I can, but you should know I'm no longer in Tucson."

His sigh of relief echoed through the SUV. "I need access to the parts of Lotería that are biometrically locked, and I need camera feed access so I know where Ryan is in the building," he said.

I scoffed at his request. "You're going to need more than that." I yanked my laptop out of the backpack at my feet, placing it in my lap. "I know you're used to working with shit resources and intelligence, which is ironic, but that's not how I work." My fingers flew across my keyboard. The phone was tucked between my shoulder and ear as I worked to get everything he'd need. "A message is coming through. You'll find the blueprints to the club and a link to watch the live feeds from the cameras."

Relief flooded my veins when the grainy feed popped up on my screen. Ryan was currently walking into Lotería, guns blazing. Caleb jerked the car to the right, taking us away from our penthouse.

"Well, our girl is currently blowing holes in people. I'll be watching the feeds for when you and Dex arrive."

I rolled my eyes at Dex's amazement that I knew he was with Gunner. It was honestly a lucky guess. Gunner's file said he'd taken this undercover job in exchange for a deal for his best friend, who'd beat the ass of a man who had sold his sister. To me, it sounded justified, but the legal system was fucked.

"Damn right I'm a wizard. Now pay attention. This is important. I'll have to send the system into emergency power mode. It's the only way to override the biometric scanners. All the house lights will cut out, and the emergency lighting will trigger. Be aware that a fucking annoying alarm will also sound, but the chaos will probably help you out. The doors will still require a code to enter, but the scanner will be disabled. I'll change the code to four zeroes when you arrive. Got it?" My fingers were flying across my keyboard as I called out the instructions.

Caleb's deep voice barked out instructions of his own. "Kenji, tell Gregori to get to the warehouses now—we need to blow the fuckers. The plan has changed and we're moving on Dominick."

This hadn't been part of the plan. We were supposed to kill Maxim tonight, and then in the following days, we'd do Dominick.

Caleb's eyes found mine once more. "The news of what's about to pop off in Tucson is going to spread fast. We can't afford for Dominick to find out we've taken out Maxim."

He was right.

We pulled up in front of my uncle's house. Déjà vu hit me at the sight of the arched black doors of the brownstone.

"The camera feed doesn't show anyone else but him and a few guards," I said, watching as Dominick poured himself a finger of whiskey in his living room.

"Everyone knows what they're doing?" Caleb asked, his voice steady.

I nodded, checking the slide on my gun before tucking it back in the band of my pants and looking up to lock eyes with him and Kenji. Kenji's face was pulled into a frown, deep creases marring his forehead.

"Hey," Caleb placed a hand on his shoulder, "she's going to be fine. She's fucking Cain. She lives for this shit."

Affection bloomed in my chest at his words. As much as we'd fought, Caleb had never made me feel less-than.

I chuckled. My abilities were the only thing he'd actually liked from the beginning.

My eyes fluttered closed when Caleb leaned forward and cupped my face before pressing his lips to mine. This kiss was soft and gentle.

Loving.

When he pulled away, my eyes popped open to find him staring at me intently.

"Don't tell me you love me," I whispered.

Caleb's face paled, and what looked like disappointment flashed across his face. "You don't feel the same way?" His voice was quiet and lacked the authority I was used to. Instead, it was laced with hurt.

I clamped down on his wrist, keeping his hand in place as I turned and placed a kiss on the palm. "No, that's not it at all. I love you so much it scares me. Because losing you, any of you, will feel like a crucial part of me is missing." His eyes widened in surprise, and Kenji's hands stilled from whatever he was doing when he heard me say *any of you*.

"I don't want you to tell me you love me, because it feels too much like you're saying goodbye," I said.

Caleb's thumb stroked my cheek as Kenji crawled into the back seat and held me tight in his arms. It was as if they sensed the emotional breakdown I was having. My heart wanted to open up and love while my mind attempted to keep us shielded in safety.

"People leave after they tell me they love me," I whispered, thinking about the only other man I'd loved. Thought I'd loved.

"Scar, you listen to me right now." Kenji wrenched my face toward his, pressing his mouth to mine in a claim. "We fucking love you, and we're going to tell you every fucking day until the devil takes us, and then we're clawing out of hell and haunting your sexy ass until you join us," he said.

"I love you, Scar, and I don't give a shit if you don't want me to tell you. Because you deserve to be told how special you are. Now go fuck up your uncle," Caleb said, sealing his speech with a kiss.

A rock settled in my gut, and I hopped out of the SUV. I'd just been told that I was loved, and the man who'd made my life a living hell was about to have his life snuffed out at my hands, and yet something felt…wrong.

I checked my phone once more before approaching the doors of the brownstone. I'd already unlocked the doors and system at Lotería for Gunner, but I wanted to check the feed one more time before I was unavailable.

My heart stopped in my chest at the sight of Ryan locked in a room. She didn't realize that Gunner and Dex were pinned down. I tapped into the intercom system at the club.

"Nice job, bitch. Now get your ass to the cargo bay. Your man needs some help, and I would hurry if you want to take care of Mario before the authorities do," I told her. How ironic that I was about to go in and exact my own justice.

"Scar?"

"Yup. Your man called in a favor. Now get going." I paused. "Oh, and Ryan…don't be too hard on him when you find out the truth," I said before shutting down the feed. I saw the way Gunner looked at her, and all that he was giving up to gain her. She was going to be pissed and feel betrayed. But the bigger wound was that she would feel she was unlovable, but that was a fucking lie. The same one I'd told myself before these men.

She'd be fine. She had to be.

I pounded on the door. The heavy thud mimicked the

beating of my heart. There was a mix of anticipation and utter calm swirling through my veins. The door was yanked open, and one of Dominick's personal guards stared down at me, disgust clear on his face.

"What the fuck are you doing here, traitor bitch?"

I pushed past him, making my way toward Dominick's office. "Oh yes, because I had a fucking say in that shitshow of a situation. Where's Dominick? I have shit on the Syndicate to tell him."

I didn't wait for his answer as I stormed into his office.

Dominick lounged in his recliner, feet propped up and crossed at the ankle. Cigar smoke filled the space, burning my lungs. His cold eyes slid to where I stood at the doors.

"Well, if it isn't my bastard niece. Come crawling back to ask for forgiveness? Has Callahan already tired of your pussy?"

I ignored the insult, turning to close the doors to the office, but a large hand halted my movement.

"What the fuck do you think you're doing?" the meathead guard sneered.

"I have shit to tell Dominick that I'm sure he wouldn't want your pea-brain to hear," I snapped back, looking over my shoulder to my uncle.

Dominick's gaze trailed over me. I kept my body relaxed and slightly hunched over. I wanted to seem as unintimidating as possible. His eyes narrowed on my face, like if he squinted hard enough, he'd be able to see my thoughts. I had to give him something, or he wasn't going to let me in.

"It's about Maxim Petrov," I said.

That got his attention. His eyebrows hit his hairline, and he sat up straighter. "Leave us and close the fucking door behind you." The guard turned to leave. "And check the perimeter. Full scope," Dominick said, giving him a pointed look before sliding his attention to me.

But I stayed relaxed, thankful that I'd made the guys go

check on Niko at the warehouse. Kenji had bitched the whole time, not wanting to leave me, but Caleb told him I could do this shit on my own.

This time, the click of the door sounded like the slamming of the gavel of Dominick's sentence.

"What the fuck is it you want, Scarletta?" he asked, taking another puff of his cigar, the smoke wafting in the air between us. "Shouldn't you be with your *husband* and the men you whore yourself out to?" he asked. His condescending tone grated on my nerves, reminding me of all the lectures he'd given me over the course of my life. Every moment was an opportunity to make me feel less-than.

"They're busy at the moment," I stated, moving closer, blood roaring through my veins. This moment was the culmination of everything I'd worked for my whole life. Every cell in my body screamed for me to pull the trigger. That he didn't deserve to breathe one more breath.

He grunted a response. "Why the fuck are you coming to me now, girl? You made it clear where your loyalties lie when you stole my daughter's fiancé," he sneered, spit flying from his lips.

"I didn't have any fucking part of that. I didn't even want to go to that party, remember?" It wasn't difficult to sound convincing since everything I said was the truth. I discreetly flicked the lock on the handle before moving farther into the room and plopping down in the chair in front of him. "I didn't have a chance to come sooner. They've kept me locked in the apartment," I said, eyeing how he shifted in his seat.

His hand was slowly reaching for the Glock I knew he kept hidden in the crevice of the chair. Thankfully, I hadn't fully relaxed in, and my position would make it easy for me to leap behind the desk when he drew his firearm.

Because the fucker definitely would.

"You always were a stupid fucking girl," he sneered. "You

didn't look *locked up* when you perched your ass on that bike and shot at my men."

I caught the movement of the black barrel as I threw myself to the side, scurrying behind the desk as a shot rang out and hit to the right of where I'd been sitting.

"Your shot is as fucking trash as you are, Dominick," I called out, poking my head out and firing off a shot of my own. Blood and muscle matter exploded from where the shot struck him in the shoulder of his dominant arm.

His strangled yell was music to my fucking ears. The beast lurking beneath my skin roared in victory at the bloodshed of our enemy.

"Are you a shit shot with your off hand too?" I taunted, rolling across the floor as wood shrapnel rained through the air where his bullet hit the desk. My manic laughter echoed through the room, combining with another pained yell as I hit Dominick in the other shoulder.

"Fucking bitch," he yelled.

I used his momentary distraction to rush him, knocking his gun loose as I plowed into him, his body colliding with the bookshelf. The butt of my gun struck him in the temple, and blood seeped from the head wound.

"I'm going to fucking kill you, Dominick," I seethed. "And it's going to be long, drawn out, and painful as payment for all the shit you put me through."

Ice chilled my veins when he laughed. His body gave out below me, but his laugh sounded as if he was the one who'd won.

"What's more important, Scarletta? Your revenge, or those men?" he asked, his eyes glazing over with a crazed look. "Because you can't have both. I bet you choose revenge. I fuckin' ruined you for love. You don't fucking work right, do you? Your head is too fucked up to care for others." He was rambling nonsense, but the words caused my heart to pound.

"This is my fucking city. You don't think I know what

happens in it?" he yelled out. "I know everything, and you're as pathetic as your whore of a mother. If you want to spread your legs, I'm going to at least get some money for it. So thanks for bringing your pussy to my doorstep. I was going to have to send Enzo to collect you after he buried the bodies of your men in the rubble."

My hands moved on their own, instinct and skill taking over, smothering the panic threatening to drown me. "Fuck you, Dominick." I pressed the barrel of the gun to the tender flesh under his chin. "What the fuck are you talking about?"

"Those boys are about to be on the news. Three men killed in a warehouse fire," he said, his voice thick with gloating. An evil sneer curled up on his ashen face. "Did you know your mom moaned with pleasure when I fucked her before selling her? She didn't want you. I asked her if she wanted to keep you, and she said no."

I cut off the self-loathing that wanted to creep in. I kept my face neutral, knowing I needed him to keep talking. "Now, these three will be gone, and Enzo is married. Who will you have if you kill me? Admit it, Scarletta, I raised you well. Taught you how to survive. You let me live, and this will all be forgiven. Things go back to the way they were. You don't even love those fuckers."

His words snapped me out of the trance I'd fallen into.

I dug the barrel in deeper. "You didn't teach me how to survive, Dominick. You helped me turn into the beautiful fucking monster I am, and I can't fucking *wait* to paint the walls with your brain matter. Splatter the fucking walls like a macabre piece of art." I leaned closer, hissing in his face, lapping up the fear in his shit-brown eyes. "But that's going to have to wait, because you're going to be a gift to the Circle. They are going to *love* when I deliver Maxim's killer."

His face blanched, his eyes widening the second before I slammed my gun into his temple for a second time and knocked him out.

His head snapped back as blood pooled under his body. As much as I wanted to kill him, I wanted him to suffer even more. Saving him to be tortured would be even sweeter than a quick death. And right now, I didn't give a fuck what happened to Dominick, because I was terrified at the idea that any of my three men were in danger.

I shut all my emotions off before the terror caused me to freeze.

My body moved on autopilot. The cries of Dominick's men were muffled, barely registering as I moved like a blur through the home, riddling each man with bullets.

I was numb to the world, scrambling to keep my fractured heart intact, because I knew my uncle. The men I loved really were in trouble, and I would need every skill I had to keep myself from falling apart before I could save them.

I wouldn't be able to check on the men I loved if I died in this house.

"Where the fuck is Enzo?" I yelled in the face of one of the men who was bleeding out. His head lolled to the side, his eyes unseeing. Warm blood coated my fingers as I dug them into one of the bullet wounds. His pained cry was music to my ears.

"The warehouse. He's at the warehouse by the docks."

A gunshot echoed as I placed another bullet in his brain before stepping over his body. I shot off a text to my cleaner, instructing them to come secure Dominick's body, forcing myself to operate as if my men were fine.

FORTY-ONE

NIKO

IT'S GETTING GOOD. OR BAD…

I DIDN'T KNOW why I'd been surprised that Scar had access to a cleaning crew, and a damn good one at that. The lounge off the dining room was already beginning to look back to normal. In a few hours, no one would guess we'd just offed a member of the Circle in there.

The vibrations of my cell phone drew my attention away from where the guys were scrubbing blood off the floorboards. "They aren't done yet. It's only been maybe twenty minutes, Caleb," I said, rolling my eyes that he was already calling.

"Scar's at Dominick's."

Every muscle in my body tensed with those words. What the fuck did he mean she was at Dominick's, and why was his tone laced with worry and pride? Out of the three of us, Caleb was the one who never doubted her abilities, so the tremor of concern had me on edge as I stormed out of the room. I didn't even fucking know where I was going, but I wanted to already be moving toward the goal.

"What the fuck happened?" I asked, practically running to my car, ready to run every red light in the city to get to her. Fuck, I'd plow through people and cars if I had to. The muggy night air wrapped around me like it was attempting to smother me. My heart was already threatening to send me into an early grave with how quickly it beat.

"Gunner called her. Ryan was taken by Mario, so he and some guy named Dex are raiding the club to get her back. The straitlaced agent is going rogue for his woman." Respect and understanding were evident in Caleb's voice. The agent just gained some points in our book. "Sergio is still nowhere to be found, and I doubt Mario is going to survive this showdown. I know if I were in Gunner's shoes, I wouldn't let the slimy fucker live."

"That's fucking great, but what does that shit have to do with our woman being in the home of the man who abused her?" I spit out. Fuck, I wanted to shoot something or someone.

Caleb's voice remained steady, helping to keep me grounded in reality instead of flying off into a murderous rage. "News of that shit on the West Coast is going to move fast…"

Understanding bloomed in my mind, but the reality didn't make me any less tense. "It's going to cause us problems over here if Dominick hears about Mario being offed. He'd want to know if Maxim had any part of it," I said.

Our plan had been to frame the Mafia for Maxim's death since there'd need to be a fall guy for when the Circle came looking for their man. We'd hoped that they'd then reach out to Cain or us to take Dominick out.

Two birds, one stone. Get in the Circle's good graces so we could keep an eye on the fuckers and kill off Dominick and Enzo. But now…

"What does this do to our plan?" I asked, hopping into the front seat.

"I don't know exactly." Caleb paused. His uncertainty had my gut clenching and my knuckles whitening against the leather steering wheel. We didn't like to run into shit half-cocked, and this felt an awful lot like doing that.

"We just dropped Scar off. She's going in to face her uncle. There was no other way to make it work so quickly. I told her to do whatever the fuck she needed to do to come out safe. Fuck the plan if she had to," he said.

I nodded in agreement before realizing he wouldn't be able to see it. "Yeah, I agree. We'll figure the rest of the shit out, even if we have to execute every motherfucker who stands in our way with our bare hands. She *needs* to be safe," I growled out.

"I told her I loved her, Niko."

My brows hit my hairline. His voice was soft and vulnerable, reminding me of what he'd sounded like when we were teenagers. What happened to Jessica had hardened him, all of us really, but Caleb turned callous toward the idea of love and relationships.

Scar had stormed in and fucked that all up for him.

Kenji and I had known he loved her. We could see it in the way he acted around her, but I hadn't been sure *he* knew he did.

"She has to be okay. She has to come out of there okay." Panic was starting to seep into his words.

"Caleb," I barked, starting the engine, "tell me where the fuck to go and what's next. We have to do our part, or her risking her ass is going to be for nothing."

He'd pulled me out of my own thoughts enough times that I knew we needed something to focus on. Something to do.

"Fuck, you're right." I could picture the way he was probably running his hand through his auburn hair, pulling at the messy strands. "Meet us at the warehouse. We're almost there. Gregori is arranging the call for the drop so we can get the Yakuza leaders there—"

"And my dad and brother," I bit out, anger and anticipation thrumming through my body like an electric current.

"Exactly. We have to blow those fuckers up tonight. I already called Rowan. Genius bastard has been poisoning our Da for months now, so he's going to take care of him."

The knot in my stomach loosened a bit as Caleb ran through the plans. Maybe this wouldn't be a complete shit show. But something still nagged at my mind.

"Where the fuck is Enzo in all this?" I asked, pulling out of the parking lot and onto the street.

"No fucking clue. He wasn't on the cameras at Dominick's brownstone," Caleb replied.

"Get Kenji on that. That fucker will put a snag in our plan if we don't take him out too. Otherwise, he's going to seat himself on Dominick's throne, and we'll be back to square one."

"What? You don't think he'd want to work with us after we tell him we're fucking his girl?" Caleb asked, barking out a laugh.

It helped relieve some of the tension building in my body.

The corners of my mouth pulled up into a smirk. "Should we tell him how good our cocks look filling her up?" I asked, snaking through the streets toward my destination.

"We'll send him a video of it, but we'll make sure all he sees is Kenji's ass thrusting in and out of her." Caleb's tone changed from playful to serious then. "Be careful, brother. We'll see you soon."

I drove in silence the rest of the way, unable to handle any more noise with all the voices clamoring in my mind. Gravel crunched under my tires as I pulled through the chain-link gates. The nondescript metal warehouse was eerily quiet tonight. Normally, there'd be a guard rotation around the exterior, with two men walking the gravel perimeter and the third guarding the main entrance.

But the building was empty tonight.

During my recon, I'd only spotted a motion-activated flood light at the side door and another at the old cargo bay entrance. The metal roll-up doors looked fairly new, unlike the rest of the decrepit industrial building. I'd rigged the place with explosives over a week ago. We'd wanted it prepped so we could pull off the job at a moment's notice.

I'd never imagined *this* situation.

I spotted the black SUV tucked away out of sight. There shouldn't have been anyone around to see us, but it was better to be safe than sorry. After the meeting with Gregori, we'd agreed that he'd pull all his guys when we gave him the call to make contact with the Yakuza and Bratva. His job was to let them know about the drop. Then when they got here to inspect the product, we'd blow the fuckin' place sky high.

"Hey, big boy. Ready to have a barbeque?" Kenji asked the moment I stepped out of my car. His words were playful, but his body was on high alert. His eyes kept darting around the abandoned lot, his hand twitching like he wanted to be palming his katana.

My large palm landed on his shoulder, pulling his attention to me. "She's going to be fine. We're going to blow these fuckers up, and she's going to hand her uncle his ass. Then the four of us will go on a fucking vacation," I said, giving Kenji an encouraging squeeze.

The confidence in my voice was all bullshit. I was scared shitless that this would all go to hell. But we were fucking demons in human flesh.

We'd deal with what the devil dealt us.

Death was etched on Caleb's face when he rounded the front of the vehicle. We were ready to shed blood and bring about the reckoning we'd planned for years. Whatever the cost to keep our found family safe, we'd pay it.

Caleb opened his mouth to speak when a light flickered on over by the warehouse, causing all three of us to still.

"That light is motion activated," I said, palming the gun

tucked in my waistband. I caught their nods of agreement in my periphery. Before we were able to investigate, two blacked-out Escalades pulled up outside the warehouse.

Hatred flooded my system, coloring my vision in red as my father and brother exited one of the cars—Kenji's family the other.

"Fuck, I wish I was running my blade through their chests. Hearing the shattering of bone as I rammed it through their flesh to their fucking blackened hearts," Kenji said, practically vibrating with anger.

"Easy, brother. You'll be able to hear their cries as they burn."

Caleb's tone was so sinister it sent goose bumps erupting on my skin. None of us said a word as we waited for them to all disappear into the warehouse. Tension was building in my muscles, violence coiling at my core. I wanted to bathe in their blood and desecrate their graves under my feet as I danced on their bodies in victory.

Actual crates of product had been dropped off. We needed them to be distracted long enough for us to lock them in.

The time seemed to slow as they scurried in like rats, but the slamming of the metal door behind them sling-shotted us into action. My neck was damp with sweat as I ran in a crouch across the graveled landscape. I'd convinced myself Scar was fine, and we needed to execute our part, because otherwise, she'd be pissed. The fabricated reality was the only thing that kept me here, chaining the doors shut instead of speeding across the city to her.

"You got all of them?" I asked when we met back at our vehicles.

"Everything on the south side of the building is locked down," Kenji answered, a sheen of sweat glistening on his brow under the dull lighting.

"Same with the east side of the building," Caleb answered.

I nodded and pulled out a small control. "All right, then. Cover your fucking ears, boys."

The ground shook with the impact of the explosion, the sound nearly deafening. "Fucking hell, Kenji. How much fucking C4 did you use?" I yelled out. My ears were ringing, and I couldn't gauge how loud my voice was. Caleb and Kenji both looked slightly disorientated because of the blast, but it only took a moment for sounds to come rushing back to full volume.

"What? I wanted to make sure it worked," he replied with a shrug of his shoulders.

Agonized yells rang out in the night air, but I couldn't bring myself to have an ounce of sympathy for any of the fuckers trapped in that warehouse. They'd made the lives of so many fucking hell. They deserved to burn for it.

"Can you pick out which scream is hers?"

That voice sent chills up my spine. Every muscle was on high alert as I turned and aimed my gun at Enzo's head. His coffee-colored eyes glistened with hate as he leaned against the hood of our vehicle, hands casually tucked into the pockets of his jeans.

"What the fuck did you say to us?" Caleb asked, his voice low and menacing.

"I asked if you could pick out Scarletta's scream." He canted his head toward the inferno. "It's been a little while since the whore let me fuck her, but I think I can still pick out her voice." The smile that appeared on his face was downright evil.

Caleb's body tensed, and even in the low lighting, I could see the color draining from his face.

"You're lying, motherfucker," Kenji bit out, his knuckles white against the hilt of his katana. There was a slight shake in his voice, a thread of uncertainty.

"Am I?" Enzo asked, uncrossing his legs and looking perfectly at ease. I glanced at Kenji, who was watching the asshole's every movement for a tell. "I know you saw the light come on before they got here, right? Who do you think set it off? Her uncle was going to sell her ass after that stunt you four pulled, but this is better. That fucking bitch deserves to die for leaving me."

Truth rang out in his words.

I took off for the fiery building, ignoring my brothers' shouts as I called out the name of the woman I loved. Smoke smothered me, burning my eyes and lungs as I pressed through an opening created by the flames consuming the building with their greedy maw of destruction.

"Kolay."

The heat of the warehouse did nothing to thaw the ice that ran across my skin at the boom of my father's voice. I turned on my heel and came face to face with the man who'd tormented me since birth. His face was blackened with ash, the skin on his hands burned away, yet he still had a gun clutched in his palm.

"Kolay, this was you, wasn't it?" He barked out a manic laugh—like a man who knew he'd already been summoned by death and was prepared to be pulled under. "To think I thought you were the weak son. Tainted by your American blood. But you're just like me, no?" he asked before a fit of coughs.

"I'm fucking *nothing* like you," I sneered, the barrel of my gun pointed directly at his head.

His beady eyes narrowed on me. "No, I suppose you're not. Because it looks like you rushed into this fiery grave to save someone." He spit on the ground in disgust. "What a pathetic thing to do. You deserve your death."

The twitching of his wrist was the only clue I got of his intentions.

We fired at the same time, but the shots were nothing but whispers compared to the roar of the fire. I doubted my brothers had even heard it.

They won't have a clue that I've been shot.

My teeth jarred as my knees hit the concrete, pain radiating from the hit I'd taken. But the physical pain was nothing compared to the crushing reality that there was no way I'd be able to make my way through the carnage to find Scar. Not even the fact that I'd killed my father could soothe my agony.

I cried out her name until my lungs burned from the heated air and exertion. Each moment seemed to slip, my brain no longer able to make heads or tails of time. Tears streaked down my face.

I wished I'd heard her tell me she loved me before I died.

FORTY-TWO

SCAR

GET YOUR TISSUES OUT, OR NOT. MAYBE
YOU DON'T CRY EITHER.

FUCK.

None of them were answering their phones.

I'd raced through the streets of New York on the back of a stolen bike. I couldn't even remember getting on the bike or how I'd managed to navigate my way to the warehouse.

My heart stopped in my chest at the sight of smoke and flames dancing against the night sky. A scream ripped through my throat as I leaped off the bike and sprinted toward where bodies huddled outside of the building.

"Caleb, Niko, Kenji," I yelled, running faster and faster toward the three men I loved. Blood heated in my veins when I saw two familiar forms hovering over a body sprawled out on the floor.

Caleb's voice boomed over the crackling of the fire and the snapping of timber as the warehouse was consumed. Relief swept over me, making me almost collapse.

"Who the fuck was he planning to sell her to?" His voice vibrated with rage. Kenji's katana was pressed into Enzo's chest about three inches. Blood drenched his shirt as it leaked from the wound. "I swear to God, Enzo. I will keep you alive only to continue to torture you for the rest of your pathetic life. Because *nothing* is worth living for without that woman. And your fucked-up ass left her and then planned to help *sell* her when you couldn't have her."

Rage raced through me, making me see red.

"Caleb, Niko's still in there. They haven't fucking come out yet." Kenji's voice sounded panicked, and it tore at my soul to hear, even as my mind tried to wrap around his words.

Blood spilled from Enzo's mouth as he let out a cruel laugh. "That fucking bitch is probably already gone, and your Russian brother is dead from running after a ghost. Idiot ran in there thinking I really had tied her up inside. I don't give a shit what you do to me, Caleb. I still fucked you over," Enzo taunted.

"You always were a cocky motherfucker." I moved forward, my gun hanging loosely by my side, savoring the way Enzo's eyes widened at the sight of my bloodied body.

"Scar," Kenji called out in relief, but I couldn't look at him. I needed to handle this shit before the last bit of my resolve faded away.

"Where the fuck is Niko?" I pressed the barrel to Enzo's forehead, the black a stark contrast to his pale face. "Now, Enzo. I already put a bullet in your boss's brain without blinking. I'll blow your fucking head off without an ounce of remorse." The lie fell seamlessly from my lips. I would put a bullet in Dominick's brain—just not yet.

His eyes flicked to the building before settling back on me, and dread filled my being.

"He's in the building," I whispered, the reality of the news still processing.

"Fuck, he's still in the building," I called out, sprinting toward the flames. "Get someone down here to help. Now," I yelled over my shoulder, ignoring the shouts of protest from Kenji and Caleb and their frantic footsteps behind me.

I banded an arm across my mouth as I burst through an

opening. Smoke filled the space, making it impossible to see more than a foot in front of me.

I screamed as part of the building crashed down behind me, effectively blocking the way I'd gotten in, and I looked around, frantic. Caleb and Kenji were shouting from behind the wreckage, but I could only be glad they were safe outside. I'd find another way out. My eyes stung and my lungs cried out for fresh air, but I didn't give a fuck. Niko was somewhere in here. I hoped I wasn't too late.

He would've tried to get out.

The man was a fucking fighter, and he would've dragged himself to a fucking exit. I moved toward the door, keeping my eyes low. The flames were still concentrated at the back of the building, but they were quickly surging forward.

A lump lay on the floor only feet from the main exit. I shot off a text to Caleb and Kenji as I sprinted over.

The room blurred further as tears welled at the base of my lash line before spilling over and running down my dirty cheeks. I raced to his limp body, screaming for help at the sight of blood pooling where he lay.

So much blood. Too much.

I yanked off my shirt, pressing the fabric to the gaping wound and choking down a sob when it instantly turned crimson.

My emotions warred with one another. Crippling pain ripped through me, worse than any physical wound I'd ever endured, while numbness snaked its way through my body, attempting to preserve my shattering soul.

Embalming it in its broken state.

"Don't you fucking dare leave me," I cried out, smearing crimson over his ashen skin as I stroked his face.

"Scar." My name was weak on his lips, and it hit me like a physical blow. "You have to get out of here. I need you to be okay."

Of course he was trying to make *me* feel better as he lay there bleeding out.

A cold hand stroked my face, brushing the salty tears away, only for them to be replaced by more.

"But I won't be okay if you don't come with me, Niko." I pulled at his arm, seeing if I could move him, but he didn't budge. A sob caught in my throat at the realization that I wouldn't be able to get him out. Not alone. "I'll be a shell without you. I already feel grief draining every ounce of color from my world. You can't leave me." I buried my face in the crook of his neck, sobbing. Helpless to stop him from dying.

"They're on their way, Niko. They're almost here. Don't leave me. Promise me," I sobbed.

"I'm sorry I couldn't stay, *solntse*." His hand came up and stroked my hair. The touch was so weak compared to the strength of the man I knew. "I love you, Scar. I love you with every fiber of my being and every beat of my heart. Death won't take away how I feel for you. Take care of them," he rasped, the words barely above a whisper, as if it hurt to speak.

"Niko?" I pulled my face from his neck. "Niko!" Panic stung my throat.

"No!" I roared. He lay still head lolled to the side—chest unmoving.

My mind and soul fractured, splintering into a million pieces that would never be whole again, and I knew without a doubt it would be the same for the other two I loved. We were a unit, a team.

A family.

Everything went black after that thought. Somewhere in the distance, a woman wailed, crying out with so much pain in her voice that she must be dying.

It took a moment to realize the sound was coming from me.

FORTY-THREE
KENJI

BROTHER-HUSBANDS...LIKE SISTER-WIVES BUT WITH DICKS

I STOOD at the table beside Caleb, watching the rise and fall of Niko's and Scar's chests. A white gauzy bandage was wrapped around Niko's midsection, covering the wound that had been stitched closed. We'd found them lying in a heap and surrounded by a pool of blood just inside the burning warehouse. The sight had nearly killed me when I thought they were both dead.

"We won't live without you two," Caleb yelled as he sank to his knees, cradling her limp body in his arms.

We had a few firefighters in our pocket, and they'd rushed over when we made the call for help. I'd watched in horror as they placed Niko on a backboard. Blood had leeched from his body at an alarming rate, and I couldn't stop seeing it flash in front of my eyes, and reliving the moment.

My heart was pounding. Failing.

Death would be the sweeter option to the grief threatening to consume me. The weight of a reality in which she didn't exist was crushing. Hopeless.

It hadn't hurt this badly when my father had beat me and told me I was worthless. That I knew I'd survive.

This? I didn't.

"They'll both live."

The squat man's announcement yanked me back to reality as he bagged his tools. The dark tones of Caleb's room pushed the panic away. We had a doctor on our payroll for emergencies like this, but never had we needed to call him for something so serious. Caleb had insisted they both be placed in his bed to be tended to, and he hadn't left Scar's side since he'd picked her up off the floor. Rowan was busy cleaning up the mess that had been left behind at the warehouse.

"She is suffering from smoke inhalation and appears to have some scrapes and bruises. I'm not sure those are related to the fire, though." He looked over at where Niko lay, pushing his glasses up the bridge of his nose before turning back to Caleb and me.

"He also suffers from smoke inhalation on top of a gunshot wound. He's lucky it missed his heart. I dug the shrapnel out and cleaned and stitched it. He'll need to wear a sling for a bit, but otherwise, he will be okay."

I let out the breath I'd seemed to be holding since Scar got the call that turned this night on its head.

"It's a good thing you're a universal donor, Mr. Kenji, or Mr. Niko would have been in a dire situation. Please make sure you take it easy. You gave a lot tonight," he said as he scrunched his nose in concern.

The fact that he remembered we preferred not to go by our last names brought a smile to my face.

"I'll make sure he takes it easy, Dr. Pont. I don't need the health of another member of my family in jeopardy," Caleb said, cutting me a look that made me snicker.

"Caleb? Kenji?" Scar called out, her voice barely above a whisper. I rushed to join Caleb at her side, where he'd been stroking her honeyed hair, careful not to jostle her or Niko.

"We're here, baby," I called out, gripping her free hand.

Her beautiful eyes roved over both of us. "You look like

hell," she said. The tension in the room broke, and I let out a laugh. Of course she'd wake up with all her sass intact.

"That will happen when the love of your life decides to fucking run into a burning building," Caleb bit out, giving her a scowl.

She smiled at his bitching, reaching up to rub her thumb across the crease in his brow. She turned her head toward Niko, watching the steady rise and fall of his chest. The weight on her shoulders visibly lifted with every breath he took in.

Her attention swiveled back toward us, a sly grin on her lips. "How do you feel about a plural marriage? Because I think you would make great brother-husbands."

Caleb let out a bark of laughter, pressing his lips to hers in a smile.

"Do you want three wedding rings too?" he asked as he pulled away.

She smiled softly, looking at all of us with affection. "Being a family and cared for is all I've ever wanted, and you three are my heart and soul."

EPILOGUE: SCAR

PUSH HER. I DON'T KNOW THAT BITCH

THE REPETITIVE THUMPING of fingertips was the soundtrack to my thoughts. The thump-thump helped calm the itch to stab the woman who was making dick-me-down eyes at Caleb. She'd already eye-fucked Kenji and Niko.

"Ryan, if you don't tell your girl to back the fuck off my husband, you're going to be paying workers' comp. Because the bitch is about to *fall* off a stage," I gritted out.

The new cartel kingpin glanced over her shoulder toward the table our men were sitting at. Well, she had one man, while I had three.

"Push her. I don't know that bitch," she said with a shrug, but her body went rigid when the woman ran a manicured finger over the tattoos on Gunner's arm. I chuckled at the way she shot up out of her seat, ready to storm over. She always was the shoot-first, who-gives-a-fuck-about-questions kind of woman. My hand landed on her forearm, stilling her movements.

"Remember the night I was here installing the security?" I asked, quirking an eyebrow.

Her face morphed from a murderous rage into a conspiratorial grin. "Scar, this is why I love that evil genius brain of yours." She yanked me up, dragging me behind her toward the dancers' dressing room entrance. "Come on, Nikki is supposed to be on next. She'll love this. She and Dex are in some fucked-up standoff where the goal is to flirt with everyone possible to piss each other off. Oh, and they're fighting over Robert too."

I laughed. "I knew I liked her. And are you talking sexually fighting over him?" I asked while shouldering people who wouldn't move out of my way.

Ryan paused, looking back at me, her manicured brows scrunched in confusion. "Huh. I don't actually know," she responded before continuing to weave through the patrons celebrating the reopening of Lotería. The club had been closed for *renovations* for the last few weeks.

"You don't even notice the bullet holes you riddled this place with," I commented, snickering at the glare Ryan gave me. "Don't be pissed at me. You're the one who stormed in here like you were in a Bruce Willis movie."

"Okay, Scar, we can't all be fucking John Wick and take people out with pencils or whatever the fuck you use."

"I use a gun as often as you do, but I try to hit the fucking person and not the walls," I said, laughing when she flipped me off before glancing over my shoulder toward the boys. The bitch was still at their table, batting her lashes like she had something in her eye.

"Those assholes should've told her to fuck off already. They deserve what's coming," I said as we pushed into the dressing room.

In their defense, they all looked uncomfortable, and Niko might have been telling her just that based on how he was flicking his hand toward her. But Ryan and I weren't going to miss out on our chance to be petty. We needed some fun after the last few weeks of straight fucking chaos.

Tits, glitter, and perfume were everywhere when we entered the posh dressing room. The walls were lined with vanities, each with a lit mirror hanging above it. There was a whole wall dedicated to racks for the dancers to hang their costumes and store their shoes. Lotería was a gem of a club. Ryan had something special with this place, and I was glad she'd decided to stop running guns out of it.

She was still running them, just no longer out of the club. We'd partnered with her and the Skeletons of Society MC to expand the Syndicate's operation. With Mario and Sergio gone, Ryan had seamlessly slid into the position of kingpin.

It wasn't quite the same situation with me and the Mafia. I'd always been a pariah in my uncle's organization, so there was no way that his men would accept me with open arms the way Sergio's had with Ryan.

So I'd burned the fucking organization to the ground.

When I told Caleb and Kenji how I'd kept Dominick alive so our plan would still work, they both sank to their knees and gave me so many orgasms that I thought I'd pass out. Poor Niko couldn't participate since he'd still been on bed rest, but the fucker loved to watch and direct, and I'd made sure to take *good* care of him with my mouth after.

The call I'd made before I raced to the warehouse was to my cleaners. I'd instructed them to store Dominick in the holding cells under my apartment building. It had been a herculean feat not to put a bullet in his brain that night, but fuck if I wasn't happy I'd waited.

Two-ish weeks after all the shit went down, I collected on Gunner's favor. One of his remaining connections in the FBI walked in to find a compiled package of evidence against the Mafia. There was no way they could say no to prosecuting the remaining members with the amount on the thumb drive. The lawyers didn't have to do shit to prepare for the RICO case.

I'd always known the years of blackmail I'd saved would come in handy. I'd made it look like Dominick was the leak of the intel and threw in some shit on the Circle, too, to get

Dominick on their radar. Not even twenty-four hours went by, and the Circle contacted Cain to put a hit on the don.

I told you I'd paint the walls with chunks of your fucking skull.

Those were my last words to Dominick before I blew a forty-five-caliber hole in his head.

"Nikki." Ryan's yell pulled me back into the moment. The blond bombshell spun around, a giant smile on her face, but her eyes looked…haunted. I'd heard about the shit that went down here while I was busy in New York—the secrets that managed to rear their ugly heads. Nikki had her own monsters to slay, and it looked like she was worried about them coming to collect.

"Hey, what are you two doing back here? Coming to join in on the fun?" she asked, rolling a stocking over her ivory legs before attaching it to the garter around her thigh.

"Actually, yeah, we are. Have any spare shit?" I asked.

Her blue eyes bounced between us, the sparkle finally reaching them. "Oh, fuck yeah, I do. Holy shit, this is going to be so fun."

Thongs, bras, and an assortment of shit I wouldn't even know how to put on all went flying as she dug into her bag. "Those fuckers aren't going to know what to do. Should I place bets on which one of them hops up on the stage first to yank you off?" she asked.

"Caleb," Ryan and I responded, looking at each other when the answers came out simultaneously.

Gunner was possessive of Ryan, but he was still groveling for the shit he'd pulled. Niko knew he'd just punish me in the bedroom for showing my tits and ass to a room full of strangers, and Kenji would probably run up on stage for a lap dance.

Caleb, though? That grumpy fucker was going to yank me off the pole and carry me to a dark corner and fuck me.

And my core clenched in anticipation.

I peeled off my clothing. All my underwear and bras were

scraps of lace these days, so all I needed was the spare pair of stockings that came up to mid-thigh.

"Nervous?" Nikki asked me, handing me a pair of platform heels.

"Not even a little," I said, winking at her.

"Well, you look fucking hot with that sheer bra and matching cheeky underwear. I want a bra with a fucking skull covering the nips. Where did you get it?" Nikki asked, reaching out and snapping the strap.

My lips pulled up into a smirk. "I don't know. You'll have to ask Kenji. I don't buy any of my lingerie anymore."

Ryan popped up from where she was slipping on her shoes. "And *this bitch* let one of them coat her chonies in cum after she watched him fuck his hand."

Nikki's brows nearly launched off her forehead. "Fuck. Why is that hot?"

"I ask myself that same question every single time I think about it," I replied as we approached the stage entrance.

"All right, ladies, you two take the stage and pole at their table, and I've got the main one. Have fun," Nikki said, throwing a kiss our way.

Ryan laced her fingers with mine and led us toward their table. "*Vamos, chica.*"

The lights dimmed, and my attention went to the stage at the center of their area. I took a deep breath as we stepped onto the platform. The men hadn't yet noticed us. The stage and pole were a few feet from where they sat. The distance was to keep space between the dancers and grabby hands.

Nothing was planned. It was all about the feel of the music. The steel was cool against my heated palms as I gripped the pole and slowly walked around in a circle. Don Omar's "Dile" started playing over the house speakers, and all the lighting turned crimson.

Tossing my head back, I let my hair trail down my naked back as I ground my hips to the rhythm of the music. My nipples pebbled against the skimpy, sheer bra, and my ass pretty much hung out of the cheeky cut underwear. I hoisted myself up on the pole, twisting to the side to hook my leg and spin.

I looked over to find three sets of eyes latched on to me. The way the tendons in Caleb's neck were straining against his skin made me chuckle. Served the asshole right. I moved to the open floor and started shaking my hips down to the ground, thrusting my breasts at the guys. I mimicked the way I'd ride their cocks.

Of course, Kenji hooted and stuck a ten in my bottoms. I tossed the bill back at him.

"You better up the currency, Kenji," I called out as Ryan sank to her knees next to me.

Gunner barked out to the guys not to fucking look at her, which was a pointless threat because their attention was *glued* to me. Backing up, I jumped up high on the pole and tossed my head, sending the honeyed locks everywhere. I slid down the pole, spread my legs, and bent forward, rolling my body back up again, performing a sexy flip and landing in the splits.

I'd thought about being a stripper at one point, and even had a pole at my apartment. I liked killing more, but fuck, was there a high that came with writhing your body to music. When I turned, I came face to face with my three guys.

Holy shit. Caleb stood at the center, his arms flexed against his chest, a murderous expression on his beautiful face, but he hadn't hopped up there and yanked me off yet. So I did the appropriate thing and blew him a kiss as I dropped to my knees and crawled over to him.

"Better get out the big bucks if you want to take me home, baby," I purred, gnawing on my lip as he struggled to get his hand in his front pocket with the bulge he was rocking. Caleb fished out his wallet, and he held out his Amex, curling his fingers in a *come here* motion.

Fuck.

His finger pulled my bottoms away from my skin, the touch searing as he tucked the card against my pelvic bone. Kenji repeated the action on the other side, while Niko tucked his into the cup of my bra just as the song ended.

"Get off the stage, wife," Caleb said, his voice coated in lust.

I'd barely survived the ride back to the safe house. I was dying to have their hands run up and down my body, and I desperately wanted a cock wherever I could put one.

Niko carried me over his shoulder into the bedroom of the safe house. The assholes hadn't let me put any clothes on when they'd dragged me out of the club, and when I protested too loudly, Niko slapped his hand on my ass, being sure to catch my pussy with his fingertips.

Now I sat in the middle of the bed with a naked Niko cradling me from behind as Caleb prowled toward me. A moan escaped me at the sight of my husband stripping down as he approached. His breath touched my face, lips hovering over mine.

"Wife, we're going to fuck this pussy so you remember who it belongs to. And the bitch who made you decide to teach us a lesson? I told her to fuck off. She was just slow to get the message," he said, nuzzling his nose into the curve of my throat.

My nerve endings were already lit, but his words ratcheted them up higher. I leaned in to kiss him, starting the kiss gently and putting all my love for him into it. His breath hitched, and he thrust his tongue into my mouth, forcing me to open wide before kissing his way down my neck as a naked Kenji climbed up on the bed, his full lips replacing

Caleb's. Niko's solid stature supported me from behind, his bulge digging into my ass.

I ran my tongue over Kenji's lower lip, biting him hard enough to taste blood. He pulled back and looked at me. The onyx color of his eyes somehow glowed. "It was fucking hot to watch you." He kissed me back with an almost painful intensity.

I welcomed the pain. It meant we were all together, and nothing would break that.

"Were you wet dancing for us?" Niko asked, rolling one of my nipples between his calloused fingers, his cock pulsing.

There were hands all over me, not a single part of my body left untouched, and I was so consumed with their attention I couldn't manage anything other than nodding my head.

I wanted to touch everything. My hands caressed over broad chests and tense abs, alternating between all three of their bodies. Caleb kissed and licked down my body before he plunged his tongue inside my pussy, sending a thrill through my core.

"Fuck, this dripping cunt tastes like heaven," he growled into my pussy as Niko kissed over my neck and reached down to swirl his thumb over my clit. The move had me bucking off the mattress against Caleb's face.

I opened my eyes and looked up at Kenji, licking my lips. I wanted his cock. My eyes dropped—he was already thick and pulsing with desire. Without thinking about it, I ran my fingers over the ridges of his stomach and wrapped my hand around his cock, gliding my thumb over the sensitive underside of the tip.

"Kenji, I want you in my mouth. Now," I said breathlessly.

His breath caught in his throat as he scrambled to his knees beside me. I wrapped my lips around him, groaning in satisfaction. He didn't push into me, letting me savor the feel of silky skin against my lips and tongue.

Caleb hit a spot that made my legs shake as my orgasm

erupted through me. Before I could even recover, he sat up, pulling my ankles onto his wide shoulders, and drove his thick length inside me. The move had me moaning around Kenji's dick.

"Fuck. Keep fucking her like that, Caleb. I love when she moans around my cock," Kenji said, his head thrown back.

"Hold on. Niko needs to get in on the action this time. The doctor's cleared him now," Caleb said, pulling his cock out and yanking me forward so my breasts smashed against his chest as he pulled me off the bed for a moment.

"Niko, on your back, legs on the ground. You might've been cleared, but you're going to let our girl do all the work," Caleb said, slapping my ass. "Get up there and ride his cock like our good little slut."

I straddled Niko's broad frame, getting lost in the haze of lust as I sank down on his thick cock. I barely registered the whispered *fuck* out of Niko's mouth as he filled me. Niko was at the edge of the bed, so there would be access to my ass and throat while I rode him.

Kenji came back beside me and gripped a handful of my hair, forcing his cock back down my throat, moaning in satisfaction.

"Lean forward, baby girl," Caleb said, gently pushing me forward. He pulled my cheeks apart, spitting right on my asshole, and then he swirled his tongue where he intended to stick his cock.

"God, this is so fucking hot to watch," Kenji commented, encouraging me to continue bobbing my head up and down on his cock.

I jumped at the sensation of cold lube hitting my asshole before Caleb pushed the pad of his thumb past the tight ring. Both Niko's and Kenji's cocks twitched at the moan I let out. He worked his thumb inside me until my body relaxed.

More lube hit my ass, and the wet sounds of Caleb

slathering it on his cock filled the room. My skin itched with anticipation.

"She's excited, brother. Her pussy has my dick in a vise grip," Niko murmured, kissing up my throat.

"Good, she's going to enjoy her body being used. Hold her ass cheeks open for me, Niko. I want to watch my cock slide inside."

His words were so dirty and erotic, they had my breath picking up.

Niko's calloused hands held me open for Caleb as he slid in, inch by inch. The stretching sensation was a bit uncomfortable, but fuck, did being this *full* feel amazing.

Hot, pounding lust grew in my abdomen with every thrust until I felt that blinding wave hit me again. Caleb buried himself deep inside me, his fingers leaving bruises on my hips, and Niko pounded from below, his body grazing against my aching clit.

I increased my pace on Kenji's cock, wanting to make sure he would reach his release at the same time as us.

"Fuck, I can't wait to shoot a load down your fucking throat. If you're a good girl, I'll clean up the cum that drips out of your pussy and your asshole," Kenji growled.

Holy shit.

Kenji's words sent me over the edge. My body clamped down on Niko and Caleb when I came, shivering between the two bodies forcing me to feel so much pleasure. They couldn't hold on either. Caleb gasped as his cock tightened, and he exploded, filling my ass, and Niko let out a deep groan when he did the same, coating me with streams of cum.

Words sounded like they were coming from far away, but I still heard them.

They loved me.

And I loved them.

We all collapsed in a pile—a hot, sweaty, totally satisfied pile.

"God, I'm so fucking glad we drugged and kidnapped you," Kenji said, kissing the top of my head, and causing all three of us to bust up laughing.

"I thought about slitting all your throats in your sleep," I said nonchalantly. Caleb stiffened at my back, and I looked over my shoulder at him.

"I'm concerned about why the first thing I thought when you admitted that was *that's hot*," he responded, kissing me.

A smile so wide it hurt was plastered on my face as I drifted off to sleep. No matter what shit this life or the Circle would bring to our doorstep, I had everything I wanted right here.

CITY OF SALVATION

ONE
NIKKI

WHY FILE FOR DIVORCE WHEN YOU CAN
PUT A HIT ON YOUR HUSBAND?

THREE YEARS EARLIER

"...UNTIL DEATH DO YOU PART."

Here's to fucking hoping.

As if my husband-to-be could hear my thoughts, onyx eyes met mine. Cruelty shone from within their inky depths as his gaze dragged down my body. It didn't matter that we were in the Lord's house or that a priest stood not two feet away, performing our wedding ceremony. Yuri was still blatantly undressing me with his thoughts.

It took all I had not to bolt back down the aisle.

He knew what lay under the layers of lace and tulle that swathed my body, having already *checked out the goods*. Sick fuck had made me strip down naked in front of my own father a few weeks ago, telling him he wouldn't accept the offer if I wasn't up to his standards. I'd been poked and prodded like a piece of meat at the market. It was a pretty accurate comparison.

Shame—that was Yuri's favorite control tactic.

I'd seen it clear as day as he'd made me stand there in front of his men, their dicks hardening behind crisp suit pants, fingers furling and unfurling as they held themselves back from reaching out. They were accustomed to being able to touch the women Yuri *acquired,* but none of the other girls had been engaged to him.

Bile gathered at the back of my throat. The memory had me fighting the urge to throw up all over the Bratva leader's leather dress shoes, but instead, I stood there—the picture of a good Bratva wife. For now.

If control was what Yuri wanted, he'd chosen the wrong woman. He wouldn't use my body against me—I wouldn't allow it.

My freedom might've been sold, but my obedience and submission weren't for fucking sale.

ALSO BY MARIE MARAVILLA

Skeletons of Society

Syndicate of Sins

City of Salvation

My sweeter side, Marie M.

High Sticking the Heart

HEY BOO...

STABBING IS FROWNED UPON IN REAL LIFE...

So I did the next best thing and wrote it in my books (okay, they don't stab in my hockey books, but you bet your ass they are petty).

Writing a book was only supposed to be a bucket list thing to check off; now, here we are. My author brand centers around writing unapologetic feminine rage with FMCs as badass as the boys who fall for them. And now I am trying my hand in the sports romance world!

I currently live in Tennessee and try to survive the cycle of working, writing, mom-ing, and consuming questionable amounts of caffeine.

Keep up with new releases, signed copies & goodies, audiobook deals, and general chaos at:

authormariemaravilla.com

instagram.com/authormariemaravilla

tiktok.com/@authormariemaravilla

ACKNOWLEDGMENTS

Thank god I have amazing people in my life to help me through this book, because it was an adventure. *Skeletons of Society* brought me so many amazing book friends and so many of them were a part of making this book happen.

First of all, thank you to my husband who supports me without question. Then my editor, Beth, who I sent my manuscript to basically without an ending and she told me to rest. Which, I often have to be told that's okay. Ana, my cover designer. Thanks for making my books beautiful.

Then to my amazing alpha readers, Halle, Lex, Caitlen, and of course my OG alpha reader Ashleigh. You all were amazing and held my hand as I tried to narrow down which of the five versions I should actually stick with. And my PA/Friend Lindsey, I hope you got all the heart flutters and coochie twinches.

And to you, the reader! Thanks for taking a chance on my work.